The Riveting, Action-Packed New Adventure Of
EX-Policeman, Ed Cody — The Man Who Can See
The Future: He First Appeared In
Cries from the Darkness–Michael Fisher's
stunning first novel

Ex-cop Ed Cody, haunted by the kidnap and murder of his beloved wife and by his "gift" of premonitions and visions of future crimes that will take place, returns in this compelling mystery, hot on the trail of his buddy's murderers in a savage world of Mob violence, drugs, and corruption in the infamous Kings Cross section of Sydney, Australia.

Cody, accompanied by his two sons, is in seclusion recovering from his wife's death. Their mourning is interrupted by a desperate letter from his buddy Tommy Creager's daughter: Tommy's been killed in an obscure New Zealand town, and she needs Cody's help.

Once down under, Cody begins his pursuit of Creager's killers. His search leads, again and again, to Griffin "King of Sin" Brown–the head of the Sydney underworld–and increasingly into a Mob war on the verge of exploding. As the trail he follows gets hotter and bloodier, Cody is haunted by ever more hideous criminals. And he alone must piece together the puzzle of Creager's murder–before his enemies silence any surviving witnesses and possibly Cody himself.

THE NIGHTMARE MAN

Michael Fisher

A division of Shapolsky Publishers, Inc.

The Nightmare Man

S.P.I. BOOKS
A Division of Shapolsky Publishers, Inc.

For any additional information, contact:

S.P.I. BOOKS/Shapolsky Publishers, Inc.
136 West 22nd Street
New York, NY 10011
(212) 633-2022
FAX (212) 633-2123

ISBN: 1-56171-223-X

10 9 8 7 6 5 4 3 2 1

Printed and bound in Canada

About the Author

MICHAEL FISHER was a producer and a screenwriter before turning to fiction with his novel *Cries From the Darkness*. He has written and produced more than 30 hours of prime-time television and theatrical motion pictures, and divides his time among New York, Southern California, and Australia.

1

On the day he would be murdered, Tommy Creager woke a few minutes before six. The sky was gray, and it was raining steadily against his hotel-room window. He didn't like Auckland. He thought the city dull and ugly. He didn't like the face he saw in the mirror, either. Too much booze, too much weight had bloated the looks of the onetime TV anchorman.

He ordered food, a large breakfast, and then showered and shaved. Room service came while he was dressing. Later he retrieved his rented Toyota from the car park himself. He hated confronting the cheerful doormen, who would happily bring the car up seemingly without even the expectation of a tip. He drove west. . . again.

It was insane. Every third day. It was no system. Just every third day he had to drive the 288 kilometers, almost 180 miles – he still had to convert things like that in his head to make any sense of them. Through the countryside that started five minutes from the heart of Auckland. Rolling green hills dotted with sheep, picturesque farmhouses. Forests and mountains and streams, all of which looked like they belonged on postcards and calendars. Even that had become oppressive to him. It was like being force-fed vanilla ice cream morning, noon, and night.

The meeting place was in a small coastal town named Tauranga. A parking lot that fronted on a slate gray sea. He waited. Behind him was a large green playing field. Closer were public rest rooms that brought in a small but steady stream of traffic – trucks, cars, workmen, tourists. It could be a long drive between public toilets in this country, he had found out. He waited and tried to think through the chapter on Jack Ruby and Clay Shaw. But, as always, he ran into the same problem: There was nothing new. Nothing fresh. Nothing concrete. There hadn't been in all the years he had been working on the book, and he thought about the letter he'd written the Garrison estate and decided – as he had a number of times before – that he would find it and mail it this time when he got back to Sydney.

He waited.

It was going on noon. He was getting hungry

He waited. It was insane; every third day, the drive and then the waiting. He was supposed to wait until five, but he had changed that the first day, when at a little after three the playing field had filled with boys in short pants, loosed from school. . . . He might be dying of cancer. He knew he was. It was a secret he kept to himself, a knowledge that had spurred him to dig up the manuscript again, try to finish it, try to leave something behind to show that he had been here. He knew he was dying and he knew he had been drinking too much the last couple of years. He had botched the job in Singapore. Probably because of his drinking. He was forty pounds overweight, and there were times, blocks of time, when he was drinking that he didn't know where he had been or what he had done. He was slipping, he was secretly dying. But enough was enough; he wasn't going to sit in a parking lot not fifty feet from a public rest room with fresh-faced little boys in short pants traipsing in and out. Christ, wasn't there enough indignity to his life without someone thinking he was parked there because he was a pervert?

"G'day," the silver-haired man called from the beach where he was walking his dog. Like the water and the sky, the beach was gray; it had no sand but was instead made up of millions of varied shells. The slim, middle-aged man who wore a black stocking cap and a stubble beard, crunched over them and climbed the two-foot sea wall to the parking lot.

"Christ, he's coming over," Creager thought. The last time he'd been here the man had talked to him for over thirty minutes .

"You must like it here. A good place to think, huh?"

Creager had told him he was a writer and that he got his inspiration by staring out to sea. The silver-haired man told him about a Zane Grey book he had read once when he was young and that he had always wanted to visit America but never had, dollar was too dear now. Besides, he was too old. What part of America was he from?

Indignity, that was what this was all about. They were punishing him for Singapore. The long drives out here. . . the waiting for contact. What contact? Why here, in this godforsaken place?

"I was talking to my sister about you the other night," the silver-haired man called out. He was almost at the car window. Likable, Irish, pie face, the kind that seemed familiar. They were alone now:

Tommy Creager, the silver-haired man, his dog. The parking lot was empty. The playing field waited quietly for the shout of boys.

Creager thought about his daughter. She'd be fourteen now – no, fifteen. Christ, he hadn't seen her since she was twelve, hadn't even written her for months.

"My sister's a big fan of the American telly."

Creager never saw the gun. He was too busy feeling guilty about his daughter. The slight silver-haired man just slipped it out and fired twice, silenced .22s half an inch apart on his right temple.

Creager had just decided to send his daughter a nice wool sweater, one of the colorful ones he'd seen in the hotel shop. . . when everything stopped.

2

The wind from the north was warm and growing stronger, and Cody, without having to think about it, knew that there would be rain again tonight. It was almost February, only a little more than halfway through the wet season. He read the newspaper clipping a second time, folded it up with the letter it had come with, and returned both to the envelope.

"So who is M. L. Creager?" Patrick asked eagerly, pronouncing the name Crayger. The letter for him was a connection to the outside world, home, California.

Patrick had been snorkeling with a couple of friends when the postman, one of the other boy's older brothers, had called to him that there was a letter for his father. Patrick, who would be thirteen in a few weeks, had then run all the way back around the crescent-shaped harbor to their fifty-six-foot ketch. He was blond and very tan and wore only a pair of cutoffs and the hint of a singsong Samoan accent he'd picked up in the last couple of months.

"Creager," Cody corrected. "You remember Mary Lou and her dad, they used to come to our place a lot during the summers, before we had the boat, when I was still on the police force."

"Was he the guy who was on TV?" Patrick asked.

"That's right."

"That was a real long time ago." The boy said.

"Right. Somewhere back in the stone age, about five or six years ago," Cody smiled.

The boy grinned, "I remember the girl used to have a crush on Damien and she'd follow him around everywhere and he'd get real mad at me when I teased him about it. . . . Why did she write you?"

"Someone killed her dad. She wants me to find out who. She says no one else cares."

The boy considered and then asked, "In California?"

"No. He was killed in New Zealand. A small town along the coast. Two small caliber bullets in the head, so the newspaper says."

Neither father nor son spoke for several moments. But the boy sensed a change in the other. It was as if his father was becoming like he was before. Before his mother had disappeared. Before all that time later when they had learned she was dead. It had been almost five months since then. Five months and now it seemed like his father was coming alive again and the boy knew what question to ask. "Are we going to New Zealand?"

"There was a time in my life when Tommy Creager was my best friend. . . my only friend." Cody finally answered.

And the boy knew that that meant yes and inside was happy, but tried not to show it. His father was coming alive again. It was as if they could all come alive again. . . .

Cody watched the boy run back down the jetty and then onto the esplanade, hurrying in the late-afternoon sun to rejoin his friends. He and his sons had been in Apia for almost three months. Too long, Cody knew. Originally they had planned to be here only four or five days, long enough to restock and refit the boat, and to see Vailima. Ann had especially wanted to see Vailima; it was why Apia had become one of their scheduled ports on their trip around the world. But then Damien, his eighteen-year-old, had had an appendicitis attack on the voyage there from the Hawaiian islands. The appendix had burst over thirty hours before they could reach port, and when they finally did, Damien's temperature had been steady and burning at 105 degrees, and Cody had sensed the doctors were afraid. He stayed with his son days and nights in the hospital without sleep, willing himself to keep awake, as if by doing so he could hang on to the boy's life. His life, his sanity, so fragile. He couldn't lose another, not after Ann. He couldn't lose Damien, too. And then the danger had passed.

In the days when Damien was regaining his strength, Cody and Patrick had begun to explore and wander the island. Once outside Apia, they found Upolu startling in its beauty and contrast. Dramatic six-thousand-foot mountain peaks plunged down into tropical forests that spread in many places all the way down to beautiful, isolated palm-tree-lined beaches and crystal-clear lagoons. In their wanderings most of the villages they came upon were clean and orderly, and with the exceptions of telephone and electrical wires and occasional TV antennas, they gave the impression of not having changed with the passing generations but instead being blissfully caught somehow in a Polynesian time long ago.

Weeks had passed. Damien had fully recovered. But even then the days continued to drift without Cody making any plans to sail on. . . and for a while Cody convinced himself that they needed this time, in this place away from the rest of the world. It was a time of healing and reordering their lives after the months of anguish, the months Ann had been missing. . . and then finally having to accept her death and the fact that she had been murdered so senselessly. Brutally. She, the person they had all loved most in the world. And it still hurt when they thought of it – the pain, the fear she must have suffered – and at times it made them angry and at times it made them cry.

The weeks stretched into a month and then another, and over and over again he found himself drawn back to Vailima, the house Robert Louis Stevenson had built and spent the last years of his life in. Ann had admired Stevenson, especially for his famous letter in defense of Father Damien of Molokai; Father Damien, the leper priest, had been one of her heroes. Gradually, Cody grew aware that Vailima and the whole of the island had become part of Ann for him, interwoven with the memories of her, and that his reluctance to sail on came from the fear that he'd somehow be leaving her behind. It was as if he were trying to hold time in place, trying to keep the love and memories from fading. And as the days had continued to pass, he had begun to drink again, for the first time since her funeral. First only at night, but then gradually the days, too, became a muddle and his voice too often angry, and one dinner he had raged and seen tears in his younger son's eyes. He slept on deck that night, and a soft rain washed his face. . . and he knew he had to let her go.

The next morning he'd apologized to his sons, as best he could. Still they lingered another few days. . . only now he didn't know why. And then finally in the early morning of the day he planned to visit the harbormaster to chart out the next leg of their trip, it had begun. He had awakened with his body both chilled and sweating, and as he'd gained consciousness a terrifying sense of despair and fear and imminent death washed over him. He quickly got out of bed then and retrieved his Walther, the clock on the bedside table read a few minutes after three. He hurried silently, anxiously, down the passageway. First to Damien's cabin, where he was relieved to see the eighteen-year-old sleeping peacefully, safely. For a moment Cody's eyes went to the wall next to the boy's bed, where the silver-and-gold crucifix that had first rested on his mother's coffin was hung. But he couldn't linger; the sense of fear and death still hung over him.

Across now to Patrick's cabin. Dodger and UCLA posters decorated his walls. . . and again, relief; the blond, tanned boy slept undisturbed, one leg dangling off his bunk. And as he'd watched his youngest son, the despair and fear drained away, and Cody wondered if it was only the remnants of a nightmare. But even as he did, he knew it wasn't.

He'd returned to his cabin and lay quietly on his bed for some minutes before it came back – only this time, after the initial wave of despair and fear, he was suddenly on the edge of a great bottomless darkness. . . and then after several icy, silent moments, there were two shots, the sound and flame, and searing, hot pain. And then darkness again, and cold, and then a terrible sense of dread. And when it was over Cody was once again bathed in sweat, and he knew they had to wait in Apia. He didn't know for what or who or when. . . he only knew.

The image had returned three more times that week. And when Patrick had brought the letter and clipping from Tommy Creager's daughter, Cody knew who it was who had been killed.

3

A street boy who looked to be nine or ten popped the can of beer. He had blond hair, freckles, and a naturally pretty face, though at the moment his features were softened just a bit by drunkenness. He smiled a boasting smile, put the can of beer to his lips, threw his head straight back, and held it there as the amber liquid flowed into his mouth and down his throat and the other kids around him, mostly in their early teens, watched with various anticipations. Some of them were street kids too; others, just kids out for a bit of Friday night raging at Bondi Beach – which, as the the crowds attested, was Sydney's most popular oceanside suburb.

"John Dory and chips," the waitress announced cheerfully as she placed the plate in front of the silver-haired man.

Fitzwilliam – for that was the silver-haired man's name – briefly turned his attention from the contest down the footpath.

"Thank you," he said.

"Enjoy your meal," she answered with a smile that lingered a moment too long before she moved off. He made note of it and then turned his attention back through the low Plexiglas that separated the terrace of the restaurant from the main walkway of Bondi. At first, moving groups of pedestrians blocked his view, but when they did clear it was just in time for him to see the freckle-faced youngster finish his beer in one chug-a-lug, snapping his head back down and throwing the now empty can into the air with a happy hoot.

"He's a bloody drainpipe," one of the other kids said and the freckle-faced boy grinned and money exchanged hands. Then a police car crawled near and the Friday-night kids melted into the crowds moving up and down the walkway along Campbell Parade.

Fitzwilliam turned his attention back to his meal. John Dory was his favorite fish, and a couple of bites revealed that this piece had been cooked to near perfection. He poured some more white wine and, out of habit, checked his watch. Only twenty after ten. No worries, plenty of time, he thought. He had determined the previous week that the fire would best be set after midnight.

He enjoyed it here, this open-air restaurant, this table where he could watch the crowds amble by, some happy, some drunk, some sexy. A blonde with bouncing, red-clad breasts moved past him, and he knew now for sure that when it was all over he'd need a woman tonight, and he knew it would be rough and it would be violent and he would beat the shit out of her, and he thought about the waitress who had flirted with him. She was in her thirties, her body firm if a little too full, and he knew that on most nights she would do. But not tonight. Not after he had done his job. He didn't want anyone to remember him in this area. He had been to Bondi only three times before. First that afternoon a little over six weeks ago when Brown had showed him through the empty disco. Then, after he had gotten the go-ahead, he had returned twice more, on his own, Friday nights. He wanted to see it when it was full, as it would be when he did his work. He wanted to make sure he had a way out.

* * *

By the time Fitzwilliam had finished his dinner and the bottle of white wine, he was feeling a pleasant glow. The waitress with the full, firm body had brought him a "complimentary" glass of port with his check. He had been tempted, but then decided that for tonight, anyway, both were too dangerous. So instead of waiting for her to return, he left enough cash to cover the bill and slipped out of the patio restaurant and onto the wide footpath along Campbell Parade.

Almost at once he was jostled by the crowd hurrying this way and that. But instead of being irritated he found himself amused, teased with a sense of nostalgia, and he knew that this was one of the things he had missed most those six years, four months, and twenty-three days in prison. This was one of the things one never thought of until it was denied – the warm, crowded, midsummer nights strolling along the shore. People in holiday moods, laughing in place of the slightest smile because life was so sweet. It brought back his fondest memories of when he was a boy of twelve and thirteen and fourteen, when he and his mother and two sisters lived up in Surfers Paradise. Surfers before the high rises. Before the glitz. Golden days, warm nights, when it seemed for weeks at a time he lived in nothing more than a pair of shorts. On the beach, surfing, running with his friends, and when he got hungry the trudge up to Jim Cavill's hotel where his mother worked as a waitress.

"Got a dollar, mister?"

The boy's voice brought him back to the present. He wasn't more than fifty meters from the Galah. A large pink neon outline of the bird blinked on and off over the entrance of the disco where Tina Turner's voice splashed out onto the festive coming-and-going customers. The front door, Fitzwilliam knew from his first visit, was merely an entrance to an enclosed staircase leading to the main room on the second floor.

It was the freckle-faced boy he'd watched earlier chug-a-lugging a beer. Up close he could see that the boy's face was grimy around the ears and hairline, and his eyes were blurred from alcohol. His clothes consisted of a pair of shorts and a light blue Manly Sharks football shirt, both filthy and worn around the edges.

"What's your name?" The silver-haired man asked.

"Colin," the boy replied guardedly, ready to run.

"What a good name," Fitzwilliam said with a genuine smile. "That's my name."

He looked at the boy a moment longer and then pulled out his folded money. He started to peel off a five, but then the glow of the alcohol and his boy-hood memories nudged him on into magnanimity, and he pulled out an orange twenty-dollar bill and offered it to the boy, who suddenly looked frightened.

"I don't do any sex stuff," the boy said weakly.

Fitzwilliam was for a moment mortified at the misunderstanding, and then angry, but the latter he cloaked better than the former. "I don't want you to. I just want you to take care of yourself, young Colin."

The boy considered for another moment, then snatched the proffered twenty-dollar bill and darted off into the Friday night.

Fitzwilliam was angry with himself. He shouldn't have had more than half a bottle of that wine; the extra had lured him into relaxing. And that was something he couldn't afford. Not tonight. The sense of well-being he had experienced just moments before had vanished. Now the night was just warm and sticky, the crowds of people around him noisy and rude, the boy his childhood had befriended just another unpleasant street kid. Sydney seemed to have so many of them these days.

He watched the outside of the Galah for another hour and a half until, one by one, most of the other shops and restaurants had closed and the foot traffic along the Campbell Parade had quieted. The disco itself was of course as alive as before. Its music alternately bleeding and blaring out to the ocean-side street-front. Satisfied that it was time, he walked the two blocks up to Ramsgate Avenue, where he had parked the car.

As he neared the blue Holden on the empty street, a chill settled in on him. Not fear, only awareness. For he knew that how he fared in the next ten minutes would determine how he would spend the rest of his life – and, for that matter, how long that would be. If things went well he would be one step closer to the enormous prize of money that awaited him less than two weeks down the line. If things didn't go well, he'd be dead. It would have to be dead. He'd never go back to prison.

He opened the boot of the Holden and lifted out a pair of three-liter gas cans. Their contents sloshed from side to side as he set them on the curb. He closed the boot and looked both ways again. The street was still deserted. He picked up the cans and started back to the beachfront. Half a block down he turned into a side alley. He felt safer now, off the main street. He knew this side alley would take him almost all the way to his destination. . . almost all the way to the Galah.

4

It was a late and lazy Saturday morning when the Cody boat, *Ann's Dream*, sailed into Auckland harbor. Since just before dawn a friendly, steady wind had pushed them up the New Zealand coast. Now as they neared the city, under the warm summer sun, they found themselves in a world of dozens upon dozens of smaller, weekend sailboats, and with shouted help from one of them – a family of four, off to find a picnic spot – the Codys learned where to find customs.

"They all sound like we're in an English movie," Patrick grinned.

"Get used to it, little brother," Damien said. "I got a feeling that as long as we're here, we're in for a lot of that."

Besides having a heavy New Zealand accent, the middle-aged clerk at the customs office also had dandruff, bad teeth, and apparently a dislike for either Americans or working on Saturdays. He was a man seemingly devoid of any sense of humor, and appeared suspicious of anyone sailing around the world. Despite the fact that they were the only people on the visitors' side of the counter, he managed to keep them waiting off and on for more than an hour while he retreated for various reasons to the inner recesses of the complex – the last time, they realized with the help of a reflection in a glass door, for a tea break, at which they must have been the subject of conversation, for it was then that a woman with close-cropped orange hair, cup in one hand and cookie in the other, came out and stared at them for several moments, sighed, and then retreated back inside.

Finally the clerk returned, this time with a look of resolve, along with cookie crumbs at the corner of his mouth. He informed Cody that the boat would have to be searched but that the search couldn't take place until Monday, when there would be a full staff on. Until then it would have to be impounded.

Cody's first instinct was, of course, to get angry –
but he hadn't spent twenty years on the Los Angeles
police force without learning how to handle minor
bureaucrats with penchants for petty tyranny. Over
the years he had found that success had come for
him most often when he had managed to sow in
those mindlessly obstructing him the seeds of fear,
the idea that a great mistake was being made that
would later come back to trouble, haunt, and other-
wise embarrass them. And so to this end Cody, who
up to then had maintained a friendly attitude,
became crisp and courteous to a fault as he produced
some letters of reference brought along for just such
an occasion. The first was from an assistant chief of
police in Los Angeles. This impressed the clerk, who
hadn't realized that Cody was an ex-policeman. The
second letter was from Professor Eric Trapper at
UCLA, the parapsychologist who had worked with
him the last nine years and had become a close
friend. The third – and for these circumstances the
one that Cody considered his ace – was from his con-
gressman and suggested that if further help were
needed, this letter would serve as a reference at the
local U.S. consulate.

The clerk, beginning to feel unsure of himself, acquired a new politeness but still hesitated. He looked
around for support from the woman with the
cropped orange hair, but she was nowhere to be
seen. Cody had one letter left in his arsenal, and
though he had appreciated it when he'd gotten it, he
had always questioned its value. Right now, com-
pared with the other three very official looking letters, it might appear silly, but Cody observed the
resolve returning to the clerk's face. He figured he

had nothing to lose. He didn't want the boat impounded for two days.

"There's one more," Cody said, infusing his voice with some importance as he handed the clerk the fourth letter.

It was written on a single piece of paper, in a grammar-school-like scrawl, and it simply said, "Ed Cody is a good friend. You can trust him." It was signed with the same name that was printed at the top of the page: Gene Autry.

The clerk melted and a smile creased his lips. "You know Gene Autry? The *real* Gene Autry?" he asked in wonderment.

"When I'm in Los Angeles, sometimes I have breakfast with him at a restaurant he goes to out in the Valley."

The clerk couldn't stop grinning. He was like a little boy waiting for his birthday party to start. What was Gene Autry really like, he asked Cody, who told him, "Just like he is in the movies," and the clerk volunteered that he used to go to his movies every Saturday when he was a kid.

"There aren't stars like him anymore," the clerk said.

Cody agreed, and the rest was easy. Thy boys were brought back to the tearoom and given milk and bickies (short for biscuits, which is what cookies were called here) by the lady with the short orange hair, while Cody was allowed to use the phone and the clerk himself used another to call around until he found a nearby marina that could take their boat for a few days.

On the radio in the tearoom the newscaster talked of the disaster in Sydney, twelve hundred miles away; a terrible fire in a disco the night before, thirty-seven dead so far, many more in the hospital, but the volume was low and the cookies were good and the lady with the close-cropped orange hair wanted to hear what it was like in Southern California, so no one paid attention.

* * *

Joe McCabe finally got to Cody's boat at about ten to six. He had shaggy, shoulder-length salt-and-pepper hair and a crooked, friendly grin. "Sorry I'm late," he apologized. "I would have been here about two hours ago, but my ex-wife decided to pull one of her shit acts – oh, excuse the French," he added quickly as he spotted Patrick, then offered a wink and a shrug in the direction of the boys as further apology, and a friendship was begun.

McCabe's arrival was the result of two long-distance calls Cody had made to a man named Charlie Haines, the "police editor" on a paper in Long Beach, California. The first call had been placed the night before Cody and the boys had sailed from Apia. Yes, Charlie had heard about Tommy Creager's death and had been depressed about it. He'd tried unsuccessfully to find an address on Tommy's daughter so he could send her a note of condolence, and then, unable to turn up any old cronies who cared enough, had gone off and gotten drunk on his own for his old friend.

"Who killed him?" Charlie wanted to know.

"That's what I'm going to try and find out," Cody had answered. "But the trail's pretty cold. The murder is almost six weeks old. I'm going to need some help, all the information I can get."

Charlie said he wasn't sure he knew anyone in New Zealand, but that he'd beat the long-distance bushes and see what he could turn up. Cody should call him back as soon as he got to Auckland. So Cody had, from the customs office, and Charlie's answer had been Joe McCabe.

"Joe's a good guy and a good investigative reporter. He's a New Zealander but he's knocked around the world, he knows his stuff. He said he'd dig up everything he could for you." Charlie then gave Cody Joe's local numbers – office, home, beeper – and got Cody's promise to let him know what turned up.

In exchange for a cup of Kona coffee, McCabe gave Cody a crooked grin and a large envelope filled with newspaper clippings on the Creager murder.

Factwise, there wasn't much more than Cody already knew. Tommy Creager, an American journalist stationed in Sydney, had been found shot to death in his rental car in the small coastal town of Tauranga. Speculation in a couple of the tabloids ran rampant. One headline shouted: "Aussie Mob Rubs Out American Journo." A second, dated a couple of days after the murder, read, "CIA Linked to Tauranga Murder?"

"Any strength to these headlines?" Cody asked.

McCabe squinted and rocked his head from side to side as if what he was about to say could be true or not. "Rumors are the best I've been able to pick up. I've made some calls to guys I've worked with before over in Sydney."

"And they put Creager with the mob and the CIA?" Cody asked with mild incredulity.

"Officially. . . " McCabe shrugged. "No one knows why he was killed. It doesn't seem to make sense." McCabe squinted again, choosing his words and measuring his tone. "I mean, from what I hear he was pretty much of a washout since he came Down Under. Word is he was usually bombed. I know he was the couple of times I met him – you know, at press functions. I mean, the deal is, no one can figure out why anyone would even bother to kill him. . . and if so, why all the way over here? Why not just run him over with a truck some night when he's staggering home from some pub in Sydney, or tie some weights around him and drop him in the bloody harbor? There must have been a million ways to save the airfare."

"I get the point," Cody agreed. "What about unofficially?"

McCabe rocked his head from side to side once more. "Not a lot better, at least as to why someone would bother to bring him all the way over here to do it. But apparently he was friendly with one of the big boys of crime over there in Sydney, a guy named Griffin Brown. What I hear is, he used to spend a lot of time at Brown's house, on his boat. Took Brown's wife to restaurants; it's said they used to get on real good – she's a lush too."

"Any reason why this Brown should want to kill him?"

"No." McCabe shook his head. "I could only get the vaguest of speculation on that. Maybe he crossed Brown. Maybe Brown caught him in the sack with his old lady." He paused and lit a fresh cigarette from the one he was smoking, and then continued with squinted concentration. "The most interesting was that last year there had been some rumors that Creager had been used as a go-between when Brown was trying to make peace with another underworld biggie. There's some thought his killing could have fallen out of that. But you still have to ask yourself, Why in New Zealand in a little town two and a half hours from Auckland and the hotel he was staying at?"

"What hotel was he staying at?" Cody asked, seeking a string to pull.

"Hilton. Very nice. He'd been there six days. The police are pretty certain, by the way, that he made at least one other trip to Tauranga."

"They know what he did there?" asked Cody.

McCabe shook his head without conviction. "The only reports they have just say he sat in his rental car, in the same parking lot he was killed in. Sat there for at least several hours, then drove back to Auckland."

"Meeting place," Cody thought out loud and then pressed on. "What about the CIA?"

McCabe grinned. "Sounds a bit like the cloak-and-dagger boys, doesn't it? But no one I talked to could link Creager to the CIA."

"The headline must have come from somewhere," Cody said.

McCabe nodded and his grin broadened. "You have to understand, we're a bit behind the rest of the world down here in the forsaken colonies, and consequently we have some of the last true relics of the Empire – to wit, some of the last genuine British Labor Union Communist paranoiac thinkers. And a good smattering of them are journos, who of course automatically despise most Americans on principle and suspect any one of them who lives better than they do – which is almost all of them – of being a CIA operative."

Cody considered for a few moments before speaking. "I'd like to see where Creager died."

"I thought you might," McCabe said, pleased with himself. "I've talked to the police in Tauranga, told them I was doing a piece on the murder, and after many sighs and groans and some mildly rude speculation as to my ancestry and observations that there had already been enough stories about it, they agreed to have one of their people show us exactly where the shooting took place and let us have a look at their reports and photos. So the only question is, when do you want to go?"

5

It was a little after eight in the morning when they all four packed into McCabe's cluttered nine-year-old Toyota and rumbled off toward the city. It had been decided that the boys would be tourists today and to that end would be dropped off at a sight-seeing bus company on Queen Street, in the city. And with sixty New Zealand dollars borrowed from McCabe in Damien's hand, plus the name of the marina scrawled on a piece of paper so they could cab it back when their day was done, the boys were set.

Queen Street, which runs through the business heart of Auckland, was quiet on this sunny Sunday morning. It seemed to the Codys to be a curious mixture of a double handful of glimmering new high rises scattered amongst the many more, squatter, more traditionally British-looking buildings – one of which, Patrick realized, housed the first McDonald's they had seen in almost three months. So it was with visions of McBreakfasts dancing in the boys' heads that Cody and McCabe dropped them off and headed out of the city. In less then ten minutes they were on a road slicing through rolling green hills, dotted with sheep.

"You know, until I started looking into him, I never knew Tommy Creager was such an interesting fella," McCabe said, breaking the silence that had stretched since they had dropped thy boys off. "I mean, like I said yesterday, I'd known Tommy slightly – you know, bumped into him a couple of places – but I never knew he'd been in Dallas the day Kennedy was shot."

"It's really what launched his career," Cody said, surprised by his sudden sense of melancholy for his dead friend. "He was just a kid reporter on one of the local channels when it happened. . . and suddenly his face was on TV screens all across America. He was half a block away when Oswald shot Tippit down, trying to make his getaway. He was at the movie theater when the cops caught Oswald. And three days later he was even in the basement of the police station when Jack Ruby showed up and shot Oswald."

"Holy shit," McCabe said almost wistfully, "what a run of luck."

"Yeah," Cody said after a moment, for the first time not sure if he liked McCabe. "Tommy used to say that those were the three luckiest days in his life. Of course he only said it when he was bad drunk."

McCabe squinted, this time without a grin, as he glanced at Cody. "I didn't mean for it to sound so damned callous. . . but you know us newsos. We're the only people in the world more cynical than cops, aren't we?"

"Yeah, I guess you are," Cody said, and then smiled.

McCabe grinned crookedly in return and lit another cigarette. As Cody had realized the day before, the reporter was a nonstop smoker. He had already gone through half a pack of cigarettes since leaving the marina, and by the time they crested the hill and started down toward Tauranga, he was peeling open a second pack.

"There she is," he coughed. But Cody already knew it. A feeling of cold and darkness had come upon him in the last few moments, and now as they approached the town a sense of madness flashed through him. It could be any quiet beach town in the States, he thought. A McDonald's dominated the major corner. A little way down the main street was a Pizza Hut, and not to be outdone, the Colonel was selling his chicken here too. But the stench of corrupting death was on him. Death and fear and sorrow.

"Stop the car," Cody said quietly.

"We're still a few kilometers. . . " McCabe started.

"I said stop the car." Cody's voice was terse and commanding.

McCabe pulled over. Cody climbed out onto the shoulder. A string of pleasant, modest, mostly brick homes and apartments lined the highway here and on into town. The sense of death, the stench of corruption – both had faded now. Cody stood for several moments as if to get his bearings and then started back up the road. Walking at first and then breaking into a loping run.

"Jesus," McCabe said to himself. A chill ran up his back, and all at once he knew that the stories Charlie Haines had told him about Cody were true.

There was a ringing in Cody's ears. He stopped now and looked around. Some children were playing on a nearby lawn with a plastic water slide, laughing and shouting with happiness. Puffs of white clouds dotted the bright blue sky. The day was hot, in the 90s. . . and the sense of death and fear and sorrow had passed.

He looked back to see McCabe approaching, fearful and inquisitive, and Cody knew now what motivated the man with the crooked grin.

"That's why you agreed to help, isn't it?" Cody said. "You want the story. Not just of the murder, but mine too."

McCabe searched uncomfortably for the proper words and finally managed, "That would be nice." Then, after a moment: "I wouldn't print anything about you and your family that you didn't approve of."

"That would be nothing about the boys and very little about me."

"Okay," McCabe agreed.

Cody's instinct was to believe him, and after a moment he nodded. "I have to warn you, it could end right here. Dead end in Tauranga. I don't always get. . . flashes that I can find meaning to."

"If it ends here, it ends here," McCabe assured him sincerely.

"Sometimes I don't know what the hell I see," Cody mused. "Some people call what I have a gift. It's a gift I'd happily pass on."

They stood in silence for several moments, and then Cody started back to the car.

"Cody," McCabe called to him. "Why did we stop?"

"Someone died here," Cody answered. "Somewhere near here. One of these homes."

"Died. . . you mean murdered?" McCabe pressed.

"No, that's the odd part. Cancer, I think. Long and painful." Cody stood remembering the last days he'd spent at his mother's bedside so many years ago. He had been fourteen, she but thirty-eight, and the smell of her degenerating flesh had never left his memory.

"What does it mean, then?" McCabe persisted. "Does it have something to do with Tommy Creager's death?"

"I don't know," Cody said simply, then turned and continued to the car.

McCabe watched a moment, perplexed, then followed Cody back to the car. As he slid in behind the steering wheel, Cody was drawing a circle on a local map. When he was done he handed it to McCabe, his hand trembling.

"Get the local paper to give you the name of anyone who died here in the last two months."

"Are you alright?" McCabe asked.

Cody stared at him a moment, and for a split second, just as it had happened a few moments before when he had returned to the car, everything was black and he could hear the screams. They were far away, but he could hear them, and he could feel and taste the stinging smoke. He was back now, in the car, in Tauranga. "You can forget what I said out there. . . it's not going to end here," Cody said, his voice quiet but intense, reflecting the horror he sensed. "What happened here is only the beginning."

And for one of the few times since he had become an adult, Joe McCabe was truly frightened.

6

Fiona Brown wailed and sobbed inconsolably. For her lost life. For her lost sons. The sweet, innocent, happy boys they had been. . . the vile, evil men they had grown into, in their father's image. Only now they had lost more than he could ever lose, they had lost their immortal souls. And then for a tingling moment she tried to believe that they hadn't. She tried to believe that maybe in the last moments when the fire had been all around them and the walls of the disco were collapsing in on them – maybe then, in their pain and fear, the evil that had taken over their spirits had been stripped away, and her little angels, like they had so many years ago on their first communion, returned and asked God to forgive them.

"Oh my God, I am heartily sorry for having offended thee." She could see seven-year-old Kevin, with his turned-up little nose and eager sincerity. He used to come to her, even then at that innocent age, and try to console her after Griffin had been mean to her, yelled at her, humiliated her in front of the children and the servants and sometimes even guests.

At first young Kevin had been confused and frightened that his father would treat his mother that way. Then, when he overcame his fear, his emotions changed to anger and a rage to revenge. But Fiona would only cry more and tell the boy, "He's your father, you must love him, no matter what," and, "The fourth commandment tells us to honor our father and our mother. We must do what God tells us to, no matter how hard it is." And then they both would cry and kneel and pray for his father, her husband, in front of the shrine to Mary she had in her bedroom. They prayed the rosary and she sipped gin. She remembered the last with regret.

Only all the rosaries couldn't transform Griffin back to the warm, loving man she had married, or help with her need for more and more gin. As the years had gone by, the only change seemed to be that Griffin didn't even give her the dignity to yell at her anymore. And he began to be openly seen in public with other women.

"I'm not going to ask you again." Griffin's hard voice cut through her gossamer reveries. He wouldn't go away. "Tell me what you want done for the funeral, or I'll take care of it myself. I'll have them both –" he paused to fight his emotions "–what's left of them, cremated."

"No," she wailed, "you will not!" Her voice rang with a righteous anger. "You destroyed their lives, you're not going to destroy their eternity."

"Then what?" Griffin asked.

She was flustered for several moments. She didn't like having to make decisions. Not worldly decisions. Not decisions that affected anyone outside her room. Then the inspiration came to her and she crossed herself in gratitude. "Monsignor Ahern will help me. We'll plan a wonderful funeral mass. We'll have it said in Latin. That will be beautiful, won't it?" She wasn't talking to her husband now, but to the sea of three dozen or so plaster faces that had over the years come to populate her room. The Blessed Virgin, the Sacred Heart. . . mostly statues of Mary and her son. But there were others – Francis of Assisi, Ignatius Loyola, Stephen the martyr, Rose of Lima – so many others.

"The monsignor is downstairs," Griffin reported.

But she wasn't on his plane anymore. The plaster faces were crying. She knew they would. She could no longer remember when she had first started speaking to them or, more important, when they had begun talking back.

"Rejoice, your sons asked for my forgiveness before they died," the Infant of Prague said.

"They will have to spend a good deal of time in purgatory," Saint Francis added. "But with your prayers they will eventually join us in heaven."

She was so happy she began to laugh, and then she realized that her husband was shaking her.

"For Christ's sake, Fiona," he hissed. "Just this once can't you snap out of it!"

"I want to see the monsignor."

"He's downstairs," he repeated impatiently. "He's been there for an hour."

"Why didn't you tell me?"

Griffin Brown sighed. He too now wondered why he had bothered, why he hadn't just turned her over to the fat, pasty-faced priest. Brown was still tall and trim and had his hair, which his barber kept the proper shade of reddish brown. He liked to think he could still pass for a man in his early fifties. . . but today he felt every one of his sixty-two years. "Kevin and David were our sons. I thought their funerals were something we should decide upon between us."

"You poisoned their souls," she said. "Poisoned their lives."

Griffin Brown turned without another word and left his wife's sanctuary. She began to weep again, but then remembered the promise of heaven after purgatory and her joy returned. She found her glass of gin where she had left it, next to Saint Hillary, and drank it down.

7

The screams were louder now. The fire all around him. The stairway collapsing. A girl, she looked to be sixteen, her blond hair on fire. . . . It had hit him all at once when he had stepped out and into the parking lot where Tommy Creager had been shot to death.

"Mr. Creager's rental car was parked just here," announced the young constable whom they had followed over from the local police station.

"There's been a fire, or there's going to be one," Cody said. The smoke was stinging his eyes. He felt off balance, as if he were going to fall. The words came out of his mouth without his having formed them in thought. "A lot of people trapped, burned to death. . . " And then it was gone, and there was only the blue sky and the blue sea and the gray beach made up of the millions of seashells and summer Sunday kids and adults splashing in the gentle surf.

And behind him the green playing field was filled with picnickers and a cricket match. . . and he was cold, bone-chilling cold.

"Excuse me?" the crisp, red-cheeked young constable asked, thinking he must have missed something.

Cody turned a hungry gaze on the young man. "Has there been a fire in the last month or so, a bad fire, a lot of people killed?"

"No sir, not in Tauranga," the constable answered. He was sure now he had missed something along the way.

"Oh, shit." The words escaped from McCabe's mouth.

Cody looked at him. "What?"

"No, it couldn't be." McCabe squinted and grinned slowly, not ready to accept the connection.

"Tell me what couldn't be," Cody pressed.

McCabe, uneasy, kicked at the ground. "I mean, it could make sense in a way, but Jesus Christ, how would you. . . " He broke off and just stared at Cody a moment. "Oh, shit." He suddenly moved to his Toyota and returned with a folded newspaper from the backseat. He found the second-page article and offered it to Cody, explaining as he did. "There was a fire in Sydney last night, Bondi Beach. A disco went up. The police know it was arson – shit, the place was bloody well firebombed. Thirty-seven people died. Two of the dead ones were sons of Griffin Brown – you remember, the underworld boss I told you was linked with Tommy Creager."

They rode in almost silence all the way back to Auckland. At one point Cody asked the reporter how much he knew about Griffin Brown. Not very much at all, McCabe had to admit, but he promised to start making phone calls tomorrow.

It was a little past five when he dropped Cody at the marina and the late afternoon shadows seemed rich and warm against the water. Damien had found a Catholic church about a mile away that had a six p.m. Sunday mass, so they all trooped up there and Cody heard the familiar words and watched his sons go to communion, but his mind couldn't get away from the memory of the flames and the screams. Of people dying. Of Tommy Creager at his house in Playa del Rey, laughing and telling stories.

About halfway back from the marina they stopped at a little restaurant overlooking the bay. They sat in the patio and the locals looked at them curiously. Patrick clattered away about the great old museum they had been to and Cody tried his best to listen and smile appropriately. . . but Damien was aware that his father had deeper, more troubling thoughts on his mind.

"How did you do today?" Damien asked his father.

Cody considered before speaking. "It was a long ride. Two and a half hours each way. Got me thinking, it's been a long time since you boys have seen your grandmother."

"Not that long," Damien said quickly.

Patrick counted, "October, November, December, January and February. . . almost five months."

"We could afford the airfare for you two," Cody went on. "They have flights from Auckland direct to Los Angeles. You two could meet me back here in two or three weeks."

"You're going after Mr. Creager's killer and you don't want us in the way," Damien stated.

"It's not your being in the way," Cody said. "It's just that it could get dangerous."

"Any more dangerous than us sailing around the world in a fifty-six-foot ketch?" Damien asked. "We're doing that because we always wanted to, it was our family dream. We've been talking about it as long as I can remember, you and me and Mom and Pat. . . . You can't pack us off to Grandma's when we run into a storm out there."

"That's different." Cody said.

"No it isn't." Damien insisted. "Pat and I talked about it today. Mr. Creager was your friend. I remember he was at the hospital every day when you were shot and afterwards he came out to the house all the time. . . I remember Mom saying if it hadn't been for him keeping the rest of the press away, she didn't know what would have happened to you."

"Then you can understand why I have to do this for him," Cody said.

"I can understand why we all have to do it for him," Damien urged. "We're a family. We're all we have left. We're not giving you away that easy."

"Mom would want us to stick with you no matter what," Patrick added.

And then the waitress came with their plates of fish and chips and they ate in silence for some moments, and Cody knew that he needed and wanted his sons to be with him as much as they did. There was a special bond between them since Ann was gone. But he also knew he had to protect them .

"If I take you with me, you have to do everything I tell you," Cody said.

"We'll do whatever you say, Dad," Patrick agreed earnestly.

"We will," Damien added.

No one spoke for several moments and then Patrick began to grin, he couldn't help it or stop it, he knew that he and his brother had won and now Damien was grinning too.

"Your grandmother was right, you know. She said I was crazy to try and raise you two all by myself," Cody said.

"She's got it backwards, Dad," Damien said with a grin.

"Yeah," Patrick added. "We're the ones who are raising you."

And Cody laughed.

8

It's a war, Billy, that's what it is," Griffin Brown said. "Jesus, I never thought the bloody Chinaman would go this far."

They were in the main cabin of Brown's seventy-foot yacht that was secured to the private jetty behind his Point Piper home. Up in the house, on the second floor, his wife sipped gin from her inexhaustible supply and communed with her plaster saints and her fat monsignor. Down here, Brown poured himself three fingers of Black Label and talked to his oldest and most trusted friend, in a voice remarkably calm, if strained. But after he'd splashed in the soda and raised the glass to his lips, a sudden surge of anger and frustration swept over him, and instead of tasting the Scotch he hurled the glass against the teakwood paneling, shattering it. "Goddammit, Billy, why does he have to be so greedy. . . we had an agreement!"

Billy moved to retrieve the broken shards of glass. "We should have killed the little chink bastard last year instead of making a deal with him," he said. Billy Packer, only five foot five himself, had thirty years ago – when he'd first met Griffin Brown – been a professional boxer. Though he continued to this day to work out, he had managed over time to add about two pounds a year to his once wiry frame, so that today he was a balding fireplug of a man.

Billy finished picking up the glass, deposited the pieces in a wastebasket, and then made Griffin Brown another drink. The older man sighed as the ex-boxer placed it in his hands. "How are the ladies?" Brown asked.

"They're scared," Billy answered. "They think if someone can firebomb the Galah and kill the boys to get at you, what's to stop 'em from blowing up a few whorehouses?"

Brown was suddenly angry again. "Tell them Griffin Brown is going to stop them," he snarled. "Me and you and all the others who work for me. You tell them what happened last night was a surprise. . . only the Chinaman doesn't have any surprise left."

"You don't have to convince me, Grif," Billy said. "But they are scared."

Brown sighed again. "I guess we can't blame them. Triple normal security, make it around the clock. . . and make sure the girls know about it."

Billy shook his head with some concern. "That could stretch us kind of thin. I've already moved some people around. . . thought we better protect the bars first. I got Tony Walker, Bill Anderson, and Mende moving in over at the Scorpion, and Ted Roberts, Stanley, and Burns at the Regal."

"That Burns is a rum bastard," Brown mused. "I thought he was living in Bali drinking until he puked, and sodomizing little native boys."

"They threw him out."

"Who did?" Brown asked.

"Bali. . . I mean the whole country," Billy added, smiling.

"Then what the hell are we doing with the slime-ball?" Brown demanded, a snarl edging into his voice.

"He's off the drink. . . and he's the best man I can get right now," Billy answered.

"Then get the next-best man. I don't want the son of a bitch around," Brown pressed. "Do you under-stand?"

"Consider him gone," Billy said simply.

Brown hesitated, then downed half his drink and sighed again. "I don't mean to be angry with you, Billy."

"I know," the small, bulky man replied.

"I still want to triple security for the girls," Brown went on. "What if we close the Sixpence until this is over, spread the girls over the other places?"

"We should be alright then," Billy said. "That leaves the gambling clubs."

Brown considered a moment. "They won't go after the Cowboy, we're too well protected there. As for the Manly operation, if we haven't got enough men to secure it properly, we'll close it down for the duration too – which, believe me, won't be long. This is going to be one short fucking war." He started to put the glass to his lips again, but his hand began to tremble so badly that he had to bring the other one up to steady it. He drained the glass. He looked at his friend. The cabin was painfully quiet for some moments before Billy spoke.

"I know there's no way I can say this, and maybe I don't even have the right. . . " Billy's words came out haltingly. "But your boys were like my own kids. How many afternoons like this did we play cricket with them up there on that lawn? Or go out on the boat with them, fishing and swimming?"

"Jesus, Billy, you're going to make me cry," Brown said and started out the door to the rear deck. Then he paused, turned, and looked at his friend, tossing him the empty glass. "Bring me another, will ya, Billy?" Billy started to move to the Scotch, then changed his mind and followed his friend outside. Griffin Brown was on deck, staring out at the water, as Billy came up and put his arm around him, laying his head on Brown's shoulder and then hugging him hard for several long moments before speaking. "I would have rather died myself than see the boys hurt. Mandy cried her eye out when she heard. She and the grandkids are going to say a novena for them."

He raised his head up now and after a moment spoke again with words he had practiced. "As for me. . . I'm going to kill Wang myself. And believe me, I'm going to make him pay. I'm going to cut the little slant - eyed bastard up in pieces. I'm going to bring you his balls in a jar."

This promise made, Billy returned inside and poured three fingers of Scotch and added the splash of soda just the way Griffin Brown liked it. Then he took it out to his friend, and as he came out the door he laughed.

Brown glanced at him curiously. "Something funny?"

Billy grinned. "I was just remembering the time you first got this boat and you had this big party and it was Kevin's birthday, he was fourteen or fifteen."

Brown grinned back, remembering the day nearly eighteen years ago. "Fifteen."

Billy went on happily. "And Fiona had her priests here."

"And nuns," Brown added, almost laughing.

"That's right," Billy gasped with an even bigger smile as he remembered. "There were nuns, a whole bunch of them, gee. . . and an ambassador."

Brown nodded with pride and humor. "The German ambassador. . . and the lord mayor, a couple of MPs – oh, this was a boatload of some very respectable people."

Billy was fighting tears of laughter. "And you had this hooker, she was supposed to be from a fashion magazine – what was her name? Tina. . . Tina!"

"Tanya," Brown popped in a moment later as he remembered.

"Yeah," Billy recalled. "Chrickey, did she have some great tits."

"When you're just turning fifteen, great tits are very important," Brown said with a misty smile.

"Only neither Kevin or anybody else knew she was a hooker. Kev thought she was straight, only every time she moved past him she'd feel him up. . .

stroke his joint – geez, I'm the only other one on board who knows who she is and I'm about to split a gut and I think young Kevin's going to pole-vault off the boat if something doesn't happen. . . and all them priests and nuns and ambassadors are around making their happy talk and she finally gets him downstairs. . . and how many times did he come?" Billy asked and for the first time saw his friend was crying.

"Three." Brown said. "The first time before he could get it out of his pants."

Billy nodded and tried to smile. "He was one tired puppy when he blew out his birthday candles that day."

The two old friends looked at each other through the tears and over the past. Almost a minute went by before Billy spoke again. "Geez, Grif, you think we'll ever have good times again?"

9

The silver-haired man answered the phone on the second ring. It wasn't the call he was expecting. He listened to the husky female voice.

"Colin, I thought you should know: Two people have been asking questions about the shooting. One's a local journo named McCabe, the other an American named Cody. I think he's an ex-policeman. I also think they're headed your way.

10

It was just noon on the day of the funeral mass that the Codys sailed into Sydney Harbour. Damien

guided the fifty-six-foot ketch through the massive
heads and then dipped gently south to Patrick's giggles as they moved past Lady Jane Bay, which they
quickly realized was one of Sydney's nude beaches,
for this was a hot, sunny day and the small patch of
rock and sand was well populated. Patrick waved
and was waved back to, which of course only
brought more giggles.

They sailed on, past Watsons Bay and Parsley
Bay, and like the sea the sky was a rich blue. The
homes they saw on shore were neat and attractive,
and many of them had red-tile roofs that gave them
a Mediterranean feel.

On past Shark Island and into Rose Bay, where
they watched a seaplane taxi through seemingly
dozens of wind surfers and small sailboats and then
rise above them like a large gull and bank off to the
open sea.

Beyond Point Piper and its mansions, they sailed.
Past the majestic opera house and under and beyond
the famous bridge. Finally they reached customs and
with little trouble conducted the necessary business,
and by three in the afternoon they had sailed back
up the harbor and secured a berth at the Sailing Boat
Club in Rushcutters Bay.

"It's a nice-looking city," Damien observed with
a smile tinged with an underlying tone of sadness.

The three of them, Cody and his sons, were
walking across the park that fronted Rushcutters
Bay, in the direction the boatman at the marina had
told them would lead them to Kings Cross. "I don't
know how long you've been at sea, but the Cross is a
pretty wild place at night – nothing you can't get
there," he had said, winking knowingly at Cody.

King's Cross also promised shops and restaurants and, most important for them now, banks, where Cody could cash some traveler's checks for Australian money.

"It *is* a nice-looking city," Cody replied to his son. Then he added, "Thinking about Mom?"

The tall, bronze eighteen-year-old darted a look at his father that reflected a hint of surprise. "Yeah, I guess I am, a little. . . she's part of it."

"What's the other part?" Cody asked.

Damien smiled and shrugged. "It's hard to put into words. It just seems strange that we talked about sailing around the world for so many years, and I guess I never really believed that we'd do it. And yet here we are, and we are doing it. . . but without Mom."

"Hey, look!" Patrick called excitedly as he ran ahead to get a better view of a cricket match just ahead.

Seeing a cricket match was something new and different for them, but Cody sensed that the younger boy's enthusiasm was also sparked by a desire to break away from conversation and the talk of his late mother. They had all learned that an unexpected remark, or even just hearing a song she used to like, could still sometimes trigger a melancholy that might last for hours or even days.

"It's a trip she would have wanted us to take," Cody answered his older boy once Patrick was gone.

"I know," Damien said, managing a smile. "I just wish she could have been here."

"So do I," Cody said after a moment. And suddenly he wanted a drink, desperately.

They caught up to Patrick on the fringe of the cricket oval and stayed and watched the game and its white-clad players for some minutes with a mix of bafflement and curiosity.

"What's the score?" Patrick asked an elderly lady after a particularly good hit that saw the batsman running back and forth between the wickets several times.

"Oh, I think they're nearing a century," she said with the smile of an aficionado.

"Great," Patrick responded with a wide perplexed smile, which he played to his father and older brother. . . and then added when the elderly lady was out of earshot, "Whatever that means."

* * *

Despite the boatman's lurid implications, the shopkeepers of Kings Cross obviously had worked hard to make it a pleasant area, at least in the daytime. There were tree-lined streets, a nice park with a huge spraying fountain, outdoor restaurants – and as if that weren't enough, right in the heart, just to finish the all-around wholesome image, a clean and sparkling McDonald's. All off which attracted families of eager tourists who happily trooped from one souvenir shop to another. But Cody also noticed that mixed in among the storefronts were nightclubs and bars. Many had old-fashioned neon signs hanging over their fronts, and all of them exuded a general aura of sleaze. Some were just opening up now that it was late afternoon, their sidewalk pitchmen trying to lure passersby into seeing girls, girls, girls. . . and on the sidewalk a crusty, bearded man in filthy, tattered clothes and equally filthy bare feet stood and urinated into the gutter, as the hookers who couldn't wait for night to fall, the ones with drug hunger in their eyes, lurked hopefully in doorways.

The Codys found a bank, and then – to the amusement of the boys – a pay telephone in the form of a squat orange box with a receiver on top, which had been placed on a stand and wheeled onto the sidewalk outside the news agency it was in front of. Cody made several calls and finally located Joe McCabe, who had flown over two days before to try to get a head start. They agreed to meet at Archibald's, an outdoor restaurant on the park.

* * *

McCabe arrived just in time to hear Patrick's fervent "Oh, gross!" as the boy discovered that Australians think it's a neat idea to put a slice of beet root on your hamburger. The offending vegetable was quickly removed, but the damage had been done. The hamburger patty, the lettuce, and the bun were all stained and flavored with the dark red juice.

They all agreed, even McCabe, that beet root on a hamburger was disgusting.

"You know, when I look back, I should have known. . . that was the first sign," McCabe mused, squinting contemplatively into a cigarette. "My ex-wife loved beet root. Enough said? She still grows them in her garden. I suspect she used to grow nightshade out there too. You know, just for shaving off a little at a time into my morning coffee or whatever." He rolled his eyes and offered his familiar crooked grin, which he now turned on the passing waitress as he ordered a beer.

"What have you been able to dig up?" Cody asked.

McCabe squinted again and stamped his cigarette out in the ashtray. "You want my opinion?"

"I have a feeling I'm going to get it whether I do or I don't," Cody answered.

"That's true," McCabe said as he took another cigarette out of his pack. "Just think of it as a warning label like they put on these things: Doing what you came here to do is very liable to be not good for your health."

"You want to expand on that?"

"Sure," McCabe said. "Let's start with Tommy Creager. I've talked to some of the best crime hacks who have been around this city for a long time. Not one of them sees any possible connection between Tommy being killed and the disco fire, which they all point out was over six weeks later. . . . I mean, the ones who didn't come right out and laugh in my face probably thought I was on something." McCabe broke off briefly to light his cigarette.

"Okay," Cody said after a moment.

McCabe looked at him curiously. " 'Okay'? I'm not sure what that means."

"It means, Okay, maybe your crime hacks are right. . . maybe they're not," Cody answered. "But I'm going to have to find that out. Because whatever the answer is, it doesn't change what I came to Sydney for, which is to try and find out who killed Tommy Creager. If that leads to the disco fire it leads to the disco fire; if it doesn't, it doesn't."

McCabe exhaled a cloud of smoke unenthusiastically. "The problem with that right now is that two of Griffin Brown's sons were killed in that fire. . .

and he's not a man to be crossed. From everything I hear, this town is a powder keg – which, incidently, we happen to be, this very moment, sitting right on top of."

"What do you mean?" Cody asked.

"See that place down the street?" They followed his indication to a light-colored, four-story brick building on the corner, a large neon cowboy hanging off the front. "The Cowboy Club is Griffin Brown's main operation, his headquarters. By Kings Cross standards, upscale. There's a bar and restaurant on the ground floor, and the next two floors up. . . " McCabe paused, glanced at Patrick and reconsidered his words, "He's got ladies of the evening working, high class, high priced. Top floor is the gambling club – blackjack, roulette, two-up."

"Isn't all that illegal here?" Damien asked.

"Of course," McCabe nodded.

"But then. . . I mean, if you could find out about it in a couple of days, why can't the cops?" Damien persisted.

"Oh, the cops know," McCabe said, offering a rather jaded smile. "But they don't even bother to raid the place anymore. Every time they did in the past, Brown was tipped off. Believe me, Brown is the biggie. He owns three or four other brothels around here and a couple of bars, where supposedly some heavy-duty drug dealing goes on."

"This guy's into drugs too?" Cody asked.

"Oh, he's an all-around fella," McCabe answered with a wink. "For years the newspapers here have referred to him as the King of Sin." The humor left him now as he continued. "There are some people who think he's one of the major drug suppliers on the east coast of Australia. . . the same people think that's probably what was behind the firebombing at the disco. Brown's two sons who were killed were supposedly his right arm, especially in the drug business."

"Competition moving in," Cody thought out loud.

"Right," McCabe nodded. "The most likely candidate, though no one can prove it yet, is a fella named Henry Wang. He runs brothels, gambling dens, and drugs out of Chinatown. He's also supposed to have a very nice restaurant down there, top food."

"Don't the cops close anything down?" Patrick asked in mild amazement.

McCabe grinned. "From what I hear, not unless you miss a payment. There's a lot ot folks here who say the cops in Sydney are a lot like the police force you Yanks used to have in Chicago in the 1930s."

"Which means we can't expect a lot of help if Dad starts looking into Griffin Brown," Damien said.

"It's more than that," McCabe answered, growing serious. "Griffin Brown buried his two sons today. The feeling around town has been that once that's happened, all hell is likely to break loose. I'd hate to see any of us get caught in the cross fire."

Cody looked to his two sons, whose eyes never wavered, then turned back to McCabe. "We'd hate to get caught in the cross fire too. But Tommy Creager was my friend."

McCabe exhaled and sank back into his chair. "Why did I have a feeling you'd say that?" He squinted at his watch. "In that case, I've got a date in about twenty minutes."

"Anybody special?" Cody asked

McCabe looked pleased with himself. "Well, as it happened, last night, going against the conventional wisdom of my crime hack friends, I renewed an old acquaintanceship." McCabe rolled his eyes appropriately for effect. "She's blond, blue-eyed. . . and unfortunately weighs about eighteen stone." He coughed and chuckled. "And if you want to know how much that is," he said to Patrick, "multiply eighteen by fourteen, because fourteen is how many pounds there are in a stone." He looked back at the others now. "She also happens to work for the coroner's department, and after an evening of rather romantic wining and dining, she said if I showed up at her office a little after five, when most of her bosses have just gone home, she'd find an empty room for me and let me have a look at the medical reports on the people killed in the fire. You see, in a rather romantically indiscreet moment, she hinted that I might find something of interest in them. . . but that was all I could get out of her, because I think after she said it she wished she hadn't." He consulted his watch again. "I'm going to have to get moving." Cody stood up with him. "I'll find you at Rushcutters Bay when I'm done. I wouldn't think that will be much before seven-thirty or eight."

"Or maybe a lot later, if your chubby friend gets romantic again," Patrick teased.

McCabe looked at the boy and grinned, then turned to his father. "You have a cruel son."

"Before you go," Cody added, causing the other man to pause. "Have you been able to find out where Tommy Creager's things are? I'd like to have a look at them."

McCabe shook his head. "Nothing for sure. My best guess is that they're still at his place. He had a terrace house over in Paddington." He fished a folded piece of paper out of an inside pocket, used it first for a reference and then handed it to Cody as he talked. "Lived there with a woman named. . . Jill Edwards, from what I hear a rather unsucessful would-be filmmaker, scriptwriter, that sort of thing. She still lives there, or at least her answering machine does. I've been trying her since yesterday afternoon, left half a dozen messages."

"How far is Paddington from here?" Cody asked.

McCabe shrugged. "Maybe ten minutes by cab."

11

Some boys were playing cricket in the middle of the narrow, tree-lined street as the cab carrying the three Codys interrupted their game.

The streets of Paddington were narrow, as were the houses, which had mostly been built in the 1850s. They were terrace houses, one upon the other, sharing common walls, and most trimmed with wrought-iron fences and balconies.

The cab crept along for another half block before number 157 was spotted. It stopped, and Cody paid the driver with the unfamiliar currency and stepped out into the street. As he did, he momentarily found himself on the edge of darkness once more. . . and he could hear the screams again and the panic, and the smoke stung his eyes.

"Dad, are you alright?" Damien asked.

And then he was back in Paddington and the cab was moving off down the street. The screams and smoke and panic were gone. . . but there lingered for him a sense of uneasiness.

"I'm fine," he finally said.

Unlike most of the other homes on the block, 157 was badly in need of a coat of paint. The whole place looked tired; even the windows seemed to sag. The only bright spots were half a dozen pots of geraniums in a window box inside the rusted, waist-high wrought-iron-fenced enclosure, which itself was only about three feet deep and ran the length of the twenty-foot building. A middle-aged woman in a summer print dress was watering the flowers.

Down the street the cricket game had resumed, and with it the sounds of a passionate argument. Angry, high-pitched children's voices accompanied Cody as he crossed the street to the house where Tommy Creager had lived. . . and a settling chill, a sense of foreboding grew as he neared it.

The woman in the print dress looked up at him with a jerky, nervous movement and then avoided his eyes. She was somewhere in her mid-forties and wore her dark brown hair in pigtails, as Judy Garland had in *The Wizard of Oz.*

"Hello," Cody said and smiled. But her only response was to move to the faucet to turn off the water. "I'm looking for Jill Edwards."

"I can't help you," she said, her words coming out in quick spurts. "I don't know where she is." Once the water was turned off she kept her eyes to the ground and moved to get past him and out the gate.

"You're taking care of her flowers, you must have some idea," he continued, keeping his tone friendly.

"I don't," she insisted, slipping by him and hurrying the twenty feet down the sidewalk to her own wrought-iron gate. It was then that he caught his first glimpse of the silver-haired man. He was sitting in a car, half a dozen houses away. Cody saw him, but it didn't register; his attention was on the woman, and for a flash the screams and the smoke were back. . . and then gone again.

"Do you have any idea when she'll be back?" Cody tried.

The woman with Judy Garland's hair opened her own front door and now for the first time stared at him for several long seconds, as if trying to memorize his face, and then finally said no. She disappeared inside, slamming and bolting the door.

Damien and Patrick joined Cody at the gate.

"Friendly lady," Patrick offered.

"She's scared," Cody replied.

"Of what?" Damien asked with surprise.

"At the moment, me," Cody said. "Or maybe anyone who's asking about where to find Jill Edwards."

"You think she knows where she is?" Patrick asked.

"She's watering the lady's flowers and probably picking up her mail. She knows something. The question is, what? And what is she so jumpy about?"

Cody also wondered what he himself was so on edge about. Why the flashes of the fire again? Was it just being near Tommy Creagers house? Was it the woman? Was she lying? Was it something else? And then the sound of the cricket game down the street tugged at his attention. "There might be another way to find out where Jill Edwards is," he said.

"What do you mean?" Damien asked.

Cody smiled. "One of the first things you learn when you're a street cop is that if you ever want to know something about a neighborhood, you ask a kid who lives there. The neighborhood is his whole world. He knows all the shortcuts, the best hiding places. . . and all the gossip."

* * *

Patrick munched on an apple he'd bought at the corner shop and watched the cricket game up close for several minutes before a truck came along and forced the boys to the side. "Hi," he said to the nearest boy, whose name he had overheard to be Daniel. Daniel was short and good-looking with a mop of black hair that he kept brushing up and off his sweaty face. "I'm just moving in up the road," Patrick added.

"Yeah?" Daniel responded with a thick Australian accent.

"Yeah," Patrick answered.

"You a Yank?" Daniel asked.

Patrick smiled. He'd never been referred to as a Yank before. "Yeah, I'm from California."

"You ever been to Disneyland?" the red-headed boy with glasses wanted to know.

Patrick nodded. "Lots of times. . . . You guys live on this street?"

"Most of us do," Daniel said. "Hedgehog's my cousin, though, he's from Adelaide," he added, indicating a round boy of about twelve with a shock of blond hair that stuck up like a brush.

The truck had cleared, and then another car. Patrick knew that the game was about to resume. "My dad's talking about buying that run-down place there, number 157."

"One fifty-seven?" The red-headed boy repeated as if someone had just offered him a snake.

"What's wrong with it?" Patrick asked.

"Just you gotta be crazy to live there. That's the ghost house," Daniel said.

"Come on," Patrick laughed.

"No, it's true," a tall, skinny boy named Basil interjected. His voice was at the cracking age. "Back during World War II there was a guy who lived there who used to strangle women. They found six bodies stuffed down his well."

"The ghosts of two of 'em women walk around the place at night. They say that anyone who lives there comes to a bad end," Daniel added solemnly.

"I wonder if they walk around naked when they're haunting," Hedgehog asked, to predictable giggles from the others.

"It's really true about people coming to a bad end," Basil went on. "The last guy who lived there, he was a Yank too. . . he was murdered over in New Zealand."

"And his girlfriend, she thinks someone's trying to kill her now," Daniel added.

"How d'you know?" Patrick asked.

"She told my mum. She said that once, after her boyfriend was killed, someone broke into the house. And she thought someone was watching her for a while. . . and then he wasn't. And then a couple of days ago she thought someone tried to run her over and she was really scared and couldn't sleep, so she took off and she's hiding out in her brother's place in Hornsby."

"Maybe it was just one of the ghosts trying to run her over," Hedgehog offered with a lurid grin. "One of the naked ones with big boots."

But nobody thought it was as funny the second time around.

Patrick looked convincingly apprehensive, mainly because he was. "I think I'd better go tell my dad maybe it's not such a good idea buying that place. See you guys," he said, and headed up the street. Daniel, Hedgehog, and the others resumed their game.

* * *

"She's hiding out at her brother's place in some town called Hornsby," Patrick related eagerly to his father and brother.

"Hornsby," Cody repeated, to get the sound of the word in his head. Then he smiled at his youngest son. "Good work."

"Thanks," Patrick said, brimming with pride.

"The only question is, where's Hornsby?" Damien asked.

"If it's in the Sydney area, a cabby should be able to tell us," Cody said. "If it isn't, somebody will know. In any case, we should catch a cab to take us back to Kings Cross so we can pick up some groceries for the boat. On the way Patrick can tell us anything else the boys told him."

They headed off in the direction of the cricket game, the way they had been driven in, knowing that the main street they had driven over on was one block up. And it was as they were passing the boys in the street that Cody heard the sound of the car starting, and suddenly he knew. For a split second he was on the edge of darkness again, and the flames and smoke and screaming were back, but he knew he couldn't linger here, he knew the approaching car was danger. He forced himself to whirl, and the flames and smoke and screaming were gone; he was looking back down the narrow, tree-lined street and his hand was reaching for his Walther, which in the same instant he knew wasn't there. The car was pulled halfway out of its parking space, idling. . . and through the reflections on the windshield he could catch jigsawlike pieces of the face of the man with silver hair. And it seemed as if for a moment, even at this distance, their eyes locked. But now the car was moving again, and Cody looked for cover, first for the boys and then himself – and then he realized the danger for the cricket players.

"Out of the street, boys, out of the street!" he shouted, and the game stopped momentarily as young eyes considered him as if he were somewhat loony. The car was all the way out in the street now, but instead of continuing down toward them it turned, stopped, and backed up, repeating the action several times before it could completely turn around on the narrow street. Then it drove off in the other direction.

Cody watched the car disappear around a bend. He was at first confused and then embarrassed, mostly for his sons. He had thought his "gift" was warning him of danger, but he reasoned now that he had obviously misread whatever the flashes were revealing, and he silently cursed the nine-year-old

bullet still lodged in his skull. The bullet and the following coma that had changed his life.

"Sorry boys," he called to the cricket players and
then looked to his sons. They had been through awkward moments like this before. "Sorry," he repeated
to them quietly, and they resumed walking

"On second thought," Daniel could be heard saying, "they're just the right people for old number
157," and the others laughed.

12

Cube steak sizzled with butter and fresh-chopped
onions in the frying pan atop the stove in the galley.
Patrick was cooking dinner and watching a game
show on a TV set they had rented in Kings Cross. On
their return to the Cross from Paddington, they had
spent a little over an hour shopping at various shops
– grocery, fruit and vegetable, butcher, and, happily
for Patrick, a TV rental place. For they had learned in
New Zealand that the American set they had on
board, something called NTSC, was useless in both
New Zealand and Australia, which used the
European PAL system. On the screen the audience
screamed with delight as a woman won six-thosand
dollars. The bouncy, curly-haired host now gleefully
threw the money, in a bundle, to her. . . as overhead
thunder rumbled and a rain began to fall on the deck
above.

In his cabin, down the passageway, Damien tried
to study Latin, but his mind was wandering easily
tonight, Damien knew he was where he wanted to
be, at least for now: with his father and brother. But

he also felt alone, almost cast adrift from the rest of the world, from the friends he grew up with, the duplex in Playa Del Rey where they used to live. Along with the vision of the house on the beach where he had grown up, he saw his mother and for a moment almost cried. But it was more than missing a peer group or wanting to go home again. He knew he was no longer a child and that he soon would have to move on and try to discover the purpose of his own life. For he believed there had to be a purpose, an order to life, a God who loves us despite the monstrous things that are allowed to happen. Though he didn't fully realize it, he believed because his mother had taught him to believe since he had been a little boy. He believed because without believing he couldn't have coped with what had happened to her.

"Hey, Damien," Patrick called.

"Yeah?" Damien answered.

"Dinner's almost ready, think you could find Dad?"

"Sure," Damien answered, welcoming the distraction.

The storm was coming in from northeast, through the heads; lightning forked and crackled above the harbor. Damien hurried down the jetty, through the warm rain that was increasing in intensity. He spotted his father coming away from the squat orange pay phone by the marina office. They were both soaked by the time they came together and stood now in the rain as they talked.

"I'm going to have to go to Hornsby," Cody said.

In the cab ride from Paddington back to Kings Cross they had learned that Hornsby was a suburb of Sydney, about forty minutes north from the other side of the bridge. The driver also volunteered that the best way to get there, especially for people who didn't know the city, would be by train. All they had to do was catch the train into the city at the underground station in Kings Cross and then transfer at Town Hall.

"Did you talk to her?" Damien asked

"No," Cody answered, as a loud, snapping clap of thunder sent them back toward the boat. "They don't have a phone book in the marina office that covers the Hornsby area," Cody continued. "I tried information; it rang about fifty times, and then when they finally answered, the operator said he couldn't possibly give me all the Edwards listings in the Hornsby area and then hung up."

"Charming," Damien said, smiling. They had reached the boat now and climbed on board, but before going inside Damien paused and looked at his father for a long moment. "Let me go with you."

"I appreciate the thought," Cody said. "But I'd feel better if you stayed here and kept an eye on Patrick."

Damien nodded. "I saw you put your Walther on. Should I have your spare gun handy?"

And Cody thought about the firebombed disco and the flashes of fire that he saw, and he felt sure that they were connected but he knew he couldn't prove it. Not yet. Maybe never. And he thought of Tommy Creager shot dead in a parking lot in New Zealand and then of the frightened woman in Paddington with the Judy Garland hair. . . and of her neighbor Jill Edwards, his dead friend's girlfriend, who was now afraid someone was trying to kill her.

"Yeah, the gun could be a good idea," Cody said after some moments. "I don't know if there's any danger yet, but. . . "

He let the rest of the sentence drop. Damien understood.

"We'd better get in and eat some dinner," the eighteen-year-old responded with a businesslike smile, "or Pat's going to be awful mad at us."

Patrick was a good cook, and they all ate well. By the time dinner was over the rain was coming down harder, but the lightning and thunder, at least for the present, were farther away. It was almost eight o'clock, and there was no sign of McCabe. Cody, now having changed into some dry clothes, felt he couldn't wait any longer, and so grabbing a rain slicker he headed out, down the jetty and then, as they had this afternoon, across Rushcutters Bay Park, this time in quest of the underground train station.

13

The rain was steady as Cody moved past the fountain and across Macleay Street, and he could see how with the coming of night the pleasant, clean, tree-lined streets of Kings Cross became transformed in their gaudy attire. Raucous music blared from half a dozen bars and clubs as he made his way down the sidewalk, past the hucksters and pimps and hookers who, because of the rain, were working from doorways and from under the permanent awnings that most of the storefronts sported. A drunk and flabby bare-breasted blond hooker waved and called for trade from an upstairs window, seemingly oblivious to the rain that slanted in on her and made her skin glisten and her hair soaked and bedraggled. Cody moved past the McDonald's and a quarter of a block later finally reached the underground station and turned into it. As he did, a smoky-gray Rolls-Royce glided past.

The Rolls-Royce pulled to a stop a block later, in front of the Cowboy Club. For some moments after the car stopped nothing happened. Then, all at once, three men, their right hands under their sport coats, rushed from the entrance of the Cowboy to positions of cover, facing the three different approaches to the club. Finally, after all-clear nods, Billy Packer emerged from the front door and moved to the Rolls, whereupon the back door opened and Griffin Brown stepped out.

"I thought these days were over twenty years ago," Brown grumbled as they moved purposefully toward the club. His head was splitting from the physical and emotional drain of the last few days, and he was more than a little put out at having been summoned here, to his own club, for a meeting.

"When I kill the Chinaman, they'll be over for good," the stocky ex-boxer replied. "We got men in upstairs windows across the street too."

And then they were inside. It took Griffin Brown's eyes a few moments to adjust to the darkened light of the bar. The place was packed and the crowd verging on noisy. "Any problems?" Brown asked Tim Lake, a large, bald-headed man who for the last several years had sat every night behind a podiumlike counter next to the front door.

"Nothing special, Mr. Brown," Lake returned.

Brown considered the bald Goliath a moment. "I appreciate the flowers you and the others sent."

"We all felt real bad for you, Mr. Brown, for Kevin and David. We just. . . ahhh. . ." Lake was stammering. He was clumsy with words. He could break up a bar fight in a matter of seconds and wasn't afraid to use the sawed-off shotgun he kept under the podium in front of him, but right now he was tripping over emotion.

"Lakey's offered to help out on the Chinaman if I need him," Billy Packer interjected, breaking the awkward moment .

"You're a good man, Tim," Brown nodded. "I won't forget you."

His eyes adjusted, he and Billy Packer started through the barroom.

"Who exactly is here?" Brown asked.

"The whole gang: Mooney, Jacklan, and Horowitz," Billy answered.

"Horowitz?" Brown snapped, surprised and irritated. "He can fly down to give me shit about the delivery, but he can't make it a few hours earlier for my sons' funeral?"

Mickey Packer, Billy's compact, muscular, twenty-four-year-old son, opened the door marked EMPLOYEES ONLY at the end of the bar and let his father and Griffin Brown through. Mickey, whose job it was to sit at the end bar stool and control who went in and out of the door, had been born without the ability to hear and consequently no words were exchanged, but Brown patted the younger man on the arm as he passed.

"What about Nicholas?" Brown asked once he and Billy were alone, walking down the corridor that ran the length of the building.

"I'm sorry, still nothing yet. I've turned the heat up on everyone," Billy said apologetically.

"Jesus, you'd have thought he'd at least have called his mother. . . " Brown sighed as they stopped in front of a double door covered with heavy red leather upholstery punctuated with brass braids.

"We've got Fiona's phone tapped. . . nothing. Unless she's contacting him through one of her priests," Billy offered.

"Those fat, lazy bastards. They just want to sip wine with her and eat at expensive restaurants," Brown said bitterly and sighed. "I want Nicholas found. It's important now."

"I'm doing everything I can," Billy assured him.

Brown nodded and then turned the doorknob and entered the room. Shauna was the first person he saw. . . and for the first time today the tension left him. Shauna was black and stunning. Her shiny, low-cut dress clung to her shapely body. She glided toward him and touched his hand, and the touch bespoke sympathy and love and that she was with him. At first her voice was low and all business: "Jacklan's nervous and getting drunk, Mooney's bored, and the Jew's bitchy, dangerous." Then she turned back to the room with her professional smile. "Well, gentlemen, can I freshen anyone's drink before I leave you to your business?"

"I'll have another," Jacklan said, holding up his glass. But as she moved for it, Mooney beat her to it.

"I'll get it for you myself, Jack. . . I'd still like to catch the ten o'clock plane," he said as he moved to the chrome-and-black-marble bar. "After all, you're not a difficult man to please," he went on, putting a couple of ice cubes in the glass and then filling it with vodka.

Brown nodded to Shauna, who left now.

The room was decorated with a mix of brass and chrome and black leather furniture, black marble tables, and of course the bar. "It looks like a Japanese whorehouse," Brown had said with an incredulous laugh when he'd first seen it. The redecoration of the room had been a birthday present from his son Kevin a few years before. At first he'd thought his son had done it as a bad joke. . . but when he realized the boy actually thought it looked good, he had left it as it was. Now, being in it for the first time since the two older sons had been killed, he knew he'd never change it.

"You boys wanted to see me," Brown said, giving Billy a nod that sent the stocky little man to the bar to pour three fingers of scotch and splash it with soda.

"Before we talk business," Horowitz said, "let me say you have my sincerest sympathies as to your sons."

Horowitz's words might have concerned the loss of a couple of station wagons, for all the warmth and compassion they conveyed, and Brown knew they were offered in such a fashion to aggravate him. . . and in so doing, challenge him. "You're very kind," Brown returned flatly, not taking the bait. "Now, I've had a few long days. What is it you wanted to see me about?"

"The bloody Chinaman is who," Jacklan said with concern. "He says he didn't do it."

"Jesus. . . what did you expect him to say?" Brown snapped angrily, knowing his temper was shorter than it should be. "Yes, it was me; I fire-bombed the bloody disco'? What's the matter, Jacko, is the vodka finally making your brain simple, or does the Chinaman think we're all stupid? That we don't have memories? Flaming petrol cans is how he took care of his problems a few years back."

"That's different; they were other chinks," Jacklan pleaded. "They were trying to open up their own gambling club in Chinatown. He wouldn't dare hit you."

"And if someone wanted to make it look like it was the Chinaman who did the Galah, the same kind of firebombing is exactly the way they'd do it," Horowitz added firmly.

"I think what they're trying to say, Grif, is that the heat's on pretty good right now," Ian Mooney offered. In his late fifties, balding, and with a cherubic face, he was called the Professor, for that's exactly what he looked like. In point of fact, he'd had his first brush with the law as a teenager and had spent the better part of his twenties in various prisons. But as he'd grown older, he'd grown smarter, and prison was avoided. Not success, though; for the past dozen years or so he'd controlled most of the drugs, prostitution, and gambling in Melbourne. And now he was trying to be a calming voice.

"There's already talk of a royal commission. . . " Jacklan said in a near whine, unable to control the slur of his words.

"Stuff the royal commission," Griffin Brown said defiantly. "You think I'm afraid of any fucking politicians? If they get to be trouble we'll either bloody buy them, or if they can't be bought, bloody kill them. But my guess is that we'll buy them, like we buy everyone else, like we've bought you all these years, Jacko. And now, what a prize we have: a bloody drunk deputy commissioner of police." Brown glared down into his own drink and suddenly threw it against the wall. This was getting to be a habit, he realized. And he knew that until this was over he should stop drinking and wondered if he could. He was in the trenches again, his back against the wall.

"Grif, you've got to slow down and listen," Horowitz said.

"Why? Because you say so, you Jew bastard?" Brown was beyond anger now. He was ready to kill, and the others sensed it and instinctively threw a glance at Billy Packer to see if he had a gun in his hand. He didn't.

"You didn't even have the decency to come to my sons' funeral. . . or even send flowers," Brown went on vindictively, "So you just shut the fuck up." He looked to the others and knew they didn't dare speak. His tone lowered now, but was no less deadly. "The first man I ever killed, I killed in this room. I was nineteen years old. I cut his bloody throat from here to here," he said, drawing a line with his finger from one ear to the other. "I cut it so hard I almost cut off his head. . . it fell over backwards, and there was only a flap of skin at the back of his neck to hold it on."

"Well, I'll be damned," Mooney said with a dawning smile of admiration, "that was Paddles McGuire. . . so it was you."

"That's right," Brown said and then added pointedly, "and he was my friend. And I'll tell you what: Right now, other than Billy Packer, the only people I see here are a couple of business partners and a drunken cop." Brown paused, and the room became silent again, the impact of the last words not escaping Mooney, Horowitz, or Jacklan. Feeling fully in control, Brown continued matter-of-factly. "You know, for the first couple of weeks Paddles was gone, everyone thought he'd just gone off drinking and whoring like he was wont to do and left me in charge. And by the time what was left of his body had popped up in the harbor, I was in charge. You see, by then I had convinced his solicitor to draw up and execute the transfer of ownership on this place, and I'd brought a few solicitors of my own, some cops, and, with Billy's help, killed four other men who would have stood in my way."

"Let's see," Mooney said, displaying a scholarly interest, "that would have been Ernie, Paddles's brother. . . Richie Brennan. . . "

"It doesn't fucking matter, Ian," Brown snapped. "The point is, I did what I had to do to make this place mine. . . just like when I was eleven years old and my old man got killed building the Harbour Bridge and I had four sisters and a little brother and a drunken mother to take care of. That winter, we ended up living in a house made out of cardboard boxes and rope right in the middle of Hyde Park. There were thousands of us living there and it seemed like it rained every bloody day and we spent half our time in soup and bread lines. And then first my little sister Colleen died because there wasn't enough food and there wasn't any medicine, and then my brother Teddy died. . . and I knew that we'd all die if I didn't do something, if I wasn't strong enough to make it different. There was a kid named Cecil, he lived in a tent near us. He had a cricket bat. One night I snuck in there and stole it. The next day I went walking until I could get my courage up. . . I must have walked my legs off. I ended up down on Bourke Street near Liverpool. There was a little Italian grocery. I went inside with my bat and this little old man asked me what I wanted. I hit him with the bat as hard as I could; I got him just below the hips and he went down screaming like hell. And I grabbed a loaf of bread and eight pounds, six, out of his cash box and ran as hard as I ever had in my life. We ate like kings that night. . . ." And for a moment he was back there in Hyde Park, in the rain, eleven years old, and he could smell the corned beef they'd cooked up that night and see the faces of his little sisters and his mother. The room was quiet, and he knew he had been rambling and sensed that the others were trying to decide if they should be afraid of him because he might kill them or because he might be losing his grip. "Jesus, Billy, get me another drink," Brown said. For the moment the energy seemed to drain out of him, as his ex-boxer friend moved to the bar to comply.

"We're just asking for a little time, Grif, until the shipment's in," Mooney said, once again trying to restore calm.

Ian and I have a lot of money tied up in that shipment," Horowitz added. "We put it in on your word. Your word and the promise that Kevin and David would take care of everything."

"They did take care of everything," Brown responded in a low growl, his ire building again.

"They were bloody geniuses," Mooney interjected quickly to soothe the waters, then continuing with an admiring smile. "It was nothing any of us old war-horses would have tried without them, I'll tell you that. Really in today's world, using our combined cash to buy weapons, we trade the weapons for raw opium, smuggle it into Marseilles in soccer balls, have it refined into first-grade heroin. . ."

"What do you want?" Brown interrupted, his voice tired. When Billy Packer put the drink in his hand, he took a long pull from it.

"Wait till the shipment's in before you go after Wang; it's only five more days," Horowitz said.

"I learned a long time ago that whenever anyone attacks you, you bloody well better hit back fast and twice as hard," Brown growled, but without bite.

"But according to Jacko, you can't even be sure it was Wang," Mooney said.

"That's right, Grif," Jacklan added earnestly. I swear to God, I'll find out who did it. . . and when I do, I'll put a bullet through his head myself. But if you go after Wang now and it wasn't him. . . if you start an all-out war. . . I won't be able to control it. Jesus, it could wreck everything for all of us."

"If it wasn't the bloody Chinaman, then who the hell else would it have been?" Billy Packer interjected angrily. "All you guys are worried about is your six million you both put up. Well, Grif put up six million *and* the lives of his sons." Billy was on the edge of tears. Brown put his hand on his friend's shoulder.

"From what I hear, your son Kevin was quite a cocksman," Horowitz said. "How do we know that guy who threw the petrol cans wasn't just some irate husband or boyfriend?"

"It was the bloody Chinaman," Billy said fervently. "You wouldn't let him in on this deal, so now he's getting even. I say we've got to hit him now or he'll think he has us on the run. And the Galah won't be the last place he goes after."

"Look, Grif, I don't know who did it," Mooney said with some urgency. "Maybe it was the Chinaman; if it was, if you can find that out for sure, then I would expect that you'd do the same thing I would: You'd kill the little bastard and to hell with consequences. And Grif, I've been your friend for over twenty years, I'd be right there with you. The six million dollars I put up isn't important; we take risks in our business, we all know that. If it's the Chinaman then you've got to do it, and when you do you've got to do it good, so that no other little slant-eyed bastard will ever try to go after one of us again. You'll have to kill him and his wife and his kids and any other member of his family we can lay our hands on. But if it isn't him and we start this bloodbath. . . Jacko's right, there'll be a royal commission and so much heat. We could all lose everything. starting with the shipment, to everything, we've worked for over the years."

"We don't even know for sure if the Chinaman did it," Horowitz repeated quietly.

Brown sighed and after a long moment looked to Billy Packer. "What have you got working?"

"Tomorrow morning, early. He'll never get out of bed."

"Just until next Tuesday," Mooney appealed.

Brown considered for some moments, then looked to Billy again, "We'll hold off on the Chinaman."

"Geez. . . " Billy said with sadness and disappointment.

"But Jacko," Brown went on to the police official, "you get to that little slant bugger and tell him if I even think he's coming near one of my places, what I'll do to him and his family and his friends will make the rape of Nanking look like a bloody Girl Guides picnic."

14

The train arrived in Hornsby a little past nine, and by then the summer storm had all but passed. Only glistening streets, cars, and buildings, plus occasional faint flashes of lightning on the horizon and distant rumbling of rolling thunder lingered.

Cody's route from Kings Cross, as the cab driver had outlined, had been pretty straightforward. Shortly after leaving from the underground station, the commuter train had emerged on an elevated track, where it had traveled for no more than three or four minutes across a low-rise section of the city before moving underground again. Two stops later, still underground, it arrived at the cavernous Town Hall Station, where Cody had to change trains. He had ended up waiting almost thirty minutes for the

one to Hornsby. This time, however, once they rolled
out of the station, they left the underground behind
for good. The train swayed and clicked gently, first
through the outer parts of Sydney and then through
the suburbs, one stop after another: Crow's Nest,
Roseville, Killara, Pymble. . . and as the train rolled
on, Cody realized that in an odd way, despite the
dark tensions caused by Tommy Creager's death
and all that had seemed to follow – the disco fire,
and now, Jill Edward's fear that someone was trying
to kill her – the ride was proving relaxing, giving
him needed time to think. For he had realized this
afternoon in Paddington that even if he found her,
simply making contact with Jill Edwards would be a
tricky problem. If she was scared enough to flee here
for refuge, a stranger showing up on her brother's
doorstep or even phoning was not likely to elicit
admission that she was there. As he had waited for
his connecting train back at Town Hall, it had still
seemed an insoluble riddle. But then somewhere
between Killara and Pymble the tumblers had
clicked in as he recalled something McCabe had
mentioned that afternoon at the outdoor restaurant:
She was a would-be filmmaker.

* * *

There were sixteen Edwards listings in the Hornsby
phone book he came across on the station platform.
On checking the change in his pocket, he realized
with some consternation that he had enough for only
two calls. He either had to get lucky or else hope to
find someplace open in the little town, which from
here looked pretty much shut down for the night.

"Hello?" the old woman's voice said.

"Is this the Edwards residence?" Cody asked into the phone, affecting his best Australian accent.

"Yes, it is," the old woman replied.

"I'm sorry to bother you at such a late hour, but my name is Ed Cody, I'm with the Sydney film office. We have a project here submitted by a Jill Edwards, who we're most anxious to get together with."

"I'm sorry," the old woman said. "There's no Jill Edwards here."

The second number he tried didn't answer. The third did, but they hadn't heard of Jill Edwards either. Out of change, he headed for the sleeping town.

* * *

It was a clean and pretty little town in a plain way. The buildings were mostly made from pale-colored brick. Every third shop seemed to be a real estate office – and every shop seemed to be closed. He walked for several blocks on the curving main street, until, up ahead he could see some lights. Cody quickened his pace and didn't pay any attention to the passing car until suddenly its brakes screeched, and because of the wet street spun out, doing a complete 360-degree turn before coming to a stop near him. By then, Cody's hand had found his Walther, holstered behind his back, but a moment later the driver's face – which turned out to be Joe McCabe's – leered up at him with a crooked smile.

"Now here I am, sacrificing my body and what tiny shreds of dignity my ex-wife left me," McCabe

whined with a grin, "to the whale who ate
Wellington so we can discover the secrets of the
coroner's office. . . and you're off having all the fun."

"Did the coroner's office have any secrets?"
Cody smiled back.

"A couple," McCabe nodded, squinting. "Let's
find a pub; I'm bloody parched."

They found one – those were the lights Cody had
spotted – a block and a half away, which with the
exception of a video rental shop across the street
appeared to be the only place in Hornsby still open.

By the time they had parked, piled out, and started inside the pub, McCabe had explained how he
had gotten here. He had, as he told it, been so
"delayed" with his chubby lady-friend from the
coroner's office that he had borrowed her car to
drive over to Rushcutters Bay. There, of course,
Damien and Patrick had told him of Cody's de-
parture for Hornsby a good twenty minutes earlier.
The next forty minutes had entailed a mad dash
across the Harbour Bridge and up the Pacific
Highway to catch up with him

Throughout the telling of his saga McCabe managed to maintain his offhand, wisecracking persona,
but Cody sensed a facade. Something McCabe had
learned had shaken him.

"We're closing in thirty minutes," the bartender
announced as they sat down.

McCabe ordered a middy of Toothey's, which
turned out to be a moderate-sized glass of beer.

Cody considered beer himself, but his adrenaline
was working; it was beginning to feel like one of
those nights, one of those cases. Acting like a cop
again, he realized, grudgingly, that he was dragging

back all the old habits. "Double vodka, splash of soda," he ordered, turning to McCabe. "What did you learn from your chubby friend?"

"First, that she loves it when I talk dirty," McCabe grinned, lighting a cigarette with a slight tremble to his hand that hadn't been there earlier. "Second, she wished she'd kept her mouth shut last night when she told me there might be something interesting in the reports. It seems that today some people have been putting pressure on. A high-ranking cop — commissioner, deputy commissioner, she wasn't sure which — came through and passed the word to everyone that this case was under tight investigation and all autopsy reports were to be kept strictly confidential. Anyone caught leaking them would be fired and possibly prosecuted."

"Nice, soft touch," Cody commented.

"Yeah, really," McCabe agreed with a quick, nervous smile as he sucked on his cigarette. But then the smile vanished. "What's buried in those thirty-seven autopsies are a couple of heavy-duty items."

"Such as?" Cody asked.

"Well, you have to remember, this disco, the Galah, was owned and operated by two of Griffin Brown's sons — Kevin, the oldest and apparently his old man's favorite, and his slightly younger brother David, the business whiz. They, by the way, apparently didn't care for each other a whole lot."

"Both of them were killed in the fire," Cody said.

"Well, sort of," McCabe responded with the hint of a satisfied smile.

"What are you getting at?" Cody asked.

"What my friend knew yesterday was pretty interesting. . . but not as good as a report she saw today." McCabe spoke quickly now, confidentially; he enjoyed this part of being a reporter. "What she knew yesterday was simply this; – David Brown, thirty-two years old, died of smoke inhalation. . . " McCabe paused just a moment for effect, "while unconscious."

"Do they know why he was unconscious?" Cody asked.

"It wasn't because part of the building fell on him," McCabe answered. "According to the medical report, it looks more like a blow to the back of the head with something like a tire iron. They think he was unconscious before the fire started."

Cody considered a moment. "So he didn't just die by happenstance. Somebody wanted him dead, and used the fire. . . "

"It gets better," McCabe interrupted. "His older brother, Kevin, the heir apparent to the King of Sin's empire, was dead before the fire even began; someone had slipped something nice and smooth and sharp – like an ice pick – into his heart. . . then splashed him with petro."

"I'll be damned," Cody said with surprise.

"Yeah," McCabe nodded. "It changes the whole game, doesn't it?"

Cody pondered, drained his drink, and signaled for a second. "Only slightly," he said finally. "On the surface it sounds like what you talked about this afternoon. . . a major power move in the Sydney underworld."

"It does that," McCabe responded.

"But. . . " Cody said with a troubled look, and then didn't speak again for several moments. Something doesn't make sense here. If the goal was to kill

Griffin Brown's two sons – and apparently that was the goal – and they got close enough to actually kill one and render the other unconscious, meaning they could have easily killed him too. . . why go through the charade of firebombing the disco and killing all those other people?"

"To cover their tracks?" McCabe offered.

"That's not usually how people like Griffin Brown or. . . who was the man you talked about from Chinatown?"

"Henry Wang," McCabe answered.

"Or the Henry Wangs or any gangsters I've ever brushed with operate. If they're going to make a move, they make a move; there's rarely any subtlety, anything cleverly clandestine, just usually a few car bombs and a lot of bullets."

"Maybe we have a better class of underworld types Down Under," McCabe remarked with a twinkle.

Cody chuckled, then grew silent for several moments. "I'll ask you another question: Kevin and David Brown, the apples of their old man's eye, right arms of his organization. . . they'd have to have been well protected, surrounded only by the most trusted members of the organization. So how could Henry Wang or anyone else, for that matter, get someone close enough to kill one brother and leave the other unconscious?"

"I don't know," McCabe said.

"I'll give you one possible answer. We could be talking about someone who's already inside the Brown organization."

"A traitor," McCabe offered.

"Exactly," Cody nodded, "which could explain

why they might try to cover up their work with the fire. . . and why later they'd want to suppress the autopsy reports. I'd like to know who that police commissioner was."

"I'll see what I can find out," McCabe said.

Cody finished his second drink and considered a third, but then decided against it. "Now reach with me," Cody coaxed the reporter. "Tommy Creager, killed in a lonely parking lot in New Zealand. He'd spent a lot of time with the Brown family, drinking with the wife, going to restaurants with her. Is it possible he knew who the traitor was? Or would have after the disco fire?"

"It is a bit of a reach. . . " McCabe said, doubtful.

"But it's possible, isn't it?" Cody urged.

"It's possible," McCabe finally agreed.

"And if knowing the identity of the traitor was the reason Tommy was killed. . . it could also be why someone's trying to kill his girlfriend now."

* * *

Using a pair of pay phones at the back of the pub, they split up the remaining Edwards listings. McCabe got lucky on his second call and frantically waved Cody over to take the receiver. "A man answered, I gave him the bit about the film office, he got excited and said to hold on."

Cody took the phone and his body went icy cold.

"Hello," she said.

And he was falling into the darkness and he could see and smell the rotting flesh and suddenly feel a crushing, stinging blow across the face.

"Hello?" she repeated.

He was coming out of it. It had probably lasted less than a second. He felt weak, drained. He felt she should be dead, or would be very soon.

"My name's Ed Cody," he said.

"From the film office?" she asked, a hint of apprehension edging into her voice.

"No," he answered, "I'm from California. I was a friend of Tommy Creager's. I used to be a cop. His daughter asked me to try to find out why he was murdered." There was silence on the other end. "What I've found out so far leads me to believe you're in danger. I'd like to help you."

"Oh God," she said and then dropped the phone.

Voices echoed in the room on the other end – a man's voice and that of a badly frightened Jill.

"Who are you?" the man demanded.

Cody repeated the information and then added, "Ask Jill if Tommy Creager ever told her about a cop he knew in Los Angeles who was shot in the back of the head, execution style, only he didn't die, the bullet hit and went around his scalp; he spent four days in a coma and when he came out he could see things – only bits and pieces, but they usually had to do with violent crimes."

Muffled voices on the other end. "What do you want?" she asked when she finally came back on the line.

15

McCabe pulled his car to a stop in front of the house where Jill Edwards's brother and his family lived. It was in a neighborhood of small working-class homes and, like several others on the block, was made of white clapboard and built on a raised foundation that allowed cooling air to flow underneath. The small front yard, which had a waist-high wire fence around it, was overgrown with weeds, colorful flowers, and children's toys. In the near distance lightning lit up the sky, and moments later thunder boomed and rumbled. A new storm was coming in.

Cody and McCabe climbed out of the car and into a light rain. Next door a dog began to bark and a woman shouted for it to shut up. It didn't. On the porch of the Edwards house, the front door, behind a screen door, opened and the partial silhouette of a mannish figure with a flattop haircut appeared, but then Jill Edwards voice spoke and Cody was on the edge of the endless darkness again, and he knew violent death was very near.

"Are you Cody?" the silhouette called out in a frightened voice.

"Yes," he answered.

"Who's that with you?" she demanded to know.

"His name's Joe McCabe," Cody said. "He's a newspaper reporter; he's been helping me."

"Oh, no. No reporters," she said in near panic. "You didn't say anything about reporters."

Both Cody and McCabe knew they were about to lose her.

"I'll wait in the car," McCabe called up to her.

But on the porch the silhouette had turned back and was having a muffled conversation with a man's voice – Cody guessed it was her brother – and then she stepped away from the door and the brother filled it, pushing the screen door open and turning on the porch light over his head. He looked to be several inches over six feet tall and at least a hundred pounds overweight. He was wearing shorts, no shoes, and a tank top. His hair was rich brown and combed in a pompadour, his sideburns full and reaching down to his jawbone. He vaguely reminded Cody of someone, but for the moment he couldn't think who.

"What paper you from?" the man on the porch asked in a husky, slightly slurred, familiar voice.

And now Cody did know – madness – they had found an Australian Elvis.

"Right now, the *Auckland Times*," McCabe said, exchanging a quick, curious glance with Cody, "but a lot of my features are published over here and in the U.K. and the States. "

No answer from the huge, oval Elvis; his large body just swayed in the doorway.

"I worked for the *Sydney Morning Herald* a couple of years ago," McCabe continued.

"You know anyone in the "Entertainment" section?" the bloated King asked, losing for a moment the Elvis voice.

Cody nodded for McCabe to say yes. He did.

The King pondered a moment and, after regaining his husky voice, said, "All right, both of you can come in."

"I'm Taylor Edwards," the large man offered as they reached the porch. It was raining harder now and he reeked of alcohol and his eyes weren't interested in Cody. "Maybe you've heard of me?" he added hopefully.

McCabe squinted and did his best to oblige. "I'm not sure, maybe I have," he said and winked at Cody.

But Cody wasn't paying attention. His ears were ringing and he was hot; a sense of dread had filled him as he approached the house, and then he stepped into the living room and the walls were bleeding and seemed to quake with violence and impending death. And he was falling. . . off the edge of darkness. . . when he heard a child's voice say, "Shhhh!" and another's giggle. And suddenly he was back in Hornsby, where a large black-velvet painting of Elvis in his white sequined jump suit dominated the far wall of the pigsty of a room. Littered throughout were empty beer bottles, McDonald's wrappers, paper cups, and dirty dishes, some of which looked to date back at least a week. A pair of blond, five and six-year-old bare-topped children in pajama bottoms peered into the room from under a pair of saloon-like swinging doors. And she, Jill Edwards, stood at the entrance to the kitchen, tall and hard looking. Her slick flattop was black.

"I told you kids to get to bed," Taylor Edwards said in his own voice.

The blond heads disappeared in silence. Cody noticed that all the walls were filled with Elvis memorabilia.

"You'll have to excuse the mess; my wife's visiting a friend up in Gosford," the huge man offered.

"She's bloody well left you," Jill said, her voice taut, and Cody sensed she was lashing out to relieve her own tension.

"She hasn't left me," he returned tightly, seeking to close off this line of discussion.

She looked at Cody and her whole body suddenly quivered. "How do I know you're not here to kill me?" she asked, close to tears. "How do I know you're who you say you are?"

"Tommy Creager's daughter is named Mary Louise," Cody answered, reaching into his pocket.

"Anyone could know that," she challenged, still frightened.

He pulled out the envelope he had first received in Apia and walked over and handed it to her. She wiped her eyes and took the letter out and started to read it.

"Why do you think someone is trying to kill you?" he asked quietly.

She lowered the letter and, drained and still trembling, said, "Shit. Can we sit down?"

They did, in the kitchen. She managed to clear enough trash and dirty dishes off the table to make room for herself, Cody, and McCabe to sit there. Taylor brought them all beers and then loomed above them self-consciously. There was more Elvis memorabilia in the kitchen, but with a difference: Now it was Taylor appearing as Elvis. "That was me at the Easter show," he said, handing McCabe his beer and indicating a framed photo on the wall next to him.

"Taylor's an Elvis impersonator," Jill said in a monotone. "He's really quite good; he came in second on *New Faces* once."

"That's great," McCabe said, and then glanced at Cody. "*New Faces* is a TV talent show."

"I sang 'Heartbreak Hotel'; people generally think that's my best number. I've got it on tape, if you'd like to see it later."

There was only silence. Cody had to fight for concentration. The sense of violence and death packed the room around this woman. . . and yet there she sat, untouched.

"I think I'm going crazy," Jill said shortly with a sense of despair. "I've got a three-hundred-pound brother who thinks he's Elvis Presley, and someone's trying to kill me."

"Let's start from the beginning," Cody said. "Do you have any idea why someone would want to kill you?"

She shook her head and sounded like a frightened little girl. "Noooo."

"Then tell me, what's convinced you that someone is?" he asked.

She looked at him and put a trembling hand to her mouth. "What makes *you* think someone is?"

No one spoke for several moments. McCabe squinted and lit another cigarette. Bloated Elvis topped off his beer with several ounces of Jack Daniels.

Outside the rain was pounding down on the house's corrugated metal roof, and Cody had to raise his voice to be heard. "Tommy told you about me."

"Yes," she nodded, looking for a moment like a child afraid of the dark.

"So you know that sometimes I see things, flashes. . . . I have to tell you, I don't always know what they mean. Sometimes I'm right and sometimes. . . ." He paused for a moment; there was no easy way to say this. "Right now, every instinct tells me you should be dead."

A small sound of fear came from her throat.

"It doesn't mean it has to be," Cody added quickly. "What I see doesn't have to come true. Sometimes what I see can be prevented. But you've got to help me. What made you think someone was trying to kill you?"

"I just had this feeling the last few days. . . " she said in a quavering voice that then broke off. "Oh, shit, can I have one of those?" she asked, gesturing to McCabe's cigarettes.

"No worries," he said, opening the half-filled box and offering her one, and then, once she'd taken it, setting the pack down between them. "If we run out of these, I've got another pack in the car."

She lit the cigarette herself and after inhaling deeply seemed to calm down a little. "I had the same feeling after Tommy was killed. . . even during the funeral. . . that someone was watching me."

"Ever get a look at who it was?" Cody asked.

She shook her head as if in confusion. "Those days after Tommy was killed, I wasn't thinking straight. I thought maybe this guy with real light hair, real blond or white. . . but I couldn't be sure."

And Cody knew he had found the first link, as he remembered the silver-haired man in the car that very afternoon, down the street from her house. "Go on," he urged.

"I don't know," she shook her head uncertainly. "During the funeral itself someone broke into the house. Turned the place upside down. Tommy's papers were thrown everywhere. But some money was missing too. And the cops said that happens a lot, people's houses getting robbed during a funeral, and after that it didn't seem like anyone was following me anymore. So I thought I just must have been going crazy before. . . you know, imagining things. Only then last week, I started seeing him again."

"The guy with the white hair?" Cody asked.

"Yeah. Then three days ago I was over in Balmain. There's a film company there that likes one of my scripts and we had one of those real long lunches – you know, where you drink a lot of wine and talk about how great the movie is going to be and what actors you're going to put in it, and piss on anyone who says it isn't commercial – and I'm walking back up to Victoria Street to try and catch a cab and I'm crossing this narrow little lane when this truck comes racing down on me and I try to run out of the way, only it follows me up onto the footpath and I just barely manage to duck into a doorway and it crashes into the front of the building and skids off and finally slams into this really nice restored Holden before it stops." She paused a moment, still shaken by the memory. "And I saw the truck move. . . and I knew he had put it in reverse and was going to come back, only then a lot of people who heard the crash came running out, and so he put it back into the other gear and drove away."

"Did you get a look at who was driving?" Cody asked.

"No. Not really. It was dark," she admitted, "and I was kind of full of wine. After, I was really shook. Some people helped get me a cab and I went home that night and I was really scared. The wine was making me sleepy, only I couldn't sleep, so it ended up giving me the worst bloody headache. . . and I kept thinking someone was going to break in and kill me. The next day I took off for here."

"Okay, let's get back to Tommy," Cody said after a moment. "Can you think of any reason why someone would want to kill him?"

She almost laughed and then cried. "When he'd get drunk sometimes, he'd say the CIA was after him and that they'd probably kill him someday when he got too close."

"Too close to what?" McCabe piped up.

"Who really killed JFK He was working on a book about that. He had been for years before I met him. When he really used to get shitfaced and feeling sorry for himself, he'd say that it was because of his investigation of the Kennedy assassination that they had him blackballed on American TV. Don't you see what a joke it is?" She was crying again. "Who would want to kill Tommy? He was bloody well all used up."

"Tell me about his relationship with the Browns," Cody said.

"Browns?" she asked blankly.

"Griffin Brown," McCabe said. "And his wife."

"Oh, Fiona. . . ?" she said as if coming out of a fog.

"Shit," Taylor said and belched, then continued in his Elvis voice. "No wonder there's people trying to kill you, sis. Griffin Brown. . ."

"Shut up with your bloody Elvis. You don't know anything," Jill snapped.

"I put the food on the table," the large man bellowed, suddenly looking confused as he focused in on McCabe. Then he lurched out of the room.

"You were telling me about Tommy's relationship with the Browns," Cody reminded her.

"Tommy and Fiona were just friends," she explained sadly. "She likes going to restaurants, the best places – Doyle's on the Beach or Chiswick Gardens, Natalino's – or sometimes on nice days out on the harbor on her yacht. Only she doesn't like going alone. . . or drinking alone. There was

Nicholas, of course, and she has some priest friends who go out with her from time to time, but no one regularly. No one who would drink with her all day. Not like Tommy did. They were perfect for each other. I mean, it was weird, like some bloody Italian movie – the aging but still beautiful, ignored wife of the powerful crime boss, and the still very charming, still almost handsome once-famous TV newsman. Each of them so desperately missing something they had once had, and knowing they'd never have it again. And drinking all day and laughing and laughing at each other's stories, no matter how many times they'd heard them before." She was near tears again now, and to hide it she tipped her beer up and drank until it was gone.

Out in the living room a videotape blasted and they could hear an announcer say, "And now from Hornsby, contestant number six, Taylor 'Elvis' Edwards!" And then as if responding to the audience applause on the tape, the real Taylor appeared in the doorway. "That's me on *New Faces*," he said, and, moving over to pick up the bottle of Jack Daniels, lost his balance and fell down. He sat on the floor for several moments trying to get his bearings. From the living room he could be heard singing "Heartbreak Hotel."

"You wonder why I'm going crazy?" Jill asked, taking another of McCabe's cigarettes and lighting it.

"I should have won that night," Taylor slurred in McCabe's direction. "I was thin then – well, not as fat. You should see. You could write a story about me. Put me back on top. I should have won, goddammit."

Outside, lightning flashed brightly, and a crackling, banging thunder followed right on top of it and seemingly rocked the house. Sitting on the kitchen floor, Taylor "Elvis" Edwards was messing his pants. "Oh, shit," he complained, rolling over to his knees and managing to climb to his feet, then staggering, with the bottle of Jack Daniels still in his hand, to the doorway. "Heartbreak Hotel" was nearing its finish. "Bastards," he whined. "I should have won. . . . Dirty bastards." And then without a backward glance he disappeared into the living room.

"He's crazy since his wife left him," Jill offered.

Cody nodded and then returned to the subject at hand. "These outings with Brown's wife and Tommy. Were you ever invited along?"

"Almost all of them, in the beginning." She paused and turned to McCabe. "You've been a big help with the cigarettes so far. . . but there's a box of wine in the fridge that I'd kill for right now."

"Done," McCabe said with a squinting twinkle and got up and moved to the refrigerator just behind him.

"Fiona used to like to have me along to keep Nicholas company, take him to the shops, play cards with him," she went on, turning her attention back to Cody.

"Who's Nicholas?" Cody asked.

"Her son. Her youngest son."

"He's a new one on me," McCabe said as he sat back down at the table with a couple of glasses and a flagon-sized box of Chardonnay.

"It was Kevin and David who were killed in the fire?" Cody asked to clarify.

"Yes," she said. "They were his older brothers, much older. They were in their thirties. Nicholas turned eighteen a couple of months ago. . . just before he disappeared."

Cody suddenly felt cold, the words hitting him like an unexpected body blow. For a moment his ears rang, and he had a sense of Ann and the desperate anxiety of the months she had been missing. "Wait a minute," he said, his voice hollow. "This Nicholas. . . disappeared?"

"Yeah," she nodded. "That was crazy too. I mean, where would he go? He wasn't like the brightest kid I ever met. Fiona used to baby him. He was kind of quirky, too. He even stopped going to school a couple of years ago and just spent his time with his mother and some of her priest friends."

"Tell us about his disappearance," Cody pressed. His instincts were telling him that the missing boy had something to do with Tommy Creager's murder and all that followed, but he also knew his instincts were clouded because he was on the edge of his own personal nightmare. And at the same time he felt a twinge of guilt, because he realized that even though word of someone disappearing had affected him, it didn't strike home as deeply as it had several months before. Ann was slipping away. Forever. And the guilt flowed into a sadness, and he wished he could be alone, but he knew that wasn't possible now.

"There's not much to tell," the woman with the black flattop replied. "One day he was just gone, and nobody knew where he went."

"Did Tommy have any idea what happened?" Cody asked.

"He thought he did," she said, growing misty for a moment. "Tommy said that whenever Fiona and her husband would talk, which wasn't very often, they used to have raging arguments over Nicholas. Nicholas hated his father. One day when we were over at Luna Park – Nicholas used to like to go on the whip, ride after ride after ride, and he always wanted someone to go with him. . . if I was along that day it was me – anyway, he said that once, when he had been twelve years old, he had tried to kill the old man. And then he laughed and laughed, but it wasn't because he was happy, and then he said in this really weird voice, 'Someday he'll wish I'd killed him then.'"

"How long before he disappeared did he say that to you?" Cody asked.

"I don't know," she sniffed, pouring some more wine into her glass. "Maybe a couple of weeks."

She finished the wine and tried to light a fresh cigarette but lit the filter instead.

"You were telling us what Tommy thought," Cody said.

McCabe lit a cigarette and passed it to her. She took it gratefully .

"Tommy said the old man was determined that once Nicholas was eighteen he was going to make the boy work for him. . . or at least for one of his brothers. Tommy said Nicholas used to shriek like a bloody baboon whenever the subject was brought up."

"And so when he turned eighteen, rather than go to work for the old man he disappeared?"

"That's what Tommy thought," she said, pouring herself another glass of the boxed wine.

"Is there any reason Griffin Brown may have thought that Tommy had something to do with the boy's disappearance?" Cody asked after some moments.

"You mean enough so he might want to kill Tommy? I thought of that. But that's crazy too. I mean, one night about a week or so after Nicholas was gone, he came to our place with a couple of his heavies. . . "

"Griffin Brown?" Cody asked for clarity.

"Yeah. . . he was drunk and he accused Tommy of helping Nicholas. Tommy denied it. But Tommy had been real nice to the kid. Fiona used to give him money to buy him presents and candy for him. And the way she wanted it, the boy was supposed to think the presents were just from Tommy. I mean, it was really stupid, these two hopeless bloody alcoholics partying it up every day with this idiot kid and a gaggle of priests." She broke off and drained most of the wine from her glass.

"What happened that night?" Cody pressed.

"There was a lot of shouting," she said, refilling her glass from the box. "Tommy kept swearing he didn't know where Nicholas was. . . and I know he didn't. He said he'd asked Fiona, but she would only smile and say she didn't want to talk about it. That night we thought Tommy had convinced Brown that he hadn't had anything to do with it. . . but maybe we didn't." Her voice broke on the last words. "Is that why Tommy was killed? He didn't know anything. I told you, it's crazy."

"And back to the same old question," McCabe interjected. "If it was Brown, why kill Tommy all the way over in a remote part of New Zealand? If Griffin

Brown wanted him dead he would have had it done easily, here in Sydney."

There was the sound of glass breaking and then the scream of a child from another room, followed by Taylor's angry voce.

"What the bloody hell is that?" McCabe asked.

"Oh, shit, it's Taylor," Jill said. "He lays into those kids every time he gets mad or something goes wrong."

The screaming was from pain now, and the trio in the kitchen could hear flesh hitting flesh. Anger filled Cody as he rose to his feet and moved toward the sound of the children's screams.

"Taylor, look out!" he heard Jill cry as he crossed the filthy living room, and as if in response the screams became whimpers as he moved through the saloonlike swinging doors. The passageway was dark. He knew that Taylor Edwards was waiting behind one of the two closed doors down the hall. Suddenly Jill was on him, smelling of wine and cigarettes and absence of deodorant.

"Listen, he's stopped," she pleaded. "It's okay now, can't you see?"

"How often does he do this?" Cody asked.

Her lip trembled. "Sometimes they're bad kids. . . " she said, knowing it was a desperately stupid answer. "Shit, I need a cigarette," she whined, and slunk back to the swinging doors.

Cody moved down the hall. The sounds of the children whimpering, trying to be quiet, were coming from behind the first door. Cody tried to turn the knob. It was locked.

"Stay out of here," Taylor shouted belligerently from the other side.

Cody stepped back now and with one movement kicked it in. The room was dark. The children's sounds were coming from the right-hand side. He couldn't see them. He couldn't see the King, either.

"You kids get out to the kitchen with your Aunt Jill," Cody said.

"My kids aren't going anywhere," the Elvis voice hissed from the dark, and Cody, determining that the huge man was in the back of the room, reached his hand in and found the switch on the wall, turning on the lights.

The children cowered on a filthy bed. The blond girl had had her pajama nightie ripped off one leg and pulled down to her ankle on the other. The boy, who seemed to be a year younger, had blood circling his left eye. His mouth was also bloody; it looked as if his front tooth had been knocked out. The obese Elvis still wore his tank top but was naked from the waist down. He had an erection and was holding a cricket bat, ready to swing. His voice came out throaty, the best of the older Elvis: "You take one step in this room and I'll split their heads open."

McCabe was at Cody's side now. "Jesus, here's a warm family moment for the kiddies' memory banks."

As McCabe had spoken, Cody had reached around his back and pulled out his Walther, which he now leveled at Taylor's head. The large man looked truly surprised to see the gun. "You start to swing that bat and there's going to be two dead Elvises. Now slowly, fat boy, put it down."

"You haven't got any right," Taylor complained, but he lowered the bat and his erection melted. "You're a bloody Yank. This is a family matter."

"Go on, kids, out to the kitchen," Cody said.

The boy started, but the girl was afraid to move, so he waited by her. "She needs something to wear," the boy said with a bloody lisp owing to his broken tooth.

"See what you can find," Cody said to McCabe.

"Top drawer," Taylor said. "I did their laundry yesterday. . . . I take good care of them."

McCabe found a red-and-white dress and some boys' underpants.

"This do?" McCabe asked the little girl. She nodded ever so slightly and he smiled and threw them over to her.

"Go on now," Cody said, and the two children scurried from the room.

"Nothing happened in here," Taylor said.

"Is that why you ripped her pants off and had yours off too?" Cody asked, closing the distance between them.

"It's not my fault," the fat Elvis whined. "My wife left me. A man's got his needs, you – "

Cody's foot caught him square in the crotch before he could finish, and the huge man gasped and moaned and folded over as best as his bulk would allow. The next sound he heard was the breaking of bone as Cody's knee found his cheekbone, toppling Taylor to the floor. "Not my face, not my face," he pleaded, "I'm a performer."

Cody looked around with disgust, then offered his gun to McCabe, who pulled back. "I'm afraid, I'm afraid of those things," the journalist protested.

"You only have to be afraid when someone else is pointing it at you," Cody said, forcing it into his hand. "Now if the son of a bitch moves, pull the trigger and you'll be doing the world a big favor."

By the time he reached the kitchen the little girl was cleaning the boy's eye wound with a wet paper towel. Jill was standing away from the pair, taking a long drink from a tumbler of white wine.

"What did you do with Taylor?" she asked.

"Are you totally fucking useless?" he asked her. But she only shuddered and finished her wine.

Cody moved to the children. "Let me help," he said, taking the wet towel from the girl and getting a better look at the boy's wound. "You're going to need some stitches, but don't worry," he grinned, "I've had plenty of them. They don't hurt."

"I know," the boy said.

"Are we going to Grandma Sally's?" the girl asked.

"Is that where you usually go when this happens?" Cody asked in return.

"Yes, she's nice," the boy said with his broken-toothed lisp. "She doesn't hurt us."

Cody looked over at Jill, who stared back at him like a frightened animal. "Get Grandma Sally on the phone and tell her we're coming over," he said.

16

Like a great bird of death, the black winged shadow moved effortlessly through the steady rain, over the rooftops of the homes and buildings of Rockdale. Closer and closer to earth, until finally Quantas flight 718 direct from Hong Kong, with screeching tires, touched and splashed down runway 07 at Sydney's Kingsford Smith Airport.

The flight, like several others, had been delayed in a holding pattern offshore, as pilots waited for the incoming series of late summer thunderstorms to either pass altogether or to space themselves apart enough to allow for a landing.

In all, the storms had delayed Quantas flight 718 by just over forty minutes, which had, as the time passed, made the silver-haired man increasingly nervous as he waited in the parking lot. He knew that in all probability the flight was held up because of the weather, but he couldn't be sure. And as the steady rain filmed over his windshield, he pondered the other possibilities that could account for the delay. Had they been spotted? Had they been stopped going through passport controll? And most important, was he in danger? He didn't like being here. Alone. Exposed. Not in command of the situation. He knew he could easily get information about the flight by going into the terminal, but if it had gone wrong, that could be a trap. He considered driving to a pay phone to check on the arrival time, but decided against it, for if they came into the parking lot while he was away, then they'd be lost, unsure of what to do. He felt the gun in his pocket for reassurance. At least he had that in his control: his resolve to never allow himself to be returned to prison.

The minutes dragged by. Shadows became enemies; passing cars, danger. He tried to think of other things. Happier things. More positive things. Five more days and it would be over, he knew. Five more days and he would have enough money to live out the rest of his life and live it well. He'd buy a place in the Bay of Plenty, and he'd have his own jetty and a thirty-two-footer, and he'd grow grapes and apples and oranges, and he'd be a free man – for the first time in his life he'd be free. And whenever he felt like raging and fucking his brains out and living the hot life he'd just take a three-hour plane ride to Brisbane and have one of those chauffeured stretch limos drive him down the coast, to a fancy hotel in Surfers. . . back in Surfers Paradise, where he had spent the best years of his life. Where he and his mother and sisters may have been poor, but they'd been together. . . They had been a family then. And he knew when he had the money he'd take care of his sisters too. He'd make sure that they lived well. And he thought about them, all of them, back there in Surfers, in the golden days. Meanwhile, outside the rented minivan the rain still poured down. He struggled to remain in his daydreams, but the nagging, passing minutes wouldn't let him.

Finally, when it was half an hour past the time he thought they should be out of customs, he couldn't stand the not knowing any longer. So he left the rented minivan and trotted through the puddles and downpour to the international terminal. He reached the entrance, his hand resting on the gun in his pocket. He wasn't afraid. He took a breath and moved through the door. It was warm inside, the air heavy and stale. A couple of hundred people milled about, waiting for international passengers to appear from the blocked-off customs area. No one seemed to pay any attention to him. He moved to the television screen displaying arrival times and saw that the flight from Hong Kong was delayed, which immediately set his mind at ease. So much so that he thought about going upstairs to the airport bar and having a drink, but then he decided against it. It was a long shot that anyone would recognize him, but he didn't want to take the chance of later being identified as having been here tonight. . . especially if somehow everything went wrong and the boys' arrival was traced back to this time and place. So he returned to the van and waited.

* * *

Flight 718 from Hong Kong was less than half full — welcome news to the passport and customs officials, who were already on overtime because of the rain delays. They were tired and in the back of their minds just a bit worried about getting home tonight. Which roads would be flooded out? At least one main road always was. This flight 718 was the last international arrival of the night. End of shift was near, and so while none of them shirked their duty, it seemed the 168 passengers managed to move rather quickly through the official process of entering Australia. . . including the four Hong Kong teenage schoolboys and their rather pretty teacher, Loretta Chang.

The silver-haired man was dozing in a dreamy world somewhere between a picturesque home in the Bay of Plenty and his boyhood in Surfers Paradise when Loretta Chang tapped on his window. Quickly alert, he rolled it down. She stood under an expensive white umbrella, her face reflecting restrained impatience. Behind her he could see the boys sharing a pair of umbrellas. They wore dark blue, well-fitting raincoats. Their hair was trimmed neatly. Jesus, he observed. The oldest didn't look more than fifteen.

"Are you Fitzwilliam?" she asked with a well-bred English accent.

"Yes," he nodded. "Get in."

Without expression she moved away from the driver's side and led the boys around to the sliding doors, which she pulled open for the four young men. A couple of the boys exchanged words in Chinese, and the others laughed lightly. Loretta Chang waited until the last boy was settled, then pulled the sliding door closed, opened the passenger door and climbed into the bucket seat next to the silver-haired man.

"They look like choirboys," he said with a small smile.

"If you provide the weapons promised, they'll sing the song you want," she answered with her own smile, which touched on arrogance.

17

"I keep coming back to Griffin Brown thinking that Tommy might have helped his son Nicholas disappear," Cody said, breaking a silence that had lasted over twenty minutes, ever since they had left the little house in Hornsby. They were crossing over the Sidney Harbour Bridge in a misting rain. Cody was in the backseat; the boy with the blond hair and the broken tooth, who needed stitches, was asleep in his lap; his sister was curled up on the seat next to them. "It just doesn't make sense. Why single out Tommy? I know you said that Tommy had been nice to the kid, but there must have been a lot of people who were nice to him. What about the priests?"

"According to Tommy, Brown raised hell with them, too," Jill answered after a moment. Sitting in the front passenger seat, she turned her head halfway back to speak. The silhouette of her jutting chin, sharp nose, and crown of flattop hair made for an almost surreal profile.

"So what you're saying is that Tommy wasn't singled out?" McCabe asked as he drove.

"Noooo," she said and the feeling of hopelessness was back in her voice. "I don't think he was."

"And since there hasn't been a recent rash of priest killings that we know about. . . " McCabe left the rest of his thought dangling for Cody to pick up.

"It probably means young Nicholas Brown's disappearance wasn't the direct reason for Tommy being killed," Cody finished, providing McCabe an answer he hadn't expected.

"Direct? You think it might be an indirect reason?" McCabe asked.

"My guess is it fits in the pattern somewhere," Cody answered.

"What do you mean, pattern?" Jill asked as if some new horror had just been sprung on her.

"Nicholas disappears," Cody started, "then a couple of months later his two older brothers are killed. Somewhere in between, Tommy goes to New Zealand and is shot. . . and now someone is trying to kill you."

"But how do you know they're connected?" she demanded with a whine.

He knew there was no way he could explain. There was no way to tell her about the screams he had heard and the eye-stinging smoke he'd felt, first in New Zealand and then here in Sydney, outside her terrace house. He was sure Tommy's murder and the disco firebombing were connected, but at the same time he knew he couldn't be sure. He knew he could never be sure of what he saw in the flashes. . . if they were things to come or things that had happened. . . or things that might be. "I don't know for sure," Cody finally answered. "But twenty years of being a cop tells me they probably are. Do you know why Tommy went to New Zealand?"

"No," she answered, shaking her head. "Sometimes he made trips like that. I'd know something was up a couple of days before, because he'd get real crypticlike. Then an envelope would arrive; it would always have an airline ticket and money in it."

"How much money?" McCabe asked. They had left the bridge now and were stopped at a red light. In a doorway they could see someone huddled up in a cardboard box.

"I don't know," Jill answered. "Maybe a couple of thousand. He usually gave me four or five hundred of it for the house. Once he bought me a sweater he knew I liked." The memory brought her back near tears.

"But you don't know who sent the money or the tickets?" Cody pressed.

"No."

"Could it have been from his work?"

"No," she said again.

"How can you be so sure?" Cody asked.

"Because he always had to call and tell them he was taking time off."

"Could it have been from Griffin Brown?" Cody went on.

"It could have been from the bloody man in the moon," she snapped. "I told you, I don't *know*! Jesus, I could use a drink."

"Did you ever ask Tommy where they came from?" McCabe offered, trying to lighten the tone.

"Not after the first couple of times," she said wearily. "He said it was something he had to do. He said it was top secret, but that was stupid. He said someday it would all be in a book he was going to write. . . once he finished the Kennedy one."

"How often did he take these trips?" Cody asked.

"Three, four times a year. Once to Tokyo, couple of times to Hong Kong and Singapore. Once to Auckland. . . " Her voice trailed off like a little girl's.

Cody thought for several moments before speaking. "When I knew him, Tommy was always making notes to himself. Do you know if he made notes on these trips?"

"Why wouldn't he? Our place is filled with his notebooks. It looks like a bloody library," she said with desperate exasperation. "Everything from courtroom testimony to conversations he overheard in pubs. The last few months he even made notes on how many times he shit every day," she said, laughing and nearly sobbing simultaneously. "He thought he had cancer. You know, of the colon. He thought he was dying. He told me one night when he was really drunk. . . and then made me swear I wouldn't tell anyone else. Tell anyone? Shit, there were times I almost wished it were true. I mean, how long could he go on at the end of the rope? Doesn't God owe us the dignity to let us end with at least our head above water?"

She was looking at him now and her eyes inadvertently dropped to the broken boy in his lap.

"You let your brother do this," Cody asked, "and you can talk about human dignity?"

* * *

They rode in silence the rest of the way to the suburb of Kingsford. The rain had stopped. Grandma Sally lived in a block of pale brick apartment houses. She was waiting out front as they pulled up. Thin and blond, she had an expression that seemed to perpetually anticipate something going wrong. She saw Jill get out of the car first and moved toward her.

"What happened?" she asked.

"Taylor," Jill answered, and that seemed all the explanation necessary.

Cody was out of the car now, carrying the sleeping boy.

Grandma Sally saw his face and shuddered. "Oh God."

"He needs to see a doctor," Cody said.

"I called Dr. Donovan; he said he'd come over as soon as little Taylor got here," the older woman said, and then turned to Jill again. "Where's Kathy?"

"I don't know for sure, I think she took off with Doug. He's playing some dates in Newcastle." Jill answered.

McCabe was trying to lift the little girl out of the backseat when she awoke.

"Grandma," she said sleepily, and then ran and wrapped her arms around her.

"It's alright, honey, it's alright," the older woman said as she picked the little girl up. She then glanced at Cody. "Could you bring him in?"

Cody nodded and then followed her into the building, McCabe and Jill trailing behind.

The boy had stirred himself awake by the time they'd come in the front door of the third-floor apartment. Cody let him down and he ran with familiarity to find a black-and-white cat that he picked up and now carried around like a rag doll. The cat, whose name was Dinky, didn't seem to mind. The place was small and inexpensively furnished, and there were more framed clippings of Taylor "Elvis" Edwards on the walls and one of Queen Elizabeth.

"I want the keys to the house in Paddington," Cody said to Jill.

"Why?"

"Because maybe the answer to why Tommy was killed and why someone is trying to kill you is there, somewhere in Tommy's notebooks," he said, more curtly than he intended.

"But I told you, someone already broke in there, during the funeral. All of his papers were gone through, they were everywhere."

And suddenly for Cody the sense of death was back, and there was a hard, crushing blow across his face. He winced and recoiled, and for a moment he was on the edge of the bottomless darkness.

"What's wrong?" she asked.

And then he was back in the tiny apartment, but he could still smell the stench of corrupting flesh. His legs felt unsure and he didn't understand how she could be here, still alive.

"There's death all around you," he said, and she cringed again. "They didn't find what they were looking for," Cody went on with words he hadn't formed consciously, "or they wouldn't be trying to kill you now. . . and the white-haired man wouldn't have been waiting down the street from your place this afternoon when I was there."

"Oh, shit."

Cody looked at her curiously for a moment without speaking, trying to pull up a memory. . . and then he had it. "Did they get to his metal box?" Cody asked.

"You know about that?" she asked with surprise.

Cody glanced at McCabe, who was looking curious. "Tommy was always afraid he'd fall asleep some night with a cigarette going and burn the house down, so whatever he was working on that he thought was important he'd keep in a little metal box."

"So that it would survive the fire," McCabe grinned. "Sounds like a clear-thinking journo."

"I don't know if they did find the box," she said. "He used to keep it in an old refrigerator he had up in his office. It was on the third floor. Tommy always said house fires didn't get hot enough to burn a refrigerator." She was on the edge of tears again. "I've hardly been up to his office since he. . . If the metal box is there, it'll be in his fridge."

"Give me the keys," he pressed, and she fumbled for them in her purse and finally gave them over with a shaking hand.

"The little one is for the alarm," she said. "It's just inside the front door."

"The doctor is on his way," Grandma Sally announced as she approached them.

"Good, now call the police," Cody said.

The two women stood in silence, avoiding his eyes.

"What's been done to those kids is a criminal offense," Cody stated, feeling his anger building. "And it's not the first time, is it? I mean, you people have this down to a routine: Elvis mauls his kids, someone calls Grandma Sally, Grandma Sally calls the doc. Then Elvis the child beater, the child molester, sobers up and all's well again and the kiddies go home. . . until it happens again. Well, that's not good enough this time."

"Taylor's my son," Grandma Sally finally said in a tiny voice.

"Taylor's a monster," Cody replied. "Those are your grandchildren, they're the ones who need your help."

Grandma Sally tried to think of something else to say but couldn't, so instead she turned and moved away.

"Jesus," Jill stammered. "I swear to you, until tonight I never knew he was doing any sex with those little kids." Her eyes went pleadingly to McCabe. "Could I have another cigarette?"

He took a few out of an almost full box, put them in his pocket, and then handed her the box.

"I'll call the cops," she said. "I'll tell them everything I know."

18

"Jesus," McCabe said. "It's like a bloody bad dream that keeps winding tighter and tighter. Who in the hell do you think paid Creager to take those trips overseas? I mean, it does sound like the CIA, doesn't it?"

They were driving through the Sydney streets again, but Cody was only half listening. His own mind was trying to make sense out of what he had learned tonight, trying to fit the pieces of a puzzle together, only he knew he didn't yet have enough pieces to know what they meant, or even if all the pieces were from the same puzzle. From Tommy's murder to the firebombing of the disco. . . and of course the murder of Griffin Brown's two oldest sons. But what enemy of the Browns could have gotten close enough to them? Did Tommy know who the traitor was? Is that why he was killed? And who bought the police commissioner to cover up the autopsy reports? And where did eighteen-year-old Nicholas's disappearance fit in. . . or did it?

McCabe pulled the car to a stop in front of an all-night chemist shop and Cody became aware that the reporter had been talking to him.". . . going to get some smokes, and some batteries for the flashlight."

"Sure," Cody said.

McCabe managed a lopsided grin and moved inside. Cody fought a yawn and realized he was extremely tired. He looked at his watch; it was after midnight. He sighed and stepped out of the car to breathe the night air. The streets were still wet but the rain had stopped, and above, the clouds, brushed apart by the warm summer winds, now revealed a pitch black sky that sparkled with stars, and he thought about his son Patrick and the boy's renewed enthusiasm for astronomy since they had started the trip. And who could blame him, he thought. When you're on the open sea and a thousand miles from the nearest land, the stars and constellations become

almost alive in their clarity. He smiled as he recalled
the twelve-year-old's excitement the first night he
saw the Southern Cross, which of course can only be
seen in the Southern Hemisphere. "It's actually
called Crux Australias," the boy had chattered. "The
five stars of the Southern Cross are on the flags of
Western Samoa, New Zealand, and Australia." And
with a sense of melancholy, Cody realized that
Patrick would be thirteen in four days. He and
Damien had listened and nodded and done their
best to look interested when Patrick had talked on
and on almost nightly about the skies above, because
they knew that astronomy was one of his passions. . .
as it had been for his mother.

* * *

"Ready," McCabe coughed.

Cody became aware that the salt-and-pepper-
haired man must have been standing there for some
moments.

McCabe threw him a small flashlight still
encased in it's clear plastic packaging. "They were
on sale," he grinned. "Thanks," Cody said.

"You getting anything?" McCabe asked awk-
wardly. "You know, I mean, you seeing anything?"

Cody grinned and shook his head. "I'll let you
know when the spook show starts."

* * *

It took only a few minutes to get back to the narrow
streets of Paddington.

"You know, there's another reason Creager might have been taking those trips out of the country," McCabe offered. "But you won't like it."

"Because he was a bagman or a mule for Griffin Brown?" Cody asked with some irritation.

"It would make sense," McCabe shrugged. "I mean, if he was bringing drugs or whatever into the country for Brown, that would explain why they were so friendly. Reporters, or at least famous ones, usually have a pretty easy time getting themselves through customs."

"If Brown and Tommy were so friendly, then why did Brown think Tommy helped his son Nicholas disappear?" Cody jabbed back, realizing that he was jumping unnecesarily to the defense of his dead friend. In fact, he knew McCabe's questions to be legitimate.

"Maybe they had a falling out. Maybe Brown felt he had to kill him just to shut him up," McCabe suggested.

"Then I'll ask you your favorite question," Cody replied. "Why all the way over in a remote town in New Zealand? Why not right here in Sydney? He goes out for a boat ride one day, gets drunk as usual, and falls overboard."

"I don't know," McCabe shrugged, deciding it was safer to stay quiet for now.

The possibility that Tommy had been running drugs or money had been the first thought that had come to Cody's mind when Jill had told them about the trips. He had rejected it because of what he remembered of his friend. Tommy Creager had been a lot of things, but mostly he was an alcoholic who, despite his name recognition from those heady days in Dallas and later as a network correspondent in Vietnam and later still for his anchor jobs in New York, L.A., and finally San Diego, knew he was not as good a reporter as everyone seemed to think he should be.

The fact was, as Cody had pieced together over the span of their friendship, Tommy had been a victim of his own success. He had been catapulted to the top in Dallas that November 22, 1963. He was only twenty-two then, thrust out of his league, and sadly had spent the rest of his life desperately trying to recapture the glory, to maintain himself in the big leagues, only to find himself slipping, year by year, farther down the ladder. When Cody had known him, Tommy had had problems with booze and self-esteem, but he'd held onto the set of standards he had started out with. And every once in a while, because of them, he had lost the chance to break a big story. Cody remembered hazily the night in the hospital nine years before when he'd come out of the coma and had told Pyne where to find the man who had shot him. Shot him in the head. Left him for dead. Tommy Creager had been there, at the beginning. The first time Cody had *seen* something. The first of his flashes. The Nightmare Man, the other cops would later call him behind his back, and a lot of them never wanted him to return to duty. A lot of them were afraid of him. But Tommy had been there, in on the beginning of what could have been a big story for him. Only he never broke it. Because of Ann and the kids and, as he would grin at Cody over his glass of scotch, "maybe a little bit for you too." For Tommy had known that breaking the story would have made Cody a circus freak for the media, and that Cody and Ann and the kids' lives would never be the same again. No. The Tommy Creager Cody had known wouldn't be a bagman for a gangster, or mule drugs. And yet with a sense of sadness he also knew he hadn't seen Tommy in almost five years. Five years in which he had slipped even farther down in his career spiral.

They had pulled up in front of number 157.

Cody stepped out onto the pavement, and for a moment the sadness turned into a sense of fear. He was suddenly back on the edge of the endless darkness, and once more he could hear the screams and smell the smoke, and he knew that angry death was near. His hand reached back and touched his Walther.

"Maybe you should stay here," Cody said.

"Why?" McCabe asked.

Cody didn't speak for several moments. When he did, he turned toward the reporter, but his eyes looked through him and his voice, almost hollow, told of what he sensed from the darkness. "Someone's been murdered here, or is going to be."

"Jesus," McCabe said, gamely attempting after several moments a variation on his crooked smile, but not quite succeeding.

"Maybe if I just stayed behind you."

"At your own risk," Cody answered starting across the street, where the sense of death and violence embraced him.

He unlocked and opened the front door, and as soon as he did the stench of a decomposing corpse filled his nostrils.

McCabe, just behind him, turned away. "Whew, someone's ripe!"

Cody covered his face with a handkerchief and moved inside. The alarm control was where Jill had said it was, beeping with a little blinking red light. He turned the small key she had given him; the beeping stopped and the blinking red light was replaced with a steady green one.

"Jesus, I'll open some windows," McCabe said, moving into the living room, following the beam of his flashlight.

Cody using his own flashlight moved deeper into the house. The stench of death was coming from upstairs.

On the second floor he found her. She was naked. On the bathroom floor. What was left of her face had been bashed in by repeated blows from a bloodied tire iron that lay nearby. A small animal, perhaps a rat, had eaten away part of her left foot. Her hair was dark and matted with blood, but he could see it was cut short. . . as if for a flattop.

Madness.

Jill Edwards was dead at his feet. And she had been dead at least three days.

19

The basement room was sweltering and dimly lit. The pair of electric fans the silver-haired man had brought in earlier in the day did little to help. The four Chinese boys had stripped down to their boxer shorts, neatly folding their clothes for future use. Two of them now rested on the mattresses that had been laid out on the floor for them. The other two were playing Nintendo games that the silver-haired man had also set up for them earlier in the day.

The phone rang at exactly 1:00 a.m. Loretta Chang looked up from the table where she was checking over, for the second time, the four Tec-9 series machine pistols. At first glance, she had been upset. "These are brand-new," she had complained. But the silver-haired man had reassured her. "Just well taken care of. . . I've fired twenty clips from each of them, that's seven hundred and twenty rounds apiece. Believe me, they're smooth as silk."

The silver-haired man crossed the room and picked up the phone on the second ring. "Fitzwilliam," he answered, and then listened for several seconds. "Yes," he said, "everyone's here and happy with the equipment."

He listened for several more seconds, and then a smile creased his lips. "Yes, very surprised," he replied, and then hung up.

"We're on schedule," he said to Loretta Chang.

20

Cody picked up the framed photo next to the bed. It was a shot of Tommy Creager and Jill. The Jill he'd met out in Hornsby. Not the dead one on the bathroom floor. In the photo they were on a boat; it looked big and expensive, and his dead friend's face was happy and bloated from too much booze.

It all made a sort of mad sense now, Cody realized, why he had kept seeing death and violence around her.

"Jesus," said McCabe, still standing in the doorway to the bathroom. "I wonder who she is?"

"Someone thought she was Jill Edwards," Cody said, and picked up the cordless phone next to the bed and punched out Grandma Sally's number, which he'd written on a scrap of paper. He scanned the rest of the room with the flashlight. There was nothing of immediate interest. He was moving into the hallway when Jill answered.

"The cops there yet?" Cody asked.

"No. Not yet," she answered, her voice sounding tired and shaky. "But I did call them. The doctor is with little Taylor now."

He said nothing for the moment. He'd found a second bedroom. . . and what he had been looking for. Women's clothes were scattered on the floor. A large floppy purse on the bed. He moved to it and dumped out its contents.

"Is that all?" she finally asked.

"I need to ask you something," he said after another delay as he went through the wallet, looking for identification.

"What?" she asked, fear creeping back into her voice

He found the driver's license. There was no picture, but the height and weight matched close enough. "Who's Mandy Hattmann?"

Jill seemed to gasp on the other end. "She's my cousin. She lives in Melbourne, but she travels a lot. She sells makeup."

"And she wears her hair in a black flattop?"

"Yes," she said. "We both did it, as sort of a lark, about a year ago, for a photo layout. We just both sort of kept it."

"Let me guess: When Mandy's in town, she stays here."

"Yes. . . "

"She has a key to the place?"

"Yes. *Why?*" Her voice rose anxiously.

"I'm afraid someone thought she was you," Cody finally said. "She's dead."

"Oh, shit," Jill wailed.

"Hang on, goddammit," Cody insisted.

"What am I going to do?" she sobbed after some moments.

"Nothing. The safest place you can be right now is where you are. Out of sight." Cody was talking quickly, trying to calm her. "As long as the people who did this think you're dead, you're going to be okay."

"But I can't stay here," she moaned hopelessly in a child's voice.

"Why not?" Cody asked.

"My mother overheard me calling the police on Taylor." Her breathing was choppy now. "She called me a whore and a traitor. Shit, she came at me with a knife. She wouldn't have stopped if the doctor hadn't come then."

Cody, aware of McCabe in the doorway, glanced up at him now and sighed, covering the mouthpiece with his hand. "Grandma Sally's turned nasty."

"I thought she might," McCabe said. "Reminds me of my old mother-in-law."

"Oh, noooo," he could hear her wail on the phone now.

"What's wrong now?" Cody asked.

"The cops are here," she whined, closing in on a sob. He knew he was near to losing her.

"Listen to me!" His voice was hard. "Do you want to stay alive?" No answer. His tone became impatient. "It's not a tough question. Yes or no; you want to stay alive?"

"Yes," she said finally.

"Then do exactly as I tell you: First, you tell the cops everything you know about your brother and what he's done to his kids. If you lie or try to hold anything back, I'll find out, because I'm going to get a police report, and if you do, I'm going to goddamn well find the people who are trying to kill you and then tell them exactly where you are. Do you understand?" He knew he was bullying her, but he didn't care. He was tired and his friend Tommy was dead and so were a lot of other people, and she was the only live link he knew of and he couldn't let her cave in on him.

"I understand," she said, her voice flat and devoid of resistance.

"When you're done giving your statement to the cops, go downstairs. Mr. McCabe will be waiting for you in his car. He'll take you someplace safe."

"What if he's not there?" she asked in a scared, little girl voice.

"He'll be there," Cody assured her. "Now go do what you have to do." This time he didn't wait for her to respond. His thumb pressed the disconnect button, and then he threw the phone onto the bed.

"What about us?" McCabe asked. "Shouldn't we be calling the cops ourselves?"

"I don't think so. Right now the people who wanted Jill Edwards dead think she is," Cody said, slipping the dead girl's wallet into his pocket and then stashing her clothes and purse in nearby drawers. "If we call in the cops right now, first off we'll have to tell them that the real Jill Edwards is still alive and is the one who gave us the key to get in here. And then they'll want to know why I'm here and why I'm carrying a gun and what you're doing here, and sooner or later all of that will get back to the police commissioner who was trying to cover up the autopsy reports. Because if this is connected to the fire, you've got to know he's going to be on the lookout for the discovery of her body."

"Enough said, enough said," McCabe agreed, managing a small smile and raising his hands and flashlight beam in mock surrender.

* * *

Cody watched McCabe drive away as he stood at the window of the bedroom Tommy had shared with Jill. The body of her look-alike lay a dozen feet away. He tried not to breathe deeply. They had opened half a dozen windows, but the air was still foul. The odor of death seemed to cling to the walls, floors – everything that was in the house. He made a quick, semi-thorough search of the bedroom. Jill wasn't much more of a housekeeper than her brother. The room was cluttered with magazines and dirty underwear, ashtrays filled with cigarette butts and empty wine bottles. She had apparently already cleared out Tommy's clothes and belongings.

He was about to leave and move upstairs when something in the bottom of an empty drawer caught his eye. It was the corner of a photograph stuck under some papers. He could see the face of a younger, less boozy Tommy Creager and the blue of the ocean behind. . . and Cody's stomach felt numb and his legs seemed unsteady. He pulled the photograph free. It had been taken where he had thought. Tommy was on the deck of the Cody family house in

Playa Del Rey. He had his little girl with him and they were both smiling at the camera. She was pretty and chubby and looked to be six or seven. And in the background, blond three-year-old Patrick in bright red swimming trunks was pulling at his mother. Only her head was blocked out by Tommy's, so all Cody could see of Ann was one of her arms and part of a leg, and he had to sit down on the edge of the bed and for some moments thought he was going to cry. And then he heard the car pull up outside.

Cody moved back to the window. It was a police car, its blue light flashing silently. A lone cop got out and waited as the woman from next door with the Judy Garland hair hurried out into the street. Talking and pointing to the house Cody was in.

Cody knew he had to work quickly now. Once the cop moved close enough to one of the open windows he'd get the unmistakable whiff of death, and backup support would flood in.

A light from a street lamp partially lit Tommy's office on the third floor, which was much as Cody had expected. . . and not a lot different from the one he remembered from California: a modest-sized room crammed with makeshift bookcases overflowing with books and magazines and newspapers and notebooks. . . Tommy's notebooks, everywhere. His desk was a large old dining-room table, again piled high with papers and notebooks, the only relief being a lap-top computer that sat like a shrine in the middle of all of it. Someone, no doubt the cop, was using the heavy knocker on the front door now, banging and banging.

Cody moved through the shadows of the room

to the old refrigerator that hummed with a steady rattle and seemed to lean against the wall behind the desk. A piece of moldy cheese and a half loaf of equally green-black bread shared the top shelf with a dozen cans of club soda. On the second shelf was what he was looking for: Tommy's metal box, about a foot square and four inches high. Cody pulled it out, then squatted down so that he might rest it on his knees, and then, pulling back the fastening clasp, he opened it. A couple more of Tommy's handwritten notebooks, plus some photographs, lay inside.

In the glare of the refrigerator light he looked through the photos first. Most had been taken on a yacht or at outdoor restaurants. The cast was almost always the same, the two stars being Tommy, looking boozy and fleshy, and an older woman who Cody was certain must be Fiona Brown. She was small and looked to be in her early sixties. Her hair was frosted gold and usually styled into a sporty, windswept look. Her clothes vere colorful and flowing and very expensive looking. In most of the photos she was smiling or laughing and had a drink in her hand. The one constant was that in all the photos her eyes were hidden behind a pair of large dark glasses.

Some of the recurring supporting cast included Jill and a scattering of cherubically smiling, middle-aged priests – sometimes in their clerical attire but more often in awful sport shirts and pants, which made Cody realize that this must be a worldwide compulsion shared by all Roman Catholic priests.

Then, of course, there was the missing boy, Nicholas. At seventeen he was tanned but soft looking, almost pretty, with curly, brownish blond hair. But even in the photos there seemed something odd about him. Another layer. In about half the photos he was in, he didn't seem to be in tune with the others. His eyes either strayed or else just remained pensive while everyone else laughed. And now he was missing. . . vanished. Just like Ann had. Even though that was the only connection, a sense of melancholy swept over him.

Nicholas was identified on the back of several of the photos. On one Tommy had written wryly, "Another charming lunch. Nicholas talks alternately of becoming a priest and of chopping his father into little pieces with a butcher knife."

There were the others, too: the older brothers now murdered, Kevin and David. Both athletic looking, tanned, and handsome. David with dark, straight hair; Kevin with the dirty-blond curls of his youngest brother. On the back of one of the photos of the three brothers Tommy had written "Herod's pigs?"

He found those words scrawled several more times in one of the notebooks. The page was made up mostly of doodles and then words written at various angles: *"Herod's pigs?. . . Herod's pigs?. . . Did Oswald pass the paraffin test? Was it rigged?. . . What is Griffin up to? What now? Why risk all for drugs?"*

Cody flipped through several more pages. They seemed to be filled with Fiona's rambling accounts of her early life with Brown. One underlined passage detailed how she had delivered a paper bag filled with cash for Griffin to the wife of the state premier. On another page was an account of how one night she had heard her husband order Billy Packer to kill a rival, and a week later the rival's body had turned up in the harbor.

So Tommy had been doing research into Griffin Brown. Using his wife as a firsthand source. Had Brown found out? Is this why Tommy had been killed? Because of the bitter, alcoholic memories of an old woman? He hoped not. It all seemed a bit tasteless, a bit sad. He hoped his friend hadn't slipped as far as that. He hoped that maybe Tommy's notes of her memories were just fulfilling his insatiable need to make notes. . . but he suspected they weren't. He slipped through several more pages until he came to one with a big star. Tommy had been discouraged on this page: "This is ludicrous. . . tonight she was so drunk she thought I was the prophet Samuel and told me Griffin is Satan. That's why he's so successful and never been caught or gone to prison. She told me of a night – long after Griffin had lived in her bedroom or had sex with her – that he appeared in her room with his head in the form of a goat's and his body that of a Greek God's, and he had then raped and committed sodomy on her in every way he could, all night long. He had left her just before dawn, bloodied and with fang marks on her breasts. She's sure that he had tried to kill her that night, and that it was only the power of her wailed-out prayers, combined with the power of her saints there in the room with her, that had saved her. . . " Cody started to move on to another page, but downstairs the banging on the front door had long stopped, and now he could hear a second and then a third car pull up.

Carrying the metal box with him, Cody moved to the window. As he had suspected, three police cars with their flashing blue lights were now down on the street. He counted four police officers, two heading for the back of the house. He waited several seconds and then carefully opened the wrench door that led to the wrought-iron balcony.

It covered about two-thirds of the twenty-foot front of the building. There was no way he could jump the fourteen or fifteen feet to the matching balcony on the next house over. He looked and then reached up, tugging at the rain gutter. It was rusted and rotted through, nothing he could dare to try and hang onto as he made his way over to the other balcony. There was no way of escape from here. Then, as he stepped back inside the room, he felt a sudden draft of icy cold air. . . and he could hear a woman weeping and thought about the ghost that the boys playing cricket down the street had told Patrick about, and then the cold and the woman's weeping were gone, replaced by the sound of men's voices on the floor below. One of them was coming up the stairs now. Cody stepped into the shadows behind the door. The police officer pushed the door fully open, glanced around, but not behind the door, then retreated down the steps.

"Nothing up here," he reported to the others as he reached the bottom.

"Chrickey, she had a nice pair of tits," another voice said.

Cody found a trap door that led to crawl space in a cramped attic and pulled himself and the metal box up into it and then replaced the trap door. It was dark and musty. He was exhausted. He could hear sounds of activity below and knew there was nothing he could do but wait. Wait and maybe sleep. For he knew it would be hours before they were done down there. Years ago he had taught himself how to sleep for short periods of time; how to relax and concentrate, eliminating all outside thoughts and emotions. He managed to lie down, using the metal box as a hard pillow, and fatigue swept over him. . . . No time to concentrate; no time to block all thoughts. . . . And as he started to slip off he could hear someone coming back up the stairs, and the feeling of cold came back over him and again he could hear the woman weeping. He thought of the dead woman on the bathroom floor and of Tommy and his bizarre relationship with Griffin Brown's wife. . . and of the night of madness when she had been raped and sodomized by the goat-headed Greek god. And he thought of Brown's two sons, alive and healthy and handsome in the photographs, now dead. And the other boy, the one vanished. . . and as he saw young Nicholas, the cold moved over him again and he heard the weeping woman once more, and as he did he realized that the weeping woman's voice wasn't a woman at all, it was young lost Nicholas. So afraid. . . so afraid. And then the thoughts were gone and Cody was in a deep, dark sleep. . . for seconds or minutes or a thousand years.

21

Henry Wang listened to the police commissioner. They were sitting at a table in his restaurant, the Golden Fish, which took up the entire second floor of the six-story building he owned on Dixon street, in the heart of Sydney's Chinatown. On the first

floor was an import shop, which like the Golden
Fish was a favorite of tourists. It sold everything
from cheap Hong Kong toys to ivory carvings, fine
silks to rosewood dining-room sets and large teakwood chests. It was, in fact, hidden in one of those
chests for almost thirty-six hours without food or
water that Henry Wang had managed to illegally get
ashore eleven years before. His uncle, who at that
time owned this building and a number of other
businesses – all of which were now Henry Wang's –
had been in failing health and had needed him.

The probleln was, Henry, then thirty-one, had a
rather impressive police record in Hong Kong, making an entry visa for Australia, even as a tourist,
impossible. So in Hong Kong, other family members
came together, and eventually arrangements were
made that first saw Henry get a job on a freighter
carrying the teakwood products into Sydney. Of
course, by the time the freighter had arrived,
envelopes of money had already changed hands and
the customs official on the dock that day passed the
consignment of teakwood chests through without
examination. Later, further monies were paid in
Hong Kong and Sydney and Canberra, and in Hong
Kong police records disappeared and in Canberra
and Sydney two members of Parliament and one
prominent government minister spoke publicly of
the good character of their friend young Henry
Wang. Within a year of his arrival he had attained
permanent resident status and was a respected
member of the community. A little more than three
years after that, when his uncle died, Henry took
over the family businesses.

The police commissioner was finished speaking.

Henry Wang said nothing for several long moments. His eyes scanned the large room. Only a dozen or so customers were left. At a table of eight, the people were drunk and laughing loudly. Most of the tables were already cleared and had their chairs placed on top of them, upside down. Near the entrance to the kitchen, the cleaning crew waited with their vacuums for the last of the guests to leave.

"I don't like being threatened, commissioner," Wang finally said. He didn't like dealing with Jacklan. The policeman was a puzzle that he hadn't yet been able to sort out. He felt the man put on the face of a crooked, not very intelligent cop. But Wang sensed a cunning behind the facade. He reasoned that Jacklan had risen too far in both the police department and Griffin Brown's organization to be as stupid as he sometimes appeared. It was that cunning, Henry felt, that made the commissioner unpredictable. And dangerous.

"Goddammit, don't take it that way," Jacklan said. His body ached for a drink, but he didn't want to show weakness in front of the Chinaman. "Griffin is really edgy right now. Christ, two of his sons have been killed!"

"Which, no matter what I say, he thinks I was responsible for," Wang returned accusingly. Then he turned his head to Li, one of the two bodyguards sitting with them at the table, and spoke to him in Cantonese. Li got up and signaled the cleaning crew with a wave of his arm. They moved out and began to vacuum, and then Li himself left the table.

"Listen," Jacklan implored, "I told you I was able to convince Griffin you weren't behind the firebombing. . . or at least I convinced him to wait."

"Wait for what?" Wang demanded.

"To find out who did do it," Jacklan said. "Sooner or later someone's going to talk. We'll find out, and you'll be in the clear."

"And until then, I'm to behave myself, like a good little boy," Wang said sarcastically. "What about the Jew and the Professor? They're the ones I'd be looking out for if I were Griffin Brown. They're the ones he's doing the big deal with. They're the ones most likely to double-cross him so they can move in and take all the heroin for themselves."

Jacklan's nerves were raw. He really needed a drink now. He wasn't to be disappointed. Li returned to the table with a bottle of vodka and a glass of ice, which he placed in front of the commissioner. A flash of shame went through the cop. The bloody Chinaman knew more about him than he should, he mused. Christ, he wanted a drink, but he'd be damned if he'd take one now. He stood up instead. "I told you, there have been rumors the last couple of weeks that you were going to pull something."

"The rumors were unfounded," Wang stated flatly.

"Goddammit, it doesn't bloody matter," Jacklan said loudly. "The fact is, they were out there. They said you were still pissed off because they didn't let you in on the deal. They said you were going to pull something to save face. The fact is, I saved your life tonight. I talked Griffin Brown and the Jew and the Professor out of killing you. I talked them into waiting. All I'm asking you to do is to keep a low profile for a week or so until all this sorts itself out."

"You mean until the big delivery takes place?" Wang mocked.

Jacklan, realizing his hand was shaking, sighed, picked up the glass and threw the ice cubes out on the floor, then filled it with vodka and drank it down with one pull. "It doesn't matter what I bloody mean," he hissed at Wang. "I'm just telling you, if you got anything planned outside of Chinatown in the next week or so, call it off. 'Cause I gotta tell you, Griffin Brown sees one bloody Chinaman anywhere near the Cross in the next few days, and this whole fucking town is going to explode."

Jacklan refilled the glass, only halfway this time, downed the drink, and then threw the glass on the table, turned, and marched out of the restaurant.

Henry Wang said nothing. He didn't move a muscle. He waited until the big cop had left the restaurant, then turned to Li and addressed him in Cantonese. Li nodded and then moved to the bar, where he picked up the house phone and began to dial. Henry Wang watched and promised himself that soon, very soon, he would personally shoot Police commissioner Jacklan's eyes out.

22

The door opened and the silver-haired man stepped out into the narrow street. He looked both ways and then just stood and listened for several moments. He could sense no danger. He returned to the door and nodded to Loretta Chang, who was waiting just inside. She moved back down the hallway to the door that led to the basement stairs.

The four boys, wearing just their boxer shorts, were asleep now on the mattresses. She moved quietly to each one of them, shaking them gently like a mother would her sleeping child. As they stirred awake she spoke to them in Cantonese. Each rose without protest and began to dress. A few minutes later, like ducklings following their mother, the boys trailed Loretta out of the building and across to the van, where the silver-haired man was waiting with the engine running. Each of the boys was carrying a raincoat folded over his arm. . . and under each raincoat was one of the automatic weapons Loretta Chang had checked so carefully.

"How far is Kings Cross from here?" she asked.

23

He saw her first in the reflection of the window he was looking out of. The penthouse window overlooking the harbor. Shauna was standing naked in the doorway behind him, and he found himself surprised that with all that had happened in the last days he could be aroused. But he was. He turned away from the window and looked back at her. She smiled. Her ebony body was perfect and sparkled now with beads of water from the shower she had just stepped out of.

"Jesus Christ," Griffin Brown said, "you are beautiful."

"So are you," she purred, and moved over to him.

He laughed and then sighed. "I'm one tired old son of a bitch, is what I am."

Her hand found the front of his trousers. "That doesn't feel too old or tired to me."

He smiled again and this time put down his scotch.

They made love.

"You should sleep," she said afterward.

"I know," he answered, his voice tired. "But every time I close my eyes. . . everything starts spinning. I see Kevin and David . . . and the bloody Chinaman." He sat up abruptly.

"Griffin, you're exhausted."

"God, I miss those boys," he said, getting up and moving back to where he had left his scotch. "It's like someone reached into my chest and pulled my heart out. Sure, we had our differences." He paused and almost smiled. "There were times you could see it in their eyes. . . how much they would have liked to see me out of the way. . . how much they wanted to take over everything, *now*. But they knew I was still too tough. They knew I may be old and tired, but I'm still bloody king of the hill."

"Come to bed," she said.

He moved to it and sat on the edge. "I feel so bloody empty," he said. "Like a beaten team."

"Don't," she protested.

"Christ, Shauna, everything I've got – the clubs, the bars," his lips found a wane smile, "my bloody fucking empire, and now I have no sons to leave it to anymore."

"You still have a son," she said.

Her words snapped him out of his melancholy, "Nicholas? That's a bloody laugh. He's the one who actually did try to kill me, remember? Of course, he was only twelve then." He grinned darkly.

"I remember."

"Besides, he's bloody crazy," Brown said dismissively. "And no one even knows where he is."

"Maybe he's with the Chinaman," she said, using words as a surgeon would a scalpel.

But this time he didn't smile or look surprised; he just nodded. "Nicholas and the Chinaman. . . yeah, I've thought of that possibility."

"It could explain a lot," she said. "Why he disappeared. Why the Chinaman didn't have to send any of his people to firebomb the Galah."

"All right," he snapped. "I don't want to talk about it now." He looked over and saw she was hurt, so he managed a smile and tried to make a joke out of it. "I'm sorry. But you know that if it is Nicholas working with the Chinaman, I'm certainly not going to leave my empire to him."

She moved across the room naked and poured herself a drink. Jesus, she was perfect, he thought.

"He wasn't the son I was talking about."

He looked at her a moment and then realized. "Kelly?"

"Our son." She nodded and turned back to him, and remarkably he could feel himself being aroused again.

"But he's only a boy."

"He's almost sixteen."

"He's. . . " He started to speak again and then stopped.

"Half black? Is that what you were going to say?" she asked, starting back toward him.

"That doesn't matter," he said, standing up to meet her. When her breasts nuzzled into his chest, she reached down and took ahold of him and then smiled. "In one way he's more your son than any of the others," she said. "Don't you remember, when you gave him your traditional gift for a boy turning fifteen, he was the only one who taught the hooker something new?"

Brown grinned and nodded. "Makes you wonder what they're teaching them at Jesuit schools these days."

24

Cody slept fitfully in the crawl space. He was back on Terminal Island in California. Empty, ugly, rain-swept streets. In the parking lot, against a rusting car. He was there on his knees, his hands handcuffed behind him. His partner was already dying. Writhing on the ground, moaning in pain, his hands also handcuffed behind his back. Circling around his partner was Tucker. Tucker the Maniac. He liked to kill girls and carve crosses into their foreheads. He waved and pointed his .38 at Cody and shouted out the Twenty-third Psalm with the passion of a crying, sweating evangelist: "He maketh me to lie down in green pastures, he leadeth me beside still waters. He restoreth my soul. . . " Now Tucker was arguing loudly with his brother. His brother wanted to leave. His brother was telling him, "You're fucking crazy, man," and Tucker was raising the gun and then he shoots his brother in the forehead and it explodes in blood and orange, and now Cody knows his only chance is to run and he tries, rolling over and gaining his feet. Running now. Running. Tucker is screaming at him. It seems miles. Tucker is screaming. Now hot pain cuts through Cody's body, and he's falling and falling. . . and then Tucker is staring down at him, his eyes glinting with a fanatic's desire, and shouting, "Surely goodness and mercy will follow me all the days of my life, and I will dwell in the house of the Lord forever. . . " And then Tucker's gun explodes with orange fire and the sound of a shot, and everything is red now, electric red, and his ears are filled with a high-pitched tone and Tucker's shouted words "The Lord is my shepherd, I shall not want. . ." And now someone else's voice: "Pulse, there's no pulse," and he's on the edge of endless darkness, and he knows he's falling. "Paddles. . . clear!" and his body leaps. "Again!" And once more his being is jolted and then everything is red again – bright electric red – and the high-pitched tone is splitting his head, growing louder and louder. And now he sees himself in a hospital bed. Sees himself as if he's floating above. Nine-year-old Damien is here, trying not to cry. "Papa," the boy says, and then it's bright electric red again and the ear-splitting high-pitched tone is back, and now we're in a basement, dirty and clammy. Tucker is here. . . leering toward us. He's reciting the Twenty-third Psalm again, only his words are garbled and drawn out and then he's gone again, replaced by the bright electric red and the ear-splitting high-pitched tone. And then Cody's back in the hospital room, looking at himself from above, only now the room is as big as a basketball court and Ann is there with little Patrick. Ann is crying. She asks a doctor, "How long can he stay in a coma?" And then he's back in Tucker's basement. There is a girl, about fifteen or sixteen. She's naked and tied to his table, and Tucker's carving a cross in her forehead. And then he's back to the bright electric red and the ear-splitting high-pitched tone, and then he's watching himself from above. In his hospital bed, and nine-year-old Damien is there again, "Papa, please don't die," and then everything becomes bright electric red again until he sees Tucker, who's dragging

explode, and then there was only white – soft, comforting white – and he rested and slept and slept, and when he opened his eyes he was still in his hospital room. Ann was there and Pyne and now, too, Captain Waters. A large man, the kind Cody's afraid of becoming, one who's been a cop too long. Whatever sensitivity he might have had as a young man had long been burned out. What drove him now was staying alive – not on the streets anymore, but in departmental politics. Right now he was trying to be compassionate. After all, Cody was a cop, one of his, but right now Cody was the focus of a very disturbing question: How had he known where Tucker was? Cody told him he didn't know how he knew and then asked.

"Did you get him?"

"Oh, we got him," Pyne beams. "Eleven girls he's murdered, son of a bitch gave himself up, quiet as a mouse."

Waters is still disturbed. "You don't know how you knew he was there?"

"No," Cody answers, trying to remember. "I just saw him in little bits. . . saw the Four Deuces. What about the girl?"

"Dead, at least for a day," Waters replies.

"What about her forehead?" Cody asks.

"He'd carved a cross in it, just like the others."

And Cody feels uneasy. But then, from their faces, so do the others in the room. . . and Cody's uneasiness grows into anxiety. How did he know? How could he have possibly known? And he has this sense of someone having cut a hole in his soul, only he doesn't know how large it is or how deep it goes, or if it would pull him down into it, falling and falling. . . . And then the soft, white sleep floods over him once more.

25

Mickey Packer carved into the two-inch steak with enthusiasm. It was cooked, as it was every night, just the way he liked it: charbroiled on the outside, the blood rare on the inside. He was sitting at the end of the bar, his shift here almost over. In a few minutes Clackers would arrive and take over the responsibility of making sure that only authorized people went through the EMPLOYEES ONLY door. Not that there was much to do, he thought; Mr. Brown had gone over an hour ago, and his dad had left a few minutes after that. Only Lady in the money cage was left, and she was behind her own three-inch steel door. And as he ate, he wondered, as he had a number of times before, how she could stand it. Being locked up in there for twelve hours a day. Watching TV and knitting and counting all the money that came through, making sure it balanced to the receipts and then putting it in the safe. The counting and all the numbers – Billy knew that would be hard for him. In the school for the deaf that he had gone to, math had always given him a headache. But that wasn't the worst part, he thought. The worst part would be being locked up in there all that time. Not seeing anyone else except when she would ring the buzzer and he'd go let her out so she could pee or make a phone call or whatever she had to do. And then he let Lady drift out of his thoughts; the steak was too good. He loved skewering big chunks of dripping red meat together with pieces of fried potatoes. He

smiled at the thought that most people would be too
tired at the end of a long day to eat such a big meal,
but he wasn't, he never was. He prided himself on
his physical condition. He was hungry and now letting Debbie into his thoughts, he was horny, too. He
knocked on the bar for Grasshopper, showing him
his empty beer glass. Grasshopper was lean and at
least six foot seven and had tattoos over most of his
body. He brought over the beer and grinned.

"Going to get yourself some tonight, Mickey?"
he asked, darting his tongue in and out of his mouth
salaciously.

Mickey grinned and nodded his thanks for the
beer. Grasshopper's question was a long-standing
joke between the friends, because they both knew
that Mickey went over to the Bayswater brothel
every night after work. Grasshopper even knew that
for the last few months Mickey's girlfriend had been
Debbie. For from his silent world Mickey had once
showed him a picture of her. It had been a high
school picture. That was the way Mickey liked to
think about her. It didn't matter to him that she
might have had half a dozen customers in the hours
before his arrival. She always put a dress on for him
when they began. A sun dress without any underwear, so he could just make out her nipples through
the cloth. He liked to rub them and rub them, and
gradually they'd pull off the dress and by then he'd
be in a frenzy and they would have sex at least
twice. In many ways. She was the best he'd ever
known. Not just because of what they did together
physically, but because she was actually nice to him.
She didn't treat him like a freak. Mickey was in love
with her. She was the first girl he'd ever asked on a

date. It had been hard. He had to get over his fear
that she would laugh at him, either in front of him or
behind his back. But he couldn't stand being without
her. So he had written the note: "Will you have
lunch with me?" He gave it to her after one of their
night sessions, and she had smiled and nodded her
head. She really wanted to. Now they had lunch two
and three times a week, or sometimes they'd take
ferry rides over to Manly, or feed the ducks in
Centennial Park. And of course he saw her every
night when he got off work, except Sundays.
Sundays he didn't work. Sundays he went with his
mother and his brother to church and just had a lazy
day around the house watching the telly or playing
cricket or rugby with the youngies while Dad usually burned the Sunday dinner on the barbie.

* * *

But Grasshopper wasn't the only person who knew
that Mickey went to the Bayswater brothel every
night after work.

Mickey, who had walked the two and a half
blocks from the Cowboy Club to Bayswater street,
now waved a friendly greeting up to the third-floor
window across the road where he knew Max Oliver
was stationed as extra security for the whorehouse
opposite him. Of course Mickey had no way of
knowing that the arm that had waved back hadn't
belonged to Max. That Max in fact lay dead on the
floor of the tiny apartment, his throat cut, his warm
blood soaking into the worn hardwood floor. Mickey
had no way of knowing that the arm that had waved
back to him had belonged to Colin Fitzwilliam.

Fitzwilliam watched Mickey enter the brothel and glanced at his watch. Five minutes, he thought, that's all the time they would wait. He knew from earlier reports that there were also at least half a dozen American sailors in the four-story brothel, along with a couple of ambitious teenagers, a couple of tourists, and of course a handful of boozing businessmen. It would be a night to remember, the silver-haired man thought.

26

A mouse nibbled on his finger, and Cody awoke with a start. As he jerked the hand away the mouse scurried for cover. It took Cody a moment to get his bearings. He sat up, careful not to bang his head on a nearby support beam. The house below him was quiet, but the scent of rotting corpse still lingered in the air. . . and for the first time tonight he recalled driving in New Zealand with McCabe, when he had told the reporter to stop the car as they neared Tauranga. His "gift" had caused him to sense the same smell then. He had thought someone had died there, and now he wondered if that were true at all. . . or if what he had sensed there had just been a premonition of what they'd found here tonight. He didn't know, and his head was still foggy from sleep. He looked at his watch: nearly three-thirty. He listened carefully now; not a sound below. Carefully, quietly as he could, he moved back the trap door to the crawl space and listened again. Silence. He moved Tommy Creager's metal box near the opening and then lowered himself down into the room below. Then, standing on a chair, he retrieved the box.

He moved to Tommy's dining-room-table desk. Notebooks and papers and scraps of paper everywhere. Cody looked at several of the notebooks, but also was well aware that whoever had broken in here during Tommy's funeral would have too and that there would be nothing of significance left – at least nothing appertaining to why Tommy might have been murdered. Most of the notebooks were what he expected – old ones dealing with the Kennedy assassination and filled with faded clippings and photographs, many of them showing a younger, thinner Tommy Creager at various sites in Dallas that had become famous during those few fateful days. Again, Cody felt a stinging sadness for his friend and his long-lost glory days.

Cody had to lift half a dozen more notebooks until he had found what he was hoping for: Tommy's address and phone book. It was red and well worn and the size of a videotape. He flipped through the pages. None of the names he glanced at meant anything to him. Then he moved to the letter "B." There were half a dozen listings before he came to Brown, Griffin, under which was written a number for both the Cowboy Club and home. Then just below it was the name Fiona and the notation "private line" and another number.

It was almost three-thirty in the morning and yet he had an overwhelming urge to call, as if he had to hear her voice. He pondered and nearly decided against it. . . but then didn't, for he had learned a long time ago – even before the bullet in his skull had brought on his "gift" – that as a cop he was usually right when he followed his first instincts. He used the phone on Tommy's desk. On the other end it began to ring and ring, and as it did a sense of coldness came over him again, and the sound of weeping seemed to be near. Six. . . seven rings. He was about to hang up when a frail, sleepy voice answered.

"Hello?" Fiona Brown said.

Cody said nothing. The sense of the weeping was closer now.

"Is that you, Nicholas?" she asked after several moments. "Is that you, darling?"

Still Cody didn't speak. But he knew now that if he was going to find out who killed Tommy Creager, he had to find young lost Nicholas first.

"Don't be afraid to talk, dear," she went on gently. "Mommy loves you. Mommy will always love you."

Cody hung up.

27

The silver-haired man was the first one through the door. He had gone out the back of the building across the street, where he had killed Max Oliver, circled around the block and approached the brothel like any other late-night customer might. As he expected, Charlie Pallero was acting as security in the front room. But what he hadn't expected was that Charlie wasn't alone. It was late and they were getting lazy. He was playing Monopoly with three hookers. One of them, a freckled redhead, was naked; another, who looked to be Greek, wore only a green sequined tank top. The third, a blonde, was in a green South Sydney football jersey. The girls fought their sleepiness and tried to look alluring as he entered. Charlie, who had been serving five to ten in Long Bay Prison when Colin Fitzwilliam had been doing his own time, showed a spark of recognition. "Hey, Law and Order," Charlie said and smiled, but that was before he saw the gun. The silver-haired man fired twice at him. The first one went through Charlie's forehead, the second superfluously into his chest. And in those moments of insanity the girls had begun to scream and try to run for safety. He shot down two of them. The last, the naked redhead, was cut down by a burst of bullets from one of the four Chinese boys, who, along with the other three and Loretta Chang, had now poured into the room.

"You said there would be no girls down here," she said accusingly.

"Didn't think there would be," he answered curtly. He was getting tired of her arrogance.

"We have lost all surprise," she continued.

But the silver-haired man didn't give a shit what she had to say. They had to finish the job. He moved quickly to the door that led to the stairway. It was locked. He stepped away quickly and barked at her.

"Blow the bloody thing open!"

She in turn spoke a few words in Cantonese to one of the boys, who now emptied his thirty-six-round clip into the section of the door that held the lock. It splintered and shattered and finally creaked open. Another of the boys ran through the doorway, his Tec-9 ready, only to be greeted by gunfire from up the stairs. The firing wasn't as rapid as a machine pistol; more like a .38, the silver-haired man thought, the weapon Tony Baker usually carried. He was the third member of the overnight security Griffin Brown had put on this place since the disco firebombing. Max Oliver dead across the street; Charlie Pallero dead in the front room; and now Tony Baker – very much alive and dangerous – alerted by the screaming hookers. But the lack of speed in firing from Tony's gun didn't matter; the Chinese boy was hit and spun backward, the front of his shirt filled with blood, and Fitzwilliam could see from where he stood that he was dead before he hit the ground.

The other three boys looked startled, but Loretta Chang wasn't about to let them move from startled to frightened. She picked up the Tec-9 from the fallen boy and charged into the stairwell firing. Fitzwilliam heard Tony's gun get off two more shots and that was all. Loretta reappeared and shouted commands at the three remaining boys, and with her leading the way they all ran up the stairs.

The second floor was in pandemonium as the four Chinese reached it. An American sailor, almost fully dressed, jumping up and down on one foot trying to pull his second pant leg on, was stitched across the front by Loretta's bullets. She moved on to the room he had come out of, replacing her clip as she did and directing the boys to other rooms. A fat, naked brunette hooker cowered in a corner. Loretta fired a burst that nearly severed one of her breasts.

Two more American sailors were trying to climb out the window and onto a fire escape from the room they had shared with a blond hooker, who herself was rapidly pulling on clothes, when one of the boys burst through the door. He fired first at the sailors, spending more than half his clip to rip their bodies open. One fell back into the room; the other, the black, fell through the window.

"Please, I have nothing to do with this," the blonde screamed.

The boy fired a burst at her that tore a red line from her belly up through her eyes.

A businessman wearing only boxer shorts stood with a handful of money, fifty and one-hundred-dollar bills extended as an offer as one of the other Chinese boys kicked the door in. He was going to say, "Here take everything I have," but he never got the chance. The burst from the Teck-9 threw him back and against the wall, only now the boy was alert. There seemed to be no one else in the room. He stood and tried to listen, but the sporadic gunfire and screams filling the rest of the house made that difficult. Something was moving under the bed. The Chinese youngster dropped to the floor, gun ready. From under the bed, a naked blond teenage boy stared back at him in terror.

"Please," the blond boy said.

The Chinese boy hesitated. He had been forced to sell his body when he was very young. It was a special shame, he thought. . . and then emptied the last twenty-six bullets of the clip into the blond teenager, wracking his body until the gun was spent.

On the fourth floor it took Debbie only moments to alert Mickey Packer to the sounds of gunfire and screams that she was hearing, and as soon as he realized what she was telling him he remembered that his father had told him to be careful. . . that they might be in a war with Henry Wang very soon. . . and now he realized that most of all he didn't want anyone to hurt Debbie. Without bothering with his clothes he grabbed his .45 and moved carefully out into the hallway. He knew he was at a severe disadvantage not being able to hear. But he had to go on. He had to protect Debbie. He had to protect Griffin Brown's brothel. Then she was at his side, helping him, being his ears. She pointed to the stairway. They moved to it, and she looked frightened at what she heard. Mickey pushed her back, indicating she should return to her room. She started, then paused, came back and kissed him on the cheek, then retreated.

Naked, Mickey started down the stairs. Halfway he could see that there was frantic activity. He moved another few steps and saw a Chinese boy reloading a clip into a machine pistol. The boy saw him and tried to start away. Mickey fired. Once, twice. . . the third bullet caught the Chinese boy in the shoulder and spun and slammed him against the wall. Mickey's fourth shot exploded the back of the Chinese boy's head. Now someone else was moving, running. A Chinese woman; she was firing at Mickey, and then for a fiber of a moment Mickey was an eight-year-old boy again, running with a rugby ball over green fields, chased by his father and laughing and laughing, and Mickey was so happy. And then for Mickey everything ended.

The shooting and screams lasted another few minutes. The special surgery took almost no time at all.

Eight minutes after it had started, with the silver-haired man coming through the front door, it was over. Now Fitzwilliam, Loretta Chang, and the two Chinese boys who were still alive ran back out the front door, across the street, and between a pair of buildings. Fifty yards beyond was a wire fence that they had previously cut. They moved through it for the second time this night and hurried down to the next street, where the van was parked.

28

The early morning streets were filled with the sounds of distant sirens as Cody let himself out the front door, and with Tommy Creager's metal box under his arm he started to walk the two blocks up to Oxford Street. As he neared it, a bearded man wearing high heels and mesh stockings stared at him from the rear entrance of a bar named Jeffie's.

"Are you with Stuart?" the bearded man wanted to know.

"I don't know a Stuart," Cody answered.

"Well, are you at least with the foam company?"

"I'm looking for a cab," Cody said.

"Shiiiit," the bearded man said petulantly. "It's only three days to Mardi Gras; I don't know how they think I'm supposed to get ready." Then he sighed. "There's a cab rank up the top and down two blocks."

Cody thanked him.

Another siren raced by on nearby Oxford Street.

"There must be a terrible something going on somewhere," the bearded man murmured as Cody moved away.

* * *

Two miles away, the ringing phone woke Griffin Brown. He realized two facts on waking: Shauna was not in bed, and there was trouble, for the phone ringing was the private line. And with Kevin and David gone, there was only Billy Packer, commissioner Jacklan, and Lakey who had the number. It was for emergencies. It had rung only twice in the last seven years: once a couple of years ago when Fiona, drunker than usual, had fallen down the stairs at the yacht club and broken her leg; and the last time, five nights before, the night the disco was fire-bombed.

"This is Brown."

Jacklan, on the other end, spoke briefly.

"Christ," Brown said angrily. "Have you called Billy yet?"

He listened again, and this time his face dropped. "Oh shit, oh shit, oh shit," he said in disgust, and then looked up as Shauna came into the room. She was wearing a sheer negligee, and he realized her hair had been brushed. For a moment he wondered why she had stayed up, why she hadn't gone to sleep, but sorrow and outside events were flooding in on him, and Jacklan was speaking again. "No, goddammit," Brown snapped, and then his voice settled with fatigue and sadness. "I'll call Billy. . . . You just clean him up, I don't want Billy to see him. . . " He broke off for a moment, the anger of the battle was returning. "Do you understand? Goddammit, I don't want Billy *seeing* him like that!" He listened another moment. "Bullshit, I'll be there in ten minutes."

"What's happened?" Shauna asked with fear in her voice after he'd hung up.

"They've hit the Bayswater," Brown said as he crossed to the closet and selected a shirt and trousers. "From what Jacklan tells me, it's a bloody massacre. They killed all the hookers and most of the customers."

Shauna had to lean on a wall. "Why? It's crazy."

"Why is because it's bloody war," he spat out, pulling on his pants. "Don't you see, they're trying to take me apart piece by piece. First the Galah, now this." He paused a moment. "Jesus," he said with a mixture of sad reflection and survival curiosity, "why didn't they just come after me? Kill me if they can? It's as if they first have to destroy me in front of the world."

Shauna's body was quaking. "The Chinaman?"

He looked at her a long moment before answering truthfully. "My instinct says yes. . . but I don't know for sure. Not yet. It's so bloody savage. Christ, it's more like a vendetta. First Kevin and David and now. . ."

He finished dressing.

"Now who?" she asked in a broken voice.

He moved to her and tried to help her to the bed so she could sit down. She was near hysteria.

"Now who?" she insisted.

He sat down next to her and held her tight. "Whoever did it apparently waited for Mickey to show up."

"Oh, noooo," she moaned. "He's. . . ?"

Brown sighed. "He was with his girl. After they killed him, the bastards mutilated him. They cut off his private parts."

"Why?" she cried.

"Christ, I don't know. But I'm bloody well going to find out."

* * *

The cab ride from Oxford Street in Paddington took Cody up through Darlinghurst and onto Victoria

Street. Many of the sirens were closer now. They were ambulances, one after the other rolling into St. Vincent's Hospital. A policeman held the cab up for several minutes.

"What's going on, mate?" the cabby asked the cop. "Bloody World War III?"

The cop shook his head with distress. "Some bloody nut shot up a whorehouse over in the Cross."

"Chrickey, pays to keep your pants on, huh?" the cabby joked.

But the cop wasn't smiling as he waved them on. Half a block farther on they had to pull over again, as two more ambulances wailed toward them and then passed. When they finally reached and turned onto Williams Street Cody could see the police activity half a block away. Though the brothel itself was blocked from view by other buildings, at least a dozen police cars were parked around the perimeter, and ambulances with their lights flashing were still actively darting about.

"Geez," the cabby said. "Some crazy with a gun, how d'ya figure?"

Cody didn't answer. He remembered what McCabe had said yesterday afternoon about Sydney being a powder keg and Griffin Brown and Kings Cross being right in the middle of it. And he reasoned that if it wasn't a crazy lone gunman, if it had been an attack on one of Griffin Brown's brothels, then Sydney was into one hell of a gang war – which Tommy Creager's killing and young Nicholas's disappearance somehow fit right into the heart of.

29

In the early-morning darkness, some of the boat owners had gotten up and were standing out on their decks, listening to the sirens and watching the strange flickering light-show of police and ambulance vehicles across the park. They sipped from cups of steaming hot coffee and tea. A happy, almost festive mood prevailed.

Cody's cab deposited him at the street side of the marina. He hadn't walked a dozen feet when he heard McCabe calling to him.

"Cody? Jesus, don't go away!" he shouted, hanging up the pay phone he was on and loping over. "Jesus," he repeated with a cigarette wheeze as he arrived. "We were getting worried about you."

"I had a few worried moments myself," Cody said. "What have you done with Jill?"

McCabe squinted an apologetic grin. "Well, a. . . you might say, she's sort of asleep on your boat."

They started back, through the gate and toward the jetty. "Sort of?" Cody asked.

"Well, passed out is probably a better term," McCabe admitted. "She was really strung out when I picked her up. Apparently she and her mother got into another shouting match when the cops showed up, and she had started telling them about what her brother had been doing to the kids. Then when you didn't show she really started to fall to pieces. She kept asking what was going to happen to her if you were dead."

"The boys hear this?" Cody asked tautly.

"I'm afraid so," McCabe answered. "But they handled it well. Damien told her nothing had happened to you, you just must be onto a lead or something." He squinted a smile again. "Patrick tried to be a good host and offered her a drink to calm down. She calmed down all right, all the way through the better part of a bottle of vodka. I see you found Tommy's metal box."

"Yeah," Cody said.

By now, Patrick, who had been waiting on deck, had spotted his father and bounded off the boat and was running toward him.

"Papa," the boy cried, hugging him around the waist.

"You're up pretty late," Cody said.

"I got some sleep," he answered, "I'm just up early. It's going to be light in about an hour or so. Thought I'd make some breakfast."

"I'm starving," Cody smiled.

"Scrambled eggs and bacon?" Patrick asked eagerly.

"You're the best," Cody told him, and the boy leapt happily back to the boat. On deck now he could see Damien, who waved to him quietly. He was the rock, Cody thought, the anchor, since Ann had gone.

"Was it worth it?" McCabe asked. "Tommy's box? I mean, what's in it?"

"A snake pit," Cody replied.

* * *

The smoky gray Rolls-Royce slid to a stop near the police barricade. Police commissioner Jacklan, who had been waiting for it, was now surprised to see Griffin Brown climb out from behind the wheel.

"Jesus," Jacklan said, "you're alone?"

"Everybody else is home. They were sleeping," Brown snarled. They were walking briskly now through the barricade of police cars, headed for the brothel. "You had promised me there wouldn't be any more trouble from the Chinaman."

Jacklan said nothing, and that was enough of an answer. Brown stopped in his tracks and grabbed the cop by his jacket. "It was the fucking Chinaman, wasn't it?"

"Jesus," Jacklan said. "I didn't even know when I called you. The son of a bitch swore to me not more than a couple of hours ago that he wasn't behind anything. . . "

Brown overrode him, cutting off his words. "What's happened since you called me?"

"We've found a couple of their bodies," the large policeman said. "Kids, for Christ's sake. Fifteen-, sixteen-year-old Chinese boys. We've also got a few witnesses still alive. The hitters were all Chinese. . . one was even a woman." He paused, trying to muster his dignity. "I wish you wouldn't treat me like this when the men are around."

Brown, whose mind had been racing both as to how to sufficiently retaliate against Henry Wang and as to what immediate security measures should be taken, emerged from his thoughts with a bitter, sarcastic smile. "You really think it would come as a surprise to anyone in this town to discover that you're in my pocket?"

Then, on Brown's lead, they continued on to the front of the building. Bodies were still being carried out.

"How did they get in?" Brown asked.

"Apparently right through the front door," Jacklan answered.

"But that doesn't bloody make sense," Brown spat out. "I've got a security man across the street watching the front of the place. Another man should have been in a locked-off front room. How does a bloody army of Chinese come in and wipe the place out without our security people at least having time to sound an alarm that could have brought more help?"

"Max Oliver was the security across the street," Jacklan answered, wishing he didn't have to go on. "Somebody cut his throat."

"Oh, Jesus. Not old Max," Brown said in a near groan. And then his mind started working again. "Max was too old and too smart not to have protected himself on a job like this. He wouldn't have let anyone sneak up on him. He would have had himself locked up in there."

"Yeah," Jacklan nodded. "You're right. It doesn't make sense. I mean, how could anyone get to him?"

"I'll tell you how," Brown said soberly. "Because Max let him in. Because whoever killed Max was someone Max knew. . . someone he trusted. Whoever killed Max was one of us."

30

If she hadn't been snoring, Jill would have looked dead, sprawled out as she was across Cody's bed in the master cabin. He had come through the cabin to use the bathroom and take a quick shower. Now, feeling a bit better and with some fresh clothes on, he studied her for a few moments. She reeked of alcohol and several days of hard living without a shower, and yet there was a definite prettiness about her, a softness, despite the garish jet-black flat top that worked to harden her. Cody wondered if it was only a defense against the rest of the world, for there was also a vulnerability about her. The vulnerability of a victim, he thought, as in the victim of a nonstop car crash of a life. And he speculated that this was what most likely had attracted Tommy Creager to her in the first place – and her, in turn, to Tommy Creager.

He removed her shoes and found a blanket and covered her up, then turned off the lights and closed the door behind him.

The aroma and sizzling sound of bacon led him to the galley.

"Few more minutes," Patrick smiled as he saw his father.

Damien was at the table, Tommy Creager's metal box open in front of him. He was looking through the notebooks.

"Find anything?" Cody asked his older son. Cody knew that a pair of fresh eyes was always helpful, even if they came with no police background. Looking at the same puzzle from a different perspective sometimes could reveal a lot. In Damien's case, he felt there was an extra chance, for in his early school years they had discovered he had a slight dyslexia. With Ann working with him, he'd eventually learned to if not overcome at least cope with his difficulty. Cody, though he could never prove it to any educators, had always tied the boy's dyslexia – which is, after all, seeing the world slightly differently than the rest of us – to a remarkable ability: to be able to sometimes solve even the most complicated riddles as easily as most people might do the simplest of math.

"I'm not sure what I'm looking for," the eighteen-year-old said with an easy smile as he put down a notebook and picked up a stack of photos. "I haven't had much of a chance to look at the notebooks. As far as the pictures, I recognize Mr. Creager," he said, showing his father a photo of Tommy with Fiona Brown.

Cody sat down across from him.

"And that would be Griffin Brown's wife?" the boy went on.

"That's her. Fiona Brown," Cody nodded.

"And two of these guys. . ." Damien asked tentatively with a new photo, "would be Brown's sons who were killed?"

It was one of the shots with all three brothers on the yacht. Cody pointed out the older brothers. "That's right; the blond one is Kevin, and the other, David."

"Then who's this one?" Damien asked, indicating Nicholas.

"The youngest brother."

"Are you sure?" Damien asked with mild surprise.

"Very sure, he's the third son," Cody answered.

"I thought Mr. McCabe said there were only two sons," Patrick piped up. He was scooping scrambled eggs onto plates now.

"That's what we thought until tonight," Cody said, and he knew he had to tell them the rest. The part that would touch them. "But the fact is, right now no one knows where Nicholas is. He disappeared. . . a couple of months ago."

"Disappeared?" Pat repeated, setting the plates down on the table. His hand had become shaky, and his voice had for a moment gained a quiver. "You mean like Mom did?"

Cody took the boy's arm and pulled him onto the seat beside him. "I'm sorry."

"It's not your fault," Patrick said. He had regained himself. Forced a quick smile and moved back to the stove.

"If it matters to you, I think Nicholas disappearing is part of everything else that has happened, including Tommy Creager being killed," Cody said.

"How do you mean?" Damien asked.

"I don't know," Cody answered, trying to sound matter-of-fact. "It just seems to be the first in a string of events. Nicholas disappears and his father becomes quite angry and accuses a number of people, including Tommy, of helping the boy to vanish. Then, a couple of weeks later, Tommy is killed."

"But in New Zealand," Damien interjected.

"I know. I can't explain that," Cody said, starting on his breakfast. "Then there's the firebombing of the disco."

"Where the other two sons died," Damien said, and almost smiled. "This is beginning to sound Shakespearian. One by one the king's sons are eliminated."

"Oh, it gets craftier than that – great food, Pat," Cody said.

"Yeah, it's really good," his big brother agreed.

"Thanks," the blond boy smiled.

Cody went on. "McCabe got a look at the autopsy reports from the firebombing. Of the two sons at the disco, one was already dead when the fire started, and the other was unconscious."

"Why would that be?" Patrick asked

"The best we can figure is that someone close to them killed them. Someone they trusted. But to make it took like an outside job, they did the firebombing to cover.

"Someone like Nicholas?" Damien asked.

"Why do you pick on him?" Cody asked in return.

Damien answered by going through several photos and then finding one that had Griffin Brown himself in the background of a party scene on the yacht. "Maybe I'm wrong, but is this Griffin Brown?"

Cody looked at it. He hadn't paid any attention to it before. "I don't know; I've never seen Griffin Brown."

"There are a hundred thirteen pictures," Damien continued. "This guy is in eleven of them, almost always in the background at some big party on a yacht, and he's always with some guys his age and his older sons, the ones who got killed."

"I don't know where you're going," Cody said.

"Maybe nowhere," Damien mused. "Just that if this is Griffin Brown, and if Nicholas is his son too. . . how come they're never in a picture together? Didn't they get along?"

Cody smiled. "You don't miss a lot. When Nicholas was twelve, he tried to kill the old man. From what I hear, the relationship didn't improve with time."

There was a knocking above and a moment later the door swung open and McCabe popped in. He looked excited. "Thought you ought to know. . . just got off the phone. The brothel that got shot up in the Cross was one of Griffin Brown's. And it wasn't any lone, crazy gunman. It was bloody Henry Wang's gang. I'm headed over there now. If you grab a camera, you could probably fake it past police lines with me, on my credentials.

Cody's instinct was to go. He wanted to see the latest scene of violence. Maybe catch a look at Griffin Brown. Maybe get some sort of sense of the evil that had been there. And yet he sensed the real answer wasn't there; it would be only the latest aftermath. More important, right now he had a twelve-year-old son, almost thirteen, who had cooked eggs and bacon for him and had worried about him throughout the night.

"You go ahead," Cody told McCabe. "I've got some thinking to do. Some eggs to finish."

McCabe squinted a tired grin and disappeared again.

31

Billy Packer bounded out of the car. Lakey, who had driven him, followed close behind as they hurried through the police line. A young cop tried to stop the aging ex-boxer. "Hey," he called out, grabbing at him, but Billy decked him with one punch.

Other cops, now alert, started to go after Packer, only to be mollified by Lakey. "Come on, boys, come on; that's Billy Packer, he works for Mr. Brown. He didn't mean any harm. His son was killed in there tonight."

Brown and Jacklan were on the third floor watching the last of the bodies being carried out when Bill Packer found them. He didn't wait for pleasantries; instead, he plowed right into the police commissioner like a charging bull.

"You son of a bitch," Billy shouted as together they slammed against a wall.

"Billy, stop!" Brown shouted.

But Billy was busy pounding his fist into Jacklan's face.

"You swore it wasn't the bloody Chinaman," Billy Packer shrieked.

Jacklan's nose was broken and squirting blood. For a moment it looked as if he were going to fall over, but instead, with a surprisingly loud and angry yell, he swung back, both fists clenched together, and struck the smaller man across the face, sending him reeling to the floor.

Billy Packer shook himself, regained his rage, and climbed to his feet. This time, however, Griffin Brown came between them.

"Billy, Billy, goddammit, stop it! Get control of yourself!"

"They killed my boy because this son of a bitch was wrong. Because he was trying to protect the Jew and the Professor and their goddamn money," Billy wept in anger.

"They killed my sons too," Brown said. "They're trying to destroy us, Billy. If we're going to survive, we can't fight among ourselves. Not now."

"I told you it was the Chinaman," Billy said bitterly to Jacklan, but his energy was draining. "Mickey would still be alive if you'd listened!"

"You weren't going to hit Wang until this morning," Jacklan said defensively. "This still would have happened."

"Yeah, only Mickey wouldn't have been here," Billy said, the tears and anger returning. "He would have been with me, setting up right now to hit the slant-eyed bastard."

"Billy, you can't blame Jacko," Brown implored. "I made the decision not to hit Wang. I listened to Jacko. He told me what he thought was true, and I bought it. If anybody here has to take the blame for Mickey, it's me."

"Oh, Jesus," Billy said and wilted. "Don't ever think that."

Then no one spoke for a dozen moments. The last of the bodies were gone, and these men under siege were alone now, standing in the third-floor corridor of the brothel. Griffin Brown, Billy Packer, and the police commissioner. Lakey appeared at the head of the stairs, and Griffin Brown glanced at him with a look that told him he was trusted, he was welcome. The floor beneath their feet was soaked with blood; the walls near their heads, splattered. Jacklan held a handkerchief now soaked in his own blood over his nose. "It won't stop bleeding," he said.

After several more moments Griffin Brown sighed heavily. "We have to hit back. . . and hit back hard."

"Jesus," Jacklan groaned.

"Shut up," Billy said to him without passion, then turned to Brown. "I'll pull the same team together I had ready last night. I'll find someone to take Mickey's place."

"No. Not yet," Brown told the ex-boxer. "I need

you to do some other things done first." He paused. His friend of thirty years looked like a wounded animal. "Are you going to be able to handle it? Or do you want me to have Lakey do it?" Brown asked with compassion.

"I can handle it."

"You sure?"

"I'm sure," Billy insisted, but then gave in to his friend's concerns. "Lakey can help me. I'll have to go home later, I. . . " He broke off, knowing if he kept talking he'd start crying again. "Good," Brown said, nodding to Lakey, who moved closer in to the conversation.

"The first thing I want is to close all the other whorehouses. Give the girls a thousand bucks apiece, tell 'em to get out of town, go on vacation for a week."

"Some of them have habits that cost that much, Mr. Brown," Lakey offered.

"Then before they leave town, have them go by and see Dom at the Scorpion. Tell him to supply them with enough to take care of their needs. The security from the brothels I want moved to the bars – the Scorpion, the Regal, and the Cowboy Club. Those will be the only three of our operations we keep open until this is over."

"When do we hit the Chinaman?" Billy asked.

"Soon enough," Brown returned.

"Jesus, Grif," Jacklan whined through his still-bleeding broken nose. "The city is going to go crazy because of what happened here. You hit Wang in another bloody shootout and everything will be out of control."

Billy started to protest, but Brown quieted him.

"That's why we're not going to hit him," Brown told the policeman. "You are."

"Oh, Christ. What do you mean?"

"What I mean is, I'm not a bloody moron, Jack. I know we can't turn Sydney into a shooting war. Not and survive. Oh, the bloody Chinaman is dead. Believe me; him and his family, they're fucking mincemeat. But I can wait for my revenge. I don't have to have it right now. I can wait. A month, three months. I can wait, Jacko. But you're going to have to help me if I'm going to wait. You're going to have to put him and his people on ice for me."

"How do I do that?" The commissioner asked in a voice that said he didn't really want to know the answer.

"It's really very simple," Brown answered. "One of the Chinese shooters lived long enough to give you a deathbed confession. . . telling you he was working under Henry Wang's orders."

"Jesus," Jacklan said, considering the consequences of such an action.

"It'll give us time," Brown continued. "Time to pull our pieces together. Time to bury our dead. . . again. Time to finish off the big shipment in four days. Time for your bosses to cool down."

"There were other cops here, street cops, who know that the shooters were already dead when I got here," Jacklan complained .

"It's your word against theirs," Brown said to him coldly. "You're the bloody commissioner, who are they going to believe?"

Still Jacklan hesitated.

"Let me put it this way, Jacko," Brown said in a tight, controlled fury: "What happens to this town in the next few hours is up to you. You tell me you're going to put the little slant-eyed bastard and his people in jail, *now*, or I've got no choice: I'll go after him with everything I've got before he's had a chance to eat breakfast."

32

The first light of the dawning sun was just coming up behind them as Fitzwilliam steered the van off the Hume Highway and onto the side road that led to the small airport.

Loretta Chang, who had wept bitter tears for some minutes after they had driven away from Kings Cross, had spoken only once on the long ride. . . and that only after one of the two boys had addressed her first in Cantonese. She had asked Fitzwilliam to pull over. The boy had gotten out and relieved himself, and then they had been on their way again.

But now, as the rural airport came into view, she began to speak. There were no more tears. Only the terse, almost arrogant tone she had started out with. "We did what we were contracted to do. You people were sloppy. It was not as promised. There were not supposed to be any girls in the downstairs. If they hadn't been there and begun to scream the people upstairs would not have known what was to come. Two of my boys would not have been killed."

Fitzwilliam saw no point in telling her that if at least one of her boys hadn't been killed anyway he would have had to shoot one himself, so as to leave a Chinese body behind. He was tired and didn't feel like getting in a verbal sparring match with her. "If

you want more money, that's not my department,"
he said with little interest.

"You people were sloppy," she repeated.

"Things happen."

"No. Not if you plan right. You people were
sloppy. It cost the lives of two of my best boys. It will
cost the man you work for much more money."

They didn't speak again until he pulled to a stop
at the side of the hangar.

"Which is the plane?" she asked.

"It's inside the hangar," he answered.

"We fly straight through to Darwin?

"I don't think so," he said. "I think you have to
stop in Mt. Isa to refuel. Then on to Darwin."

"Sloppy, sloppy," she repeated with bitterness
and then barked Cantonese orders to the two boys as
they all climbed out of the van and headed for the
hangar.

One of the boys – the one, Fitzwilliam thought
had killed the naked redhead in the early stages of
the brothel operation – turned back and gave the
silver-haired man a wave and a small smile.

* * *

If Loretta Chang had known anything about air-
planes she would have suspected her fate moments
before she did – not that it would have mattered. For
the only plane inside the hangar was a Lear jet, quite
capable of making it to Darwin without refueling. As
it was, and probably because of her fatigue, she
didn't become alert until she detected the movement
behind her. Then she whirled to see two white men
in the early golden rays of the morning sun. They

both had automatic weapons that they began to fire before she could speak.

Fitzwilliam waited until the gunfire had stopped and then got out of the van and walked over to the hangar. The man who he worked for greeted him with a smile.

* * *

Later they sipped from steaming cups of hot coffee as they watched the big tractor push the van, with the three bodies inside, over into the ditch that had been prepared for it a week before.

"We've left a bit of mayhem behind us," Fitzwilliam reflected with a near grin. "A lot of bloody bodies."

"There will have to be more before we're done," the other man said.

"I know. . . . No worries, as long as everything is going the way you want it to," the silver-haired man said.

"It's going bloody perfect."

The tractor was now using its blade to cover the vehicle with the first delivery of what would eventually be tons of earth.

"We'll still be done by Tuesday?" Fitzwilliam asked.

"Tuesday night," the other nodded. "As long as we stay on track. Griffin Brown's empire will be over and mine will have begun. Then both of us will be very rich men."

"I love it when you sweet-talk me," Fitzwilliam said with a grin and a large yawn. "When do you fly up?"

"Hopefully by late this afternoon or tonight, as soon as I get the signal that they're transferring the goods from the freighter to our boats," he said, and then chuckled

"What's so funny?" Fitzwilliam asked.

"I'm just thinking about what the faces of Mr. Brown and Mr. Horowitz and the bloody Professor are going to look like when they discover that their crates of soccer balls. . . are really only soccer balls."

Fitzwilliam grinned.

The two friends paused in their conversation, for the van was now almost completely submerged in dirt, and they watched as if at a sporting match as the tractor pushed over the final load that would forever obscure the vehicle from view.

After that the tractor kept working, piling more and more dirt into the ditch, but the silver-haired man and his friend walked away as if the home team had just won.

"I need to get some sleep," Fitzwilliam said as he yawned again. They were approaching several parked cars. "You know where I'll be. I mean, nothing's on until late tomorrow, but if something comes up. . ."

"It might," the other man said with a frown, as if he had just remembered.

"What?"

"The police; they found Jill Edwards's body last night."

The silver-haired man shrugged. "They had to find it sooner or later."

"I know," the other said. "But it's the way they found it. The police were called by a neighbor. She said she'd seen two men breaking into the place.

One of the men, she said, she had talked to that afternoon out in front of the place. He had asked her a lot of questions about where Jill Edwards was. She said the man had been with a couple of boys — one an older teenager, the other twelve or thirteen."

"Christ," Fitzwilliam said.

"Then that's the guy you saw?" the other asked.

"Yeah, shit," Fitzwilliam said.

"And so the guy you saw and the other guy who broke in there are probably the ones who were asking questions over in New Zealand."

"Yeah, I guess," the silver-haired man said with some frustration. "But what the hell do they want?" he wondered aloud.

"I don't know. That's what bothers me. What-ever they want, they want it badly enough to come twelve hundred miles to Sydney and break into Tommy Creager's house. And that kind of intensity bothers the shit out of me."

"Can you check them out?" Fitzwilliam asked.

"I'm working on it. So far we don't know much more than you told me. We did find out that McCabe had come to Sydney a couple of days ago on a free-lance assignment. The other guy. . . all we know is his name is Cody and he's supposed to be an ex-cop out of Los Angeles."

They had reached a white Ford station wagon. Fitzwilliam opened the driver-side door and then let his tired body hang on it for a moment before speaking. "It's crazy. . . they can't know anything."

The other man nodded. "You wouldn't think so. But we've got too much riding on the next few days to have a couple of loose cannons rolling around. They show up in our world again, I may have to call you early."

33

"Wang didn't do this by himself," Griffin Brown said. He had waited until he and Billy Packer were alone. They were standing in the front room of the Bayswater brothel.

"What do you mean?" Billy asked, his mind still clouded with grief.

"It's one of us. Someone in our organization, or someone very close to us, is helping him," Brown said solemnly.

"No," Billy said, "I can't believe that. That's crazy."

"Then how would he know?" Brown insisted. "I'm telling you, someone close to us knew Mickey would be here and at what time. That wasn't the Chinaman. . . that was someone close to us. Someone Max Oliver knew and trusted was let into that room across the street so he could cut Max's throat. Max didn't even like Chinese food."

Billy stared at his friend, disbelief turning to anger. "Who?"

"Christ, Billy," Brown growled. "Do you think if I knew he'd be alive right now? You're the only one I trust. That's why I waited until we were alone. We've got to find out who the traitor is."

"How?" Billy asked

"We'll start by checking and rechecking," Brown said. "Find some boys you can trust. I want to know everyone's movements for the last twenty-four hours."

"Let me get ahold of the Chinaman," Billy interrupted, trembling. "I'll save us all a lot of work. I'll find out who the bloody traitor is and take care of him in the bargain."

"We'll get to the Chinaman in our own time and in our own way," Brown insisted. "Right now, he's on the outside. And right now we have to worry about who's killing us on the inside. Your cousin Neville, up in Brisie, think he'll do a job for us?"

"Sure," Billy answered. "His wife will winge her bloody head off, but Nev will come good. What do you want?"

"Some phone taps."

"Crikey, Grasshopper's as good as they come on that," Billy assured him.

"No," Brown said emphatically. I want someone clean. . . from outside. I want Jacklan's lines plugged into."

"Jacko," Billy said with some surprise. "You think he's the traitor?"

"Billy, there are only two people in this world who I know aren't, and that's you and me. Until we find out for sure who the traitor is, we don't trust anybody."

"I'll call Nev from the house," Billy said. "He'll be down here by this afternoon."

"Good. But don't tell him what the job is until he's here. And when he's done here, we're going to have to get him to Melbourne. You or Billy Junior will have to go with him. I want the Professor's lines tapped."

"What about the Jew?" Billy asked.

"I'm going to take care of him another way," Brown explained. "I can't trust the son of a bitch, and I haven't got the manpower to keep an eye on him. Kevin Madden down in Hobart still owes me for the time I kept his kid out of prison, and he hates the Jew anyway."

Billy nearly grinned. "You going to have him kill him?"

"You have a better idea?" Brown asked.

"No. I never liked the fuckwit in the first place."

"Good, then that's the way we'll do it," Brown said, and then sighed. "There's one other person we have to concentrate on. I know it may be remote, but we can't overlook anyone at this stage."

"Who?" Billy asked.

"Nicholas."

"Geez, Grif, you don't really think. . . " Billy's words trailed off.

"Think of the possibilities," Brown explained. "He's bloody crazy. He hates my guts. And nobody knows where the fuck he's been for the last couple of months."

"But he'd never have done anything to hurt Mickey," Billy said with emotion. "They used to have fun together and, Christ, he adored his big brother Kevin. He never would have done anything to hurt him, either."

"No. Not directly," Brown agreed. "But that doesn't mean he couldn't have made a deal with the Chinaman. . . and the Chinaman's using him. Not telling him everything that's going on, other than he's hurting me. Look, if Wang's got him, then someone in Chinatown's got to know. Get some people up there, let it float around that there's a lot of money for whoever tells me where the kid is."

"We've offered money before," Billy said.

"Not fifty thousand dollars, cash," Brown answered.

"I'll get on it," Billy nodded. "But I think I'd be very sad if we found out Nicholas was the traitor."

"We're both going to be very bloody dead if we don't find out who is," Brown stated.

34

After the bacon and eggs, Cody had stayed up another hour with Damien going through the note-books and photographs from Tommy's metal box. There were more bitter, rambling accounts from Fiona, chronicling her husband's wicked ways. The murders she suspected. The politicians they enter-tained lavishly. The policemen he paid, like commis-sioner Jacklan. Then there were his "whores," as she called the women he was seen in public with. Her greatest shame was a "colored" one, a singer she knew he had been supporting for years. Fiona and she had "accidentally" met at a charity party once. Fiona was sure someone had deliberately set her up and that everyone was laughing at her behind her back. She had been humiliated and had thrown a drink in the black woman's face. That night, though she was very drunk, she remembered that Griffin had come again, as the Greek god with the goat's face, to rape and punish her.

Also scattered throughout the page were Tom-my's recurring, random thoughts on the Kennedy assassination. These would be mixed with other brief thoughts or snatches of conversations, along with doodles, endless doodles. The chronological order seemed fairly clear, the entry farthest back being apparently just over a year old. On one page: *Tension between #1 and #2 sons growing with old man.* And

Nicholas brooding over lost cat; he's sure his father had it killed...

On another page, Cody and Damien weren't sure which world an entry related to, the Browns' family life or Tommy Creager's personal quest, but it read, *Christ, off to Hong Kong again. Sometimes I feel like the Scarlet Pimpernel behind enemy lines and wonder, How did I ever get into this shit? I would be better off and probably safer breaking into the national archives and stealing the sealed reports.*

Farther into the notebook: *Hong Kong went fine. Same as usual. Another face I've never seen before.*

Next page: *Party for Nicholas on the boat, but Nicholas, pouting, stayed in his room and masturbated all afternoon. . . . Old man and David had shouting match with Kevin over money and control. Fiona so drunk she messed herself. . . . Jesus, one happy family.*

Later on in the year: *For some reason going to Tokyo is scary. I'm worried about the trips. Am I a fool? Can I trust Gallagher?*

A couple of pages later: *Do you think I should use sharp knives or poison? Nicholas asked me. For what? I asked him. To kill my father, he said. Why do you want to do that? I asked him. Because Jesus told me to, he answered and giggled. . . . Praise the lord and pass the ammunition.*

Then a few more pages on: *Big meeting on boats: old man, Kevin and David, Jacklan, and big hitters from out of town. Someone named Horowitz fronm Adelaide and one named Mooney from Melbourne. I've heard of Mooney, called the Professor. He's as big in Melbourne as G. Brown is here. . . something big going down. . . . Boys happy . . . old man happy too until Nicholas tells him he's going to be dead soon. . . Fiona laughs when Griffin gets angry. Police commissioner Jacklan, moderately drunk, as usual, gets me close and while spraying food in my face reminds me if I ever report his being here or around the Brown family, he'll personally see I end up at the bottom of the harbor.*

Some weeks seemed to pass with only sparse asides, and then: *Big money deal happening with boys, old man, Jacklan, the Professor, and Horowitz from Adelaide, who they all call the Jew behind his back. Don't know what deal is. Gallagher thinks drugs. But why would G. Brown take such a risk? He owns everything now.*

In the last page of the first notebook: *Boys flying to Europe, very happy, excited. . . Nicholas crying. "Kevin is going to bring me a present," Nicholas told me.*

Not much seemed to happen in the time period covering the next dozen pages or so. More of Fiona's bitter reminiscences, more scattered Kennedy assassination thoughts. They all made one think of so many old reruns on television replayed too often. Then: *Boys back from Europe, very pleased with themselves. . . . Old man seems happy, but sense a tension. Kevin brought Nicholas $$$ presents and toys.*

Then, on the next page: *Fiona cuts her wrists on Nicholas' birthday. I'm asked to leave. Understand this isn't the first time. . . . Fiona in private room at St. Vincent's, everything hushed up.*

Next page: *G. Brown really agitated, meeting with Horowitz and the Professor, but Kevin has taken Nicholas to Blue Mountains so he won't know about mother.*

Visited Fiona at St. Vincent's. She swears Satan/her husband possessed her, tried to kill her. Room filled with priests.

The next page had SICK written in large letters.

Fiona`returns home in time for Nicholas' big planned birthday party. I think I know now why she planned party three days after his actual birthday. She also planned on cutting her wrists. . . . Nicholas home. . . Old man, Kevin, and David flying to Melbourne.

Next page: *I have to go to Singapore, but I can't find Gallagher. I wonder if he's in Melbourne too.*

Next page: *Singapore a total fuck-up. I got too drunk. Gallagher really pissed. Says I may have wrecked everything.*

Three pages on: *Do you believe in ghosts? Nicholas asks me while we're at Luna Park. He's already been on most of the rides and eaten from all the food stands. I answer him, I'm not sure. I do, Nicholas says. My mother says the ghosts of six boys are in there, he said, pointing to the haunted house. She says they died in there because my father locked the doors and set it on fire. When was that? I ask. A long time ago, I think.*

Then near the bottom of the page: *Checked old newspaper files. . . there was a fire at the amusement park a dozen or so yeas ago. Six teenage boys died. It was called the Mardi Gras fire, happened Shrove Tuesday. Police never found out who or why.*

Next page: *Talked to Edythe, old-time crime reporter. She says rumors about Luna Park fire had G. Brown in power struggle with another gang.*

Cody and Damien had paused when they finished reading this entry. Could the fire in the amusement park and the one at the disco so many years later be related? Was it some long-delayed revenge? They realized that there was no way of knowing. Not without more information. Cody made a note to have McCabe track down Edythe.

They went on, a few pages down: *Accidently saw G. Brown at Chiswick Gardens, having lunch with Shauna, the singer. They had a boy very handsome, about 15 or 16 with them; he looks half black. Wonder if he's their son.* Then later on the page: *Edythe says yes, boy is definitely G. Brown's, boards at St. Joe's.*

Farther on: *Gallagher says I must be very careful. Careful of what? He won't tell me.*

Then on another page: *Fiona and Nicholas very excited about disco opening tomorrow night. Drove by to look at place in the daytime, Kevin there with crooked cop (?), waved.* Then halfway down the page: *Bondi Beach disco huge success. We stayed until 4 a.m. Fiona danced, mostly with priest friends, until she was too drunk to stand. Kevin grew angry as night went on that old man didn't show up for grand opening. Nicholas drunk, exposed himself to some high school girls; Kevin and David paid the girls off. Sent Nicholas home with a priest.*

A couple of pages down: *Day on the boat. Ugly tensions. G. Brown goes into a rage against Nicholas, shouting and beating him. Fiona hysterical. I'm told to leave.*

Then a page later: *Nicholas has disappeared. Fiona very upset.*

Next page: *Nicholas still gone. Fiona under doctor's care, but she tells me Griffin is afraid Nicholas is hiding, waiting to kill him.*

Near the bottom: *I'm called to the Cowboy Club. G. Brown interrogates me as to whereabouts of Nicholas. I tell him I know nothing. He threatens me. Insults me. Finally lets me go.*

Next page: *Fiona calls that night; wants lunch at Doyle's on the Beach, tomorrow. I ask about Nicholas. She laughs and says not to worry. Is he back? I ask. He will be, she answers cody. Then you know where he is? I ask. But she only answers, St. Augustine says it's best not to ask too many questions.*

Next page: *Lunch at Doyle's much the same. Fiona a happy drunk today. Dodges all questions on Nicholas.*

Shit, someone ought to tell G. Brown about St. Augustine. . . G. Brown here tonight, drunker than I've ever seen him. Raging. Accusing me of plotting against him and of helping Nicholas. I thought he was going to kill me. I think I convinced him I know nothing. Christ, I hope so.

Next page: *I have to go to Auckland; guess they're not that pissed off about Singapore.* Then: *Beginning to wonder about G. Brown. Why can't he find Nicholas? Does he protest too much??*

Then, finally, one of the pages Cody had come across earlier, filled, like most of the others, with doodles. . . and again the words *Herod's pigs?. . . Herod's pigs?. . . Did Oswald pass the paraffin test? Was it rigged?. . . What is Griffin Brown up to? Why now? Why risk all for drugs?*

That was the last entry. The rest of the pages in the notebook were blank.

Damien just shook his head when they were done and smiled. "Pretty sleazy group of people."

"Yeah," Cody nodded.

"What was Mr. Creager doing with them?" the eighteen-year-old wanted to know. "I mean, was he working on a story? It seems like a long time to be working on a story."

"I don't know," Cody said, getting up and pouring himself a cup of barely lukewarm coffee. "If the reason Tommy was killed was in that box, it hasn't jumped out and hit me over the head." He considered another moment and then sat down again. "I'd like to know why he was taking those trips."

"To Hong Kong and Tokyo and Singapore," Damien said.

"And finally to Auckland," Cody confirmed, adding, "and I'd like to know who Gallagher is too."

"Do you think she knows?" Damien asked, meaning Jill, who was passed out in Cody's cabin.

Cody shook his head no. "She told me about the trips earlier. She said Tommy would get an envelope with an airline ticket and cash. . . but that's all she knew. He wouldn't tell her who he was making the trip for, or why."

"You think what he was doing on the trip is why he was killed?" Damien asked.

"It seems logical, doesn't it?" Cody said. "But I keep coming back to his murder being connected to the firebombing of the disco."

"But that was five or six weeks later," Damien reminded him.

"I know," Cody replied.

"So how could they be connected?"

"I'm not sure," Cody said. "But I don't believe the disco fire was an isolated event. I think Tommy knew something. Or saw something."

"You think the fire was connected to the brothel being shot up last night?" Damien asked.

Cody nodded. "And to Tommy's killing. . . and the killing of the girl they thought was our sleeping princess – and, if I'm not mistaken, to young Nicholas Brown disappearing."

Both of them were tired now. Sleepy.

"But why? It's all so crazy, twisted," Damien finally offered.

"It's how a lot of the world goes around," Cody sighed. "Murder and greed and more greed. . . and desperation and pain." His thoughts had gone to Fiona: For all her wealth and former beauty, her married life had turned into an endless nightmare. And now he understood Tommy's attraction and friendship with her also.

"We should both get some sleep," Cody determined.

"You sleep," Damien replied. "I want to go through the pictures again. Besides, someone should stay awake in case she wakes up."

"You're a champ," Cody smiled and then got up and headed down the passageway to Damien's cabin. He climbed up onto the top bulk. His eyes and body ached with exhaustion. He knew he had to sleep. . . and yet he realized it couldn't be for long, for now more than ever he sensed the force of evil that they had moved into. And the clock was ticking against them, for he knew that soon the police, if they hadn't already, would discover that the dead woman they had with the black flattop wasn't Jill Edwards. . . and first there'd be confusion and then somebody would make a phone call. And then the people who wanted Jill Edwards dead – the same people, he was sure, who had killed Tommy Creager – would know she was still alive, and not long after that, if they had someone talk to Grandma Sally and she had any memory at all, they'd also know she'd gone off with a man named McCabe to meet a man named Cody. He closed his eyes and tried to search for a nothingness. His mind was racing. The people in the photographs swam through his head, as he tried to fit faces with events. Tommy Creager and

Fiona Brown. The sons. The dead sons. Missing Nicholas. Was he really missing? Was he dead? Was he out there waiting to kill Griffin Brown? Was he part of all the murders going on? And he thought about Nicholas exposing himself and the priests who took him away. Madness. The fat, well fed, satisfied priests, dancing into the early hours of the morning with Fiona. . . queen to the King of Sin. The priests laughing and drinking champagne with the drug dealers and murderers. . . and then he was back in Marina del Rey and Tommy was there and Ann, and they were all having a good time – but then his mind told him that that was impossible, because Tommy had never been to the boat. They had only bought the boat two years ago, and Tommy had left Los Angeles several years before that. And now he wasn't at the boat anymore and he could hear the weeping, and he was on the edge of the endless darkness and the weeping was becoming a sobbing, and he was filled with a sense of total hopelessness and now the darkness was taking a shape, but he couldn't tell what or who it was. . . or who was weeping. And then he was back in the Marina again and it was April and drizzling and he was working on the deck of the boat. Ann was there and she was smiling. She was going to the store. Bacon and coffee. "We need more tonic," he said, and she said, "Okay," and she was smiling but he wasn't because the Dodgers were playing on his pocket-sized radio, only they weren't playing the way he wanted them to. She was smiling. Smiling. . . and that's the last time he ever saw her.

35

Kelly, who had been awakened and told to dress twenty minutes before, now sipped a hot cup of tea and watched the driveway from the dormitory master's window. He would be sixteen in a month. He was just under six feet tall and had tawny, movie-star-handsome good looks.

"Did they say if it was anything about my mother?" the boy asked anxiously.

"No, I'm sorry." Mr. Dempsey stuttered. He had tousled gray-and-brown hair and the beginning of a middle-aged spread. "I was asleep when the phone rang; they just said it was a family emergency."

A black Mercedes swept into the school driveway.

"This is probably them," Dempsey said as he started for the door, expecting the boy to follow.

"Wait," Kelly said. He was well aware of who his father was, and since the fire at the Galah also aware of the potential danger that came with it.

The black Mercedes had come to a stop now, and Kelly relaxed as he saw Billy Packer, Jr., and Grasshopper get out. Grasshopper looked around and then raised a walkie-talkie to his mouth and spoke into it.

"Now," Kelly said, and moved past the middle-aged teacher and out the door.

By the time they reached the outside of the dormitory, Griffin Brown's smoky gray Rolls was pulling to a stop behind the Mercedes.

"What's going on?" the teenager asked.

Billy Junior just indicated with his thumb for the boy to go to the Rolls-Royce, where Old Joe, an ancient, hulking man who served as both Griffin Brown's driver and one of his bodyguards, was moving around to open the back door for him.

"Is my mother all right?"

"She's fine, kid, no worries," Joe said in his gravel voice and pulled the door open.

Inside, Kelly could see his mother and father. Griffin Brown beckoned for him to get in. He did and now noticed John Higgins, Brown's other bodyguard, seated on the other side of the soundproof glass, in the front passenger seat, and he knew something heavy was happening. A sense of danger tingled through his body like a minor electrical shock. . . and he liked it.

"What's wrong?" the teenager asked.

"You're a lucky boy," Griffin Brown said with a forced grin. "You and your mother are going on holiday to Hawaii."

"We'll have a great time," she said.

But Kelly knew she'd been crying.

"Billy Junior and Grasshopper are going to run you out to the airport now."

"What's happened?" Kelly insisted.

Griffin Brown looked to Shauna for a moment before addressing the boy. "There was some more trouble a few hours ago, at one of my businesses. A lot of shooting. A lot of people killed. I'm into a major fight right now. If I can know that you and your mother are safe, it'll be a lot easier on me." .

"Which place?" the boy wanted to know. "Where was the shooting?"

"It doesn't matter," his mother said.

"I want to know," the boy said forcefully.

Griffin Brown fought a grin; he liked the boy's fight. "The Bayswater."

"Oh shit," Kelly said. "How bad was it?"

"All of the girls who worked there are dead. Most of the customers. It was Wang," Griffin Brown told him.

The boy seemed to tremble for a moment. "If you're under attack, I don't want to run out to Hawaii. . . . Let me help."

"Kelly, don't talk like that," Shauna said.

"I'm not a baby," the boy said.

"Kelly, Kelly," the older man soothed. "A couple of months ago one of my sons disappeared. . . Last week two more sons died. You're the only son I have left; I don't want to lose you, too. Do what I tell you to do. I'm your father and I love you."

After a moment the boy lowered his eyes and nodded.

"Okay, the two of you, better get moving," Griffin Brown said, indicating the waiting Mercedes.

Kelly looked at his father and then shook his head. They started to part and then the boy leaned over to hug him. Touched, Griffin fought the urge to cry. As the boy got out of the car, Griffin hugged Shauna.

"Call me when you get to the hotel," he said.

"I will," she promised, and then followed her son into the Mercedes.

Griffin Brown watched Billy Junior and Grasshopper help his family get settled in the back of the black car, then load themselves into the front and, with Billy Junior driving, move off with some speed. Brown sighed now and sank back into his own seat.

"Where to, boss?" Joe asked.

"Home. Point Piper."

The Rolls-Royce moved sleekly through the residential Lane Cove streets, heading for Pacific Highway, which would carry them back over the Harbour Bridge. Griffin Brown allowed himself to rest. Shauna and Kelly would be safe now, six thousand miles away in Hawaii. He knew that he loved her in his own way. . . but he also knew that, like everyone else, with the exception of Billy Packer, he didn't totally trust her. She was a strong woman with ambitions for her son. At first she'd argued when he told her he was sending them away — argued so vehemently that for several moments there came alive the tiny nagging suspicion that she could be the traitor, and a wave of anger and betrayal had swept over him. . . and then she was crying. She was afraid for him, she loved him, she said, and she begged him to come away with them if there was so much danger here in Sydney. And he knew then it wasn't her, she wasn't the traitor. . . and he also knew then how necessary it was to get them to safety.

36

Cody slept for almost four hours. He awoke with a sense of anxiety and the image of Jill Edwards on a morgue table. He brushed the sleep out of his eyes and made his way down the passageway and cracked open the door to the master cabin. She was still there, sprawled out atop the bed. The snoring had stopped but she was still in a deep sleep. Still alive. Cody closed the door and moved back down the passageway. He paused at the door to Patrick's cabin. The blond boy was asleep in his bunk with his clothes on. Cody smiled and moved on.

Tommy Creager's metal box sat closed on the table, but there way no sign of Damien. Anxiety returned. He climbed the stops, opened the door, and moved outside. Damien was on deck, shirt off, dozing in the glaring late-summer sun. The heat felt good and the sky and the water were perfect. The boy snapped awake as his father approached.

"Hi," he said.

"Hi," Cody responded.

Damien started to stand up.

"Don't get up," Cody said.

So instead Damien just sat on the deck and rubbed his eyes. "What time is it?"

"Almost eleven-thirty," Cody answered, looking out through the dozens of sailboats and across the harbor. "God, it's beautiful here."

The boy passed a hand through his hair and nodded "Yeah."

"You look through all that stuff again?" Cody asked.

"Twice," Damien grinned and then added, "You have to try and find Nicholas, don't you?"

Cody nodded and then smiled with some curiosity. For him, going after Nicholas was logical; his disappearance was the first piece of the pattern that had led to all the murder and madness. But he also knew Damien's mind: sometimes the boy had unpredictable insights. "That's right," Cody said. "How did you figure that out?"

"He's the only piece that doesn't fit."

"In what way?"

"I think he's the only person his father was afraid of," Damien said.

"Because he tried to kill him?" Cody asked, genuinely intrigued.

Damien shook his head no. "Because he was the only person he couldn't control. Everyone else he controlled through fear or money and probably sometimes friendship."

"Nicholas does seem to be the fish swimming upstream," Cody agreed, and thought about the soft, womanlike weeping. Last night he was sure it was Nicholas – so afraid, so afraid – and yet now, in the bright sunlight, with all the violence of the night before fresh in his mind, he wasn't sure.

"If everything is connected," Damien stated. "His disappearance, Mr. Creager's murder, the other woman being killed, the disco firebombing, what happened last night. . . then, like I said, he's the only one who doesn't fit, especially if he's alive."

"And if he's dead?" Cody asked.

"Then," Damien said with a grin, "everything fits easily with the Herod's pigs question Mr. Creager wrote several times on the back of the pictures of the three brothers."

"I remember that," Cody said. "Do you know what it means?"

"I couldn't place it at first myself," the boy explained, "but I knew I knew it. Then, after I dozed a bit on the table, I remembered. It's from one of Pascal's *Pensées*. It has to do with King Herod, after the three wise men had visited him and told him that Christ, a new king who would reign over the whole world, had been born. You remember what Herod did to protect himself? He had all the boy children in the land under two years of age killed. Including his own sons. . . which prompted Pascal's thought: "Better to be one of Herod's pigs than his own son."

"You think Griffin Brown killed his own sons?" Cody asked.

Damien shrugged. "Mr. Creager wrote a number of times in his notebooks that there were lots of arguments over money and control and just a lot of tension between Griffin Brown and his sons. Maybe Griffin Brown decided to get rid of his competition. Maybe that was what Mr. Creager had known, or would have known after the killing had started, so that he'd have to be killed first."

Cody considered for several moments before speaking. "Pretty dark scenario. Man kills his own sons to ensure his power."

"What did you say last night?" Damien grinned. "That's how the world goes around. Murder and greed and desperation and pain. But of course that's only if Nicholas is dead. I think he's probably still alive."

So did Cody, but he wanted to hear why the boy did. "Any reasons?"

"Two," Damien said. "One is, Griffin Brown doesn't seem to be a man of great subtlety. He seems to operate rather bluntly with murder and fear, bribery and physical violence. If he wanted Nicholas dead, I think he would have found a simpler way of getting rid of him than an elaborate charade of him disappearing. The other is, Nicholas's mother doesn't seem concerned. She seems to think he's safe and sound."

Cody nodded and remembered the call he had placed to Fiona eight hours before; she had thought it was Nicholas on the line. More important, she sounded as if she was used to Nicholas calling.

"So the quest is Nicholas," Damien said.

Cody nodded. "The quest is Nicholas."

"Where will you begin?"

"That's easy." Cody answered. "With the one man who wants to find him more than I do: his father."

37

The phone rang four times before the silver-haired man came fully awake, rolled over, and answered it. "Yeah," he grunted .

"It wasn't her," the man on the other end said.

"What?" The silver-haired man asked, fighting himself awake and feeling he'd missed part of the question.

"Jill Edwards. She isn't dead."

Fitzwilliam was fully alert now, but his fatigue brought with it an edge of irritation. "Of course she is – Christ, I ought to know."

"No," the other man said. "The cops had the mother down to identify the body. She said the dead girl was a cousin from Melbourne. That her daughter, Jill Edwards, had been at her flat last night – and get this, she was with two men. She said one was a reporter, she didn't remember his bloody name, but he was a New Zealander. The other bloke was a Yank."

"Christ," Fitzwilliam said. His body had drained cold. He just didn't make mistakes like killing the wrong person. . . and yet he obviously had. "Where is she now?"

"The mother thinks she went off with the bloody reporter."

"Christ," Fitzwilliam repeated in frustration. "What in fucking hell are they after?"

"It doesn't matter. What matters is they now have her. They've come too bloody far into our world. We've got to find those bastards now. . . and put them out of their bloody misery."

38

"Cowboy Club," the voice on the phone answered loudly enough to be heard over the jukebox.

"I want to speak to Griffin Brown," Cody said. He was standing at the pay phone on the Rushcutters Bay marina. A soft, warm breeze was pushing across the blue harbor that was now dotted with sailboats. A sailing club for kids was in full swing. Boys and girls as young as nine and ten, working in pairs, their little bodies bulging with their bulky orange-and-blue life vests, were carrying their small boats to the water's edge.

"Who is this?" the voice on the other end asked.

"It's none of your fucking business who I am," Cody said with a deliberate, quiet intensity to get the man's attention. "I'm calling Griffin Brown, about his son Nicholas." Some children were laughing as they ran across the dock. On the highway, the traffic was sparse, and for Cody the surroundings brought back a memory of more innocent times when weekends were gentle and lazy, and for a moment he wanted to hang up and walk away from it all. Wake up Jill Edwards and send her on her way and set sail and take himself and his boys away from here, away from the storm of violence and evil and danger they were about to walk into. What real difference did it make who killed Tommy Creager? But in the same moment he knew it meant a lot, because Tommy had been his friend and Tommy had died seemingly without reason, without dignity, cast aside like the carcass of an animal on the side of the road, and that shouldn't happen to anyone. And in the same moment he also knew he couldn't let Jill be killed, as she most certainly would if he cast her adrift.

On the phone the song on the jukebox suddenly stopped. The man's voice sounded both earnest and nervous. "Mr. Brown isn't here right now, but if you want to hold on I could try to reach him."

"Listen carefully, asshole. . . " Cody said, glancing at his watch. It was twenty to twelve. "Tell Brown that I'll be there at the Cowboy Club at three this afternoon. If he wants to find his son, he'd better be there too." He hung up. . . and as he did knew the other reason he couldn't walk away was because of young missing Nicholas. Even though he knew that the *missing* part of it was providing the emotional, irrational pull. But how could he help it? Ann had been missing for four and a half months. Missing, missing. . . and every day it tore and dug at his gut until he couldn't sleep without the vodka and more vodka. He had been the cop, the great detective, and he couldn't even help her, the one he loved most in the world. He couldn't even find her.

* * *

Damien looked up as his father approached. "Talk to Griffin Brown?" the boy asked.

"No. But I set an appointment," Cody answered. "And gave him plenty of time to think about it."

* * *

Cody shaved in his own bathroom and didn't worry about making noise. . . but it didn't do any good; Sleeping Beauty was still passed out, sprawled on the bed, snoring again in fits and starts. Time was working against them, he knew. He needed her to put some names to the faces in photographs from Tommy's metal box, and so he had the urge to shake her awake and push her into a cold shower, but he let it pass. He'd rather have her as a friendly, if hung-over, ally than one he'd forced into service. So she could wait, he reasoned. Not much longer, but she could wait. In the meantime, there were other things he had to do. Places he wanted to visit.

As he moved back down the passageway to change into some fresh clothes he passed Patrick's cabin and saw that the boy was awake now, though still lying on his bunk. Reason told him any danger was some time away, but right now reason was fighting with a nagging anxiety at the back of his head. Damien was old enough and agile enough to take care of himself if any trouble came. . . but if Cody didn't have to leave his twelve-year-old alone, he wouldn't.

"Hi," Patrick said.

"Hi," Cody smiled back. "I've got to go a couple places. Want to tag along"'

"Sure," the boy answered, bounding up into a sitting position.

"I'll meet you up top in a couple of minutes, then. . . and bring your camera."

"Okay," Patrick agreed happily.

* * *

"Dad, I'll be alright," Damien said emphatically.

"Just keep your eyes open," Cody said.

A pair of bikini-clad, very tan, and very attractive girls in their late teens were moving down the jetty now past their boat. Damien's eyes followed them a moment. "Oh, I don't think I'll have any trouble there," the boy grinned.

"Ready," Patrick announced, popping his head outside, his 35-millimeter camera around his neck.

"You know what to ask McCabe when he shows up?" Cody asked the older boy as he moved to the side of the boat and climbed over onto the jetty.

Damien nodded. "You want the names he was supposed to get from New Zealand. . . anybody who had died in that neighborhood just outside Tauranga in the last two months."

"Right," Cody said. "And as for the sleeping princess, if she's as hung over as I think she'll be, she's going to want a lot of orange juice or soda pop and ice when she wakes up."

"No problem. What about the pictures?" Damien asked.

"If she's up to it, show them to her. If not, just try and keep her calm until I get back."

39

What's up?" Gallagher asked into the phone. In his mid thirties, he looked like a grown-up version of

Huckleberry Finn, boyishly handsome, with longish red hair and a hint of freckles. Right now he was in beach trunks and a floppy sport shirt.

"I'm not sure, mate," the man named Clint on the other end of the line said. "McClafferty picked up a sort of weird call a little while ago on Brown's direct line."

"What was it?" Gallagher asked.

"I'll play it back for you if you want. Some guy called in, wouldn't give his name. But said if Brown met him at the Cowboy at 3:00 p.m. he'd tell him how to find his son Nicholas."

"That is weird," Gallagher mused, aware of a cold chill running down his body. "Did Brown agree to meet him?"

"Brown wasn't there, and the guy didn't give them a chance to reach him. He just told them to have Brown there at three and hung up."

Outside, the car horn was honking for him now.

"Shit," Gallagher said. "Hang on a minute, will you, I was just taking my family to the beach. Then you'd better play it back for me."

"Take me that long to set up the tape," Clint said.

Gallagher went to the front door and waved to his family to be patient, and with his fingers promised he'd be there in two minutes, at which point five-year-old Arthur hit three-year-old Lara, who began to scream, which gave their mother, thirty-two-year-old Karen, the beginning of a splitting headache.

Gallagher returned to the phone, and the tape of the conversation between Cody and the man at the Cowboy Club was played.

"Could be just a crank," Clint offered when it was over.

"Could be," Gallagher agreed out loud. But he knew he couldn't take that chance. "Our bugs all still working?"

"Yeah, the ones that count," Clint said. "There's a couple on the upper floors that are fuzzy, but if Brown shows up, he'll probably meet this guy in his office, and we're fine in there."

Gallagher sighed. "Listen, I've got to do this thing with my family; I think they're ready to shoot me."

Clint laughed. "No worries, we can listen as good as you can, and if you want to listen later we'll have it on tape."

"We're going to be down at Nielson Park; I'll call you from there about three-twenty."

"Fine."

"Clint."

"Yeah, mate?"

"Just in case this guy isn't a crank, let's get the cameras working. . . let's see everyone who goes into the place from two-thirty on."

"Done deal," Clint said, and they both hung up.

Outside the horn was honking again, but Gallagher had one more phone call to make.

40

Bondi Beach was jammed with people and cars.

"It's the best surfing beach in the world," their cabby told them. But if you're going to swim, you've got to stay within the flags or you're liable to wind up on the Bronte express. "

"What's that?" Patrick asked him.

"It's a riptide that'll pull you out to sea, and if the lifeguards don't catch you, the next time anyone sees you will be when your body washes up on Bronte Beach, a couple of miles down the coast," the driver related with a grin. "But no worries, we've got the best lifeguards in the world here. They only lose two or three to the old express every year."

"That's comforting," Patrick remarked.

He let them off on the beach side of Campbell Parade. It was packed will sunbathers and swimmers and kids just running around. Patrick noticed with some interest that a number of the young women were topless.

"I think Damien is going to like this country," the boy said with a dry grin, and then added, "I might not find it too hard to swallow myself.

Cody returned the smile and then studied the shop fronts across the street. His grin quickly faded. It wasn't hard to spot the burned-out Galah. A blackened outline of the bird could still be seen over what had been the entrance of what was once an all-white building. The windows were boarded up, but fanning out from them were more blakened images of where the flames had shot out. . . and then for a few moments he could hear the screams again and know the fear and almost feel the stinging smoke in his eyes. Then it was gone. He was back on the walkway by the beach, and there was frantic shouting behind him.

On the sand, a bald-headed man wearing bikini shorts and sporting a large belly chased a boy who looked to be about ten. The man was shouting, "Thief! Thief!" and as he started to draw some attention, the boy, himself wearing only shorts and a powder blue jersey, threw what appeared to be a wallet high into the air. Cards and money slew about, as the bald-headed man halted his pursuit to try and gather his belongings. But by now other adults had joined the chase and the small boy in the powder blue jersey had to zig and zag a couple of times to avoid capture, and just when it seemed he didn't have a chance, suddenly a dozen or so kids, mostly boys, ran into the action, shouting and throwing sand into the faces of the adults, and by the time the pursuers had stopped swearing and spit out the sand in their mouths and wiped it from their eyes, the swarm of children had vanished.

"Bloody kids," a fat woman with two fat little girls complained. They were all wearing red-and-white strip bathing shits and eating ice creams.

"That kind of thing a problem down here?" Cody asked.

"Didn't used to be like this. Bloody street kids, they call them. More like beach rats down here," she finished in disgust, waddling off with her brood.

Cody turned and stared again at the burned-out building. Patrick noticed it for the first time.

"Is that where all the people died?" the boy asked.

"Yes," Cody answered, and for a faint moment the screams were back, and the fear. . . and then the soft weeping.

They crossed Campbell Parade at the crosswalk. Crowds of people shoved back and forth. Mostly in bathing suits. Hot pavement. Loud radios. Portable CD players. Squealing children. Whining children.

Exasperated adults. Sexy young men, beer loud, trying to impress sexy young women, many in bikinis. Late-summer afternoon, good times. Busy times. . . laughing. Chattering. And none seeming to notice the looming three-story relic of mass murder so near them.

* * *

Cody pushed a piece of plywood to the side and stepped into the charred ruins of the disco, and the screams and the fear and the stinging smoke with him again. He and Patrick had worked their way around to the back of the building. Cody waved to the boy, who was waiting in the alley, to come ahead.

Much of the floor above them had been burned out, but a stark, fire-blackened concrete stairway led to a portion of the second floor that still seemed to be fairly intact. Cody stood and surveyed the ruins around him, the sense of fear and pain rich in the air. "Most of them died upstairs," he said. . . and then a chill descended on him.

"Someone was dead here," he continued after some moments.

"From the fire?" Patrick asked. The sense of dread seemed to have captured the boy also.

"No," Cody said, and the words, again, came without his forming them in thought. "A body wrapped in a rug was under the stairs. . . cold and dead and wrapped in a rug."

The boy said nothing. He looked at his father fearfully, and Cody wished now that he hadn't brought him. But he also knew he couldn't stop here.

He started up the stairs, where the screams were louder, and the fears and the energy of the trapped lives were penetrating into the hall. He knew now that the doors upstairs had been locked, that people had been stranded inside. . . and he thought of the amusement park fire that Tommy had written about. . . the six boys who had died a dozen years ago in the haunted house. Locked in. . . locked in. The Mardi Gras fire, they had called it, and now Mardi Gras was only three days away again, and somehow he sensed that they were connected.

He reached the second floor. The energy of anguish was at a pitch here. In a moment of terror he saw a pretty blond girl with her hair on fire. . . a teenage boy, his face blistering from the heat. He was at the edge of the endless darkness again, the screaming and sense of pain and fear filling him, and he was falling and falling and he knew the body in the rug had been carried up here, and then his foot gave way and a charred piece of flooring slammed into his face.

"Dad, Dad!" He could hear Patrick calling desperately through the screaming. . . and then the boy was with him, pulling at his arm. He was still stunned from the blow, but the boy wouldn't give up. "Help me, Dad. Help me!" the boy shouted, and then Cody was fully back in the burned-out building and he realized he had partly fallen through the floor and that Patrick holding onto his arm was the only reason he hadn't rolled over and down onto the first floor below. Cody struggled now and tried to swing his leg back up. On the third try he finally managed it. . . only to have the floor crumble again. Again he tried and then again, and finally his leg found a cross beam that was still stable enough to use as leverage.

They sat for some moments without speaking. The sound of screaming was gone, along with the fear and pain. Now the only sounds he heard were the same as his son heard. . . the people and traffic and the sound of the surf.

"What do you think?" the boy finally asked.

"I think I'm glad you were with me," Cody smiled and his son couldn't hide the fact that he was pleased with himself.

They climbed back down and made their way through the ruined building until they reached the outside. They stood in the alley for several moments. Cody seemed to be trying to get his bearings. Patrick knew better than to speak now.

"He came this way," Cody said, starting off down the alley. But after only ten yards or so he paused, as if confused. Then he moved to a wooden gate covered with graffiti and opened it; it led to a smaller, winding alleyway. Patrick followed him as he moved into it, and it didn't take long to realize that people lived here, under the balmy Bondi skies, for the narrow alley was crowded with refuse. Old mattresses and car seats. Beer bottles, wine bottles, hypodermic needles, used condoms. But Cody's interest lay ahead, he didn't know where, but he guessed maybe why. They bent around another corner, and up ahead now they could see three teenage boys waiting in line, while a fourth was on the mattress before them, having sex with a girl.

"The cops!" one of the boys in line shouted, and three of them ran. The boy on top of the girl howled "Oh shit!" as he jumped up and grabbed his shorts and sand shoes. He looked at Cody and Patrick for a moment with a mix of fear and confusion, and then he too ran off down the alley. The girl was sitting up now, pulling a sweatshirt on. She looked to be fourteen or fifteen, and Cody could tell she was a junkie.

"You're not a cop," she said as she saw them more clearly. "Shit," she wailed in bitter disappointment bordering on tears, you're not even a bloody cop."

Cody found a twenty-dollar bill in his pocket, and as he and Patrick moved past, dropped it in front of her. "Try and use some of it to eat."

It took him several moments to regain his concentration, but the trail continued to pull him on. The tiny alley wound for another half block until it came out onto a busy street.

Ramsgate Avenue was filled with neighborhood shops. A greengrocer, butcher, dry cleaner, liquor store. The Saturday afternoon sidewalk was crowded with people doing their day-to-day shopping and others, in bathing suits, traipsing up the two blocks from the beach to where they'd parked their cars. Cody and his son stood at the mouth of the alleyway for almost a minute before the boy spoke.

"What happened here?" Patrick asked.

"I'm not sure, but I think whoever firebombed the disco came from here," Cody said. "He carried the gasoline down that alley."

Cody stood without moving for another minute or so. But nothing else was there for him. Using the sidewalks now, they walked back down to Campbell Parade and the beachfront. They bought some fish and chips and a couple of ice teas and sat in the plaza as they ate. It was mobbed with happy people in bathing suits. Children laughing and running around. Old people enjoying the sun and the feeling of having a crowd around them, of being part of life again. And all, of course, in the shadow of the burned-out disco, where once Tommy and Fiona and young missing Nicholas and the good-time priests had danced and drunk the night away, enjoying the company of the now dead brothers. Who of course had made their fortunes with death and violence. . . and off children, who would do anything – even sell their bodies and souls in alleyways – for their drugs.

"I may ask you and your brother to come back down here with me tonight," Cody said about halfway through their meal.

"I thought you might," Patrick nodded.

"You want to tell me why?" Cody asked with a curious grin.

"If that guy who set the fire did come through that alley, it was late at night, right?" the boy asked, getting an approving nod from his father. "Well, there might have been someone there who he didn't see but who saw him. . . and I get a feeling a lot of the people who live in that alley are kids – teenagers, anyway – and none of them liable to talk to cops much, no matter what."

Cody nodded and smiled. "I think you've been hanging around with detectives too long."

The boy grinned back.

41

Billy Packer's red Mercedes pulled to a stop in the circle driveway of Griffin Brown's Point Piper mansion. The ex-boxer got out and moved for the house as the front door opened and a Catholic priest, Father Larry, came out. He was portly, in his early forties, and extremely well groomed. He looked first surprised, then embarrassed, and finally properly saddened to see Billy approaching.

"Mr. Packer, I can't tell your how sorry I am. . . "

"Thank you, Father," Billy said. He had always found Father Larry to be bit of a phoney and full of shit, but he still regarded priests with a certain reverence left over from his childhood.

"Fiona is very upset," the cleric went on piously. "She had a special place in her heart for young Mickey. We were supposed to go to Doyle's for lunch today, but she just isn't up to an outing."

Billy wanted to say something about how the priest could well afford to miss a meal or two, but decided against it. "Do you how if Mr. Brown is in the house or on the boat?"

"On the boat, sleeping," the priest told him. "Fiona is very afraid for his health, with his blood pressure problems and all. The events of the last week have shaken him terribly. She still prays for his soul, you know. . . when she can bring herself to."

"That's great, Father," Billy said, resisting the urge to smash the well-fed cleric in the face. "I've got to go." And he started across the lawn for the boat.

"Mr. Packer," the priest called after him. "Fiona feels strongly that Mr. Brown needs his rest. I really must insist that you talk to her before disturbing him."

"Father," Billy said, turning and releasing a fraction of his pent-up rage, "how about you and Fiona going and fucking yourselves."

* * *

Griffin Brown's two bodyguards, Old Joe and John Higgins, were sitting in lawn chairs at the end of the dock, playing gin rummy, their shoulder holsters laid out on the deck beside them. Joe looked up and took off his glasses to see who was approaching. . . and when recognition came, stood up. "Oh, geez, Billy. . . we're. . . so sorry. . . ."

"Thanks, Joe. I need to see the boss. It's important," Billy said, and then realized someone was stirring in the lounge chair turned away from him. A moment later sleepy-eyed commissioner Jacklan sat up.

"What the hell are you doing here?" Billy asked him, his exasperation mounting again.

"Waiting to see the old man," the big cop said, rubbing his eyes and standing up. "I got to piss like a racehorse."

"Piss on yourself," Billy said irritably. "What's happened to Wang, did you arrest him?"

"No," Jacklan said uncomfortably. "That's just it. Somebody must have tipped him off. We raided all of his places, but him and his top guys have dropped out of sight."

Billy exploded. "You didn't think that was worth waking Grif up for? The man we're at bloody war with is on the loose, and you're sleeping in a fucking lawn chair?"

Billy moved over and picked up the portable phone on the table the two men had been playing cards on and punched out a number.

"Fiona said he needed his sleep," the police

commissioner said defensively. "I didn't think a couple of hours would make much difference."

"You want me to wake him now, Billy?" Joe asked.

"Yeah, Joe, please," Billy said. "Tell him that among other things it's about Nicholas. Some guy called the Cowboy and said he knew where the kid was."

"No shit," Jacklan commented as Old Joe moved down the dock to the boat.

But Billy ignored the cop and spoke urgently into the phone. "This is Billy Packer. I need to talk to Lakey." Now he turned contemptuously to Jacklan. "All right, you missed the Chinaman; what about his family?"

"They were still at the big house. They seemed kind of confused, like they didn't know what was going on," Jacklan said, pleased he had some positive information.

Billy was back on the phone. "Lakey. . . Billy, here. The Chinaman's gone to ground. But his family's still out at the big house in Hunters Hill. I want all of them fucking dead – the wife, the kids, the grandmother, anybody who's fucking moving."

"Oh, Jesus, you can't do that," Jacklan wailed.

That was the last straw. In a rage now, Billy threw the phone at Jacklan. The large cop winced and put his hands up, but the instrument hit him in the chest. Billy was shouting, the veins in his neck bulging.

"You don't tell me what to do! That fucking Chinaman killed my son. He killed Grif's sons."

"We can't be running all over the city killing people," Jacklan shouted back.

"Then what the fuck are we supposed to do?" Billy screamed back, ignoring the mounting pressure in his head and chest.

"Dig in to survive. I've already given orders for the bars to be ready to close."

"You've given orders?" Billy bellowed with a mix of amazement and exasperation. "Who the fuck do you think is running this thing? Grif wanted those places kept open."

"That was then. Only a bloody moron wouldn't know things have changed," Jacklan shouted back in defense.

"You bastard," Billy shouted, running at the bigger man and plowing into him, knocking them both to the ground.

The ex-boxer now tried to drive his fist into the policeman's face, but Jacklan was stronger than he had expected. They rolled over once and then Jacklan was on top, pounding his right fist into Billy's face. Billy responded by grabbing Jacklan's ear and pulling him down far enough to butt his head against the cop's broken nose. Jacklan yelped in pain and started to roll over, which gave Billy a chance to drive his knee into the larger man's crotch. The commissioner was in double agony now. Billy sat up and pounded his fist into the broken nose. With a gurgled howl of pain, the cop covered up his face and rolled away. Billy kicked him hard in he back repeatedly, as short, savage bursts of screams came from the commissioner, who was rolling over and over as fast as he could until he was far enough away from Billy to stagger to his feet. He weaved from side to side, his nose streaming blood. He looked around frantically for a weapon. But there wasn't time; Billy was on his feet and charging him again.

Griffin Brown had come out on stern deck of his yacht with Old Joe and shouted at them. "Billy, stop!"

But Billy either didn't hear his boss or else chose to ignore him.

He crashed again into the stunned cop, plunging the two of them over the jetty and into the water. Billy tried to hold Jacklan's head underwater, as the police commissioner thrashed and fought violently to get to the surface for a gasp of air. But once there, Billy seized his chance and grabbed the cop by the hair and pounded his head against the piling of the jetty.

"Billy, for Christ's sake, leave him alone!" Griffin Brown shouted. But by the time he and the others arrived, all they saw was Billy pounding Jacklan's head, now on a limp neck, over and over again into the piling. Blood was streaming from the commissioner's nose and ears.

"Get him out of there," Brown ordered.

John Higgins dropped into the water and pulled Billy away.

"Come on, Billy, it's enough, enough."

Billy Packer didn't resist. He was drained of energy and anger. He made his way over to the ladder and hung on.

John Higgins returned to the commissioner, who was now floating facedown. He pulled him back over to the pilings and took his head out of the water, then checked his pulse along the neck. "Christ, boss," Higgins said after some moments. "I think he's dead."

"He can't be dead!" Brown bellowed. "Get him out of there, get him out!" He shouted, hurrying to the ladder.

Old Joe, seeing John Higgins struggling with the body, himself jumped off the jetty and into the water, then splashed over to try and help.

Exhausted and in a daze, Billy Packer was still holding onto the bottom rungs of the ladder as Gritfin Brown lowered himself down.

"Help them, Billy, for Christ's sake!" Brown ordered.

Billy nodded and obeyed, pushing himself off and joining the other two men as they dragged Jacklan to the ladder.

Griffin Brown climbed down into the water to meet the rescue group. He slapped the commissioner's face. "Jacko. . . Jacko, come on! Come out of it, Jacko!"

They could all see that there was no response.

But Brown didn't want to believe. . . he couldn't believe. "Jesus Christ!" he wailed in frustration. "Let's get him out of here. . . come on!" Grabbing Jacko by the back of the collar, he tried pulling the inert body up with him as he climbed back. Old Joe and John Higgins pushed from below. But the effort was going nowhere, the commissioner being a man weighing well over two hundred pounds.

"I'll get him up," Billy Packer said tersely.

"What do you want me to do?" Old Joe asked.

"Nothing," Billy said sharply. "Just let me do it."

Billy now started to work himself under the commissioner's body so that he might try to carry him fireman style. Brown could see what he was doing and started back up the ladder. "Johnny, come with me, we can pull from up here. Joe, do what you can down there."

Billy had Jacklan over his right shoulder now and grabbed hold of the first rung out of the water. The pressure in his chest was crying out now across his shoulders. He pulled up one rung. . . and then with another enormous effort a second rung. Now his foot was able to find a rung below water. He could use his weight lifter's legs to help now. His foot found the next rung and slowly pushed the body up to the next level. He had to pause now. The pain in his chest and shoulders were making him dizzy. He had had the pains before, but never this bad. Then he could hear his friend Griffin Brown talking to him. "Billy are you alright?" But Brown's voice sounded like it was coming to him underwater. He responded the only way he could. Up another rung. . . then another. "One more Billy, one more," he could hear the voices calling. His chest and head and shoulders were pounding, but he took the next step and then suddenly the weight was being pulled off him and his own body sagged and he seemed to have only enough strength to hang on to the ladder himself.

Griffin Brown and John Higgins struggled desperately themselves to pull the large, limp body up the last couple of feet and onto the jetty. And when this was finally accomplished, they both needed to sit on the planks for over a minute to catch their breath. By this time, Old Joe had swum down to the small muddy beach and had climbed up to the lawn and made his way back to the jetty. He knelt down by the police commissioner and felt his pulse.

"Well?" Brown asked.

Old Joe didn't answer. He squeezed the commissioner's hand. Then after a moment did it again. This time he almost smiled. "I think he squeezed back," Joe announced.

"Are you sure?" John Higgins asked.

"No," Joe said after some moments, squeezing again.

"Jesus Christ," Brown lamented. "We're in the middle of the battle of our lives and this has to happen."

"I'm sorry," Billy's voice said, floating up from the side of the jetty. The pains in his chest and shoulders were receding now, and he was regaining his breath. He struggled now to climb the remaining rungs. When his face emerged over the level, he looked at his old friend.

"Did you at least have a reason?" Brown asked.

"Mickey. . . your boys. The fucking Chinaman – he missed, him; Jacklan missed him! The bloody Chinaman's still out there with his top guys," Billy said with a mournful mix of anger and melancholy.

"Oh, Christ," Brown sighed, and then didn't speak for some moments. "What the fuck is it all coming to?" Brown finally said. Then he climbed to his feet. "Okay, first let's get Jacko on board. We'll feed him some vodka, that always brings him to life."

"I don't think he's coming back, boss," Old Joe said.

"Just bloody try it," Brown exploded. "Can't anyone do what the fuck I tell them to around here anymore?"

"Yes, sir," Joe mumbled, as he and Higgins started to drag the body down the jetty.

Brown turned back to Billy now. "I want you to get on the phone; we're going to have to close everything down for the duration. The Scorpion, the Regal, even the Cowboy."

"Close them down?" Billy said, truly shocked. "But you said you wanted to keep them open."

"That was when I thought Wang and his people would be in jail."

Billy stole a look down the jetty where Old Joe and John Higgins were working to get Jacklan on the boat. He knew they must have heard the last remarks, and he felt they were deliberately avoiding his gaze. Old Joe looked up now and offered him a conciliatory shrug, as if to say, "Hey, everyone makes mistakes."

"And we've got to find Wang before he has a chance to hit us again," Brown went on.

"I told you, he's gone," Billy repeated. "But his family's still out at the Hunters Hill house. I got a team on the way to take care of them."

"His family?" Brown asked with some astonishment. "You're going to kill his bloody family?"

"He hit our families," Billy said emotionally, the pressure in his chest building again. "He killed my Mickey. He didn't care."

Brown just looked at his old friend for a long moment before speaking. "Has the whole world gone bloody insane?"

"You said it yourself, Grif, with me and the Jew and the Professor. You said if he hit again we'd kill everyone," Billy said on the edge of tears.

Brown remembered the conversation now. It seemed like a hundred years ago.

"You said we'd wait if Jacklan put him in jail,"

Billy continued. "Well Jacklan bloody missed him. He's out there and laughing at us. If we don't hit back now, the Jew and the Professor will think we're done."

He knew Billy was right, but for a fleeting moment he wondered if it mattered anymore. And then that doubt was gone. He was fighting again, the only way he knew how. "You're right, go on with it. . . but close the clubs first. And then put the word out on the street that there's a million dollars in cash for Wang's head."

Billy knew he needed desperately to sit down or lie down somewhere. He was weak and nauseated. His legs felt as if they would crumble, and the steady pressure in his chest was making it hard for him to breathe. "We can't close the Cowboy, at least not right away; some guy called about Nicholas."

"Yeah," Brown nodded, remembering. "Joe told me. . . something about some guy calling the Cowboy and saying he knew where he was."

"He said three o'clock."

"Think it's a Wang trick?" Brown asked.

"I don't know," Billy said.

"I mean, it doesn't make sense," Brown said in futile exasperation. "After all this time, someone shows up out of the bloody blue and says he knows where Nicholas is. . ." He paused and sighed; everything was falling down around him. He sighed again. "But then, what the fuck does make sense anymore."

42

The cab dropped Cody and Patrick off at the corner

of Ward and Bayswater. It was 2:15 p.m., and Cody knew he was running short on time.

"The place that got shot up is just half a block that way," their cabby said.

They followed his directions and discovered that they weren't the only ones interested in the brothel murder scene. It was the grisly novelty of the day. Two television crews were here, along with a couple of dozen scattered gawkers. The copper smell of blood was still in the air, and three smiling Japanese women were having their pictures taken at the police barricade, near the bullet-riddled front door. Across the street, a stout older Irish-looking woman wearing a scarf was kneeling on the sidewalk saying the rosary.

Cody and Patrick stood there for some minutes. Up above they could see windows on the second, third, and fourth floors that had been shot out; one splashed with blood. In time, some of the onlookers drifted away, while others replaced them. The woman saying the rosary kept saying the rosary. But there was nothing here for Cody. Nothing special that he "saw" or "felt". . . only a sense of violence and pain and murder, and he didn't need any special gift to perceive that.

43

"I'm afraid he's really dead, boss," Old Joe said. They were inside the main cabin, commissioner Jacklan laid out on the couch where so many well-fed priests had sipped wine and devoured brie and caviar. Old Joe and John Higgins had taken turns trying to bring the cop around. John had once seen a TV show about CPR and had tried to apply those methods from memory. Old Joe had tried forcing first vodka, then brandy down the dead man's throat.

Griffin Brown sat across the cabin from them, nursing a glass of scotch. He had realized in the last ten minutes that Jacklan really was dead. But he didn't say anything to stop the others' efforts. He needed the time to think. To try and understand everything that was happening to him. Kevin and David were dead. Now Jacklan. Billy Packer was his best friend, but the other three had been his three top men as far as operations went. Kevin and David overseeing the ever more dangerous drug business. Jacklan keeping the police under control.

Several times during those ten minutes Griffin Brown had fought panic. He was in the middle of a war with a powerful adversary who somehow had a pipeline into his organization, and he had been stripped naked of his best men. He knew that if he was going to survive, he had to flush out the traitor. But who was he? Nicholas? Lakey? Billy Packer, Jr.? There wasn't anyone else in the family or organization with the knowledge or influence to have struck so close to the heart of his group. He tried to think of who Max Oliver would have trusted. Let into that room overlooking the Bayswater, so that he could have his throat cut. Suddenly he thought of Fiona. His wife. His drunken, religious fanatic albatross. . . and he knew she hated him enough. She wouldn't have set out to kill Kevin and David, but the Chinaman could have tricked her. And yet in the same moment he knew it couldn't be her. They had been tapping her phones since Nicholas had disap-

peared. There had been nothing. . . nothing. But
again the thought of Fiona's hatred brought up the
image of Nicholas. Mama's little boy. Petted and
spoiled and taught to hate him as much as she did.
Nicholas. . . And now somebody had called the
Cowboy Club, saying he knew where the boy was.

"Boss," Old Joe repeated, and this time Griffin
Brown looked up. "He's really dead."

"I know," Brown nodded. "You boys better have
a drink.".

"Thanks, Mr. Brown," John Higgins said, moving
over to the bar and pouring himself half a glass of
Jack Daniels.

"You off the sauce again, Joe?" Brown asked,
finding a smile .

Joe leered a nodding grin back. "Ahhh. . . the doc
says I got a better chance of keeping the old pecker
up if I give up the drink."

"That's a hell of a choice," Brown smiled. . . and
then asked, "the question is, what do we do with old
Jacko now? We've got enough problems without the
police and the press getting up in arms over a dead
cop."

Billy Packer spoke up, his voice sounding like it
was coming from the grave. "I say we lock him
below for now. Tonight we get Billy Junior over
here. He can take the boat outside the heads and get
rid of him like he did Red Marcato."

"That's right," Old Joe chimed in. "His body
never did come up."

44

Cody and Patrick walked the couple of blocks up

from the brothel to Macleay Street where, half a
block from the Cowboy Club, he found a liquor
store. He bought a new bottle of vodka and then,
considering that Jill Edwards might be with them for
a bit, added a second to that, plus a flagonized box
of white wine. Patrick lobbied for some soft drinks
and chips and won easily.

As they came out and started across the park
with the large spraying fountain, Cody paused at an
ice cream vendor and ordered a couple of cones for
himself and Patrick. It was a quarter to three, and if
he could, Cody wanted a preview. He engaged the
vendor in small talk, first about cricket and rugby
and then about when the vendor had been in San
Francisco and then Salt Lake City twenty years
before. It was eight minutes to three when Cody
became aware of the gray Rolls-Royce as it glided
down the street and pulled up to the Cowboy Club.

"Quite a car," Cody said to the vendor. "Any
idea who it belongs to?"

"Oh, a very important bloke around here," the
vendor said. "Name's Griffin Brown."

They watched now as the driver opened the back
door of the Rolls. Even at this distance Cody recognized the rugged figure of Griffin Brown. A couple
of moments later, a short, stocky man got out after
him and followed, and Cody thought he recognized
him also, but he couldn't be sure.

"They call him the King of Sin. He's got whorehouses, gambling joints, you name it. That was his
place that got shot up last night."

"Sounds like a good man to stay away from,"
Cody smiled. . . and then he and Patrick moved on
toward the marina. It was another couple of blocks

through the Cross and then Elizabeth Bay to Rushcutters Bay Park. Another cricket game was going on, only this time Patrick didn't have any interest in watching.

"Do you really have to go meet that Brown guy?" the boy asked.

"I do," Cody answered after some moments.

They could see McCabe walking toward them from the direction of the marina.

"He seems kinda scary," Patrick said.

"He won't bother me."

"How can you be so sure?"

"Because I'm going to tell him I can give him something he wants."

McCabe was on them now. He squinted and smiled. "Hello mates, been doing a bit of grocery shopping?"

"Yeah, we got plenty," Patrick teased. "Unless you bring over your girlfriend – then we'll have to go out for a lot more."

"The boy thinks with daggers in his heart," McCabe grinned, then changed tones. "Patrick?" he said, waiting for the boy to look at him. "Would you mind running ahead? I've got to talk to your dad."

Patrick looked to his father, who nodded, and then said, "Sure," and hurried on to the boat.

McCabe waited until the boy was well out of earshot, and then the grin left his face. "Damien tells me you made an appointment to meet Griffin Brown."

"If I hurry, I'll only be about twenty minutes late," Cody answered, and they started walking again.

"Jesus, Cody. . . " McCabe said, hesitating as he struggled to find the proper words. "I mean, I know you're new here. . . maybe you don't understand. Griffin Brown is a dangerous son of a bitch during normal times. But now he's in the middle of a war."

"I guess he'll just have to take his chances," Cody said, managing a grin.

"Jesus, Jesus, Jesus. . . " McCabe said. "I've gone a long way for a story, but this is really over the edge. Is it really that important to you?"

"Tommy Creager was my friend."

"Great," McCabe said with some exasperation. "But what if Griffin Brown is the one who killed Tommy Creager?"

"I don't think he did." Cody said.

"But what if he did? I mean, Christ, your kids will be in a great situation if you turn up all full of bullets."

They had reached the edge of the marina. Cody stopped. There was no humor in his face. "It's a risk I have to take. My boys know that."

McCabe sighed deeply and shrugged.

"How about Sleeping Beauty, she finally wake up?" Cody asked, squinting his own smile and changing the subject.

McCabe nodded and grinned. "Oh yeah, about twenty minutes after I got here. . . and talk about a major hangover. People have died and looked better than she did when she got up."

"Was she alive enough to get any information out of?" Cody asked.

"It took awhile; she had three cups of coffee and then found some Samoan beer you had in the fridge. After that, she was reasonable."

Damien met them on the jetty next to the boat. Cody handed him the bag with the two bottles of vodka.

"I see you got more supplies for the princess," Damien smiled.

"Let's try to save a drop or two for father this time," Cody said with a grin as they climbed on board.

"How long will she be with us?" the boy asked.

"Not much longer," Cody answered. "She probably won't be safe here by tonight. For that matter, neither will we."

"What do you mean?" McCabe asked.

"Dad figures whoever wanted her dead probably knows she's still alive by now," Damien said.

"And after I have my talk with Griffin Brown. . . with the leaks he has in his organization, someone's going to be looking for me pretty hard," Cody added. "I thought the boys and I might be better off spending the next couple of nights in a hotel somewhere, probably in Bondi Beach. I was going to ask if your girlfriend could keep the princess for a while."

"I'll ask," McCabe said.

The boy glanced at his watch. "It's a couple of minutes past three," he said mindfully.

"I know. I just want to put some faces with names, and then I'll be off," Cody answered, opening the hatch and starting down into the boat.

* * *

"He's a priest. . . he's a priest. . . and that's Billy Packer." Her finger touched on the short, bulky man Cody had seen following Griffin Brown into the Cowboy Club.

"Tell us about him," Cody said.

She looked blank for a moment, as if the question had caught her off guard and she had to engage another part of her reluctant brain. They were sitting at the kitchen table: Jill, Cody, and McCabe, a pile of photographs before them. Damien lingered nearby, taking in the information. Patrick had absconded with the television and was in his cabin watching a rerun of *Fantasy Island*, its music drifting out from time to time. Jill had already confirmed the identification of family members and added names to the hulking figure of Old Joe and Brown's other body-guard, John Higgins.

She exhaled a cloud of smoke with a sigh. "Well, there's not much to tell. He's Griffin Brown's oldest friend. He's like his number-two guy."

"Packer." McCabe nodded now as if something was beginning to make sense to him. "I think one of his sons was killed last night."

"What?" Jill said, startled.

Cody and McCabe exchanged a look.

"There was a pretty big shoot-out last night," McCabe explained. "Apparently some of Wang's men hit one of Griffin Brown's brothels. The one on Bayswater Street. It's as bad as anything I've ever seen. They got just about everybody. . . girls and customers."

"Oh shit," Jill managed, trying to pick up her drinks which was two fingers of vodka topped off with Pepsi, but her hand was too shaky. She managed it on the second try, by lowering her head halfway to the table and then quickly bringing the glass up to her mouth.

"And these are the people who are after me?" she asked once she'd put the empty glass down.

"I don't know if it's Wang who's after you," Cody answered. "But whoever is, is connected with everything that's happening, on one side or the other."

She was frightened, suddenly near panic. "Then what bloody chance do I have?" she blurted out, trying to get up from the table. Cody pulled her back into place.

"You've got one chance, by helping us," he said.

"And you and this guy," she said derisively, indicating McCabe, "are going to go up against Henry Wang and Griffin Brown and all the people they've got."

"Have you got a better solution?" Cody asked. His voice was intense. "Think about it this way: If I let you zip from this table and you walk out of here, the next time someone's dead on your bathroom floor it's not going to be your cousin from Melbourne, it's going to be you."

She shuddered and then after some moments said, "I need a drink."

"When we're done with these," Cody said, going back to the photographs. "All right, this is Billy Packer. Is his son in one of these?"

"He has two sons," she said, and started to go through the pictures. "Billy Junior and Mickey." She stopped now and showed them a group shot taken on the yacht, pointing to a trim man in his mid twenties. He wore a mustache, and his bulging arms revealed he was a weight lifter. In the photo he was carrying several cases of beer. "That's Billy Junior," she said.

The face meant nothing to Cody. He glanced at McCabe, who shook his head.

"He's a new one on me, but I've seen that guy," the reporter said, pointing to one of the figures in the background. "He was at the aftermath of the shooting this morning, with Griffin Brown."

"That's Jacko," Jill nodded and then realized she needed to elaborate. "Police commissioner Jacklan. Brown owns him."

"In one of his notebooks, Tommy referred to Kevin being with a crooked cop," Cody stated. "Would that be Jacklan?"

She found a bitter smile. "Tommy used to say if you looked *crooked cop* up in the dictionary, it would have Jacko's picture next to it."

"The Packer boy who was killed was deaf," McCabe remembered.

"Oh, no, not Mickey," she moaned.

"If he's the deaf one, that's him," McCabe said.

She sorted through a dozen more pictures until she came on another group shot, again of the yacht. Mickey was with Nicholas, both with their shirts off, playing checkers. A blond, balding man was at the table with them. He was smiling and apparently advising Nicholas where to move, over the mock protests of Mickey. "That's Mickey," she said. "Playing checkers with Nicholas."

"Who's that with them?"

She had to search her memory. "That's, ahhh. . . Father. . . no, he's not a priest. Brother. That's it, Brother Julian, I think. He was only on one outing. He was a bad boy," she smiled.

"How do you mean?" Cody asked.

"Couldn't I have just a little drink?" she pleaded. "Just something to get me through."

Cody considered and then nodded to Damien. He brought the bottle of vodka and a Pepsi over to the table.

"I need more ice, too," she said, handing him the glass.

"You were telling us about Brother Julian," McCabe reminded her.

"He was a bad boy," she repeated. "One of the priests brought him along one day, it might have been Larry, or maybe it was Eugino – anyway, they were always bringing other priests and people looking for a handout. You know, for different causes."

Damien returned with the glass that now had ice in it. She filled it halfway with the vodka and then topped it off with the Pepsi as she continued to talk. "Anyhow, this Brother Julian makes a pitch, he runs a home for kids, you know, street kids, runaways, like that. It's up near Katoomba. Anyway, Fiona takes a liking to him because he was nice to Nicholas, and she writes him a check for five thousand dollars, and everybody's happy until a few days later when apparently he finds out who the Browns really are. Then he sends the check back, saying something like he couldn't accept money made off the misery of others." She took a pull on the drink, then added, "It was Father Larry, I remember now. He was in deep shit for a long time after that. Fiona was mad that he had brought Brother Julian in the first place. . . but he managed to suck his way back into her good graces." .

She took another long drink, leaving the glass almost empty, and then looked at them. "I don't always drink like this. But it's not every day some-one's trying to kill you."

"It's almost a quarter after, Dad," Damien said.

Cody nodded. "I'd better get going," he said, sorting through the photographs until he came upon the one he wanted and picked it up. "Walk with me, will you?" he said to McCabe.

"You were going to get the names of any people who died in the last couple of months near Tauranga," Cody said, as they walked along the jetty toward the park.

"Oh, yeah, Damien mentioned that," McCabe said, fishing for a piece of paper in his shirt pocket. "There were two of them. One an old man near nine-ty. . . Here it is. How's this for a name?" He read now. "Edwin Zenius Champion-Roberts, the last two hyphenated. Mr. Champion-Roberts, having lied about his age to join the army, distinguished himself at Gallipoli. He left six sons, three daughters, forty-two grandchildren, and twenty-seven great-grandchildren. The other was a seventy-two-year-old woman, Amanda Joyce Kearsey. She died of can-cer and left behind three daughters and a son and nine grandchildren."

"What did the old man die of?" Cody asked.

"All it said was natural causes. He apparently went in his sleep."

Cody considered. He remembered the stench of corrupting flesh he had sensed that day in New Zealand. The same smell he had remembered from when he was a boy and his mother had died of can-cer. "Let's concentrate on the woman first. We're going to need to get the names of her children, grandchildren – whoever's an adult."

"Okay, then what?" McCabe asked.

"There's an old crime reporter Tommy used to check things with, named Edythe, but a funny spelling. . ."

"I know her," McCabe interrupted. "She's one of the old crime hacks I've been talking to."

"Once you have the names, see if any of them means anything to her."

"And if they don't?"

"Then we'll have to run down all the names associated with the old man," Cody replied. "And if none of those work, I'll have just led you on a wild-goose chase."

"I'll make some phone calls while you're with our friend Mr. Brown," McCabe volunteered.

"Not so fast. There's something I need you to do right away," Cody said. They were coming on the cricket game by now, and he paused and handed the reporter the photograph he'd taken from the boat. It was the one with Jacklan in it. "I'd like you to show that to your chubby girlfriend as fast as you can; see if he's the police commissioner who was trying to hush up the autopsies. . . and if he was, call me at the Cowboy Club."

"But he works for Brown. Why would he. . . unless. . ."

"Unless he's the traitor in Brown's organization. The one who was able to get close enough to kill one of the sons and knock the other one unconscious before the fire," Cody said, finishing McCabe's thought.

"Crikey," McCabe exclaimed with some amazement. "If Jacklan is the traitor. . . wouldn't that be something? I mean, if you can't trust a crooked cop, who can you trust?"

* * *

McCabe jogged back toward the marina and its pay phone to track down his coroner's office girlfriend.

Cody walked on toward Kings Cross. The cricket game was still moving at its leisurely pace. Off to the other side, nearer the water, some children were flying kites and others were racing their bikes around a made-up circuit that included a mound they rode up and then flew off. A black-and-white dog chased them all, barking relentlessly, and the sky was clear and blue and the wind gentle, and for a moment it all reminded him of his own childhood, of lazy Saturday afternoons in Los Angeles. And in the next moment he again considered returning to the boat and walking away from all this, taking himself and the boys away from harm's way. But then he was leaving the park and starting down Holdsworth Avenue, and he knew that he was crossing over and there would be no turning back until it was over. In a few minutes he'd be meeting Griffin Brown. Dangerous and violent, right now Brown was a king under siege. But Cody knew that if he could handle him, convince Brown that he needed him, the gangster could be the first true step to finding out who killed Tommy Creager. And if he couldn't, or if he had miscalculated Brown's lack of involvement in Tommy's death, then he was liable to end up with a lot of broken bones, if alive at all.

45

"Where the fuck is he?" Griffin Brown said angrily.

They were in his black marble and brass office at the Cowboy Club. "The son of a bitch said he'd be here at three o'clock. Where the bloody hell is he?"

Billy Packer and Old Joe, who were also in the room, didn't bother to answer. They knew that Brown was only venting his frustration out loud, as he had been for some minutes. Griffin Brown sighed deeply and moved back to the bar and poured himself another scotch and then added a splash of soda the way he liked it. He sighed again and looked over at his old friend, who looked gray in this light.

"You look like shit, Billy," Brown said.

"I feel like shit," Billy answered.

"Why don't you go upstairs and lie down for a while."

"I'll be alright," Billy said. "I just need something for my stomach. Besides, I want to see this guy. . . if he ever shows up."

They all turned at the tap on the door.

"Yes," Brown barked.

The door opened and Lakey stepped in, looking rather apologetic. "It's Horowitz on the phone again. This time he has the Professor on too, a conference call. They say that they heard about the Bayswater. . . they're very concerned and want to talk to you about it "

"Bloody bloodsuckers," Brown growled. "They're getting nervous about their money again." He sighed. "That just goes too prove it doesn't take a fucking genius to see the walls are falling in."

"We'll come out of this," Billy said, his voice unintentionally husky. "Like we've come out of everything else. We'll be stronger than ever."

"Tell them I'm in a meeting," Brown ordered

Lakey. "Tell them that when I'm done I'll call them. And Lakey, send someone out for some Mylanta for Billy."

"Right," Lakey said and left again.

Griffin Brown grinned back at the others. "When I'm done, I'll call the bloody Professor. The Jew can wait; and after tomorrow and Kevin Madden's done with him, he can wait for bloody eternity."

* * *

"Whoops. What's this?" McClafferty said.

"The guy show up?" Clint asked with pointed interest. They were in their surveillance room over the bakery shop, across Macleay Street and four doors down from the Cowboy Club.

"No," McClafferty said, pulling down one of his earphones for a moment. "I think Brown's got a hit out on Horowitz down in Adelaide. Supposed to happen tomorrow."

It took a moment, and then Clint began to laugh. McClafferty laughed too, but then asked, "What should we do?"

"About what?" Clint asked. His attention had gone outside now. He had put his binoculars buck up to his eyes.

"About Horowitz getting hit. Shouldn't we pass it on?" McClafferty wanted to know.

"We do and we could blow everything we've been working on. . . I got a guy going in." He switched on the camera that was locked in on the front of the Cowboy Club. It got six quick snaps of Cody before he disappeared inside.

* * *

Lakey threw Cody up against the wall. Grasshopper jammed his .45 into the nape of his neck, pointing up.

"Move and you're dead, Yank," Grasshopper hissed.

They were in the hallway on the other side of the "EMPLOYEES ONLY" doorway that Mickey Packer used to guard. Lakey searched him for a weapon and easily found the Walther. Now he grabbed Cody by the hair, pulled it back hard, and slapped him in the face with the gun. "What's this bloody for?"

"Maybe just to show you I'm serious," Cody said.

"You'd better be bloody serious. You'd better not be jerking Mr. Brown around about Nicholas."

* * *

"He don't look good, Mr. Brown," Old Joe said quietly so that Billy wouldn't hear him at the other end of the room.

"*Shit, now they're whispering,*" McClafferty said.

"*About what?*" Clint asked.

"*I don't know. I can't hear them. . . something about a doctor.*"

"Billy, do you want me to call a doctor?" Brown asked his friend.

Billy was feeling worse than he ever had in his life. The nausea, the pressure in his chest. He was rocking back and forth gently on the couch. The question surprised him. He hadn't been paying attention for some moments. "I'll be alright," he said automatically.

Brown could see now that his friend was in bad shape. He was about to overrule him when there was another tap on the door.

"Yes," Brown called out.

The door opened and Lakey stuck his head in. "That guy's here. The one who called about Nicholas."

"Bring him in," Brown ordered.

Cody was shoved inside.

"He was carrying this," Lakey said, displaying the Walther; then, on Brown's nod, he threw it to him.

Brown looked the gun over with some curiosity. "You've got to be pretty stupid to think you can get past my people with this."

"I didn't expect to. But it's like I told your bald-headed friend, I brought it with me to help get your attention."

Brown and Cody locked eyes for several moments. They were like a pair of boxers, Cody realized, trying to feel each other out. Cody knew he couldn't let the other man get the upper hand.

"Mind if I have a drink?" Cody asked, but then rather than wait for an answer just walked over to the bar and started to pour himself a vodka.

"Where's Nicholas?" Brown demanded.

"Well, now, that's what we're all here for, isn't it," Cody said as he added a splash of soda to his drink.

"You said you knew where my son was."

"No," Cody said as he turned back to Brown with a steady gaze. "What I said was, if you wanted to know where he was, you should meet me."

"Do you know where Nicholas is?" Brown asked, anger growling in his voice.

"No. Not yet. But with your help, I'll find him," Cody said, sipping his drink as he glanced around at all the black marble and brass. "You really should think about another decorator."

"Get him the bloody hell out of here," Brown exploded.

Old Joe and Lakey moved for Cody.

"I wouldn't be too hasty; you need me," Cody warned.

Old Joe and Lakey had him now, each by one arm.

"I need you?" Brown raged. "I need a bloody fucking American to come in here and pull some cheap-ass stunt? Take him out and break as many bones as you can find on him."

Old Joe took the drink out of Cody's hand and put it on the bar.

"I warned you, asshole," Lakey said. "Now I'm going to have fun."

And then with a sudden movement Cody came alive. He broke free of Old Joe's grasp, wheeled, and drove his left foot into Lakey's crotch. The big bald-headed man doubled over, and Cody grabbed him and drove him into Old Joe, slamming them both against the bar. Now he turned to Brown and for a moment froze. Brown had Cody's own Walther pointed at him. It was obviously time to play one of his aces and hope to God it worked.

"Your son Kevin was dead before the fire started at the disco," Cody said.

A look of surprise showed on Brown's face, but before he could respond, Billy Packer was moving in on Cody. His face ashen, wheezing for breath, he brought his hands together and tried to club Cody on the back of the neck. Cody ducked and side-stepped him, and the ex-boxer staggered and fell to the floor.

"What did you say?" Brown demanded.

And Cody knew he had gained the advantage. "You heard me. Your son Kevin was dead before the disco was firebombed. Someone got close enough to him to slip an ice pick into his heart, and afterward splashed him with gasoline. . . or as I guess you call it in this country, petro."

Billy Packer groaned and then yelled and half rolled over on the floor. Cody kneeled down next to him. The ex-boxer's face was bathed in sweat; his tongue had turned black. "Call an ambulance," Cody ordered. "This man's having a major heart attack."

"Jesus, someone's having a heart attack."

"Who?" Clint wanted to know.

"I don't know. It sounds like bloody chaos over there," *McClafferty reported.*

The ambulance took eight minutes to arrive. Cody worked on Billy Packer expertly all through that period. Trying to get him to respond, trying to get the heart to start beating again. Griffin Brown went out to the bar a couple of times, yelling at people, as if that would somehow bring the ambulance earlier. But in the eight minutes that seemed to take an hour, both Cody and Griffin Brown sensed that all they were doing was futile. . . and in those eight desperate minutes an odd sort of bond grew between them.

* * *

"He's going to die, isn't he?" Brown asked Cody after the gurney with Billy Packer had been wheeled out.

"It doesn't look good," Cody said.

"Jesus," Brown murmured. "He's my best friend. . . I appreciate what you did for him."

Cody nodded. "There was a time when Tommy Creager was my best friend."

Brown looked at him with some surprise.

"I came to Sydney yesterday to try and find out who killed him," Cody added.

Brown didn't speak for some moments, and when he did an edge of toughness crept back in. "Tommy Creager? Why the hell would you think I'd know anything about that?" he asked.

"Because I think his killing is connected to the attacks that have been made on your organization," Cody said. "The disappearance of your son Nicholas. The firebombing of the disco. What happened last night up on Bayswater Street. I think someone's out to get you. But first they want to twist the knife in you. For whatever reason they want to humiliate you before they kill you. My guess is Tommy knew who, or would have once everything started. That's why they killed him."

"Tommy Creager?" The gangster repeated the name with some astonishment, as if the line of thinking had startled him. "He was a bloody useless rummy."

"Maybe. But he was still a good reporter," Cody said. "He always had his eye out for a story. He became like a member of your family because of his friendship with your wife and Nicholas. You even accused him of helping Nicholas to disappear. Think about it: Tommy was at all those parties on your yacht, drinking and rubbing elbows with your friends and business associates. There were a lot of things he could have found out, overheard. A lot of things that could have made him dangerous to the wrong people."

Brown stared at Cody for several long moments. "Who the bloody hell are you?"

"My name is Cody. I used to be a cop in Los Angeles. There are people there who think that finding people is the best thing I do. I want to find your son Nicholas, and to do that, like I said before, I'm going to need your help."

"Wait a minute. . . wait a minute," Brown said, trying to get a grasp on the situation. "You want to find my son Nicholas so that you can find out who killed Tommy Creager?"

"That's right."

Brown stared at him as if he were sure one of them had gone mad. "And you're saying Nicholas disappearing, Tommy Creager being killed, and the disco fire – where you say my son Kevin was dead before the fire started – are all part of a plan to. . . get me?"

"Your son David had been knocked unconscious before the fire also," Cody said. "And don't forget what happened last night."

Brown almost laughed. "You're either a bloody lunatic, or. . . " He paused as he realized that what Cody was saying was worth considering. "Where did you get your information about my Kevin being dead and David being unconscious before the fire?"

"From a source I have in the coroner's office," Cody said. "A source who also told me someone was trying to keep those reports secret."

"Who?" Brown snarled.

"A police commissioner," Cody answered, then adding matter-of-factly, "I'm trying to find out right now if it's your friend Jacklan."

Brown shot another look of dark surprise to Lakey and Old Joe.

"If I'm figuring right," Cody went on, "you have a turncoat in your organization. In my book, the commissioner could be a prime candidate."

Brown studied him, then grinned and shook his head. "And you've only been in town a day? Christ, what would you know about me if you were lucky enough to stay alive for a week." He moved back to the bar, trying to appear calm, but his mind was racing. You want a fresh drink?"

"The old one will do," Cody said, moving over and picking it up from where Joe had placed it.

"You really think someone's out to get me?" Brown asked, knowing that it was the same logic he had entertained earlier and rejected. "Killing me isn't good enough; they want me to suffer first?"

Cody nodded. "It's the only thing that makes sense. If they could get close enough to put an ice pick through Kevin's heart and smack a tire iron across the back of David's head. . . then couldn't they have gotten close enough to kill you?"

Brown's mood turned dark. "You make a good point. . . if everything you say about Kevin and David is true."

"Don't take my word for it," Cody offered. "You must have someone in or around the coroner's office who owes you."

Brown glanced at Lakey.

"There's that Considine guy; he fixed a few certificates for us," Lakey said.

"What do we have on him?" Brown asked.

"Oh, he's strictly a money guy," Lakey said.

Brown nodded. "Get hold of him. Tell him I want him down to the offices as soon as he can get there, and there'll be five thousand in it for him."

Lakey hurried for the door but paused as Brown spoke again.

"Lakey. . . tell him I'll make it ten thousand if he has the answer in an hour."

"Right," Lakey said, disappearing into the hallway.

Brown turned and studied Cody for some moments before speaking. "All right; let's say what you're telling me is true. What do you want?"

"Access to everything I can that belongs to Nicholas. His clothes, his room, his car."

"He didn't have a car; he didn't drive," Brown told him.

"What about a checkbook or credit cards?" Cody asked.

"He had credit cards, I think, and probably some charge accounts."

"I'd like to see his bills, then. For the period, say, from a couple of weeks before he disappeared," Cody instructed, and then had a sudden thought. "He hasn't used them since, has he?"

"Christ, I don't know," Brown answered, and moved to a wall phone, picked up the receiver, and punched out three numbers. He didn't have to wait long. "Lady, this is Grif. You took care of all Nicholas's financial stuff, didn't you – credit cards, charge accounts, and all?" He listened and nodded. "I want you to pull them all, from October on, and bring them to my office."

46

He was a very old man and he watched the late-afternoon sunlight dance on the water and his tiny great-granddaughter play on the shore. She had a stick and ran this way and that, dragging it in the muddy sand behind her. And he thought of the poem he had learned many years ago and smiled to himself as he recited it in his native Cantonese: "Ruined and ill, a man of four score; pretty and guileless, a girl of three. Not a boy, but still better than nothing: To soothe one's feelings, from time to time a kiss. . . " He lost his train of thought now as his attention went to the sound of screeching tires. Up on the driveway of the main house a blue station wagon came to a stop and four white men with big guns in their hands ran toward the front door. He knew before he heard the gunfire what he must do and so he hurried down to the muddy shore, calling to his great-granddaughter in Cantonese, which was the only language either of them spoke or understood: "Hurry, hurry!" And hand in hand they ran as fast as a slight eighty-three-year-old man and a three-year-old girl could run, until they reached the space under the jetty. There he had the little girl lie in the mud, and he then pulled a ten-foot boat over to them. It was very heavy for him. But by now he was hearing the gunfire from the house. Straining all his muscles, he finally managed to turn the boat up on its side and then, lying next to his tiny great-grandchild, pulled it over the two of them like a giant tortoise shell.

They hid there in the dark for some minutes, and in his fear the next lines of the old poem came to him: "There came a day they suddenly took her from me; her soul's shadow wanders I know not where. And then I remember how, just at the time she died, she lisped strange sounds, beginning to learn to talk."

He could hear footsteps on the jetty overhead now and held his hand over the little girl's lips, for she had begun to sing to herself. Now the footsteps were in the muddy sand, walking around and around. . . and then in the distance a car horn was honking and the footsteps receded. The very old man breathed a sigh of relief and hugged his young great-grand daughter, and his eyes misted for the others who had been in the house. The other children and their mother, his granddaughter. The very old man and the little girl hid there for another ten minutes before he lifted the boat again and then returned to the sunlight and the aftermath of murder.

47

"These are all of Nicholas's charges," Lady said. She looked to be in her seventies and wore her henna-rinsed hair piled high. Her lipstick was bright red. She had a cigarette with an inch-long ash in her mouth as she put the papers down on Griffin Brown's desk.

"Were there any charges after the nineteenth of November?" Brown asked.

"I don't know; I didn't look," she stated with the impertinence of a twenty-seven-year employee who fancied herself irreplaceable. "Is that when Nicholas disappeared?" she asked.

Cody hadn't waited for the answer. He was scanning the bills. "Nothing after the nineteenth."

"Is that important?" she asked, now sensing she might have assumed the wrong attitude earlier.

"No, it's fine, Lady," Brown said with enough brusqueness so that she would know she was being dismissed. "That's all for now. Thank you for bringing these."

"I'll need those back for my records," she said.

"You'll have them," Brown assured her.

She paused again at the door. "If you had let me know what you were looking for, I could have told you."

"I know," Brown said, and then added with strained patience, "Good-bye, Lady."

She left.

"What's this abbreviation?" Cody asked, pointing to a spot on a Visa bill. It read "DblBy."

"That's Double Bay," Brown told him.

"Where's that?"

"Just a couple of miles down Old South Head Road, two bays down. It's a very expensive shopping area."

There was a tap on the door and then Lakey entered. "Two things: There's a phone call for him, a guy named McCabe. And everything's done out at Hunters Hill."

Brown sighed deeply.

Cody picked up the phone. "Yes," he said, and then listened for some moments. "All right. I'll see you in a little while."

"He is on a boat."

"Who is?" Clint asked.

"This Cody guy. The guy phoning him said, 'I'll see you back on the boat.' "

Cody hung up. Brown looked at him expectantly.

"It was Jacklan who tried to cover up the autopsies. My source in the coroner's office identified him from a photograph."

Brown had half suspected it for the last twenty minutes or so, but now the statement seemed to knock the wind out of him. "The son of a bitch," he said slowly. *"The son of a bitch."* He looked at Cody as if he needed to explain. "He's been on my payroll for over twenty years. I made him commissioner. I paid for his promotions. The son of a bitch. You're telling me he was the traitor?"

"Looks like he was at least one of them," Cody nodded.

"The dirty son of a bitch," Brown repeated, looking to Old Joe. "Joe?"

"Looks like maybe Billy did a good thing," Joe said.

48

"This is Gallagher," he said into the public phone as he stood on a cement walkway that curved around and overlooked the beach at Nielson Park. It was crowded with children and adults playing and swimming in the soft harborside surf or digging castles or sunning on the sand. Fifty yards out, like a giant soccer goal, was the protecting shark net. Beyond, sailboats and wind surfers glided lazily across the late-afternoon skyline of the city. Gallagher was in his beach clothes, a white-brimmed straw Australian hat protecting his fair skin from the sun.

"You're missing a hell of a show," Clint said.

"Did that guy show up about Nicholas?"

"Oh, he showed up, with a few bombshells."

"What do you mean?"

"He claimed Brown's two kids were dead before the fire started at the disco."

"Jesus Christ," Gallagher said, sensing that things were beginning to unravel. He looked around now to discover an iron-haired woman only a few feet away, looking to be in her forties and wearing only a bikini bottom, staring at him, obviously waiting for the phone.

"Right now Griffin Brown's got someone down at the coroner's office checking it out," Clint said.

"Who is this guy?" Gallagher asked, finding himself focusing on the iron-haired woman's breasts and thinking they were remarkably firm and upright, considering their large size. He turned away from her.

"He says his name is Cody. He's an American and, if you believe him, an ex-cop from Los Angeles."

"What the hell does he want in this?" Gallagher asked.

"He says to find out who killed Tommy Creager. Wasn't he that reporter who got killed over in New Zealand?"

"Yes," Gallagher said impatiently. "But who could possibly give a shit about that?" he wondered aloud in exasperation.

"Apparently he does," Clint said rather crisply, anoyed to have the American talking to him in that tone of voice. "He said Creager was his best friend."

"You think this guy is for real?" Gallagher asked after some moments.

"He seems to be convincing Brown," Clint said noncommittally "He's asked Brown to help him find his kid Nicholas. This Cody thinks that if he can find the kid, he'll know who killed Creager. . . and who's been doing everything else to Brown."

Gallagher's stomach sank and turned cold. He looked around now; the iron-haired woman with the large, firm breasts was still there, but this time she winked at him. He turned away again. "I'd better get down there. Can you have McClafferty run me off a tape of everything this Cody guy's in?"

"Sure," Clint said.

"You might start running a check on this Cody guy, see what we can find out," Gallagher pressed.

"You got any ideas how we do that?" Clint asked. He still had his back up over the American getting pushy.

"Well you're ASIO. You're supposed to be the intelligence boys."

"Mate, it's four o'clock Saturday afternoon. You really think I'm going to find anyone around to run checks for me? What about your side?"

Gallagher sighed. "It's four o'clock Saturday afternoon. I'll see you in about an hour." He hung up the phone and sighed again. He'd have to take the family home now. He'd promised them they'd stay late and then have dinner out on the pier over at Watsons Bay. It would mean another fight with Karen. He wondered how many they had left.

"You done?"

He looked around to see the iron-haired woman next to him now.

"Yeah, sure," he said.

They looked at each other another moment, and

then she smiled a smile that reminded him of Mae West. "I got great tits, don't I, honey?" she said and winked again.

He laughed. "Yeah, great."

"Glad you like them," she said, and picked up the pay phone receiver and put her coins in.

49

They waited another twenty minutes, during most of which Griffin Brown sat silently, deep in thought. Making plans, trying to make sense of recent history in the light of this new information. Then Lakey returned.

"I just heard from Considine," he reported, then nodded toward Cody. "Everything he said is right. Kevin was dead before the fire. . . and David was unconscious."

Brown sighed deeply and finished his scotch. "I'll be damned."

Lakey wasn't going away. Brown glanced up at him again.

"We also just heard from Tiny. He thinks he might know where the Chinaman is."

Any sense of reflection was gone now from Brown's voice. It was sharp and crisp. "See if we can get a confirmation on that and get a team ready. We've got to go after him hard and fast."

Lakey nodded. "Will do." Then he was gone again.

Brown was a general now, mobilizing his troops. "Joe, when we go, we'll use the armor-plated Mercedes. Make sure they're ready."

"Yes, sir," Joe said and exited.

Brown looked at Cody and almost smiled. "A little while ago I thought you were a bloody lunatic. You've done a great service for me."

"I hope your friend Billy makes it," Cody said.

Brown nodded. "I meant about the information you've given me. I knew there was a traitor. Knowing who it was unties my hands. I know who I can trust again."

"Unless he wasn't alone," Cody reminded him.

"I'm going to have to take that chance," Brown said with a sigh. "You still going after Nicholas?"

"Yes."

"But if you're right as to why Tommy was killed and Jacko was the traitor. . . he's probably the one who killed or arranged to have him killed."

"I want who Jacklan was working for. Who actually gave the orders."

There was a tap on the door, followed by a breathless Lakey. "Location on the Chinaman's been confirmed."

"We'll go as soon as Joe has the cars ready," Brown said. He was going into battle and was losing interest in Cody, but he still felt grateful enough to offer, "If I can help you. . . " He caught himself and grinned. "If I'm still alive and can help you, let me know."

"I'll be seeing your wife," Cody said.

Brown sighed. "I suppose you have to. I'll call her. . . "

"No," Cody said, overriding him with the hint of a grin. "I'll contact her in my own way. From what I hear, you might not be the best person to introduce me."

This time Brown almost laughed. "Christ, you do know a lot about me. If you do find Nicholas, you'll tell me?"

"If it won't bring danger to him," Cody answered.

"If he's with the Chinaman," Brown said, and the threat was back in his voice, "you'd bloody well better tell me."

"If he's with the Chinaman," Cody answered, "you're liable to find him faster than I do."

Lakey was back. "Joe says the cars are ready."

"Okay," Brown said. He considered Cody for a moment, then picked up his Walther and threw it back to him. "Good luck to all of us," he said. Cody lingered a moment and then followed him out.

"They're out of there. They're off to hit Wang and his people, but I don't know where," McClafferty said.

"It doesn't matter," Clint replied.

"But shouldn't we tell someone?"

"Who? The police? How do we explain to them what we know without blowing our job? And besides, where are you going to tell them to go? Look at it this way: With any luck, Brown and Wang and all the rest of them will blow themselves to kingdom come. And the whole bloody city will be a better place."

50

Cody left the Cowboy Club and headed up Macleay Street. He found a cab up near the park with the spraying fountain. "Take me to Bondi Beach," he said, because it was the only destination he could think of that would have a lot of people around.

The ride took about ten minutes, during which Cody glanced back through the rear window. If anyone was following him, he couldn't tell. The cab let him off at the corner of Campbell Parade and O'Brian. Beachgoers were beginning to go home, and the sidewalks were more crowded than before. He made his way along the beachfront, past half a dozen shops and then a restaurant that spilled its tables out onto the sidewalk, with a Plexiglas screen between them and the passersby. He still couldn't detect a tail if there was one. He went in and found the bar. It looked out to the sidewalk.

"Vodka and a splash of soda," he ordered. He sat and sipped for several minutes, but his eyes stayed on the sidewalk outside. He was sure now that no one was following him. What he didn't understand was why his sense of anxiety had remained. He tried to relax and took out Nicholas's credit card bill. Then suddenly he had to look around again, for the sense of anxiety had flared. And then he knew why: The high-pitched tone was back, growing louder and louder, and he was filled with a sense of dread. But then, in a matter of moments, it was gone. He was sweating, but around him nothing had changed.

He forced himself to focus on the credit card bill. Throughout the month most of the charges were small and scattered, days apart. But on the nineteenth of November, Nicholas had spent over thirteen hundred dollars, in three stores in Double Bay. One of the charges was at Bailey's Chemist, for a little over ninety-two dollars; the next at Hart's, for three hundred and twelve dollars; and the last at The Fun House, for over nine hundred. What the hell was he doing? Getting ready for the trip? As Cody wondered, he knew that Double Bay would have to be his next stop. And then the high-pitched tone was returning, louder this time; his ears were ringing and he could smell the smoke and hear the screams. He didn't know how long it lasted. He had to hold onto the bar to keep from falling.

"Another drink, mate?" the bartender asked.

"Make it a double," Cody said, knowing there was no point in trying to fight it. So now instead he concentrated and tried to find the feeling again. Find out what he was supposed to see. But it wasn't there. Goddammit, it wasn't there. Why did it do that? Why did it haunt him with flashes of nightmares and then go away again? Nothing was there except a sense of fear.

Then outside the front window he saw the nine- or ten-year-old boy in the blue jersey and shorts who he had seen chased earlier on the beach. He and several other scruffy-looking kids were walking by, smoking cigarettes. Cody knew it was those kids – or kids like them – who they would have to make contact with tonight in the hopes that one of them might have seen the man in the alley with petro cans the night of the fire.

He finished his second drink. Neither the high-pitched tone nor the sense of fear had returned. Then, even though he was sure he wasn't being followed, he left by the back door and walked down the alley past the back of the burned-out disco. He paused and looked up at it for several minutes, but there was only silence. He continued on now, down to Curlewis Street. From there he walked another two blocks up, away from the ocean, until he found another cab. He couldn't shake the feeling of danger.

He looked around before getting in. Again he assured himself that no one was there.

But then it was back. The high-pitched tone, louder and louder, and for a moment everything was red and he was back in the fire and people were screaming. The girl with the blond hair was on fire, and he could hear Damien. "Dad, help me, help me!" And then he could see his son, his body engulfed in flames.

"You all right, mister?" the cabby asked him.

Cody had lost his balance and sagged against the side of the cab. "Rushcutters Bay marina, as fast as you can."

"Are you sick or something?"

"Goddammit, just take me there," Cody barked, climbing into the backseat.

51

The silver-haired man emerged from the shower, wrapped a towel around himself, and picked up the ringing phone. "Fitzwilliam," he said.

"I've found one of them," the man's voice said. "Ed Cody. He's an American, came into Sydney on a fifty-six-foot sailboat called *Ann's Dream*. I made some calls; he's berthed at the sailing-boat marina in Rushcutters Bay."

"What do you want me to do?" Fitzwilliam asked.

"First find out if the girl is there."

"And if she is?"

"Kill them both – and the reporter, if you can find him."

"Right there in the bloody marina?" Fitzwilliam asked, expressing some rare exasperation. "I'm not a magician; I can't just disappear in a puff of smoke when it's done."

"Colin, I don't care where you do it, or how you do it. Get hold of Jacko if you need help. It has to be done."

"I can't find Jacko."

"What do you mean, you can't find him?"

"He's not at home. He's not at his office. He's not answering his beeper," Fitzwilliam said with some impatience.

"Christ, he's probably passed out bloody drunk somewhere," the other said sourly, then continued persuasively. "Look, mate, we knew we had to take risks, and both of us have taken our share of them. But it's finally paying off, it's all happening now. I'm flying out as soon as I hang up with you."

Fitzwilliam brightened. "The call came?"

"Yes," the other man said, unable to conceal his excitement. "It's the biggest shipment of heroin in the history of this country, and we've just bloody hijacked it. We can't let anything get in the way now."

"It won't, mate," Fitzwilliam said. "I'll take care of things at Rushcutters Bay."

52

Billy Packer, Jr., came up the outdoor concrete steps two at a time and into the parking lot overlooking Simmon's Point Park and the harbor, where the two Mercedes were parked. Griffin Brown, who had been waiting for Billy Junior's return, now got out of the brown car. Old Joe and Lakey, who had been standing across the way, looking out at the harbor, came over and joined them.

"Let's hope Wang isn't listening to the news," Brown said.

"Hunters Hill?" Old Joe asked.

Brown nodded. "News reports are just coming over the radio. They haven't mentioned any names yet, but even the bloody Chinaman's liable to figure out it's his family, and it he does, he's going to fly out of there in a hurry. If it's possible, I'd like to nail the son of a bitch where he is and end this bloody thing. So the question is, Billy, can we get in? And more important, can we get out?"

Billy shrugged. He didn't know the answer to the last question. "I know we can get in. I had to go through two backyards, but I got to the house, at least to the fence behind it. There's a gate, and it's open."

"Any sign of the Chinaman?" Brown asked.

"It was pretty quiet. I thought I heard a TV on."

Brown considered. "Lakey, what do you think?"

Lakey frowned. "He's picked a pretty good place for a safe house. At least as far as being able to defend it. The street it fronts on is a dead end and faces the harbor, which means they'll see us coming if we come by car. . . and Billy says the only other way in is from here and through some backyards. I don't know. How long is it going to take the neighbors to call the cops when they see men with guns moving through their yards?"

"They won't," Billy Junior said. "I cut the phone lines for every house on the street except the Chinaman's. . . and I figure if Joe and Stanley drive around and block the road with the cars, just around the corner from the house, there isn't no one going out for help."

"Nothing against you, Billy," Old Joe said, looking to Griffin Brown, "but I don't like it. You could
be walking into a trap."

Brown considered a moment and then sighed
and nodded. "I know, Joe, but I don't see what other
choice we have. We can't let the Chinaman get away
with what he's done, and we may never get a better
chance. We've got to hit him hard and make an
example of him, or every cheap crook in Sydney is
going to try and take a bite of us. Joe, do what Billy
said: You and Stanley block the way out. Take Ted
and Mende with you; when they hear the shooting
send them around the corner and have them come in
the front."

Lakey, Billy Junior, and Grasshopper had automatic pistols under their jackets – or in Grasshopper's case under his sloppy Hawaiian shirt – and
Griffin Brown carried a .45. They waited for Stanley
and Old Joe to get the cars in position, and while
they waited they watched the sailboats in the harbor.

"The old man takes my kids out to breakfast
every Sunday," Billy Junior said softly.

"I didn't know that," Griffin Brown said.

"Yeah, Pancakes on the Rocks. Even little
Bernadette – she's only two – she insists she has to
go as well," young Billy said, fighting tears.

"He'll be taking them again; you watch," Brown
said, but he didn't believe it.

"Yeah," Billy agreed, knowing he was accepting
a lie.

"You're a hell of a man to be out here, with your
dad down," Lakey offered.

Billy Junior wiped the mist off his eyes. "That
bloody Chinaman killed my brother, and I think he's

responsible for the old man being in the hospital now. I wouldn't be anywhere else."

The walkie-talkie crackled. Old Joe's voice told them that they were in place, and so the four men with guns started down the old concrete stairway.

* * *

The little girl watched the four men as they moved across her backyard. She was six and having an earnest conversation with some stuffed toys.

"Go inside," Billy Junior told her.

But she didn't move.

"Go inside and stay there!" he commanded in a more threatening voice, taking a step toward her. The little girl got up and ran inside, frantically calling, "Mum, Mum!"

By then Grasshopper and Lakey had moved a wooden lawn table over to the fence, to be used as a step to get over it. Billy climbed up first and then helped Griffin Brown follow him. Billy climbed over and then dropped down to the other side, steadying Brown again as he made his way over.

"I'm not as graceful as I once was," Brown joked.

"The next one's easy," Billy said. "It's got a gate right into the Chinaman's back door."

The yard they were in had a pair of waddle trees in full, bright yellow bloom. A car tire, tied to a rope, hung from one of the sturdier limbs.

Grasshopper and then Lakey joined them.

"We'd better get ready," Billy said, pulling out his automatic pistol and checking it. "Once we lose the cover of these trees and go through that gate, there's nothing to help us."

The others checked their guns.

"Whenever you're ready, Mr. Brown," Billy said.

Griffin Brown nodded and smiled. He wasn't afraid, but he had a nagging feeling that he might die in the next few minutes, and he wished he hadn't sent Shauna away. The world around him had become so empty in the last few days. "When I was a kid, we had a big waddle tree in our backyard," he said. "I loved that house. It was on Sully Street, over in Coogee, and then one day the bloody bankers came and threw us out on the street." It still brought a sadness to him. He smiled now as he saw the others looking at him rather oddly. "Well," he went on, "what do you say we go kill ourselves some Chinamen."

Brown led the way now. Here he was clearly the best, instincts and experience combining with a willingness to throw himself into a kill-or-be-killed situation.

They reached the gate, and Brown opened it slightly and looked through to the structure beyond. It was a boxy, two-story house of concrete blocks, painted white. There was a porch that ran across the length of the house. It had three steps that led down to a backyard overgrown with weeds. The only sound from the house came from a TV.

Brown's adrenaline was pumping. The .45 was familiar in his hand. He had killed three men with it – or was it four?

"Let me go first," Billy said.

"No," Brown answered. If it was a trap, as Old Joe had suggested, he wanted to draw the fire. "This is my show."

Then he was gone. He burst through the gate in a half crouch and ran for the porch. Billy Junior was right behind him, and then Lakey and Grasshopper. The four of them clattered up the steps and then fanned out, flattening themselves against the wall of the house for cover. But except for the television, which was singing about Tip-Top bread, there wasn't a sound from inside.

Griffin Brown was bathed in a light sweat. His heart was pounding. More and more he was beginning to believe that this was a trap. But again there was no fear. Only a sense of what he had to do to survive. A sense he had first acquired and then developed when he had been only a boy living in the shack town in Hyde Park. A boy who had to keep his family alive. If it was a trap, then he'd go down fighting.

He reached over and tried the door, and to his surprise the knob turned. He pushed it open now with the barrel of his gun. Still silence from inside. He glanced over to Billy Junior, on the opposite side of the door, and Billy shrugged. Brown knew that there was no turning back. He stepped over and pushed the door all the way open and then moved inside.

Only the sound of the TV.

Brown moved through the kitchen with the .45 at firing level. First Billy, then Lakey and Grasshopper followed.

Gun ready, Brown spun through the swinging door to the dining room and tripped and fell over the body of Li, Wang's bodyguard.

"Jesus Christ," Brown shouted as the others poured into the room.

"You all right, Mr. Brown?" Lakey asked, helping him up as the others stood ready with their guns in case someone rushed in.

Brown grimaced in pain as he shifted his weight to his left ankle. "Ahh, I've twisted it. Give me a hand here," he said, and then, leaning on Lakey, moved back to Li's body and crouched down as best he could to examine it. Li had fallen next to the dining room table, where it looked as if he might have been playing solitaire. The cards were laid out, and next to a half-filled cup of tea sat an ashtray full of cigarette butts. Rigor mortis had set in. The cause of death wasn't too difficult to ascertain; an ice pick handle stuck out of the dead man's chest.

"Ice pick," Brown said, unnerved at the unexpected appearance of the body. "I'm told it's the way they killed Kevin, before the fire."

"What?" Billy Junior asked, truly shocked.

"It's a long story," Brown returned, anger building inside of him. "But I have a feeling someone's trying to play games with my life."

Using Lakey for support, he limped into the next room. Two more dead Chinese men. More of Wang's inner circle. They had been shot and looked as if they had been surprised, as if the killer, after silently dispatching Li, had burst in on them.

The wall next to the stairs was streaked with blood, and they followed it up. At the top they found Henry Wang where he had fallen, apparently running from his attacker. The back of his legs and torso were riddled with bullets. Part of his scalp had been blown away.

The four men stood in silence for some moments, and then Griffin Brown's anger erupted. "Goddammit," he exploded, the veins bulging from his neck. "Who's doing this to me?"

53

"Bloody tennis letting out," the cabby said to Cody. They were on New South Head road and now, just past Edgecliff, it was almost 4:30 and they had hit bumper-to-bumper traffic. They weren't moving.

"How much farther?" Cody asked

"Oh, only a few more blocks, mate. White City, where they play the tennis, is right across the highway from Rushcutters. . . "

He didn't get to finish. Cody stuck a ten-dollar bill in his hand and was out the door, running, between cars. Horns honking. Suddenly there was a small break in the traffic; a red car lurched forward and Cody had to dart and then bound over the hood. He reached the sidewalk and started sprinting.

He was nearing a cross street. The traffic was beginng to rove. But the memory of what he had seen – Damien engulfed in flames – returned, and he knew he couldn't slow down. A Bentley screeched its brakes and missed him by only inches. The Toyota behind it wasn't so lucky and plowed into the back of the expensive car.

He was running downhill. Another small street. Again he ran across it without break in speed. This time, luckily, there were no cars coming. He could see New Beach Road now, which led to the marina, and across it Rushcutters Bay Park.

Stalled traffic was blocking New Beach as he got there, so he ran parallel to the street along the sidewalk. Ahead, a group of kids, mostly boys, were skateboarding. He was almost on top of them. A boy with red hair was coming fast, straight at him. The boy and his skateboard raced up a ramp and flew off. Cody averted a collision by jutting into the street, jumping on top of the hood of one car and then over to the hood of another before he landed in the grass of the park, where he rolled, regained his feet, and started running again. A burly, angry man had emerged from his car, ready to go after Cody, but as Cody had hit the ground his Walther had come free and fallen out beside him. Cody had paused long enough to pick it up. . . long enough for the burly man to decide a dent in his hood might be lived with after all.

Cody reached the marina and paused to catch his breath and look around. No obvious signs of trouble. The sun was beginning to set. Many of the boats that had been out for the day were returning.

"Hi, Dad," Patrick said.

Cody, surprised, turned to discover the boy coming up from the marina shops, eating a red-and-green frozen ice.

"Everyone alright?"

"Sure," the boy said. "I guess."

"How long since you've been on the boat?" Cody asked.

Patrick shrugged. "Maybe twenty minutes. The lady started telling me about this movie she's written." He rolled his eyes. "It was about this alien who comes down to have a baby with an earth woman. The computer on the spaceship has picked the perfect woman. She's real smart, a lawyer, and works for the greenies. And he's made to look real handsome and romantic so she'll fall in love with him. Only somehow he gets mixed up and thinks that the woman he's supposed to have the baby with is this sort of fat lady who's already married and has six bratty kids and doesn't want anything to do with him."

Cody had used this time to survey the marina and the surrounding area once more. Still no sign of danger. But he had no way of knowing. He found a smile for his son now and teased him. "I thought you liked those kind of movies, outer space and all."

"The only outer space in this movie is in the lady who wrote it, in her brain," Patrick laughed.

Cody grinned. "I want you to do me a favor now. I want you to go back to the shops and stay there. We'll be there in a few minutes."

And even though his father had smiled, the boy knew from his tone not to question him.

"I'll be there," Patrick said.

Cody headed down the jetty. It was the end of the day, and once again a near party atmosphere prevailed on the marina. People on the aft decks of their boats were having cocktails, laughing, talking, calling over to their neighbors.

A cold feeling settled in his stomach as he neared the pen where the boat should be. . . it wasn't there. He looked around quickly. Had he made a mistake? Was he on the wrong jetty? No. It was pen 114. *Where the hell was it?* What had happened to Damien. . . the girl. . . McCabe? He continued down the jetty almost to the end. It was crazy. A sense of unreality filled his head. He turned and started back. . . and then he spotted it. It had been moved to a pen on the far side of the next jetty over. He was running again, recalling his vision of Damien engulfed in flames, and he didn't know what it meant but he feared his son was in jeopardy.

He reached the next jetty. No one was on deck. He thought Damien would have been here, looking out for him – but then, he thought the boat would have been where he'd left it. He tried to climb on board silently, which wasn't too difficult, as a dozen people on the sixty-foot sailboat beside him were singing "Happy Birthday." He moved carefully to the hatch, slipped the Walther into his hand, and then turned the handle and started down the steps into the main cabin. Damien, at the kitchen table, looked up. "Hi, Dad," he said, and then noticed the gun.

"Is everything all right?" Cody asked.

"Yeah, fine."

"What the hell is the boat doing here?" Cody asked with some impatience.

"I got to thinking about what you'd said about people looking for us," Damien explained. "I thought it might be harder for them to find us if we weren't where we were supposed to be. "

"I thought it was a good idea," McCabe interjected.

"It was," Cody admitted after a moment, offering his son a smile. "Sorry for growling at you."

"That's all right," his son replied. "Patrick was supposed to keep an eye out for you and let you know."

"He must have forgotten," Cody said, holstering his gun. "He seemed preoccupied with the princess's space aliens. By the way, how is she?"

"She's watching TV," McCabe reported. "She's gone through the best part of that bottle of vodka."

"Not to mention the wine," Damien added with a smile.

"Is your friend going to be able to keep her for a while?" Cody asked the reporter.

McCabe nodded. "She wasn't real happy about it, but then I promised her that the pleasures of my body would follow," he concluded with a heavy sigh.

"Time to go?" Damien asked.

"Yeah," Cody answered.

"I'll get the bag I packed," Damien said, and took off down the corridor.

"What happened with Griffin Brown?" McCabe wanted to know.

"A lot," Cody answered. "It was a little like being in a wartime bunker. Right now, if he hasn't done so already, he and his men are doing their best to kill Wang and his men.

"Crikey, a bloody shoot-out," McCabe said, his reporter's instincts coming alive.

Cody smiled. "Sorry, he didn't give me an address."

Damien returned now with a packed duffel bag. "We should have enough clothes for a couple of days in here."

"I guess that's my cue for getting the princess," McCabe said with a slightly weary grin. "Where will I find you, once I've dropped her off?"

"There's a hotel in Bondi Beach, lobby fronts on the plaza," Cody told him.

"I'll find it," the reporter said, starting down the corridor toward the sound of the television.

Cody turned to his son. "Once we go back up I want you to take the bag and go find your brother in the shops. I'm going to move this back to our own pen."

Damien looked hurt. "I'm sorry if I did the wrong thing."

"You didn't do the wrong thing," Cody assured him. "You did the smart thing. I should have thought of it too."

"Then why move it back?" the boy asked. "The people who own this pen are going to be gone for a week."

"Because once we're all off safely," Cody explained, "if somebody does come after us, it could be to our advantage to let him think he's found us."

From down the corridor they heard Jill's emphatic, slurred "I don't want to go anywhere!"

In the moments that followed, McCabe must have told her something to the effect that it was very likely the people who wanted to kill her would soon know she was on this boat, for the next words they heard were her bellowing. "Shit, shiiiit!"

A minute or so later she emerged, trying to look sober and wearing a pair of Patrick's cutoff jeans, one of Damien's sweatshirts, and a blond, shoulder-length wig that McCabe had brought back with him. When she saw Cody she started crying. "I'm sorry," she said, moving to him. "I'm sorry."

He held on to her. "It's all right," he said.

But she kept crying, her cheek against his chest. "I'm no good. I've never been any good. I wrecked Tommy's life and he was your friend."

"You didn't wreck Tommy's life. He loved you."

"Noooo," she wailed.

"He loved you or he wouldn't have stayed with you."

She pulled back and spoke as if accusing him. "My father tried to kill me when I was two years old.

He broke six of my ribs and gave me a skull fracture, and when I lived he said he never wanted to see me again. How can anyone love me?"

Cody looked at her a moment before speaking softly. "Your father was a fool. Everyone deserves love, and people caring for them. Tommy loved you."

She looked away from him for several moments and then said. "You don't know." Then she turned to McCabe. "I need a drink."

"Sure," McCabe promised. "As soon as we get there."

She accepted his provision and moved for the steps.

"Let me go first," Cody said, moving past them and up.

He emerged on deck and surveyed the area. There was still nothing he could pinpoint that could cause alarm.

"Come on."

McCabe and Jill followed up. She had some diffi-culty moving from the boat to the jetty, but with Damien's steadying her on one side and McCabe on the other, she made it. Then together the reporter and the new blonde weaved away.

"Can I get the lines for you?" Damien asked.

"Please," his father answered.

The boy smiled, picked up the canvas bag filled with their clothes and threw it onto the jetty, then hopped over to it himself and started to release the lines. All the while Cody's eyes searched the marina for any possible danger. But still there was none.

Moving the boat back to their assigned pen went without incident, though Cody couldn't shake his sense of uneasiness.

54

As it turned out, the best spot to watch the boat and anyone who approached it was from the fish-and-chips restaurant/bar on the main pier. It was nearing dinnertime and the place was fairly crowded, but as most of the customers were waiting for take-away food, a good number of the tables were empty. The Codys settled at a small one next to the window.

Cody knew he couldn't wait long.

"I'll be all right, Dad," Damien insisted again.

Again Cody thought of the vision of his son on fire, and again, as he had a thousand times before, he cursed the "gift" the nine-year-old bullet in his head had brought him. He knew that he could never be completely sure of the images he saw, whether they were scraps of what was or what might be. And even more he believed what the experts had warned him about from the beginning: That if what he "saw" had to do with a person close to him, the love and anxiety could invent its own visions. He was afraid for his son, but he knew that if Damien took precautions he would not be in danger.

"Promise me – no matter what happens or what you see – you won't go back to the boat," Cody insisted.

"I promise," Damien smiled. "I'm just as anxious as anyone to stay alive."

They sat for another edgy five minutes, in which Patrick managed to consume a jumbo order of fries, before the cab arrived.

"I'll be back in a couple of hours," Cody promised.

"Take your time; I'll be here," the eighteen-year-old assured him easily.

* * *

First stop was the shopping area in Double Bay, a combination, it seemed to Cody, of Westwood Village and Rodeo Drive. The streets were tree lined and gently curved, and the shops themselves all very upscale, with sidewalk cafes and, naturally, valet parking for the trendier spots.

"You know what they say about Double Bay," the cabby offered with a grin. "Double Bay, double pay."

He knew where the Fun House was, a large toy store, apparently somewhat famous. It was also, at six-twenty on a Saturday evening, closed. A sign in the window announced that it would reopen tomorrow morning at ten-thirty.

The cabby blanked on Hart's and Bailey's Chemist, the other two stores listed on Nicholas Brown's credit-card bill. Cody left Patrick in the cab and went exploring.

The chemist shop turned out to be half a block down. It too was closed, but a sign on its front door also promised that it would be open tomorrow, but in this case from noon to six.

Hart's he finally found in an atriumlike shopping mall at the end of the street. It was a candy shop, and it was open. He asked for the manager and got the owner, a tall, thin man with wiry salt-and-pepper hair and a toothbrush mustache from several decades ago.

"What can I do for you?"

Cody told him that he was working with Griffin Brown, helping him to find his missing son, Nicholas. The invocation of Brown's name had the effect Cody had hoped for. The owner's words stumbled over each other, trying to help.

"Well, I don't know what I could do, but anything. . . certainly. . . that would help. I just don't see. . ."

Cody interrupted by showing him the credit-card bill. "It's about this purchase he made on the nineteenth of November."

The tall man, jittery now, put on his glasses and studied the piece of paper, searching his memory. "Oh, yes, yes, I think I remember that. It was quite a big purchase, even for him. He just about bought us out of all our turtles, if I remember right." He turned and called to a short, pleasant-looking woman. "Lorraine?" She looked up and he moved over to her. After a brief but animated conversation, the tall man returned. "Just as I thought: Young Mr. Brown came in and bought thirty-two boxes of chocolate turtles and some loose candy that he ate while my wife was wrapping the boxes."

"All thirty-two?" Cody asked.

"Oh, yes," Lorraine said. She had abandoned her customer and come over to join them. "He made me go over to the stationer's and get six different kinds of wrapping paper, because he said he wanted them to be surprises. It seemed kind of silly – I mean, they were all the same size. But then Nicholas has always been kind of funny that way."

The tall, thin man saw his life flash before him. "My wife means funny in a cute way. We always look forward to Nicholas's visits; he's been coming in here since he was a little fella." He turned toward his wife. "This gentleman," he said with a smile through gritted teeth, "is a *friend* of Nicholas's father."

"Oh," she said. "I didn't mean any disrespect. Nicholas is a wonderful young man."

"If there's some problem about him buying so much candy at once, we'll be happy to take any back," the tall man said.

"Do you know who he was buying the candy for?" Cody asked.

Husband and wife looked at each other, and then both said No.

"I asked him," she added. "But all he would say was that they were surprises. He seemed quite happy about it. But knowing Nicholas, they could all have been for him. Like I say, he had a funny sense of humor that way, and chocolate turtles were always his favorite."

Cody considered a moment. "Do you remember who was with him that day?"

They both seemed concerned about not having the proper information. "He was alone, as far as I know," she said.

"But Nicholas doesn't drive. He certainly wasn't going to carry all of those boxes on foot," Cody suggested.

"He had me call him a cab. I remember now. He stayed in here until it came," the man with the tooth-brush mustache said. "He did that sometimes – take cabs, I mean. Other times his mother's driver would pick him up, and a lot of the time it would be his big brother Kevin."

* * *

Twilight was settling when the cab dropped Cody and Patrick off at the plaza in Bondi Beach. They registered at the hotel. He asked for a room looking north. It was on the fourth floor and had a view of the ocean to the east and the burned-out shell of the disco to the north.

Patrick had landed on the bed and was watching television as Cody poured himself a couple of fingers of vodka to which he added some ice cubes. Slowly, he moved to the window. The uneasy feeling was still with him, nagging at him. Something was going to happen, or there was something he had failed to do.

The deep purple shadows of the evening stretched across Bondi Beach. The ocean was only a dark form now, contrasted against a slightly lighter sky. A pair of tiny silhouettes of surfers bobbed on the horizon. He thought about the dark forces at war in this city and wondered which of them were still alive. Would it matter, when it was all done, who had killed Tommy Creager? Would the murderer already be dead? It *would* matter, Cody knew. Finding out who killed Tommy and why would restore some dignity to his death and consequently to his life. He wouldn't have ended just being a piece of trash cast off by a world gone mad for greed and power.

Now Cody's eyes fixed on the ruins of the disco, and he found his mind going back to the fire a dozen or so years before at the amusement park, when six boys had died. The Mardi Gras fire. . . the Mardi Gras fire. And he knew it was only three more days until Mardi Gras again. Was that what nagged at him? Was that fire so many years ago somehow the key? And for a moment, just a moment, he thought he could hear it again: the gentle weeping, so sad, so desperate.

"Dad, look at this," Patrick said, bringing Cody's attention back to the present world.

On the television, the news was reporting another mass shooting. This time in a harborside mansion in Hunters Hill. A woman, three children, and a maid had been killed, but the police were not releasing the names until next of kin had been notified. The newscast managed to dovetail that crime scene into coverage of the shooting the night before at the Bayswater brothel. Patrick was caught off guard to see himself on the screen among the onlookers from this afternoon, as the news reader talked of rumors of a gang war erupting in Sydney.

"The guy's a regular genius," Cody said with a smile.

He left the boy and the room and went down to the plaza. The evening breeze was warm, the area not very crowded. It was the lull between daytime activity, dining and night life.

Cody made his way back to the burned-out disco, pulling back the same piece of plywood as before to make his way in. It took his eyes some time to adjust to the dark and make out the various lines of what was left of the building. But he didn't move. He just wanted to stand and see if there was anything here. Anything he could feel in the darkness. And again he had the feeling that there was more to happen, much more. And yet he felt he should *know* more. That there was something he was missing.

Something he should see. Pieces that could fit but didn't. Did he know enough? He couldn't be sure. And then suddenly he felt very cold and the high-pitched tone was coming back, louder and louder, and then everything was bright red, the high-pitched tone splitting his head, and then suddenly it gave way to Tina Turner singing and the sounds of the disco above, and for a moment he could see feet, the feet of two men pulling a body upstairs. The body that had been dead and cold. And then suddenly there had been flames again and the blond girl was there with her hair on fire and her face blistering, and then he could hear Damien. Damien was calling for him. He was there now, he was on fire. *Dad, help me, help me!*

"Oy!" the cop shouted.

It took Cody a moment, but then he was jarred back.

"What the hell are you doing in there?" the cop wanted to know.

"Nothing," Cody said, and he knew he had to get back to Rushcutters Bay as soon as possible. He tried to sound like a tourist. "I'm just staying in the hotel across the plaza. I had read all about this fire last week."

"You have some identification?"

The cop studied his passport, then sighed. "This is not a smart place to be, Mr. Cody. What's left of this building could fall down anytime."

"I won't do it again."

The cop handed back his passport. "Enjoy your stay in Sydney and try to stay out of places you shouldn't be in."

Cody thanked him, and the cop was on his way.

Back across the plaza now, he entered the lobby of the hotel and picked up one of the house phones. Patrick answered on the second ring.

"Hello?"

"Pat, this is Dad. I'm heading over to pick up your brother."

"He just called. He said he saw someone hanging around the boat."

"Pat, I want you to stay in the room until I get back," Cody said, trying to sound calm. "We'll have dinner then."

"I'm kind a hungry now," Patrick said. "I was wondering if I could, like, order a hamburger from room service, just to sort of tide me over."

Cody grinned. "It probably won't taste any good at all without french fries and a malt."

"Thanks, Dad," the boy said happily.

"Pat?

"Yeah?"

"I love you."

"I know. I love you too, Dad."

55

The cab made it to Rushcutters Bay in twelve and a half minutes–no traffic this time. Cody had him drive past the marina some fifty yards. He got out and stood for several moments until his eyes adjusted to the area, and then he started back for the marina buildings.

Damien was where he had expected him to be, just where he had left him, at the little table in the fish-and-chips restaurant. The place was crowded now. Voices were loud. A man at the bar had a wooden perchlike device stretched across his shoulders. Over his right shoulder sat a beautiful white cockatoo, and over his left a pair of slightly smaller pink-and-white cockatoos. The man, who had a straight brown-and-gray beard, was sturdy and stout. He was dressed like a mountain hiker and was apparently a regular in the place because no one seemed to pay particular attention to him or the birds. Occasionally someone would offer one of the birds a peanut or a chip. But the man with the beard never acknowledged or made eye contact with them.

"When I called the hotel," Damien said, "he was here, in the restaurant."

"The man who had been looking around the boat?" Cody asked.

"Yes. He was standing in line for fish and clips."

"What happened to him?"

"I thought he was going to sit down and eat," Damien explained "But he took the food out with him. He couldn't have left here more than fifteen, twenty minutes ago."

Cody considered. "Which means he could still be out there somewhere, eating his fish and chips and watching the boat. What did he look like?"

"Five-ten, five-eleven, maybe a hundred and seventy-five pounds. He looked trim, like he was in good shape. He had real silver-white hair, but he wasn't that old, maybe mid to late forties at most."

"That's the man who tried to kill Jill," Cody said. "And probably the man who killed Tommy, or he's very close to whoever did."

"What are you going to do?" Damien asked.

"That depends," Cody said. "Did he go aboard our boat?"

"No," his son answered. "It looked like he was going to once, but then the people on the next boat over came out on deck and he just kept moving down the jetty like he was looking for another boat."

Cody thought for some moments before speaking. "If he's out there, I can't let him get away."

"What are you going to do?" Damien asked again, this time with a hint of apprehension.

"With your help," Cody said, "we're going to set a trap for him."

* * *

The silver-haired man's hands were sticky; he hated that. He bundled up what was left of the fish and chips in the bag they'd come in and dumped them in the litter bin next to the bench he was sitting on in Rushcutters Bay Park. The park was pitch black, which made the viewing of the lighted marina quite easy. He considered going back to the restaurant to wash his hands, but decided against it. He didn't want to create anymore opportunities than necessary for people to remember that he was here. He sat back down on the bench and waited. His sticky hands were driving him crazy. As far as he could tell there was no one on the boat. His instinct was to leave and come back in the middle of the night and take care of it then, when everyone who lived on the boat would have returned. He had almost decided to do just that when he saw him. The man he had decided must be Cody. The man he had seen in front of Jill Edwards's house yesterday. He was on the jetty, moving for the boat. He was alone. No sign of the girl. Maybe she was on board asleep, he thought.

Then he decided it wouldn't matter. One sure kill would be better then none. He got up from the bench and moved off in the darkness in the direction of his car.

* * *

Cody paused as he neared the boat. It was quiet here. Most of the other boats on the jetty were dark. Across the way, on the next jetty over, a party was in progress on a pair of neighboring boats. He wanted to look around, scan the area, but he knew it was very possible that he was being watched, so he just climbed aboard and moved inside. He found himself the unopened bottle of vodka and poured himself a drink, then moved to the small window that he knew looked out on the marina buildings. As he had expected, he could see the large window of the fish-and-chips restaurant. He couldn't make out Damien himself, but he could see what he was look- ing for: the candles on the tables next to the window. Damien's was second to the left. He took out his Walther and checked it. There was nothing to to now but wait.

* * *

The man with the cockatoos on his shoulders was talking occasionally now in short, angry bursts directed at the voices in his head. "I didn't want to do it. Manny was the one. He ordered the horses taken in. It wasn't me, dammit, it wasn't me." Then minutes might pass before he'd erupt again. "Saigon, Saigon, Saigon, Saigon, Saigon. . . " But like the birds on his shoulders, no one seemed to pay particular attention. He was a regular. They were used to him.

Damien almost didn't see him. He was wearing a dark coat now, which blended into the night. It was only the silver-white hair that lifted him from being a gliding shadow. He was farther, much farther along than Damien had wanted him to be before being able to warn his father. In his haste in picking up the candle on his table, he knocked it over onto the floor. By the time Damien had retrieved the candle, the silver-haired man had vanished. The boy was nearing panic. Had he got his father enough warning? He got up now and did what he knew he wasn't supposed to do: He hurried outside. He knew the railing on the perimeter of the marina would give him a better view.

Cody saw the light from the fish-and-chips restaurant disappear. He finished his drink, picked up the Walther, and moved to what he thought would be the best position to receive company.

Fitzwilliam stood deliberately in a dark shadow not twenty yards from the Cody boat. The party on the next jetty over was getting noisy. That was good. Good for him. Most of the boats on this jetty seemed to be quiet. All out to dinner, he speculated, as he slipped the half-filled bottle out of his coat pocket. His hand checked again; the cloth wick was properly soaked. He moved now, closing the distance between the black shadow and the boat.

Damien saw him now, the wisp of silver hair moving from the dark into the lighted area near the boat. Was his father ready? He had to be. *He had to be*, the boy thought.

Cody heard the soft footstep above his head. He wondered what the man would do next. Would he sneak in? Burst in shooting? And then the smell of gasoline found his nostrils, and he knew. Christ, he knew, and he was moving.

The silver-haired man flipped his lighter, and the rag stuffed into the bottleneck burst into flame.

It took Damien only a moment to realize what was happening. "Noooo," he shouted, and started to run down the jetty.

The boy's far-off shout distracted Fitzwilliam only a moment, but now as he reached for the floor to move inside it was already opening. Cody was there with his gun in hand. The silver-haired man threw the bottle down, smashing it on the deck in front of the door, which now exploded into flames. Cody was thrown back and down the stairs, his hair on fire. He fired twice from his Walther as he fell, the second bullet creasing the scalp of the now fleeing silver-haired man.

Cody slapped the flames out of his hair, then grabbed the fire extinguisher and blasted its spray in front of him as he raced back up the steps. He reached the outside. His boat was on fire, but now he was worried about his son. He could hear Damien calling, "Dad, Dad!"

He dropped the fire extinguisher and jumped over onto the jetty.

The silver-haired man was running as fast as he could and cursing himself for walking into a trap. Who was coming at him, shouting? He was a boy, eighteen or nineteen, but Fitzwilliam didn't care. He reached into his other coat pocket and pulled out the second bottle he had prepared, struck the lighter, and as the cloth burst into flame threw it at the approaching feet of the teenager.

Cody was coming around the corner onto the jetty that led to the marina when suddenly he saw his son engulfed in flames.

Damien, a mix of fear and anger now, lowered his shoulder and plowed into the silver-haired man, sending them both into the water.

The silver-haired man gasped for air and swam for escape. Behind him now he could see Cody jumping into the water near his son.

"Damien, Damien!"

"I'm all right, Dad."

They moved to a piling and held on. He looked at his son; part of his eyebrow now missing. Cody touched it.

"A little singed around the edges," Cody said with a smile, flooded with relief that his son was alive.

"I'm okay. My hands aren't burned. My face feels okay, except for. . . " he dabbed at his eyebrow.

"You don't know how good I feel," Cody said. "I saw you on fire."

"I know," Damien answered. "I saw you coming around the corner just as he threw it."

"No," Cody explained. "Back in Bondi Beach, twice – once on the street, once in the burned-out disco – I saw you on fire."

"Oh shit," Damien said as he realized what his father meant. "You must have been scared for me."

His father nodded. "I never know what I see, you know."

"I know," the boy answered.

"All the time she was missing. I always thought your mom was alive. I am some great psychic, huh?"

Damien found a laugh. "I'm glad you were

wrong about me – well, not completely wrong. But I'm alive, even if I am all wet."

Cody smiled and hugged his son, and his son hugged back.

"You blokes okay down there?" a lean man with a concerned look called down.

"We're fine," Cody called back, as he and Damien made their way over to a ladder that brought them back up to the jetty.

People from neighboring boats and some from the twin parties had hurried over and put out the fire. The damage didn't look extensive, but daylight would tell more. When the police arrived, Cody told a convincing lie.

"I have no idea who he was. I was coming out on deck and he shouted something about being his best friend and then running away with his wife."

The story drew much amusement from those who were now gathered around, drinking their beer and wine and extending their party.

Cody showed the cops his passport, which confirmed that he'd only been in the country since early the day before, hardly enough time to become best friends with someone, let alone steal his wife. It all seemed a horrible mistake. Cody gave the cops a description of the man, which only vaguely resembled Fitzwilliam, and finally everyone started to relax. Even the cops took time to have a beer.

56

The phone call came a little before nine. Griffin Brown was sitting alone. In the dark, in his office. Old Joe tapped on the door and then entered.

"Don't you want some lights on?" Old Joe asked.

"It doesn' t matter," Brown said.

Old Joe switched on a tabletop lamp. It cast shadows through the room.

"Billy Junior just called from St. Vincent's," Old Joe said. "His dad is dead."

Griffin Brown sighed and looked up at Old Joe. Their eyes met and didn't move. They had both been Billy Packer's friends for thirty years.

57

Cody and Damien found enough dry clothes on the boat to change into. They couldn't know for sure how far the silver-haired man had fled. . . or if he was done with them for the night or still somewhere out there in the dark.

The cops were on their second beers at that boat two pens away when the Codys locked up theirs and headed down the jetty. They called a cab from the fish-and-chips restaurant and had to wait almost fifteen minutes for it to arrive. Cody used part of the time to slip outside and into the shadows. He studied the area around the marina, detecting no sign of the silver-haired man. But he knew he couldn't be sure.

The silver-haired man watched from behind the wheel of his car as the cab pulled up in front of the restaurant and Cody and his son got in. He let the cab pull away and get a good block farther on before he pulled out and started to follow it, his own headlights off. Once in the flow of three-lane traffic each way, Fitzwilliam turned the headlights on. He let the cab stay a block or so ahead of him. New South

Head Road had become William Street now, and they were headed for the heart of the city. The Saturday night traffic was heavy.

The Codys were passing Hyde Park when Damien said, "I thought we were staying at the beach."

"We are," Cody answered.

"But isn't this the wrong way?"

"It's a long way," he said, glancing out the rear window again. "But a safe way, just in case we're being followed. The next time we meet the white-haired man, I want it to be on our terms."

* * *

"Shit," Fitzwilliam said as the light ahead of him changed. If he had had the chance he would have run it, but there were two other cars ahead of him that had already stopped. He watched as best he could as the cab moved three, then four blocks ahead. "Come on!" he shouted to himself. The light finally turned green. Fitzwilliam hit his horn, and the cars in front started to move. Christ, the cab was turning. He weaved sharply to get around a slower car. A car behind him honked its horn. "Stuff yourself, mate!" he shouted, then weaved again and stomped on the gas pedal. He crossed over the double lines, into the lanes meant for oncoming traffic. Horns were sounding all around him now. A truck was coming straight at him, and as he swerved back into his own lane he could hear and feel metal scraping and bending. The car he'd pushed into careened into the next lane, crashing into the car there. Both those vehicles now spun out toward a crowd of pedestrians collected on a corner, who began to scream and run. But Fitzwilliam's attention was riveted on finding the cab with Cody in it. He finally reached George Street, where the cab had turned. The light had just turned red, but this time he wasn't about to wait. As he raced into the intersection, the cars who had the green light had to hit their brakes to avoid him. But for what? Now that he was on George Street in the thick of traffic, at least forty cabs cluttered his field of vision. They were clustered in front of Town Hall Station, in front of the huge, multiscreened Cineplexes. Not only was he lost, he realized that was precisely why Cody had led him here. And he knew then that Cody was a man he had to respect.

* * *

From platform 12 at Town Hall Station they caught the train to Bondi Junction, and from there they walked up a block to the cab rank near the open-air shopping mall across from the local McDonald's. Five minutes later they were back in Bondi Beach. It was a little past nine-thirty, the sidewalks, restaurants, and shops crowded with happy Saturday-nighters enjoying the balmy evening air.

McCabe was watching TV in the lobby of the hotel when they arrived. He rose with a squint grin. "I was waiting for you upstairs, but in the presence of my scintillating company, your twelve-year-old son fell asleep."

Cody laughed. "Well, so much for that crap about youth being the fountain of truth and wisdom, eh?"

McCabe smiled. "I couldn't agree with you more. Anything happen back at the boat?"

"Oh, we had a bit of a hair-raising experience," Cody said, gently brushing Damien's singed eyebrow. "But let Damien fill you in. What I'd like you guys to do is get us a table at that restaurant around the corner. I'd like one on the sidewalk – even if we have to wait or slip the waiter twenty bucks."

"You going to get Pat?" Damien asked.

Cody nodded. "We're going to need his help – yours and his – tonight. We'll be down as soon as I've made a phone call."

"We'll see you at the restaurant," McCabe said, and they went their separate ways.

Patrick was still asleep on the bed, facing the television, when Cody came in. Deciding to give the boy a few extra minutes of rest, he moved to the canvas bag with their belongings, found Tommy Creager's address book, and sat down by the phone.

58

She had all the candles lit, over thirty of them. One for each of her plaster saints. She was lying on her light blue velvet chaise lounge, the same light blue color of Mary's veil. She had fallen asleep after dinner, eaten in her room, squab and fresh-cooked carrots and rice. She had been hungry, since she had missed lunch today. She had so much wanted to go to Doyle's for lunch, and now she had forgotten why she hadn't. Her head was fuzzy and hurt a little, and the phone kept on ringing and ringing and ringing and wouldn't stop.

"Helloooo?" she answered finally, sipping from her glass of gin.

"Mrs. Brown?"

"Yes. Who is this?"

"My name is Ed Cody. I was a friend of Tommy Creager's."

"Ooooh, Tommy," she said with a hint of melancholy. "He was such a nice man." And as she said it the flickering candles seemed to dance as if his spirit had come in with the soft, warm breeze from the harbor, and so she laughed. "He could always make me laugh."

"Tommy told me about all the good times you had together. Out on the yacht and at Doyle's and other restaurants."

"We had woooonderful times," she cooed. "He was a very good talker, you know. And a very good listener."

"I know," Cody said. "I also know Tommy was very concerned about Nicholas."

She didn't speak for some moments, and when she did it was with a sadness. "He was always very kind to Nicholas."

"Nicholas loves you very much," the baby Jesus said.

"I know, my Lord," she smiled.

"He likes so much to run and play like all boys do," Saint John Bosco said.

"Yes, yes, but he can get into his share of trouble," she reminded him with a laugh.

Cody didn't know who she was talking to, but he didn't want to lose her. "Mrs. Brown, I want to bring Nicholas home."

"Oh," she said with surprise and hope. "Is he with you?"

"No," Cody answered. "But wherever he is, I think he's very sad. With your help I think I can find him, I can bring him back to you."

"How can I help you?" she asked like a little girl.

"I'd like to meet you somewhere tomorrow," Cody said. "We can have a drink to Tommy and then I'll ask you some questions about Nicholas."

"I don't know where he is," she said.

"I know. That doesn't matter," Cody assured her. "With what Tommy told me and what I've learned myself, I feel that if you'll talk to me I'll be able to find him."

"And bring him home safe?" she asked, almost afraid of the answer.

"Yes. And bring him home safe," Cody promised. "Tomorrow, should I come to your house?"

"No," she said emphatically. She was losing her nerve. She didn't know what to do. She looked to her forest of candles and saints.

"This could be what we have been waiting for," Saint Joseph said.

"Trust him," young Jesus said. "Trust him."

"Tell me your name again," she said.

"Cody. Ed Cody."

The statues nodded. It was a good name.

"Then I will meet you, Mr. Cody," she said. "Tomorrow, at Doyle's on the Beach. I'll make a reservation for us for twelve-thirty. It will be a woooonderful table. It'll be a wonderful day."

"Until tomorrow, then, Mrs. Brown," Cody said.

"Until tomorrow, Mr. Cody. God bless you. My saints are all praying for you."

She was almost afraid to break the connection, but the the other end went dead.

"Mr. Cody said that Nicholas was very sad," she said. "When he comes home we'll make him very happy. We'll have a wonderful party for him. We'll have a week of parties for him!" She beamed, and the saints seemed to think that that was a good idea, and so as if to celebrate she finished her glass of gin and poured another, but then frowned. She'd have to ring for more ice.

* * *

Cody shook his son gently and Patrick opened his eyes.

"Hi," Cody said.

"Hi," the boy returned.

"You going to make it?"

Patrick sat up, widening his eyes to more fully wake himself up. "That depends on what's in it for me," he grinned. "Like what's for dinner?"

* * *

It was a little after ten by the time dinner was served at their table on the sidewalk. They had, of course, no way of knowing, but it was in fact the same table the silver-haired man had occupied eight nights earlier.

The late Saturday night crowds were beginning to thin now. Happy faces, drunken faces. Kids in their early teens and younger openly drank beer on the sidewalks.

Patrick, despite the hamburger, fries, and malt he'd consumed from room service, had ordered shrimp cocktail, a plate of John Dory, and fries, plus inhaled his fair share of the community Greek Salad and garlic bread. Cody and Damien had settled on just the John Dory and fries. McCabe had opted for orange roughy, proclaiming that it was a nationalistic choice, since of course the best orange roughy was to be found only in New Zealand waters.

"Besides," he said. "My ex-wife once tried to kill me because of John Dory. She served it with a sauce of hot Kahlua at a dinner party one night. It was the most god-awful taste experience I'd ever had. My crime, of course, was loudly blurting my opinion at the table. Now before you think I'm a complete rotter, I must admit that I was rather well into the scotch. . . which in any court of law in the world would be considered a mitigating circumstance. Unfortunately, my wife didn't see it that way. She threw an iron at my head after all the guests had gone." He squinted a grin toward the boys. "But God and the wheels of justice turn in mysterious ways. I got immediate revenge you see; I ducked, and the iron whizzed over my head and went crashing into our – soon to be her – best china."

"That boy," Cody said, looking beyond the conversation. "Him and his friends."

The others turned their attention to the sidewalk, where they saw the nine- or ten-year-old boy in the blue jersey with half a dozen other street kids. They were all smoking and had beers.

"You want us to go now?" Patrick asked.

"If we wait for you to have dessert, you won't be able to move," Damien said to his younger brother.

"Boys," Cody said to his sons, who were on their feet now. "Be careful: Don't go too far from the lights. Don't let them isolate you."

"We'll be fine, Dad," Damien said, and then they were gone, onto the sidewalk, drifting purposefully in the direction the street kids had taken.

* * *

For the next half hour, Damien and Patrick loosely followed the band of street boys. They seemed to move almost aimlessly, drinking beer, laughing, smoking. . . and begging. A lean, dark-haired boy appeared to be in charge. The brothers overheard one of the kids call him Brian. The blond in the blue jersey was the youngest and smallest of the group, and probably because of this was the star beggar. He was also, apparently, the favorite, always received with warm congratulations and a drink of beer when he returned with his money, or else with comfort if he had been turned down rudely. The little family of street kids floated back and forth on the block-long walkway that fronted most of the shops and restaurants, roaming from time to time into the plaza. Once a pair of policemen walked through the plaza and the kids scattered in several directions. It was some minutes later before Damien and Patrick found them again. They had joined up in frout of the pancake restaurant on the next corner over, no doubt a predetermined location.

* * *

"Hi," Patrick said as he sat down opposite Brian on a bench at a public eating table in the plaza. Brian and a couple of the street kits were sitting there while the blond boy and several others of the group begged from a large party that had just emerged from the restaurant across the way. Damien moved up behind his brother. Brian and the others looked skittish, as if they were about to run.

"We're not cops," Damien said. "Unless you've ever seen a twelve-year-old cop."

"I'm going to be thirteen on Tuesday," Patrick interjected for the sake of his own dignity.

"What do you want?" Brian asked.

"Just to talk," Damien said. "We've been watching you guys for a little while. You look like you do pretty well for yourselves. You really know this area."

"You're Yanks, aren't you?" a boy with black curly hair asked.

"Yeah," Patrick said. "We came in to Sydney yesterday on our boat."

"Yeah, sure," another said with skepticism.

"No, it's true." Damien found his wallet and from it pulled a photograph of the family standing on deck. They were younger then, by a couple of years, and he didn't realize until he had taken the picture out that his mother was in it. "We're down at Rushcutters Bay. . . we're sailing around the world."

"You and your mum and dad?" one of them asked.

"My mom's dead," Patrick said.

The blond boy in the blue jersey came back now, eying the strangers warily and handing Brian a fistful of change.

"My dad used to be a cop in Los Angeles," Damien explained. "He says that if you ever want to know something about a place, you ask the kids who live there, because it's their whole lives, they know everything about it. I bet there isn't anyone who knows more about Bondi Beach than you guys."

"You got that right," the boy with black curly hair said.

Brian took a pull of his beer. "What do you want?"

"Something you guys might have seen that nobody else would have," Damien said.

"Like what?"

"Who might have started the disco fire."

"Let's go," Brian said to his group, and they started to move.

"Wait," Patrick said, moving along with them. "My dad's not a cop now and he won't tell anything to the cops that you tell him. He'll even pay you money."

Brian paused. "If he's not a cop, why does he care?"

"Because a man who used to be my dad's best friend got killed," Damien said. "My dad thinks that the same people who did that could have been the ones who firebombed the disco."

"He thinks the guy who started the fire carried a can of gasoline down that alley back there," Patrick said.

Brian darted a look to the others.

"And since people live in that alley, maybe there was someone who saw him. . . . My Dad said he knew you guys had a tough time of it, having to live on the streets. He said he'd give you fifty dollars if you helped."

The dollar amount sparked interest.

Brian considered and then glanced at the little blond boy in the blue jersey before turning his attention back to Damien and Patrick. "We have to talk."

"Okay," Damien agreed.

Brian and his troop moved some twenty feet away and had an animated conversation, a good deal of which focused on the small blond boy. Several glances were directed back to Patrick and Damien. Finally Brian returned.

"A hundred dollars and a case of beer," he announced.

"I'll see what I can do," Damien said. "You'll be here?"

"No," the dark-haired street boy answered. "See that building across the street?"

Damien and Patrick turned and looked at the public showers and dressing rooms that fronted on the beach. The building was dark now; the area around it deserted

"We see it," Damien answered.

"Who's coming back with the money and the beer?" Brian wanted to know.

"It'll be my dad," Damien answered.

"I'll be able to tell if he's coming alone, or if there's any cops," Brian stated. "If there are, you guys won't see any of us again."

"He'll be alone," Damien promised.

Brian considered a moment. "No. Not all alone. I want him to come along," he said, indicating Patrick.

"Why?"

"Because your father's less likely to try something tricky if his kid's along," Brian stated.

"I'll tell him."

"Fifteen minutes. I'm not waiting." The street-boys' leader turned and hurried off with the others.

59

It was 11:20 p.m. when the Australian Airline jet
touched down in New South Wales, but by the time
it had moved only halfway down the Coolengatta
Airport runway it had crossed over into the state of
Queensland. This was, at least airline-wise, the
entrance to the Gold Coast. Five hundred miles from
Sydney, a thousand miles from Melbourne:
Australia's favorite resort, with its dozens of world-
class hotels, miles of beautiful beaches, and, in
places, a surf that caused part of it to be named
Surfers Paradise. As if that weren't enough, there
was also a casino, racetracks, a movie studio, and the
largest amusement parks in the country – none of
which was why the man waiting next to the Lear jet
had come here. A large white truck pulled up near
him now. The driver leaned out.

"I'm looking for a man who needs some soccer
balls."

"You've just found him," the man replied.

"Then you have something for me?" the driver
asked.

The man moved out of the shadows of the jet and
crossed to the truck. He handed a large envelope up
to the driver. The driver opened it and saw that it
was filled with hundred-dollar bills.

"Okay," the driver said and smiled. "Let's play
ball, mate. "

And in the minutes that followed the driver and
the man who paid him along with the pilot moved
the six large cases of soccer balls from the truck over
to the Lear jet.

The Lear jet would leave Coolengatta six and a half hours later, with the first hint of day. The body of the driver wouldn't be found for another three days. By then it would be floating in a residential canal in the community of Mermaid Waters.

60

Brian watched the man and the boy cross Campbell Parade. The man was carrying what looked to be a case of beer. No one else seemed to be following them. They crossed over into the parking lot, past the handful of cars that were left here at this late hour, and then strode onto the esplanade. Brian slipped back into the darkness.

"Brian," Patrick called, as they reached the building. "Brian, are you here?"

"I'm here," came an answer, and Brian stepped out of the shadows about ten paces away. He was standing on a tile bench that backed against a four-foot stucco wall which separated the esplanade from the beach.

"This is my dad," Patrick said.

Brian considered. "Throw me a beer."

Cody pulled the cardboard box open, took out a can and tossed it to the boy.

Brian smiled. "At least you didn't get light beer. I thought you'd get that light shit."

"I can't stand it myself," Cody said. "Mind if I have one?"

"No, go ahead," Brian said.

Cody opened a beer for himself. Brian seemed to relax and sat on the wall, putting his beer down and lighting a cigarette.

"I don't suppose I could have a beer?" Patrick said rather sheepishly.

Both Cody and Brian glanced at him and nearly smiled, and then Cody looked to the boy sitting on the wall.

"It's okay with me, if it's okay with your old man," the leader of the street boys shrugged with some amusement.

Cody considered. "You can have one."

"Thanks," Patrick beamed, proceeding to help himself.

"What do you want?" Brian asked Cody.

"I think the boys told you," Cody answered. "If anyone around here knows what happened the night of the fire it would be you kids."

"We know something. We can't be sure we're right, though."

"That's okay," Cody told him. "The beer and the money is for whatever you and your friends know, whether it helps me or not."

Brian took a long drag from his cigarette. "And no cops and nobody will ever know who told you."

"That's right," Cody agreed.

"My dad wouldn't lie to you," Patrick added.

Brian considered and then talked into the darkness. "Gordy, go get Colin."

Footsteps moved off in the night now. Patrick thought he caught a glimpse of the boy with blond curly hair.

"It'll only be a couple of minutes," Brian said.

"Mind if we sit down?" Cody asked, indicating the bench and wall area that Brian was occupying.

"No. It's okay," the boy said.

"You'll want this," Cody said as he got to the bench and handed him five folded twenty-dollar bills.

Brian took the money without comment. Cody sat down on the bench. Patrick sat on the wall, near Brian. No one spoke for almost a minute. Patrick sipped his beer for the fifth time. "This sure is good beer."

"You drink beer a lot?" Brian asked.

"No," Patrick admitted.

Some more moments passed before Brian asked, "How come you're sailing around the world?"

"It's just something we always wanted to do, since the boys were little," Cody said. "Finally a couple of years ago we sold our house and bought the boat. It's a fifty-six-foot ketch. You do any sailing?"

"My dad used to take me when I was little," Brian said. "But he and my mum got divorced. He lives in Perth now."

"Doesn't your mom worry about you, living on the streets?" Patrick asked.

"She's dead, like your mum," Brian said.

Cody found himself tensing. He hadn't known his boys had spoken of their mother to the street children.

"I'm sorry," Patrick said.

"She was killed in a motorcycle accident. Her and her boyfriend," Brian related in a monotone. Then he finished his beer in one long pull and threw the can off behind him into the sand. "How'd your mum die?" he asked.

Cody wanted to get up and run and take his son with him. He didn't want his boy to endure the hurt of talking about it all again. . . and then he was surprised to realize that Patrick was all right. "She was killed by a crazy guy," he said.

"That's bad," Brian said, surprised by Patrick's answer.

"Yeah, it was," Patrick went on. "We didn't even know where she was, whether she was alive or dead, for almost five months. Then the cops caught this guy. He'd killed eleven other women."

Brian was shaken by the account. "That's got to be hard for you."

"It's okay," Patrick said. "I still have my dad and my brother."

Gordy reappeared with the small blond boy.

"Colin, get us some beers," Brian said.

The blond boy spotted the case of beer and fetched one for himself, Gordy, and Brian, tossing the other two boys their cans.

"This is Colin," Brian said, indicating the blond boy. "He's the one who saw the guy. At least we think he was the guy."

"What guy?" Cody asked.

"Tell him," Brian said.

"He was a white-haired guy," the small blond boy said, popping his beer. Some of it sprayed out and he giggled, already mildly drunk.

"White haired," Cody repeated and felt a certain sense of elation, the young, freckle-faced, slightly drunk boy had finally provided a physical link between the disco fire and the attempts on Jill Edwards's life, his and Damien's lives, and most important, Tommy Creager's murder.

"Yeah," the blond boy went on. "You know, like that guy on *Mission Impossible*. I just asked him for a dollar and he gave me twenty."

"Colin was afraid this guy wanted to have sex with him," Brian said. "So we just kind a kept an eye on him for the rest of the night. He was acting kind of weird."

"How do you mean?" Cody asked.

Brian shrugged. "He just kept hanging around for a long time. . . over here on the esplanade, you know, like in the dark where he thought no one could see him. It was like he was just waiting for someone to come over or he was watching the disco. Then around one o'clock the guy leaves. That's the last *we* saw of him."

"But then somebody else did?"

"Yeah, we think so," the dark-haired boy said. "What you have to know is, we don't live in the alley. That can get rough. We're just trying to stay alive. But Spaceman, he lives in the alley. He says he saw a guy with white hair with two petro cans real late at night, heading toward the disco. Spaceman said he had taken some bad stuff and he was just like done in. He was trying to lie down because he was afraid to be up and moving. That's when he saw this guy coming down the alley with the petro cans."

"Anything else?" Cody asked.

"That's all," Brian said.

"How about you, Colin?" Cody asked. "Can you remember anything else?"

"He asked me what my name was," the small blond boy said. "I told him Colin. . . and he said that was a good name, that it was his name."

"Did he say anything else?" Cody asked.

Colin thought and then shrugged. "He said I should take care of myself."

61

Cody slept fitfully, and when sleep did come it was filled with dreams of fire. Sometimes it was the disco burning. Other times it was a surrealistic amusement park, and he could hear the screams and the desperate fists pounding against locked doors. Just before dawn he drifted off again, but this time it was the sound of the soft, sad, desperate weeping that found and woke him.

He rose at first light and dressed, then left his sleeping sons in the hotel room. Outside the temperature was already pleasant. The sky, for the most part, was clear and early morning pale blue. To the northeast, however, he saw dark storm clouds beginning to cover the horizon, and he knew that rain wouldn't be far away. Except for an occasional jogger he was seemingly alone in Bondi Beach. He walked past the burned-out disco, but it held no interest for him today. When he crossed Campbell Parade and moved to the esplanade where a few hours before he had met with the street boys, he paused and stared out at the Pacific. He wondered where they were, where they slept. . . and why children anywhere would have to live in the streets.

62

The Lear jet touched down a few minutes past 7:00 a.m. Fitzwilliam was there to meet it. When the plane finally taxied to a stop, the door opened and the man he worked for emerged, smiling, and gave him a thumbs-up. But the silver-haired man didn't smile back.

"What's wrong?" the other man asked as he reached him.

"Everything's just bloody mad," Fitzwilliam said. "Have you seen the news about Wang and the bloody fucking massacres?"

The other man relaxed. "It had to be done."

"You knew about it?" Fitzwilliam asked, caught off guard.

The other man nodded. "It became necessary. As you know, we had expected a full retaliation against Wang for the Bayswater shooting. But the old shit was too smart for that; he decided to buy time until the delivery was made. He ordered Jacklan to make up a phoney confession from one of the shooters implicating Wang, and then arrest him. We couldn't let that happen."

"You could have told me, for Christ's sake," Fitzwilliam said.

"You were asleep," the other smiled. "And last night when I talked to you I was about to fly out and we had other problems; it just went out of my head. And besides, we didn't need you for Wang."

A large panel truck had pulled up alongside the jet, and soon the cases of soccer balls were being transferred to the bed of the truck.

"Who did it, then?" Fitzwilliam asked.

"One of Wang's bodyguards, a man named Li. He's been on our payroll for almost a year. Once they were in their safe house, he killed his boss and whoever else was there. Then sat down and waited for Jacklan, who eventually showed up and killed him." He smiled. "See, neat as pie. Now Wang's out of the way, which is something I wanted to do later on anyway – and most important, all the police attention is centered back on the Cowboy Club and Griffin Brown, just the way we wanted it."

"You really hate the son of a bitch, don't you?" Fitzwilliam asked.

"For a long, long time," he said, and then asked,

"What about that other business we had? Did you take care of Cody and the girl?"

"No," Fitzwilliam admitted. "I made a run at him. But whoever he is, the guy's a pro. He was waiting for me."

"What do you mean, waiting for you?"

"I think the only reason he went back to the boat was because he knew I'd make a move," the silver-haired man said, displaying his scalp where Cody's bullet had greased it. "If I'm not mistaken, that was caused by a Walther."

The last of the crates were in place, and the driver gave a wave.

"What the bloody hell is Cody after?" the other exploded in frustration.

"We know that now too," Fitzwilliam said. "Gallagher has it on tape from when this guy went to the Cowboy Club to see no less than Mr. Griffin Brown."

"Holy shit. What for?"

"It turns out that Cody's best friend used to be Tommy Creager, and he wants to find out who killed him."

"Tommy bloody Creager. . . . Who could give a fuck if that rummy lived or died?"

"Apparently Cody does," Fitzwilliam said, and then added with some emphasis, "and somehow he's figured out that Creager's killing is connected to the disco fire and even Nicholas disappearing. He said on the tape that he thinks if he could find Nicholas he'd find out who killed Creager."

The other man was silent for some moments. When he spoke again, a cold calm had descended.

"Well, we can't let him do that, can we? Do you have any idea where Cody is now?"

"No," Fitzwilliam admitted.

"Do we have Jacklan looking for him yet?"

Fitzwilliam shook his head. "Jacklan's disappeared. Since yesterday afternoon. I just tried all his numbers again before you landed. . . he's nowhere."

"What about Gallagher? He should be able to help."

"Yeah," Fitzwilliam said, seeing the logic. "I reckon he could. I can't bloody stand the man myself. He's always either winging about his family life or sticking the white shit up his nose."

"His neverending appetite for white shit up his nose," the other man smiled, "is what has inspired him to be so helpful to us for the last six months. Get hold of him; have him meet us in Balmain in an hour. We have to find Cody."

63

Kevin Madden heard the splash in the distance and looked up from his Agatha Christie paperback. He was sitting on a camp stool in the bush, surrounded by gum trees, about six miles outside of Adelaide. He picked up his binoculars and looked down to the swimming pool a hundred and fifty yards away. It didn't take him long to spot the figure of a man swimming laps. He watched until he could be sure it was Horowitz. Then he put the binoculars back in their case, picked up his high-powered rifle, and sighted in on the back of the swimmer's head.

64

Damien found the local Catholic church. It was a few blocks over and was called St. Agnes. For Cody the mass brought with it a sense of Ann. He was sure it was the same for the boys. And the church also was a piece of home in its own way, a touchstone that didn't change, wherever they went in the world.

After mass, Patrick eagerly led the way to Pancakes at the Beach on Campbell Parade. It was a friendly place, with high-back wooden booths and all the Sunday newspapers laid out for their customers to read. The sight of the menu brought delight to the soon-to-be-thirteen-year-old's eyes. But then, talked out of the Big Stack With Ice Cream special, he settled on three pancakes, eggs, bacon, and a large glass of apple juice. Apparently concurring that that was a petite enough breakfast, Damien ordered the same. Cody laughed. "You guys eat like you're going to the electric chair." And the brothers smiled.

The Sunday papers were filled with accounts of the two mass shootings that wiped out Henry Wang and his family and associates. There were photographs of the Hunters Hill mansion, and then some more of the safe house where Wang himself had been found dead. Vague speculation in the papers referred to Hong Kong Triads being at war. And though the second and third pages covered the killings at Griffin Brown's Bayswater brothel, rumored to have been carried out by Asian hitmen, not one of the newspapers – because, as McCabe

would explain later, of Australia's rigid libel laws –
indulged in even the slightest speculation that all the
killings might be interrelated.

* * *

McCabe picked Cody and the boys up at ten. The
sky was already half covered with dark gray clouds,
and an occasional rumble of thunder could be heard
in the distance. Five minutes later, Damien and
Patrick were dropped off in Bondi Junction, where
they had learned from the paper there was a cinema
complex. When the boys were done with their outing, they would catch the bus back to the beach.

"You know the problem with New Zealand?"
McCabe asked with a squinty grin, after they had
dropped the boys off and were headed for Double
Bay. "If you want to go there, you have to call ahead
and see if we're going to be open."

"Is this your way of telling me you still don't
have the names of the deceased lady's children?"
Cody asked with a smile.

"Something like that," McCabe admitted. "It's
the weekend," he said, as if that explained everything. "In Auckland – and that's our biggest city –
the Sunday paper is printed Saturday morning, so
you can imagine what it's like in a little town like
Tauranga. But no worries. I got hold of a girl who
works in our city room, and the little darling is driving over to Tauranga as we speak. She'll root to the
bottom of it."

* * *

They had been waiting a few minutes when the Fun House toy store opened at ten-thirty. The clerk, whose name tag proclaimed him to be Uncle Stew, was short and squat with curly, bushy hair thinning at the top. Wearing a red-and-white stripped coat, he was suffering from a massive hangover and having a hard enough time remembering today, let alone a day back in November. Eventually the message that Griffin Brown would be very unhappy if he didn't cooperate made its way into his brain, and he lookd up the records.

Two shrieking, racing French children charged into the store with their mother. They didn't stop running or shrieking. Uncle Stew considered dying. He found the record of sale. It was five pages long and read like a catalog, each toy costing around thirty dollars.

"Do you remember anything about Nicholas Brown being here that day?" Cody asked.

One of the children let out a particularly nerve-splitting shriek.

"No," Uncle Stew said, wincing. "I was on vacation in November, which is where I wish to God I was now."

Cody looked through the receipts again. Thirty-five items in all, close to matching the thirty-two boxes of chocolate turtles, he thought. Whatever that meant.

"Can you tell from the handwriting who might have written up this sale?" Cody asked the bleary-eyed man.

Uncle Stew studied the papers again. "No. It could be Mary-Kate, or Carrie. . . or someone else.

That late in November is the beginning of our Christmas rush."

"Christmas," Cody said suddenly, as if something had clicked. "Can you tell if any of these were gift-wrapped?"

"If it has a check next to it, it was gift wrapped," Uncle Stew offered, as the screeching children and their mother approached the counter to make a purchase.

Cody reviewed the receipts one last time and then smiled.

"How many were gift-wrapped?" McCabe asked.

"Thirty-five," Cody answered. "Something's beginning to make sense; we just have to figure out what."

65

Gallagher parked on Waterview Street and walked the half block to the auto paint shop. It being Sunday, the store was closed. He pushed the bell and waited. After nearly two minutes the black man, Oliver, opened the door and let him in. Once he'd bolted it again, they traipsed through the actual paint shop to a metal wall, where Oliver unlocked another door that revealed the stairs leading to the second floor.

While the downstairs had been a musty, unkempt workplace, upstairs was a modern suite of rooms. In the first one Gallagher found the man he worked for, along will Fitzwilliam. Fitzwilliam was on the phone with a stack of directories in front of him. The other man was watching his fortune being made on the other side of a soundproof window. It was the clean room. Half a dozen surgically clad and masked workers were cutting open the soccer balls and extracting large plastic bags containing the white, powdery substance. Other workers were then opening the bags and refining and redistributing the merchandise to much smaller, marketable-sized bags.

"My God, you've actually pulled it off," Gallagher said with a burst of enthusiasm.

"Did you expect any less?" the other man said and smiled. Then his tone became serious. "Colin told me about this Cody paying a visit to the Cowboy Club."

"Yeah. . . Jesus," Gallagher said. "Talk about a monkey wrench being thrown into the works."

"It's a monkey wrench we can't afford," the man said. "We still have a couple of more days to get through before we pull this completely off. I want him eliminated, and we're going to need your help."

Gallagher stared at him for a moment, unsure. "What did you have in mind?"

"Cody and the girl and the reporter have apparently gone into hiding. The question is, where are they going to go? They must know we'll check any place known to the girl, and the other three are strangers. So my guess is quite simple: They've checked into a hotel."

Gallagher laughed nervously. "That makes sense."

"So, grab a phone book, Yank, and you and Colin keep calling hotels until you find the one your long-lost pal Cody and his sons checked into last night."

66

It began to rain lightly at noon. Cody and McCabe had found a small restaurant down the street from the Fun House and had sipped coffee for the better part of an hour while they tried to make sense of what they knew. Nicholas's thirty-two boxes of candy and thirty-two toy store presents were the subject of a good deal of the speculation, but to no end. Who was he buying the presents for? Were there two presents each for thirty-two people? Or one each for sixty-four? And who would these people be? It didn't seem likely that he would know thirty-two people of toy store age. Was he having a party? Was he going to a party? Did he make these purchases on the nineteenth because he knew he was disappearing the next day? Were the presents at his house? Or had they disappeared with him? There just wasn't enough information.

They decided that Cody would take a cab to Doyle's on the Beach, for his luncheon with Fiona. McCabe would stay here in Double Bay until Baily's Chemist opened.

* * *

It was pouring by the time the cab turned down the narrow street, next to the park in Watsons Bay. The sky was dark, and thunder rumbled across it. The cab came to a stop on the cul de sac that let out onto the pier. "That's it down there," the cabby said, pointing down the cement esplanade that circled gently with the sandy beach, around the bay. The restaurant, the only commercial enterprise to be seen, was some fifty yards down, and despite the pouring rain it had a double line of people waiting to get in.

A sudden booming thunder, followed almost immediately by a lightning flash, startled and sent several of the people in line scurrying away. The others, mostly with umbrellas, quickly closed ranks, lest the deserters try to return and reclaim their old positions. "I hope you have a reservation," the cabby said as Cody paid him.

Even though the esplanade was more than wide enough for a car, it was strictly for pedestrian traffic and was protected from the only street approach, here at the cul de sac, by three steel posts. Cody sprinted the fifty yards to the restaurant and was fairly well soaked by the time he reached its awning. The people waiting at the front of the line looked at him suspiciously. There were a dozen or so outdoor tables here, though only a few, closest to the building and away from the downpour, were occupied.

A waiter ignored him so he moved inside, where people were jammed at every table. Eventually he found someone who passed for a maitre d'. He had mutton-chop whiskers and wore half glasses. "I'm supposed to meet Mrs. Brown; she said she'd have a reservation."

"Mrs. Brown?" the man said blankly with the hint of a Scottish burr, shaking his head.

"Mrs. Griffin Brown," Cody clarified.

A change came over the man with the mutton chops. "Oh, yes sir, this way please," he said, ignoring the entreaties of a couple of waiters who apparently desperately needed his attention and leading Cody upstairs.

The tables in the second-floor dining room were just as crowded with the exception of the one that Cody was led to. It had been centered at the large window that overlooked the esplanade, beach, and bay. It was set for six and had a large vase off fresh flowers on it, an amenity none off the other restaurant tables enjoyed. Truly a table fit for a queen. Only she wasn't here yet – nor was anyone else, for that matter.

"You're the first to arrive, sir," the maitre d' said. "May I bring you a drink?"

"Finlandia, double, with a splash of soda," Cody ordered, as he took a chair that allowed him both a view of the room and a glimpse outside. Father Larry was the next to arrive, wearing his black suit with Roman collar and looking solemn. He found the table without direction

"You'd be Mr. Cody," the priest said as he arrived.

"That's right."

"I'm Father Holden," he said, but didn't offer to shake hands. Instead he sat down a chair away. "I had hoped by getting here early I might have a chance to talk to you before Mrs. Brown arrives."

Cody smiled. It didn't take a genius to figure out that the priest was uncomfortable. "Well, I guess today's your lucky day, Padre; here I am."

"You're an American," he said with some surprise. "But then I guess that's understandable, since Mr. Creager. . . "

He broke off as the waiter brought Cody's drink and then turned to the priest. "Mateus rosé, Father?"

"Yes," the priest said, adding quickly, "better start with two bottles; I think the rest of the party is arriving."

Cody followed his gaze out the window. A white Rolls-Royce had pulled up in front of the steel posts that protected the esplanade front vehicular traffic. He watched as a man in a chauffeur's uniform got out in the pouring rain and started removing the posts.

"I take it that's Mrs. Brown's car?" Cody asked.

"Yes," the priest answered with some restraint. "You told Mrs. Brown on the phone that you were going to bring Nicholas home."

"I told her that with her help I would," Cody said. "There's a big difference."

"What sort of help, Mr. Cody. . . financial?" the priest asked accusingly.

"You have a suspicious mind for a holy man," Cody said. "But just for the record, I'm not interested in her money."

"Then what's your game?" the priest demanded.

Cody was losing patience. "If we're going to talk about games, let's talk about yours, Father Larry. The well-fed priest who wines and dines in the finest restaurants and at yacht parties, and all at the largess of a troubled old woman." Cody knew he was twisting the knife, and he was enjoying it.

Outside, the chauffeur had finished removing the posts and had returned to the driver's side and gotten in. The white Rolls now glided toward the entrance of the restaurant.

"Who have you been talking to?" The priest's voice belied his irritation and a growing fear.

"I haven't been talking to anyone," Cody replied.

"Tommy Creager was my friend, and Tommy was the kind of reporter who kept notes on everything. I've got his notebooks. He wrote down everything, Padre. Everything that happened at those yacht parties and grand luncheons, and even the night some holy men danced the night away in a disco in Bondi Beach."

Cody had him pinned. The priest's snideness had all but vanished. "Mr. Creager was well known to have a drinking problem."

"Shut up," Cody interrupted. "You asked me what my game was? I'll tell you, it's very simple: Tommy Creager was my friend. I've come to Sydney to find out who killed him. I also happen to believe that whoever is responsible for young Nicholas's disappearance is responsible for killing Tommy."

"So you think that if you can find Nicholas, you'll find out who killed Mr. Creager?" the priest asked.

"That's the idea," Cody answered.

Fiona Brown had entered the room now, followed dutifully by Father Euginio, an Italian-looking priest. They were greeted with a wave of adulation. The maitre d' with the mutton chops and two waiters swept before them, as Mrs. Brown paused to talk and laugh with friends at another table. Father Larry spoke with some urgency now. "It doesn't matter what you think of me. My reason for wanting to speak to you was for Fiona. . . Mrs. Brown. She is my dear friend and she's been through terrible tragedies these last couple of months. I didn't want to see you raise her hopes only to have them crash down again. I don't know if she could take it."

"I didn't plan on letting her down," Cody said.

"You told her you could bring Nicholas home," the priest stated.

"I expect to," Cody responded, but then stopped in sudden realization. "But you don't think I can, do you? Why?"

"*Everyone* has looked for Nicholas the last two months," Father Larry said emphatically.

"Then maybe they were looking in the wrong places," Cody answered.

"I pray that's true. But maybe the reason no one has found him because he's dead," the priest said with conviction.

"Why do you say that?" Cody pressed.

"It just makes sense."

"No. Someone told you that. Who?" Cody insisted. "You want me to ask you in front of Mrs. Brown?"

Father Larry weighed the choice. "Kevin."

"Nicholas's older brother?"

"Yes. He made us swear to secrecy, because he didn't want his mother to know. He wanted her to have hope as long as there was a chance that Nicholas was still alive. Kevin had his faults, but he was a good brother, at least to Nicholas. He gave him the love and attention his own father never did. He was heartbroken when he disappeared, and he was almost positive that his father killed Nicholas."

Cody felt a surge of adrenalin. "Herod's pigs again," he murmured.

"What?" the priest asked.

"Just a theory Tommy was playing with," Cody explained. "Whether or not Griffin Brown was going to kill all his sons."

"My God," the priest said in astonishment, then

abruptly shifted his attention to Fiona, who was nearly upon them now.

"Father Laaaary," Fiona said in greeting, stretching out his name. He rose and gave her a dutiful kiss on the cheek

She was wearing her dark glasses, and Cody knew that he would never see her eyes.

"You would be Mr. Cody," she said, looking at him. "Here, come sit next to me."

Cody took his glass and moved to the chair beside the one she had selected. The waiters were pouring the Mateus rosé now, and she picked up a glass and smiled at Cody. "To our dear friend Tommy," she toasted. "God bless his gentle soul." The two priests solemnly joined in.

"Ha, ha!" she laughed when they were done, looking into Cody's eyes. "I knew something good was going to happen about Nicholas even before you called, Mr. Cody. You see, he'd called me the night before."

"He did?" Father Larry asked in genuine surprise.

"Yes," Father Euginio, stated, pleased that he had been privileged with the information first. "Fiona told me all about it in the car."

"Well, where is he?" Father Larry wanted to know.

She laughed again. "He wasn't ready to tell me that."

"What did he say?" Father Larry asked.

"He didn't say anything," she answered, the laughter leaving her voice. "He was just there. . . my little baby. I could hear him breathing."

No one spoke for some moments as the waiter

refilled the wineglasses. Cody ordered another vodka.

"When will you be bringing Nicholas home?" she asked when the waiter was gone.

"I hope very soon," he answered.

"We'll bring him right here to good old Doyle's," she beamed to the others.

"Mrs. Brown, I need to ask you questions."

"I know," she nodded.

He told her about the thirty-two gift-wrapped presents from the toy store and the thirty-two boxes of chocolate turtles from the candy shop that her son had bought the day before his disappearance. Both sets of purchases came as a surprise to her, and she had no idea what Nicholas might have wanted to do with them.

"But Nicholas was always a very generous person," she said, the priests heartily concurring. "All my boys were so good and so holy and generous when they were young. . . " And then she didn't speak for some moments and an air of melancholy hung over the table until Father Euginio spoke up.

"Tell Mr. Cody the story about the funny-hat contest," he encouraged, with a smile that was already almost a laugh. "That will show Mr. Cody what the boys were like, from their earliest years."

And so she told the story, and in between the wineglasses were refilled and the waiter took their orders. It seemed that many years ago, when Kevin and David were just little boys, the family had gone on a holiday together to a country hotel. And when they'd gotten to their rooms, Griffin had asked her if she had seen the poster in the lobby for the funny-hat contest to be held at dinner that night. No,

she hadn't. But just the week before they had won a
funny-hat contest at the yacht club, and so they were
all very keen to try again. Of course, what she didn't
know was that Griffin and the boys were pulling a
trick on her: There was no contest to be held that
night. But she didn't know that, so all afternoon she
worked. First begging a couple of big pans from the
kitchen, she tied carrots and leeks and a piece of corn
and some cold spaghetti from lunch and several
other very funny items that she couldn't recall.
These pan hats were for the boys: Kevin, who was
only six; and David, who was then four. For herself
and Griffin, she found two trash can lids and managed to decorate them just as outlandishly. They
were all very pleased with their funny hats, and the
magic dinnertime hour was fast approaching. Griffin
suggested that he and the boys go ahead and get the
table, so they donned their hats and left the room. Of
course, what she didn't know was that as soon as
they got out or the room, they quickly got rid of the
hats and then proceeded to the dining room as
expected. It was a grand dining room, at the foot of a
graceful, majestic stairway. And so Fiona donned
her trash-can-lid hat covered with vegetables and
started down the stairway. She was a little better
than halfway down before she realized that every
pair of eyes in the dining room was focused on her
and people were beginning to laugh. . . and in that
same moment she realized no one else had a funny
hat on. Mortified, she ran back to her room and
locked herself in. Griffin had come and knocked on
the door, trying to laugh off the incident, and when
she wouldn't respond he had turned nasty and
mocked her for being so stupid. Then a little later

there had been a tiny tap at the door. It was six-year-old Kevin, crying and holding David's hand. He was sorry he had tricked her and made her feel bad. And she slung open the door and hugged them so tightly, and they cried together and then they said the rosary.

"Kevin was always like that when he was growing up," she said, finishing the story and starting in on her appetizer of oysters Fitzpatrick.

The priest agreed.

"Whenever Griffin would abuse her – which happened more and more over the years," Father Larry explained, "Kevin and David would come to comfort their mother."

"They would cry with me," she said wistfully. "Then pray with me. We always said a rosary and asked Mary to pray for Griffin's soul."

Cody, doubtful he could endure an afternoon of rosaries with the children and funny-hat stories, decided now was the time to push. "Tommy told me some people thought Griffin Brown was Satan himself," he said, getting everyone's attention. "Does it do any good to pray for the devil?"

"I didn't always know how evil my husband was," she said after some moments.

"When did you find out?" Cody asked. "Was it the night of the Mardi Gras fire at the amusement park?"

"How do you know about that?" she asked, startled.

"Tommy Creager apparently took notes of whatever was said on our outings," Father Larry reported.

"Mrs. Brown, I wouldn't pry into your life if I

didn't think it would help Nicholas and also help me find out who murdered Tommy Creager," Cody stated. "Tommy wrote down that Nicholas had told him that his father was responsible for the fire at the amusement park. . . and that Nicholas had said that you had told him that."

"I don't want to talk about it," she said.

"Mrs. Brown, I believe there's a good chance that all the terrible things that have been happening in your life lately are tied to that Mardi Gras fire."

"Euginio," she said, "please have the car brought around."

"Mrs. Brown, if I'm right, the life of Nicholas could depend on what you tell me," Cody pressed on. Then he barked at Euginio, now on his feet. "Sit down, Padre. When she answers this, I'll leave."

The priest found his seat. "Maybe you should talk to him, Fiona. If it will help Nicholas, it'll be worth it."

She looked first at one priest then the other, and then she finished her wine. "Over the years, Mr. Cody, I grew more and more aware of how evil my husband really was. I didn't want to tell the boys. I didn't want to break their little hearts," she said, nodding a "Thanks darling" to Father Larry for refilling her wineglass. When she turned back to Cody, her look was grim. "As to the Mardi Gras fire, I'll remember it the rest of my life. Two of my friends' teenage sons died in it. I remember we had had a party at the house for Kevin and his friends, it was his eighteenth birthday. Later, the boys had gone out to have fun. Then the news came over the television that there had been a fire at the amusement park and that six boys had died. I was so afraid that my Kevin and David might have been victims. I nearly got hysterical. The doctor had to come. . . ." Now a tiny smile returned. "But then about two in the morning they came home, tipsy and laughing. They had been at a party in Randwick all the time; they hadn't even known about the fire."

"Why do you think your husband was behind it?" Cody asked.

"Because I had overheard him talking to his business associates," she explained. "He had been having trouble with the man who ran the amusement park. After the fire, he didn't have trouble anymore. I even heard them laughing about it."

67

The silver-haired man hung up the phone. "Got 'em," he said, and Gallagher and the other man looked up sharply. "At least Cody and his two kids. The son of a bitch is checked into a hotel in Bondi Beach."

* * *

Cody came out onto the esplanade and into the pouring ran. He had decided that he would call a cab from the pub around the corner. He just wanted to get out of the restaurant. Away from those people. Away from poor Fiona, living in her unhappy alcoholic haze. Away from those two priests, toadying around her, sucking up the edges of the good life, feeling important.

He was jogging to keep from getting completely drenched. He had moved off the esplanade and didn't actually see the Mercedes until it pulled across a drive-way in front of him. The driver's side window went down. It was Old Joe.

"Mr. Brown wants to see you."

"What if I don't want to see him?" Cody wanted to know.

"Then I'll have to point a gun at you," Old Joe shrugged.

"Then I'll go peacefully," Cody said, and almost smiled.

Old Joe drove slowly in the rain. One of the windshield wipers didn't work properly, which made it even more difficult to see.

The rain was steady and pounding all the way to King's Cross. Old Joe pulled the Mercedes into the driveway of a gated underground parking lot, found the clicker on the seat and pressed the button, at which the gate slowly clanked open.

"Mr. Brown is. . . not quite himself today," Old Joe said. "I don't think he slept well, with everything that's been going on."

He led Cody up the backstairs that brought them into the far end of the private corridor outside Brown's office. Old Joe knocked politely on the door.

"Yes!" they heard Brown bellow.

Old Joe opened the door and the two of them moved inside. He had been right about Griffin Brown not sleeping well. Brown looked as if he hadn't slept at all. He also hadn't shaved, and as best as Cody could remember he was still wearing the same clothes he had been in at their last meeting. He was drunk, and still drinking.

"Well, if it isn't the bloody Yank," he said, weaving. "Come in, have a drink."

"I'm fine without one," Cody said.

"What's the matter?" he snarled. "You don't want to drink with me? You didn't mind drinking with my wife, though, did you. What did she tell you?"

"That you were a shitty husband."

Brown laughed. "I was a shitty husband? She was a dead fish."

"I think I'll change my mind on that drink," Cody said and moved to the bar.

"I was a shitty husband?" he repeated to the ceiling and the walls. "You want to see what kind of husband I was," he said, unzipping his pants. "Take a look at my dick, you bloody Yank," he said, weaving back and forth and holding it in his hand. "You think anyone with a dick this size could be a shitty husband? I've fucked all the most beautiful women in this town," he boasted. "And a lot of the ugly ones too – they all loved it. Except my wife. My precious, cold-bloody-fish wife." He laughed. "You want me to tell you a story?" He finished his drink and poured another. "My wife's father was knighted by the bloody Queen. . . sir Thomas bloody Crowly. He was the commodore of the yacht club, he didn't think I was good enough to join. The pompous son of a bitch. He had me blackballed. So you know what I did? I ruined his business. I never let him know it was me. I bloody wiped him out. He would have lost everything – his house, his cars. But then I offered to help him. Not without a price, mind you. Me, the guy who wasn't good enough to join his club, I gave him enough money to carry him over. After that, Sir Thomas couldn't get his nose far enough up my ass." He laughed again and downed half his drink. "I saved his bloody ass, and then I made him eat shit every day for the rest of his life. I even made him give me his daughter," he smirked. "Jesus, she was beautiful then. I thought she was the most fuckable girl in Sydney. Jesus," he said as if remembering an electrical shock, "what's the old line about can't tell a book from its cover?" He finished the rest of his scotch, then sighed deeply and stumbled a few feet away. He stared at the wall for a moment, and when he spoke again it was with defiant desperation. "What you have to understand, Yank, is that this is my city; it has been since I fought my way up. I killed my first man in this room. . . in this bloody room. And now they're coming after me, and I don't even know who. How the bloody hell am I supposed to fight phantoms?"

There was a tap on the door, and a moment later Grasshopper stuck his head in. If he was surprised seeing his boss standing with an empty glass in his hand and his penis sticking out of his pants, he didn't show it.

"Phone, Mr. Brown, it's the Professor."

He staggered to the phone and picked it up with a grin. "Hey, Mooney. . . I'm just showing a very important person my dick," he said, and then listened. "Yes, I know the Jew's dead. I couldn't have been more shocked," he replied in an unconvincing tone. He listened again. "No, of course I'm not planning on killing you. He was a bloody Jew. He wasn't one of us. We're still on schedule." He listened again and then snarled, "Yes, I'm well bloody aware that more than my reputation is now at stake. Listen to me, the boat comes in tomorrow morning, clears customs by Tuesday afternoon and Tuesday night we bring it here and make a very profitable split." He poured another scotch and became a little embarrassed. "Listen, Professor. The other night you offered me some help: Just to be on the safe side for the next few days, I could use a couple of your guys, but only guys you can trust." As he struggled to keep his balance he glanced at Cody as if seeing him for the first time.

"What do you want, anyway?"

"You sent for me?" Cody said.

Brown weaved and then remembered. "Have you found Nicholas yet?"

"Not yet," Cody answered. "I could use some help."

"What?" Brown asked.

"A white-haired guy, his first name is Colin," Cody said. "He firebombed the disco."

"Jesus Christ," Brown said, stunned, and then turned his attention back to the phone. "Professor, do you know a white-haired guy named Colin? He listened a moment. "He doesn't know him either." Brown looked around. "Joe?"

"Not me, boss." Old Joe said. "I'll make some phone calls, though."

"You're sure he's the one who firebombed it?" Brown asked again.

"That's right," Cody nodded. "There's one more thing I'd like to know about."

"Anything," Brown said, taking a healthy snort from his glass.

"The amusement park fire. . . thirteen, fourteen years ago," Cody started, but Brown's face was growing dark and ugly.

"That's ancient history. Who the fuck cares about that?" he snarled.

"If I'm right, whoever's coming after you," Cody replied.

Brown glared at Cody a long moment and then spoke into the phone. "Professor, I'll have to call you back." He hung up and then threw the phone across the room. "Don't mess with my business, Yank, or you're going to find yourself very fucking dead."

"I'll keep that in mind," Cody said, and moved to the door and paused. "Now why don't you stick your prick back in your pants and stop acting like an asshole."

Brown sighed deeply as Cody left. "Bring me the scotch, Joe."

68

It was still raining steadily when the bus dropped Damien and Patrick off in Bondi Beach. Thunder rumbled in the distance as the boys hurried down the sidewalk to the plaza.

"Oy, Patrick!" Brian called.

Patrick turned and saw the leader of the street boys across Campbell Parade, on the esplanade. He was waving and running toward them.

"I've got to hit the head bad," Damien said.

"Go on," Patrick said. "I'll wait for him."

Damien hurried on.

Brian whistled loudly to get his attention as he ran between honking cars.

At first Damien just waved back and kept moving. But now Brian had reached the island in the middle of Campbell Parade. Traffic was rushing past him on both sides. "It's the white-haired guy, he's back," he shouted.

"Damien!" Patrick cried.

Damien had heard the warning too, but he had gone too far – he was in the plaza now, and across it he saw the silver-haired man. He'd been standing under an awning outside a take-out roast chicken shop, eating a steaming ear of corn. Now he threw the corn away and started for the eighteen-year-old. Damien turned and ran back toward his brother. Down the street, Gallagher got out of his car and started up the sidewalk.

"He's one of them too," Brian shouted. "This way!"

Damien grabbed Patrick's arm, and they moved between parked cars and waited for a truck to speed past; then they ran into the street and made it to the island. "Come on," Brian called, and darted in front of an oncoming car, which spun out on the slippery streets and missed the boy by inches. Damien and Patrick followed.

"Cody's not with them," Gallagher said to Fitzwilliam.

"Not now. But if we grab one of his kids, he won't be hard to find," the white-haired man said, hurrying between cars in pursuit of the boys. Gallagher reluctantly followed.

The three boys ran along the esplanade in the pounding rain. As they neared a water fountain, Brian called, "This way," and jumped up on the tile bench, then vaulted over the wall onto the sand, as Damien and Patrick followed. The two men were fifty yards behind and now they too moved over the wall.

The running was harder here on the wet sand. With the exception of the three running boys and the two men, the beach was empty. Fitzwilliam had his gun out now. He fired twice.

"Oh shit," Brian said in near panic.

They were coming to a down slope, at the bottom of which was the outlet for a five-foot-high cement storm drain A heavy rush of water streamed from it, at least a foot deep. Overhead thunder crackled and seemed to shake the earth, and Brian tumbled down toward the water. It wasn't until they reached the bottom that he realized he had been shot. His right shoulder was soaked with blood and he was nearing shock. "Oh shit. . . oh shit!"

"Brian, we can't stop now, they'll kill us – they'll kill all of us!" Damien shouted.

Brian understood "Come on," he managed, struggling to his feet and leading them into the storm drain. The rushing water made it difficult to move forward, but they knew they must. It was pitch dark, they were soaking wet, and now the sound of water filled their ears. Brian fell down and started to float back. Damien grabbed him and helped him up. "Colin, Colin," Brian called, and then a flashlight beam opened up ahead of them. Damien supported Brian from under his good arm as they hurried forward.

Outside Gallagher and Fitzwilliam hurried down the incline. The white-haired man saw the blood and smiled. "At least we hit one of the little shits," Fitzwilliam said with some professional pride, and then headed for the drain.

"We can't go in there," Gallagher said.

"The bloody kids did," Fitzwilliam snarled. "Get your ass down here."

* * *

The water seemed to be getting higher and harder to move against as they neared the wavering flashlight beam. Brian reeled in pain. Suddenly they could see sparks around them. "They're shooting at us!" Patrick yelled.

"Down, down," Damien shouted, trying to pull Brian to safety.

But the leader of the street boys shouted back, "Noooo," and kept pushing forward.

They reached the flashlight and found it being held by young blond Colin. Like the others, he was soaked to the skin. The four pushed around the corner into the intersecting pipe. Brian sagged against the side.

"Up here," Colin shouted and pointed his flashlight so as to reveal a concrete shelf about three feet up; it was flat space of about four feet by twenty feet. There were mattresses and toys and clothes. This is where they lived, and already everything looked soaked.

"He can't, he's been shot," Damien shouted for Colin to hear. "How do we get out of here?"

The blond boy pointed down the dark tunnel. Damien nodded, then moved to Brian's ear and said loudly, "I'm going to carry you."

Damien hoisted up the fifteen-year-old fireman style and indicated for Colin to lead the way. But the rushing water was too strong for him. Patrick had to brace him and they moved together.

Behind, Fitzwilliam and Gallagher staggered out of the drain pipe and into the pouring rain.

"They must be rats to be able to move through there," Gallagher said.

"Rats with a flashlight," Fitzwilliam returned irritably.

"Well, how was I to know?" Gallagher snapped. "If you're so fucking smart, why didn't you bring one?"

It took over twenty minutes to move what turned out to be a block and a half underground. A ladder led up to a manhole. Brian was still conscious, and they were all exhausted. Damien climbed up and after considerable effort was able to move the cover away. He looked out. They were in an alleyway behind a restaurant. He climbed back down now. "Can you make it?" he asked Brian.

"I have to."

"Pat, you go first," Damien instructed his brother. "Make sure no one's coming."

Patrick climbed into the alley and pouring rain. He could see the back of the plaza half a block away. Young Colin emerged next, shivering. Then Brian struggled up, Damien pushing him from below, so that Patrick could grab his good hand and lead him out. Brian cried in pain at the struggle. Damien was right behind him. "We have to get you to a doctor; call an ambulance," he said.

"Not here," Brian pleaded. "They'll hear."

Patrick saw a shopping cart near the mouth of the alley. "We can put him in that and push him a couple of more blocks away."

Brian nodded, yes.

Patrick ran down and retrieved the shopping cart, and they managed to lift him in without banging his injured shoulder.

"Take care of Colin, he's my brother," Brian told them as they wheeled him along the Curlewis Street sidewalk as fast as possible.

"We will," Damien promised.

"I'm going with you," young Colin shouted, jogging alongside the cart.

"They're going to put me in hospital. They'll make you go home." Brian's eyes were beginning to glaze. He fought to stay coherent. "These guys will take care of you till I get back. It'll only be a few days." They crossed Glenayr and then pushed another long block up to Wellington. Brian was losing consciousness. The others were ready to drop. The trouble was, on a rainy Sunday afternoon everything was closed. Finally they spotted a pub across the street They pushed the cart over and banged through the front doors. Everyone in the place turned and looked at them.

"He's been shot, he needs a doctor," Damien said.

"What the hell?" the bartender said. He had a red face and a bad blond hairpiece. His first instinct was to be angry but the sight of the four boys, soaked to the skin and obviously exhausted, convinced him that there might be cause for alarm.

"Let me have a look," one of the bar customers said. She was a heavy woman in a sundress, wearing sandals. The other boys made way for her as she approached. She looked at Brian, who was still in the cart, and then with her pudgy, strong hands, ripped the shirt and pulled it away from his shoulder. The wound was evident and ugly.

"Oh, boy," she said, turning to the bartender. "We're going to need an ambulance. . . and I'm going to need some help getting him out of here."

"Let me," Damien said.

Two men hurried over from the bar and the four of them gingerly lifted the fifteen-year-old out and then onto a bench that sat against the wall. He was only semiconscious, but when the shoulder was pulled the wrong way, he screamed out in pain.

"How did this happen?" the woman wanted to know.

"Two guys on the beach. They just started shooting," Patrick said.

"Colin," Brian wailed.

The small boy pushed past an adult to reach his brother.

"Do what I say. Go with them," Brian told him. "I'll be back in a few days."

"I want to go with you," the younger boy was crying.

"You can't. Trust me. Do what I say." The fifteen-year-old's words were coming in short bursts as he fought the pain.

"The ambulance is on its way. I've called the police too," the bartender reported as he moved over for a look at the injured boy.

Damien pulled Patrick aside. "We can't wait. Dad's going to be coming back to the hotel soon. If those guys are still there he'll be walking into a trap."

"But if they see you. . . " Patrick started.

"They won't see me. I'll just have to find someplace where I can hide and watch the plaza too."

"The disco," Patrick said as the thought came into his head "Up on the second floor. You have to be careful because the floor gives out in some spots, but I think you can see the plaza from there."

Damien nodded. "Okay. You're going to have to take care of the kid."

"Fine," Patrick agreed. "But where will we meet?"

Damien thought a moment. "The church. Go back to St. Agnes. Hide in the confessional at the back."

They could hear a siren approaching now.

Patrick looked at his brother. "I'm scared for you."

"I'm scared for all of us," Damien answered, and then hugged his brother for a moment before hurrying out the door.

"Hey, where's he going?" the woman shouted.

"Colin," Patrick said.

The small blond boy looked over to him.

"Here's the ambulance," someone announced, and a moment later a couple of paramedics hurried in. In the confusion that followed, Patrick and Colin slipped away and ran down the sidewalk through the rain, heading for the church.

Farther down and on the other side of the street, Damien was also running. He was nearing the alleyway that they had emerged into from the drainpipe when he saw McCabe's car pass on Campbell Parade, heading toward the hotel.

At the same time, from the other direction, the cab with Cody in it was pulling up in front of the plaza. Cody paid the driver, got out, and started to jog through the downpour to the entrance of the hotel when McCabe honked his horn several times and then called out Cody's name.

Cody turned back and saw the reporter as he was getting out of his car across Campbell Parade

and starting to hurry toward him. To meet him part-
way, Cody jogged back to the curb and the over-
hanging cover of a bus stop. McCabe trotted over,
his face consumed in his squinty grin, so pleased
was he with himself.

"Finally got some names out of New Zealand,"
he said as he reached the bus stop. "The lady who
died outside Tauranga had a son named Colin
Fitzwilliam. I checked it with Edythe. She had to dig
in her files a bit, but she pulled him up – Amanda
Kearsey's son by her first marriage. He was a cop for
about fifteen years in Brisbane – that's the next state
up, about five hundred miles away. Anyway, he got
caught with a few other guys trying to smuggle a
boatload of drugs into the country. They were arrest-
ed just over the New South Wales border, so he
ended up doing his prison time, about seven years,
at the Long Bay Jail down here. He's only been out a
few months."

"Does he have white hair?" Cody asked.

"He was born with it," McCabe grinned and
fished a piece of paper out of his pocket. "And I have
more. Maybe not as exciting, but I have more.
Bailey's Chemist. What Nicholas bought there was
asthma sprays. The man there said that Nicholas had
to use them whenever he went to the mountains."

"That's a lot of money for sprays," Cody said.

McCabe nodded. "He bought a lot of them,
enough to last a couple of months, the chemist said."

"Dad, look out!" Damien shouted across the rain-
swept plaza .

Cody whirled to the voice, but then saw his son
pointing desperately behind him, so whirled again,
instinctively pulling out his Walther at the same

time. McCabe turned too, in time to take the first bullet fired from the passing car in his neck. The next bullet hit a metal pole in front of Cody's face. Cody returned fire. One, two, three, four, five, six times. He could see blood appearing on the red-headed driver's face just before his car crashed into a parked truck.

Damien way running cross the plaza. Cody saw him and shouted for him to get an ambulance, then crouched down by his fallen friend. Cody and McCabe were both in the pouring rain now. Cody held the wounded man's head in his arms. But blood was pumping out of the reporter's neck like a small volcanic eruption, and Cody knew he would be dead in a matter of moments. He stood and began running down the street to the wrecked car.

Fitzwilliam struggled to open the driver's door and then to push the groaning and badly wounded Gallagher out onto the wet pavement. Behind the wheel now himself, he managed to back up. He could see Cody coming down the street at him. He fired once, twice at Cody, but then put the car into drive and tried to speed away. His tires spun at first, but he finally got the traction he needed and raced off as best he could, one fender scraping against a tire and the engine steaming.

Cody squatted next to Gallagher, sprawled in the street. He could see that the red-headed man was bleeding from several spots on his torso. "I'm an American, an American," Gallagher said groggily.

Cody reached inside the man's coat pocket and pulled out his wallet. The identification card listed him as an "information officer" at the American consulate in Sydney.

"Jesus," Cody said with some amazement. "You are fucking CIA, aren't you?"

Gallagher looked at him with beaten eyes, but as his lips moved only unintelligible sound came out.

"You must have been a real prize agent for them to assign you to this end of the world," Cody said derisively. You sent Tommy Creager on all those trips, didn't you?"

Gallagher nodded.

"Who killed Tommy? It was Colin Fitzwilliam, wasn't it?"

Gallagher nodded again and mouthed yes. It was hard to tell in the pouring rain, but Cody thought the red-headed man was crying.

"Why did you send Tommy on all those trips?" Cody demanded, but Gallagher was busy feeling sorry for himself. Cody picked him up by the collar. "I can finish the job now. I can kill you right fucking now. Is that what you want?" Gallagher's eyes showed fear. "Then tell me why Tommy took all those trips!"

"Drugs," Gallagher managed.

"He was bringing them in?" Cody asked.

"No," Gallagher answered. "Taking cash out to pay for big shipment."

"The one coming in Tuesday night?"

Gallagher nodded. "Yes."

Cody wasn't sure he wanted the next answer, but he knew he had to ask the question. "Was Tommy in on the deal?"

Gallagher shook his head, and if he could have laughed he would have. "He thought he was helping the good guys." Then he couldn't speak for several moments, his eyes seemed to lose focus, but then he was back again. "He thought he was undercover, busting big drug deal. . . big story."

The sound of sirens was filling the air now, and a crowd of onlookers had begun to gather on the nearby sidewalk.

"What was your job?"

"Controlling Creager. . . making contact other countries' law enforcement, making sure he was left alone," Gallagher said, his eyes rolling up. Cody shook him again.

"Are you working for Griffin Brown?" Cody asked.

Gallagher managed a sickly smile. "No. Fucking Griffin Brown, that's the whole point."

A couple of policemen were approaching now. "What's going on?"

"There was some shooting," Cody said. "I saw this man fall, I came to help him."

An ambulance pulled up.

"All right, leave him to us for now," an officer said. "We'll talk to you in a minute."

Another policeman ran up now, out of breath. "There's another one on the plaza who's dead."

"What the hell is going on?" the officer said, starting to follow the other. Two more police cars arrived with sirens blaring, accompanied by another ambulance. Cody made his way to the sidewalk, where he found Damien. The eighteen-year-old was badly shaken. "Dad, he's dead."

"I know," Cody said. "We have to get out of here. Where's Patrick?"

"I told him to go to the church and hide there until I came for him."

"Good," Cody said, starting to lead his son away,

down the sidewalk to the corner. But several policemen were there, talking and looking at him, so he
paused and pretended they didn't intend to go anywhere. A glance back to the plaza side showed that it
too was filling with police. The cops' attention on the
corner was diverted now by the arrival of another
car, with what looked to be a high-ranking officer.
Cody took the opportunity to slip the two of them
into the Pancakes on the Beach restaurant. The customers and help had all gathered at the front windows to watch the show outside in the gray of the
pouring rain.

Cody and Damien moved through the restaurant, through the kitchen and out the back door and
into the alley. Again he started for the corner, but
again police activity made him shy back. He knew
that it would take days, if ever, to explain what he
was doing here in Sydney and why he had ended up
in the middle of a shoot-out in Bondi Beach with one
man dead and another well on the way to dying.
And who would he explain to commissioner
Jacklan? He didn't want to take the chance.

He led his son down the alley now and pulled
back the piece of plywood so that they could enter
the burned-out disco. After replacing the plywood
they climbed the stairs and carefully crossed what
was left of the second floor and found a hiding spot
that gave them some relief from the rain and a clear
view of the plaza below. Someone must have noticed
that Cody was missing now, for police were running
in all directions.

69

Fitzwilliam parked the limping car in the lot behind McDonald's in Bondi Junction. He walked through the fast food restaurant and then ran through the rain, across Newland Street to the pay phones in the Oxford Mall.

"This whole thing is coming apart fast," he said to the other man when he answered. He told him about the shooting. That the reporter was dead and he thought Gallagher was too. But that Cody was still alive.

"Shit," the other man said.

"I say we move the stuff now," Fitzwilliam stated.

"We can't. It's not ready," the other man said. "And besides, until the king is dead, none of his customers are going to talk to us; they're too afraid of him."

"Then let's get him now, fuck waiting until Tuesday," Fitzwilliam urged strongly.

"How?" The other asked with a hint of desperation. "I still can't find Jacklan, and now you tell me Gallagher is dead. We've just lost our eyes and ears into his operation."

70

Cody and Damien stayed hidden in the burned-out disco for some hours, and with the passing time rain only got stronger and lightning and thunder returned, and eventually the police disappeared.

Damien told his father about Brian saving their lives – the chase through the storm drains and

Brian's getting wounded and their taking care of his little brother.

Cody sat for some time in silence and went over everything he learned in trying to find out who killed Tommy Creager. At least now he knew Colin Fitzwilliam had been the triggerman – but for who? He still didn't know who had ordered the killing. Someone out to get Griffin Brown. To fuck Griffin Brown – that's what Gallagher had said was the whole point. He knew so much, and yet something was missing. What?

In hopes that Damien might be able to see something he was missing, Cody related everything to him: From the early morning in Samoa when he had awakened to the sense of fear and then had seen what he later thought were the gunshots that had killed Tommy, to the spot outside Tauranga where he had sensed someone had died. . . and feeling that somehow it could be important. As it turned out, it had eventually led them to the white-haired man they had known only as Colin.

Cody told him about the flashes of fire he'd seen while standing in the beach parking lot in Tauranga and hearing the screams and sometimes seeing the faces, blistering and desperate. How he had sensed the same fire and stinging smoke the first time they had been to Tommy Creager's house.

As best he could he recounted his trip to Hornsby and the conversation in the pub with McCabe when he learned that the two Brown sons, Kevin and David, had been either dead or unconscious before the fire. And then about the talk with Jill at her brother's house, when she told them about Tommy taking secretive trips out of the country.

Tommy's notebooks they had gone over together, and so they talked about those for a time. Tommy's mention of the trips and worrying about Gallagher. The tension between Griffin Brown and his sons. How Fiona had been humiliated by and hated her husband's mistresses. Tommy's speculation that maybe Griffin Brown, like Herod, was planning to kill his own sons. How young Nicholas hated his father, and the nightmare stories that Fiona had related to Tommy about Griffin Brown coming to her in the night as a Greek god with a goat's head and raping and beating her. And of course the story told by Nicholas that his father had burned down the haunted house at the amusement park, killing those six teenage boys so many years ago.

Cody went on to tell Damien of coming here, to the burned-out disco, and sensing that there had been a dead body, wrapped in some cloth. It had been on the ground floor and then dragged upstairs.

He talked of his meetings with Griffin Brown. A desperate man trying to hold onto his empire and not even knowing who he was fighting. Of his luncheon with Fiona and her priests and the pathetic tale of the funny-hat contest, showing that even early on in their marriage, Griffin had been cruel to her, but that the boys had always been good and loving and had cried and prayed with her many nights as children. And how frightened she'd been the night of the Mardi Gras amusement park fire, Kevin having just gone out on the town to celebrate his eighteenth birthday.

They talked of Nicholas. Poor missing Nicholas with his thirty-two gift-wrapped boxes of candy and another thirty-two of toys.

Cody told him all he could remember, whether it seemed relevant or not, and when they were done they sat in silence for some moments until finally Damien just shook his head.

"You can't figure out what's missing either?" Cody asked with a tired smile.

"I'm not sure," the eighteen-year-old said. "But sometimes if you can't put a puzzle together, it's not that you don't have enough pieces. . . it's that maybe you've got too many. Ones that don't belong. At least not the way you're seeing them at the time."

"You have a for instance?" Cody asked.

Damien shrugged. "I can't be sure, but if what you saw was right, one thing that doesn't seem to fit is there having been a body here, all wrapped up before the fire and being dragged upstairs. I mean, why?"

Cody stared at his son for some moments. . . and then he thought he knew.

71

Fitzwilliam looked up from the basin into the mirror. His once-white hair was now chestnut brown. He felt sick inside. He knew that if Cody had talked to the police and identified him for having shot the reporter, he'd be a wanted man again. He'd never return to prison; he'd promised himself that too many times. "Goddammit," he shouted angrily, knowing that even if he got away, out of Australia on a phony passport, it would be only to a life on the run. There'd be no place for him in the Bay of Plenty, with its own jetty and a thirty-two-footer. In two days he would have three million dollars, but in two

days he'd also be a bloody fugitive. He moved into
the next room. Three guns were laid out on his bed.
An ankle pistol, a .38, and an Uzi. If he was going
down, he thought, he was going to go down in
flames.

72

Night had fallen and the rain had moderated to a
steady drizzle. McCabe's car was where he had
parked it. It was unlocked, so they got in, and after a
couple of false starts Cody managed to hotwire it.
They drove to the church and found both Patrick
and Colin asleep in the back confessional. They
woke the boys, returned to the car, and drove to
Kings Cross.

The Cowboy Club was closed. Cody had to
pound on the front door for several minutes before
Lakey opened it. He didn't question Cody's demand
to see Brown.

* * *

"You look like the cat dragged you in," the gangster
remarked, his words slurred. He was sitting sagged
in the chair behind his desk, a glass and a bottle of
scotch in front of him. Pushed to his left was a plate
with the remains of a steak dinner, and to his right
was his .45.

"I need money. A couple of thousand," Cody
said.

"Why come to me?"

"Someone tried to kill me and my sons this afternoon. I want the money to stay alive long enough to

know who wants me dead and who's out to destroy you."

Brown stared at him for a moment then picked up the phone and punched three numbers. "Lady, this is Grif. Bring me two thousand dollars." He hung up and stared back at Cody. "Did you get a look at who came at you?"

"I did better than that; I shot one of them. As far as I know he could be dead by now. He's an American, works out of the consulate, his name was Gallagher. Mean anything to you?"

Brown tried to focus his mind.

Cody continued. "The guy with him got away; he was the white-haired man I told you about. I know his full name now: Colin Fitzwilliam."

Brown struggled. "It sounds familiar."

"He was a crooked cop out of Brisbane. . . " Cody started.

"Yeah," Brown interrupted. "Busted for drugs, I think, something like that. Long time ago."

"He did seven years in Long Bay," Cody said. "Know anyone else who's done time there?"

Brown looked at him and found a smile. "Almost everyone I know, or who works for me. What the fuck you think we're running here, a Boy Scout camp?" He picked up his glass and finished it.

"How about your sons?" Cody asked.

Brown scowled. "Stay the Hell out of my family business."

There was a knock at the door, and a moment later Lady entered.

"I didn't know how you wanted it, so I brought a thousand in hundreds, seven hundred in fifties, and the rest in twenties."

"Give it to him," Brown said without looking at her. He refilled his glass and then took a pull on it. "My solicitor tells me the police will be coming for me soon." He found a smile. "Seems killing Chinamen is out of season." The smile disappeared. "And I didn't even bloody do it," he said angrily, standing up on unsteady legs. "Can you imagine, they want to get me for something I didn't even do. They can't prove anything. They won't be able to hold me – even they know that. I've got other cops besides Jacklan on the payroll, and judges. . . " His words trailed off. He stared at the floor. "I'm a very important man," he said, an began to urinate in his pants.

Cody left with him standing there silently, rocking back and forth.

* * *

He had left the boys in the car a block away on a dark street. The rain was light and steady as he walked back to them. After rounding a corner, he stepped into a doorway and stood in the shadows for two minutes. There was no sign that anyone was following him.

They drove randomly, since Cody didn't know the city. A couple of times he forgot which side of the road he was supposed to be on. Honking horns, screeching tires. They found a new, quite nice hotel in Rose Bay. They parked a block away and walked up. Cody checked in under the name of Kelly, after one of Ann's grandfathers. He explained to the clerk that he and his three sons had been on a driving tour of the country and that their rented car and all their belongings, including his wallet, had been washed away in a flash flood. But he had cash. Plenty of cash that his friend had lent him to tide him over. And the sight of cash, as always, made everything alright. He paid two days in advance for a double connecting room. Then, using the house phone, he called room service and ordered seven hamburgers and fries, three chocolate malts, and a pot of coffee. The lobby shops were still open, and he spent over six hundred dollars buying the four of them a couple of dry changes of clothes.

The food arrived at the room the same time as they did. The boys ate quietly, ravenously. Cody took a hamburger plate and the coffee and moved to the phone. In the directory he found the number for the *Sydney Morning Herald*. Calling their editorial office, he talked to three people before he found a man who knew a crime reporter named Edythe. Cody told him it was a matter of life and death. But the man was as reluctant to give out her phone number as Cody was to disclose his. They finally compromised. The man at the paper would put Cody on hold and call Edythe to see if she would okay giving out her number. Cody told him to mention that he had been working with Joe McCabe.

There was a silence for several moments. "Did you know that Joe McCabe was killed today?" the man asked.

"I was standing next to him when he was shot," Cody said.

"Jesus," uttered the other man.

Cody waited on hold and sipped his coffee. Across the room Colin talked quietly to Patrick. Patrick now came over to his father. "He wants to know if you can find out what happened to his brother," the boy said, adding quietly, "He's really scared that he's dead."

"Tell him I'll do what I can," Cody promised.

The man came back on the other end of the phone and gave Cody Edythe's phone number.

* * *

"You must be Ed Cody," Edythe said in a deep raspy voice.

"That's right."

"You have any idea who killed Joe McCabe?" she asked.

"Colin Fitzwilliam."

"Did he shoot the American embassy worker too?"

"No. I shot him. His name is Gallagher, he's dirty. He was working with Fitzwilliam. Just so you know, Fitzwilliam is the man who firebombed the disco. He also pulled the trigger on Tommy Creager."

"My God," she said in amazement. "Can you prove any of this?"

"I can prove it all," he answered. "And as far as I'm concerned, with Joe gone, this can be your story. I think Tommy might have liked it that way. But you're going to have to sit on it for at least another twenty-four hours until I can track down the man Fitzwilliam and Gallagher were working for, and to do that I need your help."

"What do you want?" she asked, all efficiency, ready to take notes.

"I want to know who Fitzwilliam was friendly with when he was at Long Bay," Cody said. "I want to know if Kevin or David Brown ever did time there, and if they did, when."

"I'm sure they did," she said. "At least one of them, I think. . . I'll check. Anything else?"

"Everything you can dig up or remember, even if it's just rumors that were going around then, on the Mardi Gras fire at the amusement park thirteen or fourteen years ago."

"Tommy had been interested in that too," she said curiously.

"If I'm guessing right, it has something to do with everything that's happened since Nicholas Brown disappeared and Tommy was killed."

"My God," she said again. "Is that all?"

"Isn't that enough?" Cody smiled.

"Okay," she sighed. "I can pull some of that stuff up here. But some of the other – like who Fitzwilliam was friendly with in prison – I'm going to have to go visiting, to the kind of people who don't have phones. Give me two hours: I'll meet you in town."

"Where?"

She thought a moment. "Let's make it the No-Name."

"Where?"

There was a smile in her voice when she answered. "The No-Name cafe. It's called the No-Name because it has no name. Any cabby will know where it is. You bring the red wine." She hung up.

Cody put the phone down and then saw the small blond boy across the room looking at him. He picked up the phone again.

"What'd you forget?" she answered on the first ring.

"There was a fifteen-year-old boy shot in Bondi Beach today. I'd like to know what happened to him."

"Will do," she said, and hung up for the second time.

"We'll find out," Cody assured Colin.

* * *

Cody finished his hamburger and then showered and changed into some fresh clothes. He knew he had to talk to Fiona Brown again. The question was how. They hadn't parted on the best of terms. If he asked her any unpleasant questions over the phone, she'd probably hang up on him. He decided to risk it. If she did hang up on him, he'd just have to find out where she lived and go over there for a face-to-face.

"Helloooo," she answered.

She was truly with the pixies tonight, Cody thought. "Mrs. Brown, this is Ed Cody, I'm calling about Nicholas."

"Nicholas," she repeated. "Have you found him?"

"Not yet. But I feel I'm very close. I need to ask you about one more thing."

"What?" she asked after some moments, her voice sounding petulant.

"Last year, you had to go into the hospital for a few days, just before Nicholas' birthday." He paused, but she said nothing. "Your son Kevin took Nicholas to the mountains so that he wouldn't know that you were ill. When Nicholas came back, did he talk about where he had been?"

"I suppose he did," she said.

"Can you remember any of it?"

"I don't see what point this can serve," she said, agitated. The sound of liquid being poured into a glass came over the line.

"I want to bring Nicholas home. It could be very important."

There was silence, and then he heard her swallowing and then cough. "He liked it up there. There were lots of children he could play with, and horses."

"Mr. Brown, is Katoomba in the mountains?" he asked.

"Yes, of course. What a stupid question," she snapped.

"Only a couple of more and I'll let you go," he said, trying to sound soothing. "Last year a man named Brother Julian asked you for a contribution to help support a home for kids he was running up near Katoomba. Do you think that's where Nicholas could have been?"

"No," she shrieked. "Why would he want to do that? He was a horrible man."

"Do you know how I can reach him?" he asked.

"Why would I know that?" she answered, her voice nasty.

"Father Larry introduced you to him; where could I find *him*?"

"He's at Sacred Heart, in Dover Heights."

He thanked her, and she slammed the phone down.

* * *

Father Larry was even less gracious than Fiona. He was busy, he told Cody. He had no idea how to reach Brother Julian, who he felt had betrayed his trust. If Cody wanted to find him, why didn't Cody just drive up to Katoomba and ask around? "Someone's bound to know where his wretched little place is."

73

The cab drove halfway down the alley and stopped. "The No-Name's on the second floor," the driver said. Cody got out and moved inside. The rain had stopped but the sky was still overcast, and it was warm and sticky.

The restaurant was a collection of vinyl-topped tables with hoop-backed chairs. The place was about half full. A waiter who looked like Moe Howard told him to sit wherever he wanted. "I'm to meet a woman named Edythe here," Cody told him.

The waiter looked around with indifference. "She's not here yet," he said, and moved on.

Cody chose a table where he could watch the stairs. After a while the waiter appeared and opened the bottle of red wine that he had brought and presented him with a tumbler to drink it in. It was another twenty minutes before Edythe appeared. She was a small woman, somewhere in her sixties, with mousey brown hair cut straight across her shoulders. She walked slightly bent over and used an aluminum cane. Moe Howard pointed him out for her.

Short of breath, she sat down without a word, poured herself a glass of wine, and drank half of it. "That's better," she said. "Time to pay the piper. I help you, you have to let me stick with you until this is over."

"You know what happened to McCabe," Cody said.

"What, am I going to be cut down in the flower of my girlhood?" she asked with a biting grin. "This is the biggest story of my life. This whole town's blowing up, and with you I can be right in the eye of the storm." Her eyes were determined.

"I'll think about it. Let's hear what you've got," he answered .

She frowned. "Where do you want to begin?"

"Anyplace you like."

Moe Howard was back with a plastic bowl half filled with sliced French bread. "What do you want?" he demanded.

"What do you have besides spaghetti?" she asked.

"Spare ribs and meat loaf."

"We'll both have the spaghetti," she said.

"Salad?"

"Sure."

Moe left.

She looked to Cody. "Whole dinner costs only five bucks. Everybody comes here, starving students who can fill up their stomachs cheap, politicians, movie people." She scratched her head vigorously. "Let's get the kid out of the way. He's at St. Vincent's. They had to cut and paste a little, but they say he's going to be fine. He'll be out in three or four days if they can figure out where to put him. He's a street kid, did you know?"

"Yeah," Cody answered, but decided not to tell her that Brian and his younger brother had been the ones who'd identified Fitzwilliam as having been at the disco the night of the firebombing.

She seemed to sense that he was holding something back, but went ahead. "Both of Brown's sons did eighteen months in Long Bay on assault and attempted-murder charges. There was some speculation that the old man set them up for the fall. That they were getting too big for their britches and he decided to take them down a notch or two. They both got out about two years ago. Both were in Long Bay the same time Colin Fitzwilliam was. Fitzwilliam and David Brown had a fistfight, they didn't get along at all. Kevin, though, made friends with Fitzwilliam. Some people say he paid off some guards, even after he was out, to make sure Fitzwilliam had special privileges. Is that any good for you?"

"Yeah, I think it might be," he nodded.

"My God, I'd hate to play poker with you," she signed.

Moe Howard returned and without a word slapped two plates of lettuce down, followed by two plates of steaming spaghetti. Then he left again. She finished her wine, poured another glass, and started in on her lettuce.

"What about the amusement park fire?" he asked after she had finished her salad in silence.

"What about it?" she asked in return, digging into her spaghetti.

He grinned. "Okay, you can tag along."

She put her fork down. "That's better. The facts I think you know. Fourteen years ago, on Shrove Tuesday, a fire was set in a haunted house attraction. Six teenage boys were killed. Officially that's all that anyone knows. A young police lieutenant named Jacklan was in charge of the case. No arrests were made."

"I know who Jacklan is," Cody said.

"Okay, that's officially. Unofficially, most people in the know were pretty sure that Griffin Brown was behind it. He and the amusement park owner were rivals."

Cody nodded. "I've heard all of this."

"Have you heard that Kevin Brown might have been involved?" she asked.

"No," he said with sudden interest.

She smiled. "This is really wild speculation, but there are certain things that have a ring of truth to them. First you need a little background: Griffin Brown is a man with a perverse idea about a young man's rites of passage. It's well documented that when one of his sons reaches the age of fifteen, he buys them a hooker. It's also rumored that when the boy turns eighteen, he makes them prove themselves in a different way. Fourteen years ago Easter came late, so Lent was late; Shrove Tuesday didn't fall until February 27, which just happened to be Kevin Brown's eighteenth birthday."

"Are you saying Kevin Brown started the Mardi Gras fire?" Cody asked.

She shrugged. "It's a lot of wisps of rumors and gossip. But the scenario goes that Kevin was ordered by his father to start the fire. That Griffin Brown promised him no one would be hurt. But then

Griffin had somebody else bolt the doors. It's well known that Kevin went on a trip that lasted almost two months after his eighteenth birthday. But as the story goes, he was so shook up by the six boys dying in the fire that he had a breakdown, and that he was really in a sanitarium all that time."

All the pieces were beginning to fit. Now Cody only had to find Nicholas to prove it.

"That's all I know," she said. "So what's the next step?"

"Do you have a car?" he asked.

"Yes."

"How long does it take to drive to Katoomba?" he asked. "

"About two hours. What's in Katoomba?"

"Pick me up down front here tomorrow morning – at, say, nine – and we'll find out together."

74

"What do you mean?" Fitzwilliam asked.

"What I mean is, the cops don't know anything," the other man said. Behind him in the clean room, the people in gowns and masks were still working. "Cody didn't talk to them. They don't even know a Cody exists. They know that there was an American helping Gallagher when the ambulance arrived, but they looked around later and he was gone."

"That's crazy. It doesn't make sense," Fitzwilliam said, startled yet again by his own dark-haired reflection in the glass.

"Caring about who killed a rummy like Tommy Creager doesn't make any bloody sense either," the other said. "But because he does, and if he can find

Nicholas before Tuesday night, he could unravel everything we've put together in the last year. Unless we stop him."

Do you really think he can find the kid?" Fitzwilliam asked.

"At this point, I wouldn't put anything past that man," the other said. "But just in case he does, it might be a good idea if you were waiting for him."

75

Cody slept soundly most of the night. It wasn't until the first light of dawn and in a half sleep that he heard it again. The weeping. Sad, sad, helpless weeping, and then he could feel a numbness taking over his body, and the weeping was becoming more desperate. A sense of fear was filling Cody. He forced himself to sit up. Now fully awake, the weeping and all that had come with it was gone again.

After he showered and dressed, Cody called the hotel in Bondi Beach and told them he had had to go out of town suddenly and that he would be back in a couple of days and for them to just keep charging the room to his credit cards. The clerk he talked to sounded bored and gave no indication that the police or anyone else might have been looking for him. He asked if there were any messages. The clerk checked; there were none.

After the call, Cody went back down to the shops and bought the boys bathing suits. They had breakfast at the poolside restaurant. Young Colin had begun to relax once he learned his brother was going to be okay. He laughed and teased with Patrick. Cody left Damien with a hundred dollars and told the boys to stay near the hotel.

* * *

Edythe was waiting for him in an old, mud-splattered Volkswagen bus when the cab dropped Cody off at the mouth of the alley that led to the No-Name cafe.

"This van is a lot like me," she said as he climbed in. "It's old and not very pretty, but it gets the job done."

"I'm kind of fond of both of you at the moment," Cody smiled.

They worked their way out of the city at a snail's pace through traffic for almost an hour before they hit the open highway. Most of the way she played a Pavarotti tape, and between the music and the thrashing sound coming from the engine there wasn't much chance to talk. As they were leaving the Plains and heading up to Springwood, Pavarotti finally ran out. Cody seized the opportunity.

"If I'm right in what I expect to find up here, we're going to need the name of an honest cop. One who'll stand by us," he said.

"No worries. There's plenty of honest cops in Sydney," she said, slipping in another tape. It was the opera *The Barber of Seville*.

The ride up the Mountain to their eventual three-thousand-foot-high destination was filled will gentle curves, a handful of tiny towns, and landscape that reminded Cody of Southern California.

* * *

Katoomba had been a mining town in the last century and still maintained much of that flavor: It had a single main street crowded with depressed-looking shops. Traffic was at a standstill, for a huge barefoot man with a full beard that came down to his chest way playing the harmonica and dancing in the middle of the two-lane road. He was accompanied by two small dogs that jumped and barked and seemingly danced with him.

Eventually the police came and, to the boos of some of the onlookers, led the huge man away. He didn't seem to mind, but waved and smiled at his fans, who cheered him in return.

Cody got out of the traffic-bound car and walked up to where the impromptu show had been going on. He talked to one of the leftover cops and got directions to Brother Julian's Boys' Village.

*　*　*

Boys' Village was a couple of miles out of town. It was set on several acres overlooking a huge green valley that seemed to stretch forever. As they pulled into the driveway they saw what was probably the original house on the property, with a wood-carved ADMINISTRATION sign in front of it, and parked nearby. From there they could also see the chapel, a barn, a workshop building, and several large cottages, plus another under construction. From another side, a cement truck rumbled out and back onto the highway.

Just then classes must have let out, for the area became filled with boys ranging in age from about ten to fifteen or sixteen. They looked like Australian schoolboys anywhere, most of them in shirts and shorts. Occasionally there was a boy who looked part aboriginal or Asian, but on the whole, like the general population of the country, most were fair skinned with blond or brown or red hair.

* * *

From a hill three hundred yards away, Fitzwilliam, with a pair of high-powered binoculars, watched Cody and Edythe move farther into the complex. Like a gambler down to his last dollar, a cold, sinking feeling had settled in his stomach. He thought of the mad irony of it all, that something he had believed to be so insignificant, the killing of Tommy Creager, was now very close to destroying everything. Everything here and now. Everything in the future.

* * *

Cody and Edythe were surrounded on all sides now by moving boys, all of whom seemed happy and gave off a feeling of wholesomeness and well-being. A red-headed boy leading a goat by a rope paused. "Can I help you?" he asked.

Cody smiled. "I'm looking for a boy name Nicholas. He's older, maybe seventeen; he has sort of dusty blond curly hair."

"Oh, yeah," the boy said craning his neck. "Old Nicky. . . I don't see him right now, but he's usually around the horses, he takes care of some of them, that's over that way," he said, pointing beyond the barn.

"You son of a bitch," Edythe growled after the boy had left. "Nicholas Brown?"

"That's the idea," Cody replied. They were both moving in the direction indicated. Edythe, despite the cane, kept a brisk pace.

"Why didn't you tell me?" she demanded.

"I wanted to make sure I was right first," Cody said. "And until I actually see him. . . " he broke off now, for they had rounded the corner of the barn. And there he was, brushing a white-and-black horse and singing to himself. Anyone who'd seen his photographs could not doubt this was Nicholas Brown.

* * *

Fitzwilliam started the car. He considered a moment and then took the .38 out of his shoulder hostler and laid it on the seat next to him, along with the Uzi. He put the car in gear now and started away.

* * *

"Hi," Cody said.

Nicholas looked up and smiled.

"Nice-looking horse," Cody commented.

Nicholas's grin widened. "She likes to pretend that she's a famous racehorse who won the Melbourne Cup. But she didn't, really."

"I'm a friend of your mother's," Cody said. "She'd like me to bring you home."

The smile left the boy's face, and for a moment a flicker suggested that he might cry.

"Would you like to go home?" Edythe asked.

Nicholas nodded.

"Nicholas, who brought you here?" Cody asked.

"I don't know," the boy answered.

"Was it a man or a woman?"

"He had white hair. I told him if he had a beard and got fat he could look like Santa Claus. But he didn't like me," Nicholas said earnestly, a slow, impish smile beginning. "When I was here and he was driving away and I knew he couldn't get me, I gave him the finger."

"Who told the white-haired man to bring you here?" Cody asked. "Was it your brother Kevin?"

Nicholas nodded. "Yeah."

"Have you seen Kevin since then?" Cody asked.

"Yeah, sure, lots of times."

"When was the last time?" Cody asked.

Nicholas became serious. "Last week. He said he didn't want me to worry if I heard on the news that he was dead. Because he wasn't. He was here and we watched his funeral on TV. He said he was pulling a trick on my father, and I said I'd like to kill my father. But Kevin said he was going to do something even worse to him."

"My God," Edythe said in amazement. "Kevin Brown is still alive?"

"What could be worse than killing him?" Nicholas asked .

"Excuse me," Cody heard a voice say loudly. He turned to see the man he recognized from the photograph as Brother Julian. His thinning blond hair was tossing in the wind. He looked frazzled. "I'd like to know who you are," the brother asked.

"We've come to take Nicholas home."

"On whose authority?" Brother Julian demanded to know.

"That's something probably better discussed while the boy's packing," Cody said, indicating as best he could that this talk take place out of the boy's earshot.

Brother Julian understood. "Nicholas, take Brandywine back to the stables now."

"I want to go home," Nicholas said.

"We'll talk about it when you've finished brushing her inside," the brother said.

But Nicholas didn't like the idea; he looked ready to pout.

"Don't worry," Cody said. "I promise I won't leave here without you."

Still he hesitated.

"I won't let him," Edythe promised in a terse voice. "Now go ahead and finish with Brandywine."

The boy frowned but obeyed, and started to lead the horse for the barn.

"By the way," Edythe said to Brother Julian. "My name's Edythe Seims. I write for the *Sydney Morning Herald*.

Brother Julian's face sank.

* * *

"I'd like to know how Nicholas Brown came to be hiding at Boys' Village," Edythe asked with a certain toughness in her reporter's voice and a hand-held tape machine thrust in Brother Julian's direction.

"That's a long story," he said with some nervous impatience.

"I'm a great listener," she snapped back. But he still showed no sign of giving an answer.

"Let me see if I can help," Cody said. "It started last year when you got yourself an invitation to one of Fiona Brown's yacht parties. You were charming and nice to Nicholas and made a wonderful impression on her. Then you gave her a pitch about Boys' Village and she wrote you a check for five thousand dollars."

"I sent that check back," Brother Julian said, his face beginning to flush with anger.

"Right," Cody said with a smile that reflected some cynicism. "Was that before or after Kevin Brown offered you a much bigger one?"

Another cement truck rumbled by, diverting for a moment Cody's attention so that he didn't see the punch coming until it was too late. The next moment he was sitting on the ground .

"I sent Fiona Brown's check back because someone told me who her husband was," Brother Julian said, struggling to suppress his rage. "I hadn't made the connection before that. You have to understand what we're trying to do here," he went on urgently. "The boys we have here are good kids, but they've been hurt and scarred. At home they've been abused, either sexually or physically, often both. Some become so ashamed and scared that they run away from home; others are thrown out as early as nine and ten years of age. The people who do this to them are their own families, for God's sake, the people who are supposed to love and take care of them – their mothers, fathers, or mothers' boyfriends – and most of the time it's because these adult figures have drug or alcohol problems, or both. So how am I supposed to tell these boys with any conviction that God loves them and we love them, and that they're wonderful human beings, and that the adults who hurt them have a sickness and need to be prayed for and loved, not hated. How could we try to rebuild these boys' confidence and self-esteem if I'm simultaneously taking money from someone like Griffin Brown, notorious for making his money from drugs and nightclubs and prostitution, who's literally made a bloody fortune trading on the misery of other human beings?" Brother Julian was now fully red in the face.

Cody had climbed to his feet. "I owe you an apology," he said.

"I'm sorry I lost my temper," Brother Julian answered.

"I'm not," Edythe said. "I liked hearing what you said. It's nice to know someone still has some principles in this world."

* * *

At about the same time, in the administration building, Brother Alfred, who at seventy-six was the oldest brother at Boys' Village, was walking around quietly cursing at himself. He had found his cigarettes, but now he couldn't unearth any matches. He had just finished teaching a terrible class in which he had lost his temper for a stupid reason and yelled at the boys. He hadn't slept well the last couple of nights, but he knew that wasn't the all of it. What was bothering him were the anxieties that Brother Julian had confided in him. His fear in the last few days that because of that boy Nicholas being here, he could bring scandal down on and thus ruin Boys' Village. He had confided to him Nicholas's true identity, and they had both seen the newspapers and the television the last week or so. It was so unfair,

Brother Alfred thought. . . and then he spotted some
matches on the window. He reached them and lit his
cigarette, and as he did he saw the car come to a stop
next to the Volkswagen, and a man get out. He had a
gun. . . he had two guns. One he put in a shoulder
holster, and the other looked like a small machine
gun. "Jesus, Mary, and Joseph," Brother Alfred said
to himself. The evil they had so feared had indeed
come, and he was filled with a righteous anger.

* * *

"Kevin Brown didn't approach me until I sent the
check back. I think his mother was in the hospital at
the time. He said that he was afraid for his brother.
Afraid what his father might make him do when he
turned eighteen. He said when that time came, in a
few months, he might ask me to keep Nicholas here
for a little while. He offered me a lot of money. I kept
turning him down. Then he told me – or a least
implied what his father had made him do when he
had turned eighteen. He implied that he'd been
obligated to kill a man."

"It's possible it was a lot more then that," Cody
said. "There's some speculation that he was tied to
the Mardi Gras amusement park fire."

"Dear mother of God," Brother Julian said as if
the wind had been taken out of him.

"When did Kevin come back?" Edythe asked.

"Mid November. He offered me money again. I
told him I couldn't accept it, but that if his brother
was truly in danger, we'd look after him as best we
could." He paused and thought. "About a week later
he brought Nicholas to us. He was like a kid at

Christmas. He had two presents for each of the kids."

"There are thirty-two boys here?" Cody asked.

"That's right," Julian answered, surprised Cody would have such information. "We have four cottages, each with eight boys, a foster mother and father, and a brother. Thanks to a nice legacy left to us by a man over up in Bundaberg, we'll soon have a fifth cottage, plus a swimming pool and tennis court for the boys."

* * *

"You. You evil son of bitch," Brother Alfred shouted.

The boys had settled in their next classes and the compound was empty – except for Fitzwilliam, who had cautiously been making his way through it, Uzi at the ready, in search of Cody. He now turned to see the ancient man in a black cassock storming toward him with a cricket bat in his hand.

"What do you want, old man?" the startled Fitzwilliam snarled.

"You!" Brother Alfred said, and swung the bat.

Fitzwilliam tried to move out of the way, but was still dealt a crushing blow on his upper arm. The old brother was swinging yet again when Fitzwilliam let loose with a burst of bullets.

* * *

Cody knew the sound as soon as he heard it. "Into the stables," he ordered Brother Julian and Edythe, pulling out his Walther."

"My boys," Brother Julian said, trying to move past Cody.

"They're going to be a lot better off with you still alive," Cody said, grabbing him by the arm.

Fitzwilliam, realizing that any surprise was lost now, ran for the edge of a classroom building.

Cody's Walther led him around the corner of the barn where he remained close to the wall, amid the shadows. The compound was deserted for the moment, save for the fallen figure of Brother Alfred. Now some curious boys appeared from a workshop area. "Get out of here! Move!" Cody shouted. The sound of his voice brought a burst from the Uzi, splintering wood over his head. Cody dove and rolled, firing half a dozen times at the source of the fire. Number-four bullet slammed into Fitzwilliam's chest; number five ripped into his right shoulder and spun him to the ground, the Uzi clattering away.

Fitzwilliam tried to reach for his shoulder holster, but his right arm was on fire and useless. Cody was running at him now. Fitzwilliam managed to struggle to his feet and ran for the entrance of the classroom building. The pain in his chest and shoulder was so great he could hardly see. His left hand tried three times to find the door handle before he managed to open it. Once inside he was aware of people, children, rushing back into their classrooms. He struggled again and then with his left hand managed to pull his .38 from its holster. Then he waited, gun ready for Cody to appear. It wasn't until he heard another outside door open and close that he knew Cody had anticipated him. He could hear Cody's approaching footsteps now. He was losing his sense of balance and wasn't even sure if he could fire straight. He started to walk, and instead found himself lurching toward a classroom door. He managed to push it open. It was a chemistry lab.

The teacher was a young, cherubic-faced man with bushy hair. Half a dozen boys of various ages were in the room. "If there's trouble," he said, "leave the boys out of it."

"Shut the bloody hell up," Fitzwilliam hissed. "You," he said, pointing to a skinny, black-haired boy. "Push that table against that wall," he said, trying to position himself opposite the door. The boy started to obey.

Cody made his way down the corridor. He burst into one room, Walther ready, only to discover seven boys and a teacher. "Get out of the building," he told them and then waited protectively in the hallway until they'd escaped through the entrance he had used.

In the chemistry lab the table had been pushed against the wall. Fitzwilliam sat against it. "You," he barked at a small redhead. "Come here." The boy hesitated a moment.

"No." The teacher insisted. "I do whatever you need."

By now, pain gripped most of Fitzwilliam's senses, leaving him as unaware that the bushy-haired teacher had picked up a small vial as he started over. Drawing close to the wounded man, the teacher suddenly threw the contents, which was acid, into the gunman's face. Fitzwilliam, screaming in agony as the liquid hit his eyes, rolled over the table and onto the ground.

"Run boys, run!" the teacher shouted.

Fitzwilliam tried to regain his bearings but his vision was almost gone now. He fired wildly several times. But then there was only silence.

"Down to shooting at schoolboys, Fitzwilliam?" Cody asked.

Fitzwilliam had to turn his head halfway crooked before he could make Cody out with his restricted vision. His face and eyes were contorted in pain. He started to raise his gun, but Cody was leveling the Walther at him, and suddenly he realized he was afraid. Afraid of dying. . . afraid of going back to prison. . . afraid that the pain would never stop. Cody was coming closer now, and then suddenly in a movement Fitzwilliam couldn't see, Cody had kicked the gun from his hand.

"Kill me," Fitzwilliam said. "Kill me."

"Is that supposed to be a favor?" Cody asked.

"Jesus Christ, can't you see what's happehed to me?" he gasped. "I can't stand the pain."

Cody was down on the floor next to him, pulling Fitzwilliam up by one hand and slamming him against the wall. Fitzwilliam screamed.

"You think this is worse than the pain the people in the disco felt, the thirty-seven you set on fire?" Cody asked.

Edythe was here now, her tape recorder pointed in the right direction.

"Fuck you," Fitzwilliam hissed.

"Fuck *you*," Cody returned angrily, jamming the Walther under Fitzwilliam's nose. The pressure from his finger was almost enough to pull the trigger, but he knew that's what the other man wanted.

"I was a cop for twenty years," Cody said, "and I saw a lot of shot-up bodies. But I've got to tell you,

Fitzwilliam, unless I pull this trigger, yours isn't going to make the morgue. Not with what you've got. They'll stitch you up, and in a few weeks you'll be fine again. And you probably won't even mind the acid scars on your face, because with what's left of your eyesight you won't be able to see them." Cody paused; he could sense the other man quivering. "Oh, you'll have a blast in prison this time, ex-cop. When they're not corn-holing you, they'll be beating the shit out of you, and it'll be for the rest of your life."

"What do you want?" he asked in desperation.

"Answers. "

"Then will you kill me?"

"If you talk fast enough. Tell me about the disco."

"I was only doing what he told me," Fitzwilliam wailed.

"Who, Kevin Brown?" Cody demanded.

"Yes," he answered, and then he couldn't see out of his left eye anymore.

"I'll send for an ambulance," Brother Julian said on entering the room and seeing Fitzwilliam.

"No," the wounded man cried out. "No ambulance."

"Tell me why Kevin Brown wanted the disco firebombed" Cody pressed.

"So everyone would think he was dead," Fitzwilliam answered, and then gasped it pain.

"That was why he needed the other body, wasn't it?" Cody asked. "The one that was wrapped and hidden on the bottom floor of the disco until just before the fire?"

"Yeeeees," Fitzwilliam said with pain.

"Who was he?" Cody wanted to know.

"Just a guy from a bar, same size as Kevin. They put Kevin's watch and wallet on him."

"Why did Kevin want everyone to think he was dead?" Cody asked.

"Go after his father. . . take over everything, starting with big drug delivery," Fitzwilliam answered in short bursts. "I told him we should just kill him, but he wanted to humiliate him first, destroy him piece by piece."

"Why?" Cody insisted.

"Hated him all his life. Said his father shit on him and his mother as long as he could remember. Said he was going to make the son of a bitch pay." Fitzwilliam groaned. "For Christ's sake, *shoot*."

"Not yet. Tell me about the drug deal."

Fitzwilliam's eyes were desperate, but he knew that Cody was his only chance. "Double cross," Fitzwilliam answered. "Kevin planned it for old man and his partners, but we stole it. Two nights ago, we and Kevin stole it. They still think it's coming in."

"Where did Gallagher fit in?" Cody asked.

But Fitzwilliam couldn't answer for the moment; he seemed lost in his pain. Cody glanced at Edythe.

"He may feel like shit, but you're making this old lady happy," she said, grinning grimly.

"Tell me about Gallagher," Cody repeated, shaking Fitzwilliam again.

"He was the key to the drug deal," Fitzwilliam managed. "It's hard to smuggle drugs into this country. I ought to know, I did seven years." He was silent for a couple of moments, trying to catch his breath. "Kevin's idea was to let ASIO in from the beginning."

"Who's ASIO?" Cody asked.

Edythe answered to save Fitzwilliam's energy. "Australian Security and Intelligence Organization. It's like your FBI and CIA rolled into one."

"Gallagher was heavy into cocaine. Kevin used him to bring ASIO in. Gallagher told ASIO he had come on this drug deal, but he wanted in, help make a big case so he could get out of CIA doghouse. They bought it. Set up listening post across from Cowboy Club. Since they wanted the deal to happen so they could make big bust, they contacted law enforcement all over world, asked them to keep hands off. . . it was bloody brilliant."

"Did Griffin Brown know about this?"

"No," Fitzwilliam said, shaking his head vigorously as if that might help relieve the pain. "They had Cowboy Club bugged. That's how we knew you were coming after Nicholas. ASIO boys thought they were building case. . . Gallagher was passing information to us." Outside they could hear sirens.

"Christ, don't let them get me," Fitzwilliam pleaded.

"Tell me about Tommy Creager," Cody said.

Fitzwilliam didn't speak for several moments. "Isn't that a bloody joke. If I hadn't killed him, you never would have been here. Everything would have been as we had planned."

"Why did you kill him?"

"I didn't want to. Kevin was afraid because Creager had seen us near the disco. . . afternoon when we were planning the fire. He was showing me place. . . Kevin afraid Creager might recognize me, and after fire would put two and two together..."

"But your mother was dying over in Tauranga, so you had to kill him there," Cody said.

Fitzwilliam nodded. "How did you know?"

"It doesn't matter," Cody said. "Kevin Brown had Gallagher send Tommy on another one of his trips? Tommy thought he was delivering money again to help pay for the big delivery?"

"Yeeees, Jesus, kill me," he begged.

"Where's Kevin?" Cody pressed.

"Balmain, second floor, Brennan Auto Paint." Fitzwilliam was in agony.

"Is that where the drugs are now?"

"You promised. Shoot me."

"Is that where the drugs are?" Cody insisted.

"Yes, pull the fucking trigger," Fitzwilliam shrieked.

The room was suddenly full of people, including paramedics pushing their way in.

"I can't do that," Cody said. "Unless you go for the gun in your ankle holster."

Cody stood now.

"You bastard," Fitzwilliam shouted, and his body lurched as he reached for his ankle.

"Look out, he has another gun," Edythe screamed.

Cody fired twice. The first bullet exploded Fitzwilliam's heart. The second, his brain.

"My God," Edythe said.

"You'd better find the phone number of that honest cop," Cody told her.

76

Wearing a baseball cap and dark glasses, Kevin Brown was walking back from Swampy Anderson's, the pub where he had had lunch, when he turned the corner on Waterview and stopped dead. Half a dozen marked police cars and half a dozen unmarked, official-looking cars that he guessed belonged to ASIO were crowded around the front of the auto paint shop. His workers, still in their surgical attire minus the masks, were being led out. Kevin Brown knew it was over. He had always had a lingering fear, even when everything seemed to be going well, that it might come to this. He knew he had to finish it now. He couldn't wait for his poetic revenge. He couldn't wait for Mardi Gras.

* * *

The parking gates under the Cowboy Club clanked open. Kevin drove his car in, got out, and climbed the stairs.

"My God, Kevin, it's you, you're alive!" Lakey said, his face breaking into an uncontrollable smile. "What happened?"

"It's a long story," Kevin said, moving to the office. "I need to see my father."

"He's going to be so happy to see you. With everything that's happened his blood pressure has gone through the roof again," Lakey chattered on. Kevin had opened the door to the office now, but it was empty.

"I can help him with his blood pressure," Kevin said. "Where is he?"

"On the yacht."

"On the yacht," Kevin repeated and smiled. "That's good," he said, and shot Lakey three times with a silenced pistol.

* * *

Fiona saw him get out of the car from her second-floor room. At first she thought she was dreaming. "Kevin, Kevin, is that you?" she shouted.

Kevin waved to her. "I'll be up to see you in a few minutes, Mum."

* * *

Old Joe and John Higgins were playing cards on the jetty when they saw him crossing the lawn. Old Joe took off his glasses and then began to cry. "Kevin, my God you're alive!" he said as he moved to the younger man and then hugged him. "It's a miracle, a miracle!" Old Joe said.

"It's great to see you again too, Joe. I always liked you, from when I was a little boy," Kevin said, and then tried to make it painless by firing the bullet through the old man's heart. Old Joe looked surprised and fell in a heap. Kevin didn't care about John Higgins; he fired into him four times before he stopped moving.

As Kevin stepped into the main cabin of the yacht, he could see his father asleep on the couch. That would make it easier, he thought. Especially with time running out. He took out the small case, set it on the bar, and opened it. The two syringes were inside. He took one out, held it in the air and tested to make sure it worked, just as he had been instructed. Then he repeated the action on the second one. Everything worked fine.

He moved to the sleeping man. Griffin Brown looked old and exhausted. His breathing was long and deep. Kevin plunged the first needle into the back of his father's neck. Griffin Brown was so fast asleep that the 50-ccs had been nearly completely delivered when he started to growl and fight the pain. Kevin held his head down with his left hand. He finished the first needle, discarded it, and picked up the second and drove it in at about the same spot. Griffin Brown was groggy and now confused. "Kevin? Kevin? What the hell is going on? What are you doing? You're dead. Let me up."

The second syringe done, Kevin released the pressure on his father and then stepped back, and for several moments he knew the greatest exhilaration he had ever experienced in his life.

"What? What were you doing? How are you alive?" Griffin Brown sputtered as he struggled still to sit up.

"I'm alive because I faked my own death, you son of a bitch," Kevin said, pleased that his father looked stunned. "I did it all. I did everything to you. I took Nicholas, I had the Galah firebombed and killed my dear brother and supposedly myself. I did the Bayswater. You should have seen Max Oliver's face when I knocked on the door he was so surprised and happy to see me and a moment later my friend cut his throat," he boasted. "I did it, not bloody Wang," he said and almost laughed. "I brought in five Chinese shooters from Hong Kong so you would think it was him. I was going to kill Billy

Packer but he beat me to it and died before I could get to him."

"Why?" Griffin Brown asked, surprised that his voice was barely a whisper. "I loved you, you're my oldest son."

"You love shit," Kevin shouted back. "You treated my mother and me like shit ever since I can remember. You humiliated her at home and in public over and over. You're a bastard." Kevin paused, his breathing short. He didn't want to cry. "I wanted to do this tomorrow night. Do you have any bloody idea why I wanted to do this tomorrow night?"

"No." Griffin Brown shook his head and realized that his right side was beginning to feel numb.

"It's Mardi Gras night," Kevin explained. "Don't you remember the Mardi Gras night when I was eighteen? You made me set the fire. I killed those six boys. There was no turning back for me after that, was there? No turning back. I had killed six people. You'd stolen my bloody soul and you thought it was funny. You fucking laughed at me when I cried." He paused again as his father began to slump. "I wanted to make it the Mardi Gras, I wanted to make it even. The same night you had done it to me, I wanted to destroy you." He smiled nervously. "I almost made it. I would have, if it hadn't been for that bloody American." His father stared with eyes out of a motionless face. Kevin found a laugh. "You don't know what's going on, do you?" It's those shots I gave you. One hundred-ccs of a very nice medicine for thinning the blood. Only I just gave you a month's supply all at once. Right now blood vessels are bursting in your brain, and you can't even feel it. Your blood pressure just exploded through the top and you're having the massive bloody stroke the doctors always warned you about. The one you made me promise I'd kill you after if it happened. Only I'm not going to kill you. No one is. You're going to be a bloody fucking vegetable. You're going to sit in a wheelchair for the rest of your life, and your brain is going to work just fine; you'll know everything that's going on around your but you'll be a bloody turnip. And people will ignore you and push you in corners for hours on end. You'll shit your pants and your minders will yell at you. You're going to live a life of shit, of total bloody shit, just like you made my mother live all these years."

Griffin Brown heard everything Kevin said, but he couldn't answer, he couldn't move, and with an overwhelming sense of desperation he knew what his son had done to him.

* * *

Kevin could see, through the front window of the boat, people coming across the lawn now. There was his mother and Nicholas with a man he didn't know, who he guessed was Cody. And of course there were lots of police.

Kevin looked at his father and then adjusted the paralyzed man's head so that he could see what was going to happen. He unzipped his pants now. "Get used to it, old man," Kevin said, and started to urinate on him. "This is how you're going to spend the rest of your life."

He finished and pulled his father's head back by the hair so he could look him in the eyes. "How's it bloody feel, you son of a bitch?"

Kevin could hear footsteps on the jetty now. He knew that there was nothing else to do. He put his gun in his mouth and pulled the trigger.

77

Cody spent the next ten days or so explaining things to the police and ASIO officials. In the end they still weren't happy that he had operated on his own, but they couldn't begrudge the fact that he had been instrumental in solving the disco murders and seizing the biggest shipment of heroin that had ever been smuggled into the country. Eventually they decided not to press any of the various charges they might have brought against him. A decision that no doubt was aided by Edythe threatening to write the full story if they gave him any trouble.

One of the bargains Cody managed to negotiate was a three-corner trade-off. Brian and Colin would tell what they knew about Colin Fitzwilliam on the night of the fire if no charges were brought against them, and if the police would see to it that the Boys' Village name wouldn't be dragged into the media. The Boys' Village part of the deal was to make a home for Brian and Colin in the new cottage – which Brother Julian was all too happy to do.

As the days passed, the Codys worked to fix their boat and took some time for sight-seeing.

The Cowboy Club had remained closed for a couple of weeks, but then Edythe stopped by the boat to inform Cody that it was reopening under new management. Shauna and her son Kelly would be running it now. It seemed that Griftin Brown had left instructions with his lawyers that if he died or became incapacitated, the ownership of the Cowboy Club would pass to them.

"Want to take a chance?" he asked Edythe.

"With you, anytime," she answered.

"Let's go see the new owners."

* * *

"The stage we've got now sucks," the handsome, coffee-colored sixteen-year-old was explaining emphatically to Grasshopper. "My mother's going to be doing two shows a night. The whole place just has to be brought up to level." He looked around now to see Cody and Edythe coming in. "We're not open until six," he said.

"We're here to see your mother, honey," Edythe said. "I'm from the *Sydney Morning Herald*."

"Grasshopper, get my mother," Kelly ordered, and the lanky, tattooed man moved away. Kelly stared at them for several moments through the half dark of the room before he recognized Cody.

"You're that Cody guy, aren't you? I saw your picture in the paper," he said and moved over to them and grinned. "You know, if you had gotten to old Griffin a little faster, like before Kevin had a chance to shoot him up, I'd still be in the eleventh grade over in St. Joe's, instead of running what's going to be the hottest nightclub in town."

"Is that what you're going to make your career, running nightclubs?" Edythe asked with a hint of derision.

Kelly read her tone and grinned again, only this time it was a tougher, almost deadly grin. "That's what we'll do for starters, until everyone knows we're here, until we've got a few cops on the payroll, and then we'll start running the girls again upstairs, and after a while the casino. After that, who knows? I plan to be a very important man in this town."

"I think that's your cue to show me your dick," Cody said.

Kelly locked eyes with him. There was no humor left in the sixteen-year-old face. His words were almost a threat. "You want to see it, white man?" he asked, prepared to open his pants. "I'm hung like my old man, and now I've got his money and power too."

"Kelly," his mother's voice interjected. "I'll take care of these people."

The boy backed away as Shauna came up. "He's Cody," he said.

She eyed the pair of them. "You're the crime reporter, aren't you? There's nothing for you here."

"Maybe I should stop back in a few months. According to your son, it'll be business as usual by then," Edythe said.

Shauna darted a look at Kelly, then back to the others. "This place has had too much bad publicity. I'd like to have a new start here. Try and have some good press."

"I can guarantee you some if you answer this man's question," Edythe said. "By the way, I heard you before, when you were doing your show at Kinsella's. You're a terrific singer."

"Thanks," Shauna said, seeming to relax a bit. "What do you want to know?"

"Family skeletons," Cody said. "Young Nicholas. Why did his father hate him? Why was Kevin so devoted to him?"

She studied him a moment and almost laughed.
"You know, don't you?"

"I have a guess," Cody said.

"The reason Kevin loved Nicholas so much," she
explained with a coy smile, "is that Kevin is his real
father. As the story goes, they had a costume party
one night. Kevin, who was about fifteen then, got
drunk out of his mind, stripped down naked, put a
goat's-head mask on, and went into his mother's
room and raped her."

* * *

It was a day before the Codys had planned to sail on
to Melbourne and then Tasmania when Father Larry
contacted them. Fiona, he explained, had just
learned that they were still in Sydney. She was hoping to thank him properly for bringing Nicholas
home by inviting him to a yacht party that afternoon. The boys were eager to attend, and Father
Larry seemed desperate to fulfill Fiona's wishes.

* * *

It was much the same crowd as he had seen in the
photographs. Fathers Larry and Euginio, several
nuns, a few of Fiona's social cronies. Even Jill
Edwards was here, hoping to talk Fiona into invest-
ing in one of her films, her brother, The Elvis impersonator, was out of jail, in therapy, and opening at
Jupiter's Casino on the Gold Coast. Billy Packer, Jr.,
guided the boat around the harbor, and a buffet of
lobster and turkey and ham and roast beef and rolls
and bread and cakes and pies made Patrick and

Damien's eyes dance. The boys met Nicholas and
played checkers and video games with him. Fiona
made a big fuss over Cody when he first arrived, but
as the afternoon wore on and the Mateus rosé
flowed, she lost interest. She was telling the funny-
hat story again when Cody finally made his way
below decks. He found the rest room he needed, and
then as he came out he heard it again, the soft, desperate weeping. This time he followed it to its source
and opened a cabin door. In the dark sat Griffin
Brown, strapped to a wheelchair. The room stank of
excrement. Brown was sagged to one side and the
eyes from his frozen face saw Cody, but he couldn't
stop weeping, weeping.

* * *

They sailed the next morning with the sun. Damien
guided them out through the heads. As they moved
down the Coast, Patrick and his father stood at the
bow and took one last look at Bondi Beach.

Later Cody would go below and write to Tommy
Creager's daughter. He'd tell her what a good man
her father was. And that he loved her a great deal.
And that when he died he had been working on a
big story. That he had been working with the government to break a drug ring. He told her that her
father had always been his friend. . . and that he had
died a hero.

Recent S.P.I.
Entertainment Books